Memoirs of a Texan: War

Historic fiction by Tim Murray

iUniverse, Inc.

New York   Bloomington

Memoirs of a Texan: War

Copyright © 2009 by Tim Murray

iUniverse books may be ordered through booksellers or by contacting:

iUniverse
1663 Liberty Drive
Bloomington, IN 47403
www.iuniverse.com
1-800-Authors (1-800-288-4677)

Because of the dynamic nature of the Internet, any Web addresses or links contained in this book may have changed since publication and may no longer be valid. The views expressed in this work are solely those of the author and do not necessarily reflect the views of the publisher, and the publisher hereby disclaims any responsibility for them.

ISBN: 978-1-4401-3250-6 (pbk)
ISBN: 978-1-4401-3252-0 (cloth)
ISBN: 978-1-4401-3251-3 (ebk)

Printed in the United States of America

iUniverse rev. date: 06/03/2009

www.memoirsofatexan.com

Contents

Foreword

April 3, 2009
Tim Murray

Memoirs of a Texan is a fiction, not the autobiography of a real person. The principal character, Jim Cobb, is not intended to represent any actual Confederate officer who served Dorsey Pender or A P Hill as an aide. Cobb is a fictional person created from my imagination. When I learned that both Generals Lee and Jackson called out to A P Hill in their dying delirium, I knew Hill must have been significant to them and the Army of Northern Virginia. Therefore, A P Hill's aide would have a prime position in observing the strategy, tactics, and battles fought by the Confederate Army in the East.

To provide Northern perspective and overall observation of the war, I added another fictional character – Sam Payne, war correspondent for the New York Tribune. Other individuals in the story are a mix of historic and fictional. Generally, officers above Colonel rank are real along with Horace Greeley, John Mosby, and other well known historic figures.

I worked to create interesting characters and stories in the context of America's most bloody and tragic war. For youngsters and other readers who may not be familiar with the Civil War, I presented the war as accurately and realistically as I could. For story purposes, I wanted Jim Cobb to experience First Manassas, the first major battle of the war, and that required bringing along the Light Division which had not been formed at the time and Dorsey Pender who did not serve in that battle. I picked the

78th North Carolina to designate Jim Cobb's fictional regiment as it appears the 78 number was somehow skipped in naming Confederate North Carolina regiments. Other historic inaccuracies are unintentional.

Many histories and historic fictions have been written about the Civil War. The question I had to ask and answer is where does my book contribute? Many books are based on the lives of Generals Lee, Jackson, and Longstreet and rightfully so. Historians consider Jackson the greatest American general and one of the five all-time best. Lee and Longstreet are also highly esteemed. But, in studying the history of the Civil War, it is apparent that A P Hill, Dorsey Pender, and Jubal Early were also unique and outstanding and, like Jackson, eccentric. Through association with the fictional Jim Cobb, I wanted to bring these lesser known great Confederate officers to life. In all three books, I worked to show how the war and his upbringing affected Jim Cobb in his personal relations and particularly how lessons learned in the war helped Cobb build a business empire in Texas.

When possible, I used personal experience and observations in describing locales and communities in the story. I resided four pleasant years in Catawba County, North Carolina where the fictional Jim Cobb grew up. I have visited often in Northern Virginia and Lafayette, Louisiana and driven along the route the fictional traveling party took from Newton, North Carolina to Beaumont, Texas. An important influence was Al Guilleau, Douglas Aircraft Director of Plans, my first boss out of college. Al served as an aide to General Spaatz, head of Allied Tactical Air Command in Europe in World War II. He was the supportive, knowledgeable superior I imagined Dorsey Pender to be for Jim Cobb.

I thank all who helped me in writing the first book most particularly Beth Carlson who worked closely with me in editing; friends in the Critters Writers Group in The Woodland, Texas who helped with many useful suggestions; Linda Honig, Jane

Johndrow, and son, Owen, and daughter-in-law, Suzanne, who read earlier drafts and made suggestions to improve the final version; Chris Mulder who illustrated the maps; and Wikipedia, an excellent information and map source.

Finally, I want to thank my wife, Jeanie, for her encouragement and support in writing the Memoirs of a Texan trilogy.

Prolog

I had a privileged life. Good parents, a family who loved me, children and grandchildren who have done well, the best associates any man could have, and wealth. If I could have picked another time to be born, I would have and avoided the misery of a terrible war. But no one has that option. The final blessing is writing my story before I die and my enemies write it for me. I may even convince the grandchildren I was once young.

I am not an interesting person, but I have met many exceptional individuals, some I claim as friends. And I survived the most violent period of our nation's history, leaving behind many who died young, ten or more I personally killed. So my book is a witness to the times I lived in. I like to think of it that way.

Like most, my life is a mix of good and bad, sometimes the same thing. Most of the men I killed were in war or deserved to die which makes their killing justified. However, I took the lives of three to prevent my going to prison. Looking back on it, they were just doing their job and did not deserve to die. I have gathered political enemies and pleased that I have. Greedy bastards who deceive ignorant voters to line their own pockets; the "rich" whom Old Testament prophets decry. They published lies about me and my family which are believed by the ignorant and gullible. Before I die, I am compelled to set the record straight.

The war sets off my life and time. It changed everything. From the war, I learned much and suffered much. My wife, family, and wealth came from the war as have undiminished memories of daily horror. I served under Dorsey Pender, the best officer in either army, and have never forgotten the many lessons he taught me. Neither have I forgotten the uncaring, wanton slaughter in every battle I witnessed.

I found, after I started, material for three books. The first book is mostly about my years in the Confederate Army, what happened to me, and what I observed in the war.

In writing my memoirs, I am blessed with the support of friends and associates. I met Sam Payne, the New York Tribune's chief war reporter, as a VMI cadet and read his articles whenever I could. In terms of knowledge gained from first hand witness of the war, Payne is the most informed man alive. Years later, we renewed our friendship and he kindly talked with me at length and loaned me his diary and relevant letters for my book. Likewise, when they learned what I was doing, Andy Blaylock, Robert Savage, Charles Savage, and other associates came by to talk and refresh my memory of incidents in our lives. They also loaned diaries, letters, and other documents to me.

In writing my story, I use first person accounts of what I saw and experienced. I have also used first person voices for Missy, Sam Payne, and Robert Savage whose stories are best written as they told them to me.

I hope readers will enjoy my story and my family not be shamed. Perhaps you can make sense of my life. I am at a loss why I was both cursed and blessed. I take comfort in 1st Corinthians 13:12 where the Apostle Paul wrote "For now we see through a glass, darkly; but then face to face: now I know in part; but then shall I know even as also I am known." I will take my chances with a loving God whom I hope to meet soon.

Chapter 1: Virginia Military Institute

Lexington, Virginia, Virginia Military Institute
Thursday, September 2, 1858
Jim Cobb

"So the uppity Morgans sent the Crown Prince to mix with us commoners here at VMI," said a lanky, overbearing red-haired cadet who stared at a fellow standing in front of me.

The young man to whom the slur was directed whirled around, grabbed the shirt of the cadet who cast the insult and closed his free hand into a fist.

"Here's something for Your Highness," the red-haired cadet taunted as he spun away and hit Morgan's left ear.

The fight was on. Other cadets formed a circle for the combatants, urging them on. "Hit him again." "You can do better than that!" They called out.

Uppity Morgan dropped his opponent but, as a gentleman, let him rise to continue the fight. Morgan hit the red-headed cadet several times in the mouth and nose bloodying his face.

Another cadet jumped in the circle and started toward Morgan with his fists clenched.

Without giving it thought, I stepped into the growing circle of cadets and pulled off the third cadet as he started to swing at Morgan. I spun him around changing the contest to two separate fistfights. Before I could say anything, he hit me in the eye with a roundhouse right. I ducked his next punch and caught him with a right hook to the jaw.

He did not get up. An upperclassman ran over and broke up our impromptu assembly.

Morgan had a bloody nose, I a black eye, and each participant got a demerit before classes even began.

Uppity Morgan grinned and said, "Thanks. What's your name, cadet?"

"I'm Jim Cobb." On arrival at VMI, I decided to be called Jim instead of James, but I knew when I went home I would always be James to my mother, friends, and acquaintances.

Morgan offered his hand. "I'm Pete Morgan. Where're you from? You talk like a North Carolina Cracker."

"You got the North Carolina part right," I responded, shaking Pete's hand. I would have taken offense to the Cracker comment except Pete grinned as he said it.

"You can see I'm not popular with some around here. They don't like Crackers either. If you don't have a roommate yet, maybe we could room together."

"You're probably as good as I'll do," I commented while pondering the possibilities of having a Virginia Blueblood roommate.

"Just keep the moonshine on your side of the room," he cracked. I laughed with him, knowing alcohol was not allowed in cadet rooms.

"Who was the red-haired fellow?" I asked.

"Lem Randolph. The Randolphs live in the next county. Think they're better than us. I showed him."

We showed him, I thought and asked, "Who was the other one?"

Pete sneered. "His no 'count cousin, Curtis Warner. Thinks he's royalty too."

"These are four man rooms," I commented. "If you don't mind rooming with another Cracker, Tom Edward needs a place to room." I pointed toward Tom standing with the cadets milling around after the fight. Tom waved back.

Pete replied, "I'm not particular. Crackers, Cavaliers, all the same to me. Bring him over and we'll get introduced."

I met Tom Edwards on the train to Lexington and took a liking to him. He could crack his knuckles as he warbled a popular tune and work in a string of jokes in a near constant banter. I considered him talented. Tom did not know anyone at VMI either. On the train, we agreed to room together.

We went to the Housing Office for a room assignment and found a smallish, forlorn appearing cadet standing beside the front door and looking for roommates. He stepped forward and, in an unmistakable Yankee accent, said, "I'm Ken Johnson and you seem to be one short for a dorm assignment. May I join your group?" and stood uncomfortably waiting for our answer.

Pete replied, "Let's see, if we take you in, I'll be in a room with two Crackers and a Yankee" and grinned. "Oh, what the hell. Come on. You see what kind of pull I have around here."

Tom and I laughed along with Pete. Ken relaxed and shook hands around the circle of his new roommates. Ken met the established standard – he was an incoming student who needed roommates – and, with a nod of heads, was accepted into our group.

* * *

Pete had a Cavalier outlook on life and, except for defending slights to the family honor, did not care what others thought of him. He seemed to float with popular opinion, but was often surprisingly thoughtful in conversations.

He charmed his classmates and, particularly, the girls. I soon learned the best place to meet attractive females was standing beside him. Outgoing and quick-witted, Pete was welcome at parties and social gatherings and, by association, so were his roommates.

The second week, Pete entered the room, threw his hat on the bed, and announced, "The faculty wives are holding a social for the first year cadets, sort of a welcoming party. They've invited the pick of local girls to join us. We're scheduled to arrive at Colonel Smith's home tomorrow at four sharp." I did not know how Pete was privy to this piece of news, but suspected he heard it from one of the girls before we were officially notified.

At the social, the new cadets, in our dress uniforms, seemed to make a favorable impression on the girls. Pete knew some, but not all of them. Regardless, they flocked around him. I was pleased with the overflow that came my way.

Pete had a strong jaw, elegant nose, and an open, friendly face. He was as how I always imagined a planter would look. After I met them, I thought Pete was a good combination of his parents' best features.

Of all the cadets, I liked Ken best. He was a devout Christian with a questioning mind, but comfortable in his faith. He never made a show of his religious beliefs or drew attention to himself. It was simply an integral part of his thoughtful and sincere personality. I came to value our discussions that covered the broad range of first year cadet experiences.

Ken could have been tedious except for another redeeming quality. He was Reverend Maxwell Johnson's son and sometimes showed the impish rebellion and humor that went with being a minister's son. If there was a practical joke to be played, particularly at the expense of one of our overbearing upperclassmen, Ken was often the leader and instigator. The pranks, though harmless, were usually clever, well thought out, and effective.

Tom Edwards did not distinguish himself in any way – with studies, drill, horsemanship, participation in discussions, or the girls. He did well enough with studies and drill to pass, but that seemed to be the extent of his ability and ambition. At the socials and dances, it was usually Tom the other cadets recruited to escort a plain looking sister or cousin. Still, I felt loyal to him, a fellow North Carolinian who had the quirky talent that endeared him to me on the train ride up to Lexington.

Lexington and Brownsburg, Virginia,
Saturday, September 18, 1858
Jim Cobb

We had only been at VMI three weeks when Pete woke up Saturday morning and announced, "I'm going home for the weekend. If you Rats want to join me, we'll make room at the table."

Tom shook his head. He had a demerit to work off. Similarly, Ken, whom I think was not that sure of Pete, let alone his family, politely declined. I answered, "Count me in." By then, I was more than ready to take time off from drills, classes, mandatory study halls, and constant harassment of upperclassmen. Besides, I was curious about Pete and figured I would know more after I saw his home and met his family.

When I received my letter of acceptance, I wondered what cadet life would be like at VMI. I talked with a few local army veterans who told me of the rigors of drill and the torture of hazing. I figured I could handle it. Then I arrived. It seemed every minute of every hour upperclassmen watched for me to commit some infraction or break one of the mind numbing rules that governed our lives. It did not take long for me to be sick of it. First day, in fact.

I looked forward to the visit at Pete's home, mainly to be away from VMI if only for a day. Besides, Pete was fun to be around, always good for a joke, and a magnet for good-looking girls.

We ate a quick breakfast at the dormitory mess and went to the stable for horses. The stableman, a retired Army sergeant, had trained his share of green Lieutenants and tolerated immature cadets. Pete treated him like a hired man and turned down several horses he brought out. The stableman smiled and went about his duties, but I saw resentment in his eyes. Pete finally settled on a spirited chestnut. I took the first horse offered and made a point to thank the stableman, a gesture Pete ignored.

We took off at a fast pace for Pete's first visit home since enrolling at VMI. I shared his excitement but more from the standpoint of maximizing time away from drill and studies. As the Morgan home came into view, Pete reached out and poked me on the arm, "Bet I can beat you home."

"You're on." I spurred my horse to get a jump on Pete who followed in fast pursuit.

First day of field exercises for the first year cadets, the Instructor pointed to me and said, "Gentlemen, you will do well to emulate, Mister Cobb" and later pulled me over to say, within hearing of the others, "You're a natural. Cavalry career waiting for you." It marked me with my classmates - teasing and challenges to beat the recognized best rider in the class. Mostly, I ignored the attention, but knew Pete would want to race me and decided it would be best if he won. I had to make it look convincing – get off to an early lead and let him overtake me without being obvious.

As we approached the main house, I saw a scrawny teenage girl sitting on the front porch wearing what appeared to be Pete's hand down pants and shirt. She seemed unmindful of our approach.

By now, Pete was well ahead. As he slowed and I caught up, he said with obvious delight, "Beat you."

"Yeah." I looked disappointed and asked, "Who's the girl on the porch?"

"My kid sister. She's still mad at me for teasing her before I left. She came out on the porch to pretend she doesn't see us. Watch. I'll have fun with her."

Pete dismounted and the stable boy took the horse's reins. I followed Pete's lead. As we walked up on the porch, Pete's sister turned her back and made a display of ignoring him and reading her book.

Pete quietly walked up behind her, reached down, tickled her ribs, and said, "Those clothes looked better on me."

She dropped her book, turned around, and took a swing at his head. Pete easily ducked, laughed, and grabbed her by the waist from behind. He spun her around so that her feet traced a circle in the air, and said, "Keep trying little one, you might even hit me someday."

They appeared playful and graceful like a ballet performed many times in the past. I did not have a little sister. I had never seen anything like it before.

She seemed furious when Pete set her down, but recovered when she saw me standing hat in hand in front of her. Pete said, "Jim, this is my bratty little sister, Missy. Missy, meet Jim Cobb, my new roommate."

I extended my hand which Missy took and self-consciously smiled as if hoping I had not seen Pete embarrass her a moment ago.

Pete put his head inside the door and announced, "I'm home. Anybody here?" He gestured and I followed him inside.

The family gathered to greet the son and his guest. Pete told them, "This is Jim Cobb, my friend and new roommate."

The Morgan house was immaculate. A sparkling glass chandelier hung above the front room, offset from the neatly carpeted staircase. Luxurious green curtains covering the windows formed a background to the freshly polished furniture. Intricately woven Persian rugs covered the floors. Most of the furniture appeared to be European, not like the varnished slave crafted stuff from our saw mill stock. This was grander than any home I had seen in Piedmont North Carolina.

Pete's father, William Morgan, a tall distinguished looking man with dark brown hair graying at the temple, had a serious demeanor I later learned concealed a keen mind. I had no difficulty believing he once commanded a ship as Pete mentioned on the ride out.

The mother, Margaret Morgan seemed startled when we met, as if she had somehow seen me before, but recovered and extended her hand. "Welcome to our home, Mister Cobb. It's always a pleasure to meet Peter's friends." She was beautiful. I had never seen anyone like her. Curvaceous figure, light brown hair, and sparkling green eyes that drew undivided attention. The Captain had married well.

The older sister, Sissy, was stunning. No other way to put it. She had her mother's light brown hair, green eyes, angelic face, and an hourglass figure cadets dream about, particularly early morning. Only sixteen when I met her, she looked and acted like a young lady, a beautiful Planter's daughter. She also copied her mother's grace and quick wit. She was perfect. I instantly decided I had to have her and counted myself lucky to get a jump on the competition.

Other than flirtations with the girls in Catawba County, I had not taken serious interest in girls. This was different.

She asked, "Mister Cobb, are you a Virginian?"

"No, uh, I'm from North Carolina." I mentally kicked myself for being inept with a girl I wanted to impress.

The day went as I hoped - relaxation in a pleasant setting with interesting company. During the day, I talked with both sisters and enjoyed their company. Pete took me on a leisurely ride around the Morgan Plantation. It, too, was impressive. Numerous slaves worked well-tended fields, work I had done on our farm in Piedmont North Carolina. The Morgans had a luxury we didn't – slaves to tend the lawn and flowerbeds.

* * *

At supper, they asked many questions about VMI. I answered some directed to me, but mostly listened and observed while Pete told his family about his life at VMI.

William Morgan did not speak as a gentleman, but what he said seemed measured and well considered. I decided he was an intelligent man who lacked formal education and talked like what he once was – a seaman. He had polite table manners, but not the easy grace and polish of a Planter. Captain Morgan was a man less intelligent neighbors might consider "coarse".

Margaret Morgan, the mother, flitted about among her husband, children, servants, and guest without seemingly finishing a thought or sentence, but she ran the house and managed the family. As she talked, I thought she could be considered superficial.

I found the younger daughter, Missy, intriguing. Although still a tomboy, she had mostly passed the stage where awkward young girls transform into refined young ladies. She had an independent mind and intellectual maturity I noticed and admired. Physically, she favored her father more than Pete and Sissy and I suspected she also inherited his intelligence. It appeared William Morgan was partial to Missy by the way he looked at her and deferred to her in the family discussions.

I got up early for breakfast Sunday morning wishing I could stay longer. However, Pete and I had to be at mandatory chapel service and decided we could make the late service at 11 am if we left the Morgan Plantation by 8 am or 8:30 at the latest. As I walked toward the dining room, I heard the Morgan parents talking in the parlor.

"What do you think of Peter's roommate?" William Morgan asked his wife.

"He's polite and well-mannered. What do you think?"

"From what I've seen, he's not like most of Peter's friends. This one has a good head on his shoulders. He reasons before he speaks. Peter can learn from him."

I could not believe my good fortune – a good friend, a second family, and maybe, by the grace of God, my future wife.

* * *

I was smitten with Sissy and resolved to spend as many weekends as possible at the Morgan Plantation. Pete was amenable. He liked having his roommate around for company and winning the races to and from school.

Starting with Lem Randolph, first day, I picked up comments and bits of conversation derogatory to Pete and the Morgans. But whatever social stigma the Morgans had in the community meant nothing to me.

After several visits to the Morgan Plantation and thinking about it between visits, I worked out a plan to win Sissy Morgan. It would not be easy. She flirted with all the cadets Pete brought home and the neighboring boys who came by regularly. I watched as she encouraged each to think her affections were meant for him alone. Peter Morgan had many friends with the local young men and among the VMI Outcasts and even some of the Cavaliers who were now attracted to his sister and the nearby hospitality of the Morgan Plantation. The prospect of a pretty sister and free food overrode whatever reservations they may have picked up about the Morgans. I was one among many.

For the cadets, the Morgan Plantation was an opportunity to escape, albeit temporarily, the rigors of life at VMI and flirt with Pete's sisters. The girls, and particularly Sissy, enjoyed teasing and leading on the young men their brother brought home to visit. I suspect it began well before Pete entered VMI.

I joined the ranks of Sissy's suitors using my inside position as Pete's roommate and best friend to defeat the competitors. However, I encountered an immediate tactical problem in courting the lovely Sissy Morgan - her little sister. Missy tagged along whenever I had opportunity to be alone with Sissy.

* * *

With Pete and Tom away from the room, I told Ken I wanted him with me whenever we went to the Morgan Plantation.

Ken gave me the knowing look I got when he knew I was working out a scheme and said, "Not a problem roomie, but what are you up to?"

"I want you to keep Missy Morgan occupied while I tend to her sister."

"I knew it." Ken laughed and slapped his knee. "I'll help, but it'll cost you."

"What's your price?"

Ken smiled slyly and answered, "Whenever I doze off in Professor Jackson's class, you stay awake and take notes for me."

I weighed my options – access to Sissy and being alert during Jackson's dull lectures or sleeping through class and no Sissy – and came down on the side of romance. We struck a deal.

"We visit the Morgans together and you entertain the little sister while I court Sissy. Right?"

Ken and I shook hands and it worked out better than expected. Ken treated Missy like a princess and Missy, in turn, gained self-confidence in the company of her brother's well-mannered and attentive roommate. She also began to blossom physically. Never a rival for her sister, but she picked up notice from others besides Ken.

Ken invited her to the cadet balls which thrilled Missy and allowed her to compete with her sister and the other girls for the attention of the cadets. Over the months we knew her, Missy completed her transformation from a gangly tomboy to an attractive young lady. Ken surprised me and himself. He actually preferred Missy to her older sister.

As I learned more about her, I guessed the key to Sissy's affection was her mother. Pete was a good friend and that would not change, William Morgan liked me well enough, Missy was, by now, a friend and confidant, but I would gain the advantage by charming the mother.

I decided the key to Margaret Morgan was her vanity. She was a pretty woman who had probably always been so and would be in the future. Everyone complimented her on her looks. I took a different tack and complimented her on her children (sincere), her charm (sincere), and her intelligence (insincere). Not that my rivals neglected Sissy's mother, but none flattered her as I did. As result, I moved up to the front rank of eligible suitors. However, I noticed Missy often turned her head and smiled when I charmed her mother.

* * *

One afternoon, in my second year at VMI, Missy said, "Ken, if you would, please wait for me in the parlor. I need to speak with Jim."

I followed Missy to the porch. She closed the front door behind us and began laughing. I joined in without knowing why.

Missy said, "You're winning. It's time to pull back on the flattery. Mother made inquiries with friends in North Carolina about you. If everything measures up, you'll be the frontrunner for Sissy."

I became giddy with the idea I was winning, but also intrigued by the precocity and lack of guile of the younger sister. I asked, "Has it been that obvious?" To which Missy replied, "Yes." And we started laughing again.

I pointed out what Missy's mother was likely to discover. "My mother is a widow and owns a large and prosperous farm. No disrespect, but it's larger than the Morgan Plantation. My father was an attorney who died in a smallpox epidemic the year before I came to VMI. My older brother ran off to sea when he was sixteen. Mother manages the farm. I hope we pass muster."

"It won't do." Missy shook her head as she spoke. "Mother wants to marry Sissy to a Planter."

I ignored Missy's comment and teased her by asking, "Who does she want you to marry?"

"When the time comes, I'll decide." She snapped her head back and frowned.

"Good for you," I replied and meant it. I admired her spunk.

* * *

I followed Missy's advice and scaled back the flattery, but continued to be the favorite with Margaret Morgan. As a consequence, Sissy attended the cadet balls and parties with me except for the one time I offended her by laughing at one of her mispronunciations.

It started innocently. Ken, Pete and I sat around the dining table enjoying a custard treat when the sisters joined us. Still learning sophistication and trying to impress, Missy asked Ken, "Have you read Victor Hugo's Les Miserables?" and made the proper pronunciation of the classic novel. Sissy corrected her and pronounced the title phonetically. Everyone at the table laughed.

When the girls were eight and ten, Margaret Morgan hired a tutor to teach her children French after she read an article about how French was the vogue in the better homes of Charleston and Richmond. Pete flatly refused, but, no matter, it was the girls who would need the added cachet to attract suitable husbands. However, it was apparent Missy was the sister who learned best.

Sissy ignored the others and turned on me. "How dare you laugh? You say you love me and here you're teasing me." Sobbing, she ran to the parlor with me in pursuit. It always worked to get her what she wanted and it worked now. She wanted to punish me and continue control of our relationship. With her back to me, she said, "I never want to speak to you again, Mister Cobb."

"Sissy, I'm sorry," I apologized. "I thought it amusing and assumed you did too. Please forgive me. It won't happen again."

She replied, "Under the circumstances, I will not attend the

Spring Ball with you. George Fisher invited me to go with him yesterday. It'll be nice to have an escort who is a true gentleman, someone who will not tease me."

I responded, "As you wish" and walked back to the dining room. Not exactly what Sissy wanted, but she played her hand and I followed suit. I invited a city girl I knew Sissy envied and detested. I also knew Fisher was a bore even with the other cadets.

As Pete predicted, Sissy forgave me and resumed our courtship after, of course, making me apologize again. However, despite her affection for me, she continued to see and flirt with other young men. I could not object as I was in no position to offer her a future until I graduated and had an army commission. Despite the coming storm, we settled into an "understanding" for our future together when I graduated.

In retrospect, it all seems insane, but young love is seldom rational. Unless I could bring up my overall rating in the last year, after Carly Bryce was hopefully gone, I would have little chance of securing a commission except if there was a war. A war would and did change everything, but I did not think it through at the time. Sissy had that effect on me. Hard to reason clearly when I put her on a pedestal and convinced myself I could have her.

* * *

As I thought seriously about marrying into the Morgan family, I wondered why they were outcasts. To me, the Morgans were polite, genteel, and friendly, a typical Planter family with pretty daughters. I began questioning to learn more, but answers from Pete and Sissy were defensive and, I thought, evasive.

I went to the sure source and asked Missy, "Can you tell me about your father? You have told me your family has low social standing in the county. I have spent time with you and wonder why. Can you help me understand?"

Missy explained that her father was born in Norfolk and literally worked his way up to ship captain starting as a ten year old cabin boy. "I've never heard him talk about his family or early years at sea" she said. "There are persistent rumors of slave trade, pirating, and rum smuggling that come up every time we seem to make progress. But whatever it was, it was behind him by the time he met my mother."

Although pirating and smuggling were all alien to me, I smiled and nodded as Missy spoke. I knew she was sincere in everything she told me. From her expression, it hurt her to speak of her family's low social standing, most particularly about the community's perception of her father.

She told me Captain Morgan gained fame in Norfolk as the youngest ship captain and owner. He was considered a prime catch by the older women. Her mother worked in the family's millinery store in Norfolk looking for a better life when she met Captain Morgan at a church social. At the time she kept company with a law clerk whose family was from North Carolina. Missy thought the law clerk may have been my father and, from what I knew of his life in Norfolk, she may have been right. Regardless of whom he might have been, Margaret dropped him to pursue Captain Morgan.

"Father may have been married earlier" Missy told me "but it was part of his past that no one else knows and he doesn't talk about it. It does not matter to me. He's a good man and has the love and respect of his family regardless of what the neighbors think."

Missy went from analytical to angry in telling me about how her father was treated. When she paused, I said, "I'm puzzled. Any man who pulled himself up from cabin boy to captain is to be admired, not looked down on."

Missy took my hand and squeezed. "Jim, you still don't understand us. You don't see the hypocrisy. A gentleman can keep a Negro mistress and even have children by her. He may drink too much, beat his wife, and cheat at cards, but selling slaves, transporting rum, and pirating are not the occupations of a gentleman. These are all things said about my father. Because of the rumors surrounding him and Mother's near constant and mostly ineffective efforts to impress, we are considered uncouth upstarts and not acceptable in polite society."

I had started Missy down a line of thought that distressed her. To lighten the mood, I put my arm around her, and said, "You're right. I am so ignorant I'm anxious to marry into your woebegone family even if my father was not good enough."

Missy smiled and playfully punched my shoulder. "Polite folks in the Brownsburg community, and I can name them, are reluctant to be seen with the Morgans. But Mother has some cards to play – her children. As you've seen, Peter is a handsome and well-liked young man. Many of the local girls are infatuated with him. Until she met you, Sissy kept a string of boyfriends."

I laughed. "Be honest. She still has a string of admirers, but, to her credit, she doesn't flaunt them in front of me anymore."

It was Missy's turn to laugh. "Thanks to you and your arrangement with Ken, I, too, have a handsome cadet to squire me around."

I blurted, "Did Ken tell you?"

"No, of course not," she teased, "but, I'd have to be blind not to see the game you two are playing."

It was my turn to be embarrassed. I had become fond of Missy and now regretted having tried to deceive her. "Missy, don't be angry. It may have started that way, but Ken has told me several times he really enjoys your company."

Missy smiled and said, "I know and I'm grateful to you for getting it started. I was the youngest girl at the last Cotillion and did I ever lord it over the others at school." She added, "Growing up we had young people at the Morgan Plantation on weekends and they sometimes brought their parents. So, Mother had the social contacts she always wanted."

Chapter 2: Sam Payne

Lexington, Virginia, Virginia Military Institute,
Superintendent's Office,
Thursday, November 17, 1859
Sam Payne

Colonel Smith's office was the same as I remembered - military, neat, and organized. A commendation for Francis H Smith as a West Point cadet corps commander hung in the same place behind the Colonel's desk. Fitting as he had turned VMI into a replica of his alma mater. I visited his office twice before I was expelled. I hoped he did not remember me but considered it unlikely.

I diffidently said, "Colonel Smith, thank you for taking time to meet with me. I believe my note explained the nature of my request. I came for your reply."

Colonel Smith looked at my letter as he replied, "Mister Payne, your request is unusual. I've never had a former cadet ask to rejoin the corps."

I shifted my weight from one leg to the other like the cadet I once was. I replied, "I wouldn't make the request if it were not for the unusual circumstances."

Colonel Smith shook his head. "I think, in the end, our presence at the hanging will be ceremonial. Little likelihood John Brown's followers will attempt a rescue. But, if they do, I want you to drop out and seek safety."

"May I take your concern for my safety as acceptance of my request?" I asked.

Colonel Smith's smile put me at ease. He said, "Yes. And the gift Mister Greeley offered the Institute did not diminish my inclination to accept. There may be other reporters in attendance, but you'll be the only one up close in a cadet uniform."

Many reporters covered John Brown, but none more diligently than I. Without Greeley telling me, I knew I had vaulted to the first rank of New York reporters and Colonel Smith now saw me as a credit to the Institute. If not in his presence, I might have felt proud.

He peered at me over his reading glasses. "I hope you understand what that means?"

I knew exactly what he meant, dreaded it and muttered, "Drill".

"You still remember the joy of cadet life?" he asked.

"Yes, Sir. The Hardee Drill Manual." How could I forget? Hour after hour on the parade ground with the mind numbing rote of the drill manual and upperclassmen hollering and cursing at my ineptitude.

"You will join afternoon drill until the detachment leaves for Harper's Ferry."

"Sir, the hanging's been moved outside Charles Town to make it more remote for anyone tempted to sneak in."

During coverage of the raid, I met a reporter, James Templeton, with the Richmond Whig. Templeton was also a college man, University of Virginia, and recently married. Figuring the Whig and Tribune had little overlapping readership, we swapped notes and observations and found it helped our stories. Templeton told me of the hanging site.

"Why bother?" Smith asked. "You wouldn't believe the requests I've received to go in as a cadet."

I could. America's leading actor, John Wilkes Booth, had joined the Richmond Grays in order to attend the hanging. I heard Colonel Smith had given a cadet uniform to Edmund Ruffin, a leading Virginia Secessionist, so he could attend. I was unsure if he had allowed others to enter as VMI cadets. I asked, "Will any of them join me in drills?"

"No. You are the only one of our guests so blessed. It will put you closer to the gallows."

"Thank you." My joy was tempered by certainty of the drills I detested and reporting the hanging of a deeply spiritual man I had come to respect.

"To help you prepare, I will assign you to the company of one of our third year officers, Bryce Carlton. I warn you he is a martinet, but our best drillmaster."

Thinking of the article I would write later, I asked, "Sir, what will be the Institute's role at the hanging?"

"Governor Wise not only accepted my offer to supply a detachment of cadets, but gave me responsibility for the execution."

"How have you organized the detachment?" I asked.

"Major William Gilham will command an infantry battalion of sixty four cadets. We will also bring two howitzers under command of Major Thomas Jackson with twenty one cadets. Professor Jackson assigned Cadet Officer Carlton to drill his detachment for service at the execution. The howitzers will be positioned on each side of the gallows and your detachment will stand behind the howitzers."

I remembered Professor Jackson from my cadet years and knew the drill would never be good enough.

"I sent for Mister Carlton. He'll take you to the Quartermaster for a uniform and then out to the field for the first drill."

I thought back to my first year at VMI and a particularly obnoxious upperclassman and commented, "As a Rat, I positively hated an upperclassman. His name was also Carlton."

"That would be Bryce's older brother, Lloyd. Fine tradition of drillmasters in the Carlton family. As an older man and out of school five years, I hope you understand the purpose of the hazing."

"I do. It's necessary to develop an officer who'll instantly obey orders. It drove me out of the Corps when I realized I could not handle the discipline."

Smith surprised me with his reply. "You're not by yourself. Many of our former students have gone on to other careers. Some, like you, have distinguished themselves."

A knock on the door interrupted our conversation.

Colonel Smith ordered, "Enter."

A cadet officer walked in, stood at attention, and delivered a precise salute.

"At ease, Mister Carlton."

Bryce Carlton spread his feet but remained stiffly upright. From what I remembered of them, he seemed the perfect cadet officer. Tall, lean, red hair with an imperious nose and air of manifest superiority.

Colonel Smith pointed to me. "This is Sam Payne, a former student who will rejoin us temporarily. He's a reporter for the New York Tribune. Mister Payne will be with us at the hanging. You may have read his reports on John Brown's raid, capture, and trial. He will report the hanging. I want you to drill Mister Payne from now until then. I expect you to be courteous and professional in your conduct with Mister Payne. Bring him to the highest level of readiness you can."

Carlton looked at me dismissively and turned his gaze back to Colonel Smith. He stiffened, clicked his heels, saluted, and replied, "Yes, Sir."

Carlton turned to me. "If you would, Mister Payne, accompany me to the Quartermaster for a fitting. In keeping with the Colonel's command, you may drill in your civilian clothes today. Tomorrow, you will drill in uniform like the cadets."

"Thank you, again, Colonel." I stiffened, and, following Carlton's example, clicked my heels, and saluted. Colonel Smith returned the salute. I followed Carlton through the door.

* * *

"How long have you been in New York, Mister Payne?" Carlton asked.

"Outside drills, call me Sam if you like."

"That won't be necessary Mister Payne. I am wondering if you're tainted with Yankee sentiment."

I began to question if a front row seat at the hanging was worth the abuse I would take from the petty, little bastard. "Good reporters don't have sentiment. I try to be a good reporter," I answered.

In a supercilious tone I already hated, he replied, "I'm sure you do. But, I've read your articles from Harper's Ferry. You're treating John Brown with undue respect."

"Letters to the editor say I do not give him enough respect. John Brown may be the most divisive man in the country."

Carlton noticeably stiffened and replied, "Which country Mister Payne? Not mine. He's a scoundrel and rabble rouser here."

"So noted Mister Carlton. Probably best if we limit our discussion to the finer points of drill."

"As you wish, Mister Payne." He appeared to have what he wanted. Someone else to torment and, better yet, a Yankee.

We continued to the drill field. Carlton marched to the front of the cadets. They quickly came to attention. I stood off to the side. Carlton pointed to me and announced, "We have the honor of including Mister Payne in our drills until after our visit to Harper's Ferry. Mister Payne's a former cadet and currently works as a reporter for the New York Tribune. He's a bit rusty on drill so I will place him between our two best cadets. Mister Cobb, Mister Johnson, make room for our new addition."

Carlton motioned me to two cadets on the back row who parted so I could stand between them.

"Mister Morgan, you're excused from further drill for the

duration. Loan Mister Payne your rifle. He'll take your place in the drills."

Pete Morgan stepped from the back row making a show of handing his rifle to me amid groans of the other cadets.

"Silence! Company, a..ten..shun," Carlton ordered.

My mind raced through the field manual I memorized as a cadet and more recently in preparation. My heart pumped and palms sweated. I was a cadet at his first drill, again.

Carlton barked, "Shoulder arms."

I brought my rifle up with my right hand perpendicular to the front between the eyes, barrel to the rear. With my left hand up, I grabbed the rifle with the right hand four inches below the cock. With a second motion, I turned the rifle barrel to the front and moved the rifle to my left shoulder while extending my forearm on my chest between the right hand and the cock. Then I rested the cock against my left forearm with my left hand on the right breast. In a third motion, I smartly dropped my right hand by my side, proud that I got through the procedure without error or pause.

Carlton stopped us and said, "Gentlemen. After all my best training, you still don't have it. Didn't any of you notice Mister Payne lagged behind? You were inhospitable to our Yankee guest. Try it again, this time to Mister Payne's pace."

I whispered to Cadet Johnson, "Real jewel isn't he?"

"You've seen nothing yet," he muttered.

Carlton called out, "What was that Mister Johnson?"

"I advised Mister Payne to hold his rifle closer."

"Now that's the spirit. The Yankees may be thrusting their hireling way of life on us, but that's no reason to be rude."

Lexington, Virginia, Home of Professor William Allen,
Monday, November 28, 1859
Sam Payne

I stood in the parlor of my father-in-law's home. A modest and genteel dwelling befitting his position as Head of the History Department at George Washington College. His home was neat and comfortable which I attributed to the Professor's house-keeper, Sukie. Professor Allen had an academic indifference to appearances. The parlor was dominated by a comfortable stuffed chair where he often sat with a brandy while grading student papers.

Each of us held a shot glass of whiskey. I hoped he now saw potential in his son-in-law.

"How were drills today?" he asked.

Thinking back to the Hardee Manual, I replied, "I remember things I hoped to forget"

"Life has a way of going back on you." Professor Allen chuckled. "I must confess when you stole my little girl and took her north, I was convinced you'd fail, come back, and admit I was right all along."

Allen took a sip of brandy and held his glass up in an apparent salute. "Now I confess I was wrong about you. Reporting is not a fit occupation for a gentleman, but you found the one publisher who elevated it to a profession."

"Father, it was you who encouraged Sam to go to New York," Mary said as she joined us.

Still the Southern Belle I married. Two years of living in New York had not coarsened her. We were married three years and the sight of her had never failed to arouse me. Underneath the fine dresses and corsets she wore, the Professor's little girl was a passionate woman I loved more each day of our marriage.

"Yes, but I hoped and expected him to fail, so I could have my girl back home."

Mary put her arms around her father's neck and kissed him on the cheek. "I'm always your girl. But, Sam's not just a reporter. He's a Lead Reporter at the Tribune."

"I'm fond of you too. How about we visit regularly and you come see us when I take all the money Mister Greeley will pay me and buy a Manhattan home?" I asked.

"Sounds good to me," Professor replied as he looked back and forth at Mary and me, "especially if you work in grandchildren along the way. But all this visiting back and forth may soon be across national boundaries. Our country is headed for separation. Have you decided in which nation you want to reside?"

I felt tension in the interviews I had conducted following the John Brown Raid, rigidity on both sides. Unless something dramatic and unexpected happened, the United States would soon separate. "It's a problem many families, including ours, will face," I allowed.

"How are you leaning, Mister Payne?"

"I'm torn." Returning to Virginia reminded Mary and me of how gracious and comfortable life is in the South. People hold doors open for others. Ask about your well-being and are sincere in doing it. Not like that in New York. People there are loud, rude, talk too fast, and indifferent to the welfare of others. "If the issue were comfort, we'd live in the South," I said. "But as you advised me when I asked about a career, the heart of the nation's economy is New York. There, even the poorest immigrant knows, if he works hard and applies himself, he can make a better life for himself and his family. In the South, wealth and prosperity come from a permanent underclass – the slaves."

Finding opportunity for a reasoned debate, Professor Allen commented, "Interesting that you frame the issue in economic terms. You've spent the past month immersed in John Brown and his cause. I would've thought you'd define the differences of North and South in moral terms."

I needed balance for my reports and had the best source of

the Southern view in my family. I said, "I need you to restore my balance. From what I know, the moral right is with the North. What's your view of John Brown and the raid?"

Professor Allen never had a son and I knew he enjoyed mentoring his son-in-law whom I hoped he had grown to recognize as a decent and intelligent man. "Remember you asked. I'm a long-winded history professor and I've read your articles with interest. Even discussed them with my colleagues and students. You write well, Sam. But, you're much too kind to that old fraud."

"Your views opposing Brown and the Abolitionists will be the first reasoned response I've heard," I replied. "Please, tell me what you think." To date, the Tribune readers were presented a South implacable and ready to secede. All based on a historically outmoded attachment to slavery. I needed balance in the stories. I needed Professor Allen's view.

"Our country grew from bondage labor. First, indentured servants, then the slaves. In the North, large plantations aren't economic. Small, privately owned farms are efficient in growing corn, wheat, barley, potatoes, vegetables, and fruit. But, in the South, we need large fields for our cash crops – cotton, sugar cane, rice, and tobacco – and that requires slaves. Over the decades, the regional differences hardened into diverse social behavior and even moral perceptions. Slavery's not economic in the North, so the Yankees demonize it while Southerners consider slavery part of the natural order."

"In the early years, many people indentured themselves just to get to America and survive," I pointed out. "They were free people who were free again when their service ended. But, not the Negroes. They are slaves as are their children and their children's children forever. All races long to be free and, in America, all races are free except the Negroes. It cannot last."

Professor Allen obviously enjoyed our debate, something I am sure he did with faculty and students at the college. But his daughter, my wife, seemed concerned our discussion would turn into a dispute. I did not reassure her. Her father was presenting an argument I would use in an article to explain the Southern view to our readers. I did not agree with him, but he made, by far, the best argument I had heard.

"The Negroes are not like other races. They are an inferior race. A few Negroes are educated, some brilliant, but most are little advanced from the jungles where their ancestors were enslaved. It's simply a fact of life. The Negro is much better off with a benign master who cares for him than in the north where Negroes compete with whites for low paying work and many starve."

"But, not all masters are benign," I responded.

"Most are," he countered, but I doubted he had seen photographs of mutilated and beaten Negroes who had tried to escape slavery.

"Our Declaration of Independence says all men are created equal. No mention of race." I looked at Mary who seemed tense. I smiled and she seemed to relax a little.

"As you have seen, the Supreme Court ruled the Negro has no rights a white man is obligated to respect."

Professor Allen seemed content. He had played the trump card; the law was on his side.

"Do you think it a just ruling?"

"I do. It recognizes Negroes as a lesser race. I've read the articles on equality of the races, but intellectuals write them. On the streets of New York, Boston, Philadelphia, and the small towns in the North, the Negro's a second-class citizen. You'd be hard pressed to find a Northern workingman who considers a Negro his equal."

Allen thumped his glass on the chair arm, apparently a signal to Sukie who took his glass, refilled it with bourbon, and brought it back to him. It gave me time to compose another question to shift the subject to what I believed was uppermost in the minds of Tribune readers.

"When all of this started, the central issue was slavery. By force of his personality and the boldness of the raid, John Brown has hardened attitudes on both sides. I'm thinking the central issue has shifted to national unity. What do you think?"

Professor Allen gave a reasoned response. "Following defeat of the British Army, the American colonies formed a nation. They entered the union separately, by colony. Ever since, regional differences and conflicts have hastened in frequency and intensity to divide us. Most recently by the actions of John Brown as you pointed out. From the beginning, Northern manufacturers favored high tariffs which protected them and penalize Southern planters and farmers. Slaveholders insist on the Fugitive Slave Law to protect their property. Northern Abolitionists detest it. Because of the unresolved and continuing differences, Southerners want to depart the Union as their forbearers came in – by state. But, if what I read in the New York Tribune and other Northern newspapers is true, the North will tolerate neither the Southern way of life nor our right to leave the Union peacefully."

"Back to my question, what do you think of John Brown?" I asked.

"He's a self-absorbed madman. He wants the nation in a bloody civil war to satisfy his ambitions."

"As you know, John Brown will be executed on December 2nd. I will be there to witness the hanging to the world or at least the New York Tribune's readers."

"How perfect for John Brown. He thinks he's Jesus Christ. Now, even better than Christ, there'll be a reporter at his crucifixion." Professor Allen set his whisky glass down on the table beside him with a thump.

"Come on, you two. There are more pleasant things to discuss." Mary focused on marriage and our home. I learned not to get into philosophical discussions with her, but thoroughly enjoyed mentally jousting with her father.

"Yes, Dear. But allow me to answer your father's question before we move on."

I turned to Professor Allen and said, "I'm fortunate. You once told me to find something I enjoyed doing and then someone dumb enough to pay me to do it. I have and his name is Horace Greeley. I think you know Mary and I love you and want the best for you. After the school year ends, would you consider joining us in our new home, maybe return to the History Department at Columbia? I worry that Northern Virginia, including Lexington, will be ravaged in the war. We'd feel much better if you were with us."

Allen reached out and took Mary's hand and mine in his. "Thank you, Sam. Your invitation means more to me than I can express. My home's here. One thing I learned well as a student and instructor at Columbia. New York's cold, wet, and full of Yankees. That'll never change. My daughter tolerates it because she loves you. You tolerate it because you're a respected reporter for America's premiere newspaper. I love you both, but I will stay here in the genteel South."

Chapter 3: Hanging

Lexington, Virginia, VMI Yard,
Saturday, November 26, 1859
Sam Payne

"Thank you, Mister Payne," Pete joked as we stood with the other cadets waiting to go to Harper's Ferry.

Pete Morgan was a handsome cadet. Taller than most with an easy smile, quick wit, and personal charm, but not as simple as he appeared. He adapted a Cavalier outlook on life and did not seemingly care what others thought of him. At the same time, he often defended his family and the Planter way of life. He, Jim Cobb, Ken Johnson, and another cadet, Tom Edwards, roomed together. Pete was the apparent leader, but mostly because the others found it easier to go along with it.

"This has to be the best two weeks of my glorious career at the Institute," Pete commented. "No drill and all thanks to you."

"You're welcome." I would have enjoyed it myself except for the drillmaster. "But tell me, how do you tolerate that son of a bitch Bryce Carlton?"

"Tolerate is the operative word. There isn't anyone of us that wouldn't kill him given half a chance." Jim Cobb's harsh words surprised me since I considered him the most thoughtful and intelligent of the group. Deep, penetrating blue eyes made him appear serious even when he wasn't. If one of the cadets made it to senior officer, my bet was on Cobb. Like Pete, Jim was a handsome young man with light brown hair, an angular face, and average height. He could hold his own with the ladies but deferred to Pete when they were together.

"Not if I get to him first," I muttered. The others laughed but I wasn't kidding. Bryce Carlton embodied everything I hated about the South – supercilious arrogance that covered generations of gross inequity to Negroes. I continued, "Sincerely, thanks, gentlemen, for putting up with me."

"Hey, you came around pretty good for an old man." Ken Johnson jumped in and lightened the conversation. If any of the cadets could be described as humorous, it would be Ken. He had the disadvantage of being short, but did not let it daunt him.

I laughed along with the others. I missed the satisfaction of serving in a unit and the camaraderie of friends like these young men.

I asked Ken, "How did you and Jim rate being Carlton's favorite underclassmen?" I'd been curious about that since that first day on the drill field.

Ken winked and pointed to Pete Morgan. "It's Pete's fault."

"Me? How do you figure that?" Pete feigned offense at the suggestion.

"No Pete. No pretty sister who prefers Jim Cobb. No jealous Carly Bryce." No one could argue with Ken's logic.

"Carly Bryce?" I asked. "I heard you call him that before."

"Yeah," Ken answered. "It's the nickname we gave our favorite upperclassman."

"Gentlemen, give me your attention," Colonel Smith ordered from the podium. He stood with Professors William Gilham and Thomas J Jackson. When the cadets quieted, he continued, "Good luck on your assignment. The eyes of the nation will be turned to the execution of John Brown and you will represent our school at the hanging. Conduct yourselves to our highest standards. It's also important you look your best. For the occasion, I've arranged for you wear new shirts."

He held up one of the bright red shirts which caused cheering from the cadets. "Wear these and return them in the same condition."

Pete whispered to Ken, "Bet we can pick up girls with those."

Colonel Smith added, "As you know, you'll be under command of Majors Gilham and Jackson."

Jackson came to the podium first as Pete said to no one in particular, "Damn. There goes all our fun."

Ken leaned toward me. "Did you have the pleasure of Professor Jackson's lectures when you were here?"

"Yep. Deadly dull," I replied. I never met anyone who could sap excitement from an otherwise interesting topic like Jackson. An eccentric man even for a college professor. Jackson fought honorably in the Mexican War and came to VMI with his wife. She died and he remarried a Presbyterian minister's daughter. They stood out on campus by their severe prohibition and Jackson's stern views on religion and life in general. He gave lectures by rote and never deviated from his script. Jackson taught artillery, a required course. Cadets could not avoid his classes.

"We'll take a train to Harper's Ferry this afternoon. Wear your school uniforms and carry your dress uniforms and new shirts. Keep them clean and shine your shoes before you dress in the morning. Report to the Quartermaster for your field kits and ammunition rations. We will bivouac with the State Militia for the night and march to the gallows for the hanging. As Colonel Smith said, make us proud of you."

Charles Town, Virginia, Jefferson County Jail,
John Brown's Cell,
Friday, December, 2, 1859
Sam Payne

Following the trial that drew nationwide attention, Judge Parker banned all press contact with John Brown. I had to respect his order, but I also had to keep articles coming to the Tribune while waiting for the hanging. I found a solution in John Avis, the jailer.

I approached Avis with an offer, "Judge Parker will not allow me to question John Brown, but I can interview you. If you would, tell me what you observe with John Brown and the Tribune will pay you ten dollars for each report."

Avis shook his head. "No, I don't want your money. John Brown is an honorable man. The nation should hear his story. I will help you for that reason."

I paid Avis anyway and pleased to do it. I was particularly captivated by his description of their last meeting before the hanging.

John Brown sat in his cell, his food uneaten. John Avis entered the cell holding a blanket, stood, and watched silently. Brown wore the same blood-caked suit from when he was captured and stood trial. He refused to have it cleaned. He would have looked lean, severe, and pathetic except for the steel gray eyes that transfixed and demanded respect. His somber face lit up when he saw John Avis. Finally, Avis said, "The day has come and the hour is fast approaching. Is there anything I can do for you?"

Brown replied no, but added that he appreciated the respect and concern Avis had given him.

"Apparently you'll be buried immediately following the hanging. The box you'll sit on in the wagon is your coffin."

Brown waved his hand as if dismissing the notion of spending the hereafter in a wooden box. "It's of no consequence. The body's corrupt. The soul lives forever."

"The entire nation has an opinion on where your soul will abide," Avis noted.

"Yes. I'm sure they have my soul going in different directions. Heaven in the North and hell in the South. I am comforted God Almighty will make the decision on where I spend eternity."

"I have nowhere near your understanding of the scriptures," Avis replied, "but I know this. Faith and faith alone is passage to heaven. I've never known anyone with more faith than you. You'll reside eternally with Jesus."

John Avis' religion was politely described as "independent". Raised as a Methodist, he became a Free Thinker. He read the Bible as a sincere seeker of truth, but did not attend church. His interpretation of the New Testament paralleled the views of Martin Luther and John Calvin whose writings he apparently never read.

"From your lips to heaven. May it be so," Brown replied. He seemed deeply affected.

"I brought a blanket. You can fold it for a cushion to sit on. The pine box will not be comfortable on the ride to the gallows."

Brown took the blanket and reached into his pocket. "I've something for you," and pulled out his father's watch. After explaining its significance to him, Brown said, "I've carried it with me since he died forty years ago. No one I'd rather have it than you when I depart."

Avis looked at the watch, fought back tears, and finally accepted it. "Please forgive me for what I'm about to do."

Brown put his hand on Avis' shoulder. "For forgiveness there must be offense. God has a plan for both of us. You're doing your duty and doing it with humanity. Nothing to forgive."

"I'll await you at the gallows."

"I'll await you in Heaven."

Temporary camp outside Harper's Ferry, Virginia,
early morning, Friday, December, 2, 1859
Sam Payne

The VMI cadets stood by to proceed to the gallows where John Brown would be hanged. I passed the time with Ken Johnson, Pete Morgan, and Jim Cobb. Other cadets milled around, cleaning rifles, dusting uniforms, chatting.

Ken sidled over to me and said, "I remember you told me you're from Pennsylvania."

"Yeah. We lived in Harrisburg. Father was a railroad engineer with the Baltimore & Ohio. My folks died from the pox while I was in school."

"Sorry about your folks."

"Thanks." My stomach knotted as I recalled getting the news. Even ten years later, part of me could not accept their deaths. I still thought of them as if they were waiting for me at our home, Father returning from work and Mother cooking one of her delicious meals.

"I grew up just down the track in Carlisle," Ken said. "We moved around when I was younger, but my father's been pastor of the First Congregational Church for the past twelve years."

"If I had known you're a preacher's kid, I would've cleaned up my language." I slapped Ken on the back to lighten his mood. He seemed tense.

"Why bother? You see it hasn't had much effect on my roommates." He pointed to Pete and Jim.

"What are your thoughts in witnessing John Brown's hanging?" I asked, suspecting I had stumbled on the rare VMI cadet sympathetic to Brown.

Ken moved a few steps away from the group, motioning for me to follow, then looked around before he said in a low voice, "I hate it. It makes me wonder what I'm doing here. Most of the cadets came to enjoy the show. The Yankee Abolitionist getting what's coming to him. Jim's different, but the few who think as I do are all from the North."

"Are you an Abolitionist?" I asked.

"Never thought much about it until recently, but, I guess I am." Ken rubbed his freshly shaved chin as he told me, "Christ taught all men are equal and I'm learning that I am my father's son. Brown complicates things. Some of the things he's done are as bad as what the slaveholders do. But, for better or worse, he carries the Abolitionist banner today."

Ken turned his head and seemed to withdraw into introspection. I left him and went over to Jim Cobb. I wanted to interview him for the current or a future article. I had not met anyone in what might fit a third category, hoping to preserve the Union and peacefully solve the slavery issue. "I understand you're from Western North Carolina."

Cobb had not heard my conversation with Ken and was still in a cheerful mood. "That's me. Newton, North Carolina nestled away in the Piedmont."

"And you're the object of Mister Carlton's scorn because you stole away Pete's sister."

"She can barely tolerate him," Cobb explained. "His family has a plantation next to theirs. After I finish with the Institute, I'll marry Sissy Morgan and be away from here and Carly Bryce."

"Something like what I did except my Carlton wasn't interested in Mary, thank God." I paused and asked the question I most wanted him to answer, "Jim, do you see this hanging differently than the other cadets?"

"Interesting that you ask." Humor had left him. Jim furrowed his brow as he commented, "In your articles, you mention John Brown divides national opinion not only on slavery, but on national unity itself. I see some of the same in school. Small group of Abolitionists, including our friend, Ken Johnson. Large group of cadets that favor slavery and secession if need be. Then there's me and a few others in the middle."

"What're your views on John Brown and the bigger issues as you see them?" I asked.

"We're headed for a war, a bloody war. John Brown and his misguided raid on the Harper's Ferry Armory hastened it."

"Are you opposed to the Abolitionists?" I wanted to make sure he represented another strain of Southern thought. I heard genteel reasons for secession from Professor Allen, but, basically, he was as pro-slavery as the rest of them.

"This will surprise you, but no," Cobb said. "My family has the largest farm in Catawba County. We built the farm and operated it with slave labor. Three years ago, my parents freed all the slaves. They're all free men and women. But, without exception, they stayed and work the farm as sharecroppers or as paid workers in the mills. The farm is more prosperous than ever."

I mentally sighed. The war could be averted if more on each side thought rationally like Jim Cobb. But they didn't. By his own description, Cobb was in a small minority that included few other than him.

Gallows outside Charles Town, Virginia,
10 AM, Friday, December 2, 1859
Sam Payne

We stood immediately behind the gallows with howitzers on the right and left positioned a little behind so as to sweep the field. Two units flanked us, the Richmond Grays and Company F of the Virginia Militia. Other companies covered the field. Cavalry troops stood two and three deep serving as sentinels. Two riders, one on a black horse and the other on a white stallion, paced around the enclosure. Other companies outside the enclosure acted as scouts. Several infantry companies guarded the jail.

Our march to the gallows had been pleasant. Cheering crowds lined our path. Pretty girls smiled and blew kisses to the cadets who surreptitiously smiled and waved back. Now everyone seemed glum.

Shortly before eleven o'clock, a squad of soldiers took Brown from the jail and the funeral cortege started toward the gallows. First came three companies, then the condemned's wagon, drawn by two large white horses. John Brown sat stiffly on his coffin. Sheriff Campbell and John Avis accompanied him.

The VMI cadets stood on one side of the gallows with the Virginia Militia on the other side. A light breeze slowly furled the state and federal flags mounted on the gallows on an unseasonably warm December day.

Major Jackson and his adjutant marched to the front of the cadets. "Company, attench – hut! Order – arms!" he commanded and then "parade rest!"

We snapped to like a rope drawn taut, boot heels clicking together. Simultaneously, we seized our rifles with the left hand near the upper band and detached them from the shoulder with the right hand, reseized the rifle with the right hand above the lower band with the little finger in rear of the barrel and the rifle butt four inches from the ground and the right hand against the hip. In the next motion, we dropped the left hand to the side and let the rifle slip through the right hand to the ground.

Without pause, each grasped the rifle between thumb and forefinger two inches from the right shoulder with the rammer in front and the butt toe against and inline with the right foot, barrel perpendicular. Then, with the "parade rest" command, in unison we spread our feet out evenly and leaned back slightly.

I felt proud of our performance. I stood with the cadets and awaited arrival of the condemned man.

The wagon came into view. Brown sat on a blanket atop his casket. His lined, weathered tan face already haunted me. Brown's pale gray eyes blazed in defiance. He wore the same rumpled black frock-coat and trousers he wore since being captured. His elbows were tied tightly behind him and his hands hung helplessly at his side as soldiers pulled him from the wagon.

Appearing calm and dignified in the face of his impending death, Brown mounted the steps to the gallows and handed a note to the hangman, John Avis. Brown cocked his head to allow the noose to be placed over his neck.

Sheriff Campbell asked Brown if he should give a private signal before dropping him.

Brown replied in a calm voice I could clearly hear, "No matter to me, but do not keep me waiting long."

He was kept waiting. The troops forming his escort filed into their positions while John Brown stood ten or fifteen minutes blindfolded, rope around his neck, and his feet on the treacherous platform awaiting execution like a soldier at attention.

Avis placed a white linen hood over Brown's head. I watched intently for any sign of shirking, but there was none. Once his knees seemed to tremble, but it was only the wind blowing his loose trousers.

Finally, Colonel Smith called out, "We are ready, Mister Campbell." Sheriff Campbell turned to John Avis who was reading the note John Brown handed him on the scaffold. Colonel Smith repeated his announcement in a louder voice. Sheriff Campbell nudged Avis, who quickly stuffed the note in his pocket, descended the gallows steps, and severed the rope that held the trap door under Brown's feet. An audible gasp erupted from the cadets as John Brown dropped through the platform opening. Brown's arms instinctively flew upward from where they were tied at the elbows. His feet jerked and his body thrashed and then still for several moments, swinging gently in the breeze.

A delayed groan on my left startled me and I turned my eyes to the tear-stained face of Ken Johnson. Ken's lips moved as if in prayer. At the same time, I heard a low chuckle behind me. Pete leaned over and whispered, "Bet he shit his pants."

I shook my head and whispered, "Shh. Major Jackson will hear you."

"Don't worry. Elder Jackson's probably praying for John Brown's soul. Once the war starts, he'll likely run off and join a Presbyterian monastery."

Before I could explain Presbyterians do not have monasteries, Major Jackson heard the talking and ordered, "Silence in the ranks!"

Colonel Smith said the final words of John Brown's hanging. "So perish all such enemies of Virginia. All such foes of the Union. All such foes of the human race."

He left the platform. Sheriff Campbell walked over to Avis who was rereading the note and angrily asked, "What were you doing that was so important you ignored the Colonel's order?"

Avis handed him the note.

Campbell snatched the paper from Avis and read it. He crumpled the note and threw it down. After the Sheriff stomped off the gallows, Avis picked it up, straightened the crumpled paper, put it in his wallet, and later showed it to me.

I, John Brown, am now quite certain that the crimes of this guilty land will never be purged away but with blood. I had vainly flattered myself that without very much bloodshed, it might be done.

Boston, Massachusetts, Home of
Reverend Thomas Wentworth Higginson,
Tuesday, December 6, 1859
Sam Payne

I became captivated with the Reverend Thomas Wentworth Higginson when Horace Greeley ordered me to end my series on the John Brown Raid with him. I researched Higginson - scholar, Unitarian Pastor, active supporter of Brown in Kansas. He seemed to be a follower of Emerson, Thoreau, Fuller and others who dabbled in muddled New England Transcendentalism. He was old Boston in heritage and outlook. His study had an appropriate musty, upper New England look. Rather than facing each other across a desk, Higginson and I sat informally in opposing chairs in the parlor. I pulled out my writing pad to take notes.

"Thank you for allowing this interview," I said.

Higginson sat primly in his chair sipping tea. He put down his cup and replied, "As you well know, it's difficult to say no to Horace Greeley."

"You're right. I've not had any success with it." I hoped to build up an informal relation with Reverend Higginson, but he dismissed opening pleasantries.

"I'm here to answer your questions, Mister Payne. Fire away."

"Following John Brown's raid, I accompanied Lieutenant Jeb Stuart and the Marines to the home Brown rented across the river in Maryland. While there, I saw a briefcase filled with documents that named you and five other leading Abolitionists as supporters of the raid. I purposely did not report any of Brown's support until it came out in the trial. A Senate Committee was formed to investigate what is termed "Brown's Insurrection". Do you expect to be contacted by the Senate Committee and, if so, what will be your response?"

"John was always meticulous. In this case, it works against me and the others named in his documentation. To answer your question, I've not heard from the Senate. But, if I do, I plan to ignore their summons." Higginson sat up stiffly in his chair. Apparently, I had got him thinking.

"You would defy the U S Senate?" I asked.

"Young man, if it has escaped your notice, we're nearly at war with the slaveholders. One spark and it will begin. Brown, the raid, me, and the others will soon be forgotten in the firestorm. This investigation will fall apart before anyone's called in for questioning." Higginson treated me like a student, but no matter. He answered my questions intelligently and gave me what I needed for my final report on the Brown Insurrection.

"How would you describe John Brown?" I asked.

"Let me reverse the question, Mister Payne. You interviewed John Brown several times. How would you describe him?" Until now, I did not know Higginson had read my articles.

"The most moral and courageous man I've ever met. Hawk faced with gray eyes that see right through you. He was, at the same time, exasperating and alluring. I may never meet his moral equal again."

Higginson smiled. "There's little I can add to your description. Human nature's quirky. Some would call him stubborn. I prefer to describe John Brown as perseverant and committed to the Cause."

"His raid on the Harper's Ferry armory seems foolhardy in retrospect. How did it seem to you and the other backers when it was planned?" I asked. By now, I had Higginson leaning toward me. He was fully engaged in explaining the Abolitionist Cause.

"None of us supported it. None. There was only one reason the raid was carried out. John Brown."

"To many, John Brown and his raid was a quixotic failure. How do you see it?"

"The opposite. It's as if we're dealing in two dimensions. All of the material facts of the raid are as you described. But, spiritually? It's far different. Brown's raid and execution have energized the Abolitionist Cause and brought moral sympathy to us as nothing else could. A clear call to arms." Higginson seemed to come out of his proper New England demeanor and became the impassioned Abolitionist I knew him to be.

"John Brown told me his backers were from the Peace Party wing of the Abolitionist Cause. Would you describe yourself and the Secret Six as pacifists?" I was unsure of Higginson's role in the raid and wanted to draw him out.

"No. We've changed. The struggle in Kansas proved there's

no moral suasion or reasoning with the slaveholders. John Brown was right all along. Freedom of the slaves cannot be won except by bloodshed. We're about to see it." I was fairly sure that it would not be Higginson's blood shed when the fighting started.

"At the beginning of my assignment, Horace Greeley told me I must interview you before I concluded. I think he was telling me you are, perhaps, the clearest voice of the Abolitionist movement. The New York Tribune has worldwide readership. What do you want them to know of the Abolitionist Cause?"

Higginson paused. He seemed to appreciate the opportunity I offered and thought the question over a minute before responding. "As children, we think in absolutes. Sweet sour. Friendly unsociable. Safe threatening. Good bad. As we grow older we learn gradations. Things become gray instead of black or white. Then there is the issue of slavery. Our Declaration of Independence states unequivocally that all men are created equal. Certainly, the Gospel extends to all people of all races everywhere. And yet, we have slavery nestled into the fabric of our nation."

"Is there any moral basis for slavery? I've read the arguments of the slaveholders and find them specious. They condemn the Negro as an inferior because they have made him an inferior by denial of basic human rights. No. Elimination of slavery's a moral imperative. No equivocation. No gradations."

"Would you characterize John Brown's raid as a provocation to war?" I asked knowing how Higginson would respond.

"It struck at the slaveholders' worst fear – a slave uprising. I'm not sure failure of the raid and his execution have quieted their fears or that it should." Higginson clinched his fist in defiance. I would put the quote at the top of my story.

Chapter 4: Gathering Storm

Harper's Ferry, Virginia,
Friday, December 2, 1859
Jim Cobb

We marched back to Harper's Ferry to board a train to Richmond. Unlike our parade to the hanging, we found no cheering crowds or pretty girls. The officers hurried us on to the train for a quick trip to the Governor's reception in Richmond. I felt mixed emotions.

On the one hand, I had opportunity to see and be seen with Governor Wise and Virginia government officials. It could only help my career if I handled myself well. On the other hand, everyone knew war was coming. Talking with Sam Payne reaffirmed my conviction, contrary to prevalent thought on campus, the Yankees would fight. From what I knew of relative resources and manpower, the North would win. For a military officer, war meant opportunity, but I believed this war would be a disaster for the South, its army, and the officers and soldiers in that army.

We boarded and took seats randomly. The train engine huffed, puffed, lurched forward and gradually gained speed on the track south. After a few miles, the forward acceleration gave way to a gentle sway of train wheels beating out a soft rhythmic clatter on the tracks. I sat with Pete Morgan and we talked about what we had seen.

"The hanging won't go over well in the North," I commented. "The Yankees consider John Brown a hero for trying to overturn slavery."

"Didn't get far did he?" Pete poked my cap causing it to tilt over my left eye.

"It's not what he did or did not do" I explained as I righted my cap. "It's what people think. John Brown's hanging will pull the country apart. The separation won't be peaceful."

"We'll leave the Union and dare the Yankees to stop us. We can lick an army of store clerks any day of the week." Pete laughed.

"Damn it, Pete, have you been at VMI over a year and learned nothing? The Yankees have more men, more cannon, more rifles, more ammunition, more supplies, more everything. What they don't have is the will to fight, but that will change when the firing starts."

Pete winked at me and said, "Don't worry, Sugar. I'll do the fighting for both of us."

I grinned back saying, "I saw how you took care of the fighting when I first met you."

Pete laughed while we took mock punches at each other.

As I horsed around with Pete, I glanced at Ken and Tom sitting across the aisle in silence and saw that Ken was depressed and Tom was not helping. Excusing myself from Pete, I crossed the aisle, nudged Tom and said, "Let's swap seats."

Now it was Ken and I sitting in silence. Finally, I asked, "Would you like to talk about it?"

"Yeah, I didn't think anyone wanted to hear what I have to say."

"Which is...?"

"We saw a man die because he opposed enslavement of other humans and the crowd applauded. Has the South lost all sense of decency?"

"John Brown died because he deliberately tried to provoke a war" I explained and found myself defending the hanging. "It's treason regardless of his reasons and where he did it. You know, I know slavery's wrong, bad wrong. But, over time, it will be resolved. Morality aside, the plain fact is slavery's no longer economic. If he had succeeded, Brown would've cost lives needlessly."

Ken shook his head and pointed out, "There's a basic flaw in your argument. The slaveholders aren't near as intelligent and open-minded as Jim Cobb. Look no further than our friend, Pete Morgan. Freeing the Morgan family slaves would mean giving up his notion of the good life. He won't do it nor will any of the other slaveholders."

Ken was right and I knew it. The short debate was as finished as it was useless. With me, Ken preached to the choir. I did not respond to his last statement, but, instead, shifted the topic to Ken himself.

"What do you want to do?"

"I must leave. I'm going home and finish college there."

"Don't be rash," I cautioned. "You have good grades and, despite Carly Brice, you're well regarded. You've put in over a year. You need to finish what you've started."

"I can't stay in a school that endorses slavery and hold my head up. But, you're right. I should finish the year and take as many credits with me as I can."

Ken would leave at the end of the second year. Nothing left to discuss. Now it was my turn to be depressed. I shared Ken's views on slavery and the bullheaded determination of the Planters to defend it. But they were my people, not his. I did not have the option of leaving. To keep my mind off the loss of my favorite roommate, I thought about what I would do when the war came and grew more depressed.

* * *

After the Harper's Ferry detachment returned, accounts of the hanging spread across campus among cadets who were and weren't there. The consensus was war with the North was inevitable. We were under orders not to do it, but I noted growing sentiment to take down the United States flag on campus and replace it with the Virginia State flag.

I regretted losing several friends, most particularly Ken Johnson, when cadets from the Northern states would leave for home. Ken was a voice of reason in a world becoming increasingly irrational. During a conversation with him, after we had been in school two months, I sorted out my new life.

The Virginia Military Institute began in 1839. By the time we entered in September, 1858, VMI traditions were well established. The original intent was to provide college education, in a military setting, for the young men of Virginia.

As at West Point and by intent, upperclassmen rigorously hazed first year students. I dutifully carried out my tasks and accepted the daily humiliation as part of the training. However, I found another aspect of VMI life difficult to accept.

As Ken and I walked back to our room from the library, we fell into the swift, crisp cadet cadence. Suddenly, Ken pulled up, began to amble, and said, "We're not in the army yet. Let's take our time getting back. I have something I want to discuss with you."

It was late October, with leaves changing colors, afternoons crisp without yet becoming cold, smoke from leaf and brush burnings scenting the air. A good time to slow down, reflect, and take rest from preparations for the upcoming mathematics test. I pointed to a bench and said, "Let's sit here and talk."

"Have you noticed that none of us were invited to join any of the riding or social clubs?" I nodded as Ken described our circumstances, "I know, for certain, you outride and outshoot anyone in our class in the drills. The rest of us aren't bad either. We know how to conduct ourselves without embarrassment to the school or ourselves. Why, do you suppose, we're not welcome in the clubs?"

"Are you suggesting there's a caste system here?" I asked with a pretty good idea of where he was headed.

"Absolutely. If you check, no cadet from the North or your home state was invited to join any of the clubs. Apparently Southerners from other states are acceptable, but not Yankees and North Carolina Crackers."

"None?"

"Before I came, I was told VMI held high standards, that it was a gentlemen's school. It is. But, what I did not understand then is that, at VMI, gentleman means Virginian. You're not a gentleman nor is Tom nor am I."

"What about Pete?" I asked.

"I don't know." Ken shrugged. "You've seen how girls flock around Pete. I'd think he would be the first invited to a social club. As best I can tell, it has something to do with his family. But, it looks like we picked our roommates well. We're all Outcasts or whatever they call the lowest caste in India."

"Untouchables" I answered and added, "I like Outcasts better."

"Maybe we can organize the other Outcasts and do things together if no one else wants us." He laughed, but it worked out as Ken suggested. Informally, the first year Outcasts ate together, sat in chapel together, and mixed with other Outcasts at parties. For the first and only time in my life, I felt the sting of prejudice, in particular, from Bryce Carlton.

Carlton had the aristocrat look – slender, tall, red haired, elegant, narrow nose, and a stately supercilious bearing, a near perfect Cavalier except one flaw. He was a self-important ass. As Sissy Morgan became interested in me, my position with Carlton worsened.

Sissy did not understand, or chose not to understand, how much misery Carlton could cause me. It started when he dropped by the Morgan Plantation before I came with Pete on one of our weekends.

He had cornered Sissy on the front porch when we arrived. She left Carlton, raced over to me, and planted a big kiss on my cheek. Something she never did before or after, sending a message that was not missed by Carly Bryce. Thereafter, I never did anything properly while under his command.

As at the Military Academy, we received demerits for any action not in keeping with school rules and traditions. The demerits could be for offenses as serious as cheating on exams or as petty as real or imagined slights in appearance. Carly Bryce handed out countless demerits and most particularly to the North Carolina bumpkins and Yankee who roomed with Pete Morgan. He seemed bent on ridding the Institute of the undesirables who mistakenly entered with our first year class.

Of course, Carly Bryce knew he could not court Sissy Morgan while persecuting her brother so he spared Pete. In fact, his obsequious behavior in Pete's presence would have been laughable if not for his malevolent treatment of me, and later Ken and Tom, when Pete was not around.

School administration used demerits to determine class standing and for punishment such as denial of weekend privileges which conveniently kept me away from the Morgan Plantation. The demerits Carlton piled on me ensured I never had a high class ranking or served as a cadet officer. I worked double hard to excel in studies and earn commendations from my instructors. No matter. Carly Bryce, by himself, ensured I would leave VMI with a poor fitness rating.

To maintain harmony within our dormitory room, we agreed to confine our conversations to the usual young male topics and avoid politics. Pete and Tom solidly aligned with the Southern Cause. Ken favored the Union and I found myself in between but mostly sided with Ken. It helped that none of us seriously tried to change the views of the others. Anyway, with hazing, Carly Bryce, and course work, we had little time for idle debate.

* * *

Beginning in the first year, I studied history and economics under Professor Stuart Rawlings Bradshaw. In many ways, I count it among the best experiences of my life.

Bradshaw was a retired army colonel who had served in many areas of the United States and, at one point in his career, was military aide to the US Ambassador to France. He retired and took a VMI faculty position when Congress reduced the army's officer corps following the Mexican War.

Bradshaw was a Virginian without the regional bias of many of the faculty and students at VMI. In appearance, he had average height, thick brown hair and deep set blue eyes. He spoke rapidly and precisely without a noticeable accent. Bradshaw saw the large imbalance in manpower and economic strength and believed the South would inevitably lose the coming war and suffer the consequences. These views made him unpopular on campus. But, not with me. I agreed with him.

Bradshaw smoked a pipe and used a Turkish Mild tobacco blend that gave his office a sweet, musty smell. He kept a world globe on his desk and shelves laden with books on the subjects Bradshaw taught with a sprinkling of classics compiled from his travels. Bradshaw used the globe and the books to illustrate and support discussion points in his arguments. His office had the homey, familiar, lived in feel of the law office of my father who also smoked a Turkish Mild blend. I felt comfortable in his office.

The similarity with and reminders of my father drew me to Professor Bradshaw initially. Long term I came to greatly admire his intelligence, insight, and analytical ability particularly the way he methodically gathered facts, identified the key considerations, and came to a reasoned conclusion. A trait I worked to emulate all my life.

Even though we had few differences in our views, we discussed and debated the coming war in detail. Bradshaw predicted the South would have initial success in the struggle with the poorly trained and organized Union Army, but, over time, would lose as Union resolve and resource advantage built. Years later I saw it happen, but felt bitter, involved, and much less analytical than I did sitting in Bradshaw's office.

As I learned, Bradshaw underestimated how close the South would make the war and how long the war would last before the North finally prevailed. We could have and nearly did win the war despite the huge strategic disparity and I never forget that either.

Our discussions covered many areas of thought – philosophy, science, economics, geography, history, industry, and religion. Initially, I felt uneasy in Bradshaw's presence, like a student reciting to a teacher. But, over time, he came to treat me more as an equal which greatly flattered and reassured his young protégé. I treasured my time with him. It broadened my mind and view of the world beyond Piedmont North Carolina and Lexington, Virginia. I doubt I could have survived VMI and Carly Bryce without my sessions with Colonel Bradshaw.

Professor Bradshaw's Office, Virginia Military Institute,
Afternoon, Monday, December 5, 1859
Jim Cobb

One week after the hanging, I knocked on Colonel Bradshaw's office door. He looked up from his papers, smiled, and asked, "What's on your mind, Mister Cobb?"

As I entered, I said, "Colonel, I'm sure you heard about John Brown's hanging. I was there and what happened bothers me."

Bradshaw looked at me over his reading glasses. "Don't just stand there, take a seat. What's troubling you about it?"

I settled in my favorite overstuffed chair, leaned forward,

and answered, "I think it means war. I talked with a New York Tribune reporter, Sam Payne, and learned much about the John Brown Raid from him. Brown rented a farm before the raid. The Marines searched the farm after Brown and his gang were captured. They found a packet of letters from Brown's supporters. He wasn't acting on his own. John Brown had financial support and backing from wealthy and influential Northerners. His capture and hanging won't set well with them. The Abolitionists will step up their pressure in Washington and the Southern Congressmen and Senators will react strongly."

Bradshaw nodded. "I think you're right. You know how popular I am on campus with my views. I would be much wiser if I kept my opinions to myself, but I'm paid to think and have opinions. I see a train wreck coming." I knew Bradshaw was at the opening of a long talk. But this was the reason I came. I needed his wisdom and insight as a sounding board to work out my thoughts.

"The army always dwindles in peace time. Americans won't pay for a large standing army and never have. The United States Army is pitiful. The South is not yet a nation and has no army. But the South has high-spirited militias."

"Do you think it possible the South could win with a victory in a major early battle before the Yankees fully mobilize?" I asked.

"Maybe. Many in the North just want the South to leave, but everyone is focused on the armies. It'll be the Union Navy that wins the war if it lasts more than two years."

I guessed where Bradshaw was headed when he asked me to point out Southern ports on the globe. "How long do you think it will take the Yankees to capture or blockade our ports?" A rhetoric question I answered with, "No more than two years."

"What will the Union blockade do to the Southern economy?" he asked.

"Strangle it."

"More than armies in the field, the Union will prevail with its navy. The South has no navy going in and will not be able overcome the Union superiority in ships and trained crews. And, as you know, the South is much more dependent on imports than the North. I think the South may get the best of the war in the field in the early going, but, if and when, the North fully mobilizes, it's all over."

I understood what he said and the reasons behind it, but said, "I hope and pray it doesn't come to that."

Bradshaw paid me a much needed compliment, "You have a mature head on young shoulders. The hot bloods eager for war now will come to hate what they long for. War is ugly, brutal, and unfair. You understand this and they don't."

"Is war inevitable?" I asked.

"That's a good question and I don't have a good answer. I doubt President Buchanan will do anything if the Southern states secede. Virginia, Kentucky, Missouri, and Maryland are uncertain. I suspect sentiments are about evenly divided in those states. If the hotheads provoke the President to send in troops, they will cross one of the Border States and it will probably push some or all of them in with the Secessionists. You're from North Carolina. How do you think North Carolina will go?"

"Pro-Union in the West and Pro-Secession in the East. I think North Carolina's split as you describe the Border States. I also think the mountain folk in Tennessee and Virginia are and will remain Unionists."

We had not discussed secession sentiment in nominally Southern states earlier. He said, "That's the crux of the problem. The Secessionists may be able to pull out without a war if they can do it without provoking the Union, but I doubt it. Passions are too high for this conflict to be resolved peacefully."

"What do you see as the basic cause of the coming war?" I asked and was surprised with his answer.

Without hesitation, Bradshaw replied, "Ignorance, blind ignorance."

I wondered what Colonel Bradshaw meant, but not for long. He proceeded to tell me, "Slavery's dying in the South, but the Planters won't give it up. It has somehow become their God given right to rule over another race. The Yankees figure they can take the moral high ground and impose their will on the South. Neither side understands the other. It will be a disaster."

"How long do we have?"

First time we had discussed a time for start of the war. "I give it two years at most" Bradshaw replied. "As we discussed, there's a possibility for peaceful separation, but after listening to the stories floating among the faculty and cadets, I doubt it. I use VMI, my friends at George Washington College, and the Lexington community as a gauge. Whatever sentiment I find here, I multiply for the Deep South." Bradshaw paused and looked at me directly. "Have you decided what you will do when war comes?"

I had not decided. Talking with him helped me organize my thinking, but did not lead me to a conclusion. "I haven't and that's why I came to see you. I think about my friends and roommates. Ken Johnson told me he is leaving. Attending a school that supports a cause he opposes is too much for him. With Bryce Carlton trying to run us out of school, it's more than he wants to handle and I don't blame him. It's likely Ken will enlist in the Northern army and I have great difficulty in thinking about trying to kill him. And the same with Pete Morgan and Tom Edwards. How could I fight against them? I could refuse to fight or leave the country, but that's cowardly and equally unacceptable. I'm stuck whichever way I go."

Bradshaw shook his head and said, "Well, Mister Cobb, you have the classic problem of every thoughtful man who entered a civil war. You understand what the others will learn the hard way. I wish I had an answer for you. Your generation has the unique opportunity to fight a civil war. Nothing you did or wanted, but simply when you were born. All I can suggest is pray hard and kiss your mother and sweetheart each time you leave them."

Morgan Plantation, Brownsburg, Virginia,
Saturday, May 5, 1860
Jim Cobb

I sat on the porch talking with Missy and Ken Johnson. It was a warm, lazy day. We entertained each other with light, amusing conversation while fanning ourselves and sipping lemonade. Bryce Carlton was also there and made a point of sitting away from Missy and the first year cadets he despised. He came to press his luck with Sissy. His sitting apart was not a problem for Ken and me. We hated him as much or more than he hated us. Missy had no use for the Carltons and Bryce Carlton in particular when she learned he persecuted Ken and me, but she was under orders from her mother to be polite to the Carltons including the younger son, Bryce.

The Carltons owned an adjoining plantation as they liked to call their country estates which were not much different than the country estates we called farms in Western North Carolina. I imagined Carly Bryce saw himself marrying Sissy, usurping Pete, and combining the two plantations when the elders passed away. The evil, self-centered son of a bitch probably had plans to kill off the senior Morgans and Carltons.

Margaret Morgan and Sissy went to Lexington to pick up stylish, new French hats ordered at the general store and had returned. The Morgan family carriage stopped in front of the main house. The footman, Scipio, hurried to the carriage door to assist the two Morgan ladies in getting out of the carriage.

Carly Bryce, who sat nearby on the porch, saw an opportunity to impress Sissy and went to the carriage door to open it for her. He did not see Scipio and the two bumped into each other.

Carlton fell and was embarrassed in front of everyone – especially Sissy.

Scipio tried to help him up, but Carlton angrily pushed him away. He got up, took the coachman's whip, and began flailing Scipio. Scipio covered his face with his arms and hands to protect his eyes and face from the lash. I ran down the steps and yanked the whip from Carlton's hand. I wanted to punch him for many reasons including his bullying a defenseless Negro boy.

Before we came to blows, William Morgan came from the house and ordered us to stand down. He asked what happened. Ken Johnson stepped forward and told him exactly what he had seen.

Morgan took the whip from me and handed it back to the coachman. He looked sternly at Carlton and said, "You overstepped your welcome here. Discipline of the slaves on this plantation is my responsibility, mine alone. You will never again touch any of them for any reason. Go home and do not come back until you can behave as a gentleman."

Carlton glared at Ken and me, spun on his heel, walked angrily to where his horse was tied, and rode off.

William Morgan instructed Scipio to go to the kitchen and get something for his welts from Sara, the cook, who also functioned as a nurse for cuts and minor illnesses. William Morgan went back into the house thinking the incident was over. Ken and I knew better.

* * *

On return to VMI, Carlton used his position as a cadet company officer to step up our harassment. We were informed by a sympathetic upperclassman that Carly Bryce told other cadet officers he wanted to see Jim Cobb and Ken Johnson gone. He asked them to join him in awarding us enough demerits to be dismissed from school before the year ended.

Pete reported this to his father. William Morgan, who never liked Bryce Carlton or his family anyway, rode to Lexington and asked for a meeting with the Commandant. He told Colonel Smith what his son said about Bryce Carlton's treatment of his roommates and the incident at his plantation. Smith listened politely, thanked William Morgan for coming to see him, and promised to look into the matter.

Professor Bradshaw told me Colonel Smith was already aware of the situation. He routinely reviewed discipline reports and knew of the demerits piled on us and the source for nearly all of the demerits - Bryce Carlton and upperclassmen the staff suspected were influenced by Carlton. What William Morgan told him confirmed what Colonel Smith suspected. He called Bryce Carlton into his office, gave him a dressing down, and, outside of drill, ordered him to stay away from Jim Cobb, Ken Johnson, and Tom Edwards in the future.

The build up in demerits given Ken, Tom, and me ceased, but none of the earlier demerits were removed so I barely passed the second year. Carlton took satisfaction when Ken Johnson quit at year end. He detested me, but could no longer do anything about it except make my life miserable on the drill field and exercises where cadet officers were in charge.

Train Station, Lexington, Virginia,
Friday, June 1, 1860
Jim Cobb

At the end of the second year, I rode with Ken and other cadets to the train station for the trip north. Ken seemed increasingly morose as the day approached. Not moody, but sad.

In the carriage, I looked at him and asked, "What are you thinking?" I knew, but wanted to give Ken a chance to express what he felt.

My question broke his contemplation. He looked up, and replied, "I feel terrible. Not only leaving VMI, but giving up good friends like you, Pete, and Tom."

With more passion than conviction, I replied, "I don't know what the future will bring, but you and I'll always be friends."

"What if you see me on the other side of a battlefield?"

"I don't know," I answered. "At this point, I just don't know which side I'll be on if either. All the right is with the Union, but how can I go to war with my neighbors, friends, and, maybe even family?"

"Do you think it'll get down to that?" Ken asked.

I shook my head. Hard to consider without becoming sad and frightened. "It's what I see right now. You and the others leaving and probably joining the Union army when the time comes."

"But we're Yankees. We never fit here. I'd think you and the rest of the Southerners would be pleased to see us go."

Ken's comment disappointed me. He did not know me as well as I thought he did. I told him, "It'll be as hard for me to go to war with you and the others who are leaving as it would be to fight Pete, Tom and the cadets staying. If this war is fought on principle, I am on your side."

As Ken approached the passenger car to board, he put out his hand to me. I shook it and wrapped my arms around him and hugged him. The best friend I ever had. As the train left the station, I felt a premonition I would never see Ken again.

Virginia Military Institute, Lexington, Virginia,
September – December, 1860
Jim Cobb

Despite the increasing probability of a civil war, I felt good about my future with Sissy, at least while I visited the Morgan

Plantation. Surely, I thought, everyone would come to their senses, a political solution would be worked out, and war averted. I took comfort in the thought I would not have to fight in a senseless war, not fight Ken. I would have my commission, take my beautiful new bride to a Western post, and start a new life in a new country where Sissy would be away from her mother. Maybe I could replicate the feats of my great grandfather when he came to North Carolina from Gloucester, England and built the Cobb Farm from the wilderness.

Even at the time, I knew it was a foolish notion that flew in the face of logic and the facts I discussed with Colonel Bradshaw. It was what I wanted to believe.

On December 20, 1860, South Carolina seceded from the Union. Other Southern states quickly followed. North Carolina wavered and Virginia and the Border States went into a period of deep introspection.

South Carolina ordered the United States to turn over the forts in Charleston harbor. As Colonel Bradshaw predicted, the incumbent President, James Buchanan, did nothing as the Union fell apart. The incoming President, Abraham Lincoln, ordered the United States forts in Charleston harbor be defended. On April 12, 1861, the South Carolina militia fired on Fort Sumter in Charleston Bay and forced surrender when Union ships were prevented from reaching Fort Sumter for reinforcement.

The war was on.

Union forces could not attack South Carolina without crossing Virginia. Virginia joined the Confederacy on April 17, 1861. Arkansas and Tennessee followed. North Carolina joined the Confederacy on May 20, 1861. But all of this was pending in December 1860.

Cobb Farm, Newton, North Carolina,
Saturday, December 22, 1860
Jim Cobb

I stood with Mother in the entertainment room filling with guests. A few of my friends went on to college, but most worked with their fathers and mothers. She looked proudly at me and said, "No mother has a finer, handsomer son. Aren't you glad now you're wearing your uniform?"

I did not want to wear it, but she had insisted and I noted the expressions of the girls and their mothers who arrived. They didn't know what to make of me. The same freckled-faced kid they saw in overalls with a file and handkerchief hanging out the back pockets now in uniform as a cadet.

Mother invited my friends from school and church along with some of the parents to act as chaperones. She hired a fiddler and made sure the guests had plenty of food and apple cider. No one ever came to a table Anne Cobb set and left hungry.

As I promised her, I was polite with all the guests and danced with as many of the girls as I could. But my affection was fixed on Sissy Morgan. I thought of her even as I flirted with the local girls. When I returned to school, I was determined to convince her to become engaged to marry when I graduated. If we somehow ended up on the Cobb Farm, I knew Sissy would like my friends and neighbors and they would like her, after all, she was perfect. They could only love her as I did.

As I talked with one of the girls, I felt a strong hand on my shoulder. I turned around and saw Dolph Travetz, a friend and neighbor who attended The Citadel in South Carolina, wearing his cadet uniform.

"Dolph, go home and change. I want all the girls to myself."

Dolph reached out for a handshake and asked, "How's it going, cadet?"

I politely excused myself from the young lady and took Dolph over to the punch bowl. As I picked up cups for us, Dolph pulled out a flask hidden up his sleeve and whispered, "Want me to spike yours?"

I looked around to make sure Mother and the chaperones were not watching and put out my cup for some of Dolph's 'shine.

"Do you know they built a military school in Charlotte?" he asked.

I saw it on the train ride down from Lexington. "Just think, we could've had a fine military education and stayed home."

"And miss all the fun at The Citadel and VMI?" We both managed to keep a straight face.

"How do you like VMI?" Dolph asked. He considered attending VMI before settling on The Citadel. His grades were good enough for either.

"Other than being an inferior, too many classes, constant drilling, and an upper classman who's trying to drive me out, it's not too bad," I replied.

"I hear they're hard on Tarheels." Dolph nodded as if he already knew about the prejudice against North Carolinians in Virginia.

"They are, but how about The Citadel?" Maybe he ran into the same thing in South Carolina where the planters also thought themselves better than us.

"They know better than to try and lord it over us. Classes are hard, upperclassmen are asses, we drill all the time, but no pecking order."

I learned Dolph's training at The Citadel paralleled my own at VMI. But each of us thought our school better. We commiserated briefly and then split up to pursue our primary mission – to entertain as many young ladies as possible before the party broke up.

Recent news of South Carolina's secession dominated conversation. The talk was about which states would join South Carolina and when. When asked, I stated my hope that a compromise would be worked out to allow the seceding states to form a new nation without interference from the United States and left it at that.

Opinion on where North Carolina should go was divided among the guests. Approximately half wanted North Carolina to join with South Carolina in a Southern nation. The other half, including Mother and me, opposed our state leaving the Union. I felt encouraged when Dolph spoke up with similar sentiments. He seemed ready to join with South Carolina, but did not welcome it. I was more interested in determining the opinions of the neighbors, and discussing it with Colonel Bradshaw when I returned, than debating with the guests.

Over the years, our family earned a grudging acceptance. The neighbors seemed convinced we were covert Abolitionists. But, on the other hand, they could not help but notice the Cobb Farm did well and became more prosperous each year. They eventually acknowledged we were fair with our mill fees and barter.

The Cobb Farm slaves were more industrious and somehow more intelligent than their slaves. Our slaves took initiative and did things without being told. They saw work brought to the mills performed promptly and efficiently without any apparent white supervision. The inner workings of our farm were mysterious and baffling to the neighbors, but they considered Mother and me decent and likable people even if we held Yankee sentiments. None of them knew our slaves were freemen or they would have really come down on us.

I came to an understanding of what my father faced during his adult life. The neighbors were not stupid, but often ignorant. Some held distrust, bordering on hostility, toward knowledge and learning. It certainly did not typify all the neighbors, but too many of them. They were far too eager to accept an easy answer and act on emotion instead of reason. The coming war was a case in point and I felt helpless in averting the "train wreck" Colonel Bradshaw predicted.

When I returned to VMI, I felt uneasy. The tranquility of Catawba County would change irretrievably before the next summer.

Chapter 5: War

Virginia Military Institute, Lexington, Virginia,
April 17, 1861
Jim Cobb

We watched a crowd gather on the schoolyard. They milled around the flagpole intending to take down the United States flag. One cadet, a Company Commander, one of the upperclassman bastards we hated, carried the Virginia state flag, folded over his shoulder, as he strode briskly to the flagpole, the crowd parted.

"I won't miss this." Tom said and took off to join the mob.

"Are you coming?" Pete asked me as he started to follow Tom.

"No, go on without me."

Pete stopped and asked, "Why not?".

"It's war." I answered, a bit miffed. "Do you understand? No going back now. Virginia's joining the Confederacy."

"Yeah, we'll be free of the damn Yankees. It's a great day for Virginia. That's why everyone's celebrating. What's your problem?"

I hesitated. What was my problem? Then I smiled and said "Nothing. I knew this day would come and now it's here. I'll join you. It's a historic day. I don't want to miss it either. I'll race you to the flagpole."

We took off to the courtyard where a spontaneous and rapidly assembled group of students, faculty, and town people celebrated. More curious than caught up with the excitement, I followed Pete into the crowd. Two cadets, the same two assigned to tend the flag, had lowered the United States flag, removed it, tossed it on the ground, and raised the Virginia flag. They hoisted the state flag to full staff where it snapped and furled in the stiff breeze. The crowd applauded and broke into singing "Dixie" while shaking hands and slapping one another on the back. More than a few flasks came out of back pockets to toast Virginia's new status as the latest Confederate state.

I picked up and folded the national flag to save it from being trampled under foot.

"What the hell you want with the enemy flag?" Pete asked. "Guess you hadn't heard. The Virginia legislature meets today to decide on our leaving the Union. Great ain't it?"

"Yeah. Explains a lot. I was at the train station yesterday. Saw what appeared to be Union sympathizers buying tickets on the trains headed north."

* * *

"It is our honor and privilege to support Virginia and the Confederacy by training volunteers who're gathering in Richmond. I expect each of you to do your duty to the best of your ability, help train the Virginia Army, and bring honor to our school. You will serve under Major Thomas Jackson who'll direct training of the recruits."

Colonel Smith stepped down and Major Jackson began explaining details of our new assignment.

Pete, who stood next to me, leaned over and whispered, "He's a lot more alive than we ever saw him in class."

I nodded but did not want to draw attention and a possible demerit by responding. No doubt the bastard, Carly Bryce, would be around to put me on report. Despite the Captain ordering him away, he kept hanging around the Morgan Plantation to court Sissy and lurking around me for opportunity to give me a demerit.

"I know a tavern in Richmond where we can get a room. We'll have fun while we're bringing honor to the Institute." Pete grinned as he thought of the earthly delights waiting in a city of compliant serving wenches who would be impressed by a VMI cadet and training officer in the new army.

Richmond, Virginia,
Tuesday, April 23, 1861
Jim Cobb

As third year cadets, Pete, Tom, and I got first pick on a room over Pete's favorite tavern. But reality fell short of expectation. We got a small room with one bed. Two slept in the bed and we took turns sleeping on the floor with a pillow and comforter. The first night quenched notions of nightly frolic with the tavern barmaids.

After repeated and futile attempts at enticing the servers, Pete gave up and returned to the room. He grumbled, "Damn wenches don't know a good time when they find it."

"Came up empty did you?" Tom asked.

"The way they act you'd think they prefer the old men."

"Yeah, the ones who buy drinks and leave something extra. Your secret's safe with us. Right, Tom?" I said.

Tom nodded.

"Not a word of this to the underclassmen," Pete cautioned. "We have a reputation to uphold. I'll make up stories to satisfy their curiosity. You back me up. Understand?"

I never had the heart to tell Pete his reputation was more in his head than in those of the underclassmen he sought to impress. "The truth will never do," I agreed.

We ended up swearing one another to secrecy, taking plain

meals, and going to our room to study or walk around Richmond when not training volunteers. Not at all what Pete envisioned before we came.

* * *

I found Richmond much like Lexington and the VMI campus – bristling with patriotism and enthusiasm for the coming war. The Virginia Militia and the citizens of Richmond worked diligently to put the city on a war footing. In a few weeks, Richmond transformed to a military camp teeming with soldiers, concerned citizens, and curious children on every street.

We were soon caught up in the frenzy. At night, the tavern filled with soldiers, recruits, government workers, and merchants drawn to profits from the coming war like bees to a hive under attack. On one occasion, we shared a table with Wallace Freeman, a state treasury official. He had ducked into the tavern for a quick meal before going back to his office for work into the night. With all tables occupied, he took an empty chair at our table, introduced himself, and motioned to a waiter to come for his meal order.

"Mister Freeman, do you think Richmond will become the Confederate capital?" I asked.

He replied, "There's no reason to keep the capital in Montgomery. Virginia will supply more troops and equipment to the Confederacy and is in the greatest peril from invasion. We must defend Virginia and Richmond from Union armies that will come down through Maryland. We need the full resources of the Confederacy and better accomplished if Richmond is the capital."

I tried to ask more questions, but Freeman waved me off and concentrated on finishing his meal. I had his name and position for my report to Colonel Bradshaw when I returned to VMI.

During my free time, I wandered around Richmond and

observed the rapid build up of armed troops and volunteers gathered in and around the city. Children, mainly older boys, gathered in the streets and played soldier. Seeing me in uniform, several saluted not understanding I was merely a cadet training officer, no one worthy of respect. I saw concern in the eyes of older women and a few older men.

I walked by the Confederacy's primary armory, the Tredegar Iron Works, several times. It seemed like a great, insatiable, fuming beast. Day and night, wagons filled with coal, iron ore, and iron scrap went into the armory and cannon and military equipment came out on the other side in a near constant flow. I did not go in, but imagined that what went on inside was hot, sweaty, and frenzied.

* * *

Following the hectic and frustrating first day of drills, I went back to the tavern for supper, tired, hungry, and ready to relax. I found every table occupied, turned to leave and eat later when I saw Captain Denham motion me over to an empty chair at his table. Denham served as Major Jackson's adjutant. No way would I go to his table without an invitation. Every cadet wanted to meet him. I felt honored.

Captain Joshua Denham recently returned from Indian fighting in the West, a rare officer who had recent field experience. His reason for inviting me to his table soon became evident.

While we ate, Denham asked, "How's the training going?"

I knew it was not an idle question. I thought for a moment before answering. I did not know Captain Denham much less what he wanted to hear and decided to just give an honest answer. "Sir, the recruits are overeager to shoot Yankees, see little use in drilling, and are difficult to train. Most are older than me and have little respect for rank. I don't lecture them. I simply point out proper military dress and procedure and that, if they want to serve in the Confederate Army, they need to learn. But, they mostly ignore orders and fool around in horseplay instead of drilling."

Denham's response surprised me but it should not have. "I agree. This rabble won't become an army unless and until there's a change in attitude. I'll include your comments in my report to Major Jackson." I swelled with pride thinking my observations might come to Major Jackson's attention. With war pending, I saw Professor Jackson in an entirely different light.

Before starting second day drills, Major Jackson called the recruits together on the training field outside Richmond. He ordered a flatbed wagon to the front of the assembled troops and then climbed up on the wagon bed and stood so he could be clearly seen and heard. The cadet training officers and Captain Denham stood to the side and watched. Jackson had fire in his eyes and gravity in his voice as he spoke to the volunteers. I had never seen him angrier or more animated.

"You volunteered to defend Virginia from an enemy who would destroy our homes and defile our sacred soil. By your actions, you disgrace our army with your careless and immature behavior. I want any unwilling or unable to train to become soldiers in the Army of Virginia to leave now and tell your mothers, wives, and sweethearts you did not care enough for their honor to defend them. We will protect Virginia with you or without you. The choice is yours. If you stay, you will obey every command given. If you continue to ignore orders of your training officers, as you have, you will be dismissed and sent home."

Jackson stopped and looked over the assembly of volunteers. They stood silent, the childish humor and rowdy behavior left them. Satisfied they understood his message, he ordered resumption of the drills and jumped down from the wagon. I saw a slight smile on his face as if he might have been pleased with himself, but it was the inscrutable Professor Jackson. No telling what he thought.

After Major Jackson's speech, no one wanted to be thought a coward by leaving and the drills went much better. Even as I barked out commands to the recruits, I thought of the mobilization taking place in the North and remained less optimistic than the other cadets.

Virginia Military Institute,
Tuesday, May 21, 1861
Jim Cobb

I went for a final visit to Colonel Bradshaw. My home state, North Carolina had seceded the previous day. Nothing either of us could say would soften what we knew would be a disastrous war. I knew too that this visit would be my last as a VMI cadet.

"Jim, I know why you came," Bradshaw said as he shook my hand. "I'm heartsick and know you are too. We both know the South is about to enter a perilous war. Now that your home state has joined the Confederacy, what're your thoughts?"

"Mostly anger and frustration. Regardless of how it turns out, I only see suffering and distress. But, now, North Carolina is in and my option to standby and watch is gone."

"Have you decided what you'll do?" he asked.

"My only 'out' is cowardice – simply refuse to fight. I can't fight with the Union against my home state, neighbors, and the other cadets. I've debated myself for months and finally made a decision. As a point of honor, I'll enlist in the Confederate Army and hope for the best."

"It may not be as grim as we've framed it," he said. "It's possible the South may achieve a quick victory and force a political settlement on the North before the war becomes too bloody." Bradshaw paused, shook his head, and we both smiled.

"Professor, my apologies, but what you just said was fanciful, not rational."

"I wish it were true, Jim, I truly wish it were." He extended his hand for a parting handshake.

I left feeling sad and anxious not only about the coming war but for loss of the familiarity and comfort of school and coming of a new, uncertain life in the Confederate Army. I appreciated Professor Bradshaw and all I had learned from him in class and, particularly, in the private talks in his office and apartment. I liked to think Bradshaw gave me the sage advice and guidance I would have received from my father, had he lived.

* * *

Tom Edwards' uncle had formed a militia company and asked Tom to join him. He hoped to be a First Lieutenant before the war started and before any of us. Pete and I went to the train station to see him off. As usual with Tom, his departure was light hearted.

"Don't kill all the Yankees. Save some for Jim and me," Pete said as he clapped Tom on the shoulder.

"You couldn't hit the broad side of a barn at ten paces. The Yankees are safe from you two," Tom joked.

"You have our home addresses. Write when you can and let us know how you're doing," I told him as I reached over for a handshake.

Tom grabbed my hand and then Pete's and promised, "I'll write" while boarding the train home.

After the train left, Pete commented, "He barely managed to survive VMI. A fresh start will do him good.

Want to bet we never hear from him again?" I shook my head and Pete moved to another concern, "Let's go over to the recruiting office. They're taking applications. Might as well enlist now as later." Pete was eager to join the Virginia Militia cavalry. I did not want to delay him and thought it would also be a good choice for me.

I always pictured myself as a cavalry officer, particularly after encouragement from the riding instructors. I had no conceit or romance of the cavalryman as a knight on a chessboard of infantry pawns that filled Pete's head. I was comfortable and skilled in riding a horse and had the patience to teach others what I knew. Some cadets were ticketed to the artillery, logistics, and other specialties, but I was recognized early as a natural cavalryman.

When we arrived, the recruiting officer, Captain Williams, who taught us horsemanship, looked at me and said, "Sorry, Mister Cobb, we can only take applications from Virginians. We don't have enough horses, saddles, uniforms, and carbines to equip everyone who applies."

Deeply disappointed, I stepped outside as Pete and other volunteers were processed. But still it galled me. Pete Morgan and other Virginia cadets I could outride and outshoot were readily accepted into the Cavalry Division of the Virginia Army. As I waited for Pete, I reviewed my options and decided to go home, join a local militia unit, like my illustrious grandfather, Elisha Cobb, and take my chances there.

When Pete came out, I told him what I planned. He seemed disappointed and commented, "I hoped we could serve together. Come home with me, spend the night, and console yourself. I know my parents and Sissy want to see you before you go. Heck, I get teary eyed thinking about you riding off to join the Cracker army in North Carolina."

* * *

Despite Pete's kidding I wanted to see my intended and the Morgans once more before entering the army. When we arrived, I found the Morgans worried and excited about Pete joining the Virginia Cavalry.

Earlier, William Morgan came around to Missy's and my thinking on the likely outcome of the war. He had invested his fortune and life in the plantation and now saw it in peril. Despite his support for the Confederacy, I knew Captain Morgan was deeply concerned about how his estate and his son, the heir to the plantation, would fare. When he came in from the fields, he found us on the front porch with Sissy and Missy.

"How far will the Union Army come down the Shenandoah Valley before we stop them?" he asked.

As former cadets and soon-to-be Confederate officers, we had no informed answer. No one did.

Margaret Morgan was preoccupied in finding a safe place to hide the family silver. Missy seemed upset. She knew more than the others – that the near universal expectation of a quick victory was delusional. I knew of the huge disparity in resources of the Union and Confederacy as apparently did she.

Missy invited me to join her in the parlor for a talk. She sat down on the stuffed and richly upholstered sofa and slapped the cushion on the chair in front of her. I sat down facing her. We had many conversations in the parlor over the years, some lighthearted, some serious as this one would be.

She asked, "We thought you would join the cavalry. What happened?"

"I'm not good enough to serve in the Virginia Cavalry. I'll go home, enlist in the Catawba County Militia, and serve there. They'll make room for me."

I worked to appear nonchalant, but failed. Her face pinched as we talked. "I know it's something you must do, but I'm concerned for you, Peter, and the others going to war."

I took her hand in mine and said, "You've always been a good friend. I much appreciate your concern for me."

"Please, Jim, take care. Don't do anything rash or foolish. I'll keep you in my prayers until I know you're safe." She was only sixteen years old, but much wiser and understanding than her years, maybe smarter than anyone I knew outside of Colonel Bradshaw and my mother. She was very dear and seemed lovely with her cute, pinched face when she became concerned. Missy would always be a good friend and, hopefully, a sister-in-law if I survived the war.

When Sissy entered the room, I excused myself, and got up to talk with her. Missy watched and discreetly left the room so we could talk alone for a final meeting before the war. Sissy looked so sad and beautiful. I began to wonder if I had made the right decision in leaving. I worried about her.

What I had to say would not be easy and looking at my beautiful intended made it more difficult. "Sissy, more than anything, I want to marry you. But, the timing's awful. I've decided to go home, enlist, and don't know where or in what position I will serve. Things are just too unsettled and confused. I could be killed in the war. It would be unfair for me to ask you to marry now."

Sissy sobbed quietly and did not look up at me. Instead she twisted a handkerchief which she periodically brought up to her face to wipe away tears.

I felt my heart break when I asked, "Will you wait until we see where I'll serve and how the war is going before we become engaged?"

I waited anxiously for her answer and imagined what she might be thinking. Would she understand the gravity of our circumstances? She enjoyed the balls, parties, and socials that would be gone or greatly diminished with all the young men going off to war. Or maybe, like Missy, she understood that whole Plantation way of life could be lost.

Sissy looked up and said, "It's the only sensible course we can take."

She understood. Relieved, I took her hands in mine and declared, "Sissy, darling, I love you. As soon as possible, I want to announce our engagement. Thank you so much for waiting. I already hate this war and what it's doing to our lives."

Sissy reached up, put her arms around my neck, pulled me

to her, and whispered, "I'm so frightened. I don't know what will become of us. Father worries we could lose our home if the war goes poorly. With you, Peter, and the others going off to fight, I don't know who'll protect us should the Yankees invade."

Sissy's body trembled as I closed my arms around her and felt her soft breasts against my chest. She gave me a passionate, not a polite, kiss I remembered fondly and often in the coming years with the companion thought "why did I ever leave her for this god awful war?"

I spent the night in the guest room but did not sleep much. In the morning, I ate breakfast with the Morgans. Sara fixed me a hearty plate of ham, eggs, and buttered biscuits. She fussed over me and kidded with me like Hannah when I was home.

After breakfast, I brought down a coachman chest with my clothes and school things. Pete stood with me as I shook hands with Captain Morgan and hugged Missus Morgan and Missy. They turned their heads as Sissy gave me a full kiss on the lips. Pete slapped me on the back and said, "That'll have to do you, Sport, until we get the business with the Yankees settled."

Captain Morgan sent me back in a coach to Lexington and I left on the train home.

* * *

I wanted to return home as quickly as possible, but nevertheless had a long, slow, and tedious journey back to Charlotte. The train stopped at every station along the track. I changed trains in North Carolina because of the track gauge difference. Several blowhards in our car made it their business to uncover Union sympathies among the passengers. I tried to ignore them but found it impossible to stop their self-righteous blustering. After witnessing them badger fellow passengers, I decided to turn the tables.

When asked when and where I would enlist, I replied, "First, tell me where you will enlist" and looked to each of the bullies for an answer.

In turn, they used the opportunity to proclaim their undying loyalty to the Confederacy as each proudly announced his intended destination. When they finished, I noted none mentioned Catawba County and felt relieved. I said, "I am pleased for you. I'll join the Catawba County Militia if they'll accept me. With luck, I won't see any of you again, but if I do, pretend we haven't met." I turned and continued reading a newspaper I bought in Lexington for the trip. I suspected most of what I read of pre-war news was untrue.

* * *

When I arrived at the Charlotte train station, Henry and Hannibal, my friends from childhood, waved and shouted, "Mistuh James, we's heah to take you home." I learned Oliver called Henry in from the field and told him to take the carriage down to Charlotte and pick up Mister James. Hannibal overheard and complained to Oliver he wanted to go instead. They got into a heated argument. Finally, in exasperation, Oliver told them they both could go.

The brothers were two years apart in age and almost identical in appearance, Hannibal slightly taller. Both young men were stout and strong from years of fieldwork. They had dark, smooth skin and kinky hair, which their mother cut short and trim. Each had a broad face and a smile that showed off near perfect, pearl-white teeth with Henry missing a front tooth from one of their numerous fistfights. I remembered them as popular with the girls on the Cobb Farm and neighboring farms which contributed to their near constant bickering.

In Mother's 'school', they learned to read and, as they grew older, read every book and newspaper they could find. Afterward, they argued about what they read and nearly everything else.

They remained intensely loyal to one another, but, nevertheless, highly competitive. They provided a running joke on the Cobb Farm even to their often exasperated parents.

At first, I welcomed their company. Henry, Hannibal, and I grew up together. Their mother, Hannah, cooked our meals and did housekeeping for the Cobb Family. She looked after us and treated me like another son. As a youngster, I worked summers in the fields and mills, beside Henry and Hannibal, my companions on numerous fishing and hunting trips.

During the carriage ride to Newton, the brothers peppered me with questions about the coming war. I told them what I knew and had seen. But, the questions did not let up. Finally, I shook my head and said, "Enough" which brought on more questions and kidding.

When we arrived home, Mother sat me down and tried to talk me out of enlisting. Her arguments were reasoned, many the same as Colonel Bradshaw and I debated. Barely twenty years old, I completed three years study at VMI, felt like a man, but beneath the confidence I displayed to Mother, I feared going to war. She sensed my unease which matched her own.

I laid out my options as I had earlier with Colonel Bradshaw. Mother listened unconvinced and pleaded with me to sit out the war. But gradually she reluctantly realized it was something I would do for all the reasons men go to war – pride, honor, adventure, and duty - that mothers, wives, and sweethearts find senseless and often heartbreaking.

She eventually relented and made a practical suggestion. "Son, when you go to the recruiting station, wear your cadet uniform. For those who don't know you, it'll be a reminder you have military training." If she had understood the casualty rate for young Lieutenants in the coming war, she would not have made the suggestion, but it worked out as intended.

* * *

In the morning I put on my cadet uniform which Mother carefully cleaned and pressed the night before. Mother updated me on the militia sponsor, Henry Wilkins. We had traded at his store in Hickory for many years. Never a hotbed of secessionist fervor, Catawba County waited until after North Carolina announced for the Confederacy before forming a militia. As an enlisted man during the Mexican War, Wilkins had "seen the elephant". He offered to outfit the Catawba County recruits in uniforms of the Confederate gray and help with purchase of rifles, ammunition, and shoes. But there was a limit to the uniforms, arms, and shoes he could afford. Mother told me many willing volunteers had been turned away for simple lack of supplies and provisions.

As I finished breakfast and got up to leave, she hugged me in a firm embrace for over a minute. To comfort her, I said, "Don't worry Mother. I'll be all right." But I knew she was far from reassured with her son going to war.

She did not look up at me, did not want me to see her tears. I put on a brave front, said goodbye, and rode over to the Catawba County recruiting center in Hickory. I brought a hunting rifle, not a favorite, and an old, muzzle-loading pistol from home to use until I was properly armed and outfitted.

I rode in mid-afternoon. It had been several years since I last saw Henry Wilkins, but he recognized me and pulled me aside for a quick conversation.

He asked, "Get my letter?"

"No, sir. I came on my own to volunteer." The question surprised me and suggested Wilkins might have something in mind for me.

"We're organizing a militia company," he said. "I'll be the Captain and my cousin, Granville Calvert, will serve as First Lieutenant. We need a Second Lieutenant and I'd like for you to fill the position. Are you willin' to serve?"

As this is what Mother and I had in mind when I rode out in my cadet uniform, I readily agreed.

Already speaking to me as a fellow officer, Captain Wilkins said, "We'll drill the company next week and then take them to Raleigh. Governor Vance ordered all our militia units to assemble there for assignment in the Confederate Army."

* * *

When the militia company volunteers gathered three days later, Wilkins offered a slate of officers for election. He headed the slate as Captain and included James Gerlach Cobb as Second Lieutenant. We were duly elected as presented. After all, Wilkins supplied the uniforms and many of the weapons. Besides, none of the men wanted the responsibilities that came with being a company officer.

During the drills, Wilkins gave confused and muddled orders. Granville Calvert, second in command, quietly took over training without embarrassing his cousin. With assistance from me, the drills went well considering the majority of the men were recruits, new to the military, and more interested in shooting Yankees than drilling. Wilkins and Calvert knew I had drilled recruits in Richmond, experience that served me well in my current assignment.

Before our leaving for Raleigh, Catawba County honored the volunteers at a reception in Hickory where we said goodbye to family, friends, and sweethearts. Apparently cheerful for the occasion, Mother, I later learned from Oliver, cried on the return to the farm. Oliver drove the carriage and also came to see me off. She thought about what might befall her son and the other men in the company as did Oliver. According to what Oliver told me, neither spoke on the ride home.

* * *

On the march to the train station in Charlotte, well wish-
ers stopped us at every town and crossroad. Old men in faded
Mexican War uniforms came out to greet and salute us. Younger
men patted us on the back. Women offered cakes, pies, cookies,
biscuits, buttermilk, apples, peaches, all kinds of treats. Pretty
girls and not so pretty girls kissed us. I found it difficult not to
be caught up in the euphoria. Even earlier doubters came around
to the notion of an independent South free of Yankee meddling
and arrogance. So did I.

We boarded the train to Raleigh with the local Mecklenberg
County units. All the boys knew we would lick the Yankees in
the first good scrap and have a "grand old time" doing it. As the
train rattled down the tracks, I heard raucous carousing and hur-
rahing. Against orders and reason, our men had climbed on top
of the train cars and took whisky bottles with them. It was hard
to restrain their excitement and enthusiasm.

The officers tried to control them, but finally decided to
give up and reassert command when we arrived in Raleigh, the
only workable decision we could make. One of the Mecklenberg
County Captains, an attorney, held out for strong discipline, but
Wilkins talked him down. I was proud of our Captain for showing gumption and common sense.

Calvert commented, "Damn fools. One of 'em's goin' to get
lickered up, fall off, and probably kill hisself."

"At least it's not malicious or insubordinate. Just stupid," I
pointed out.

"Yeah. They had help in their tomfoolery. The Mecklenberg
boys egged 'em on. Some of 'em even joined in the hurrahin',"
Wilkins added.

"You heard the company names floating around?" I asked.

Calvert grinned as he obviously had and said, "We can't go to
war without a proper name."

"Lincoln Killers? Tarheel Avengers? Piedmont Posse?"

"Will the boys do better when they sober up?" I wondered.

Granville Calvert was a big, sandy haired man with a bushy mustache that, in his words, tickled the tender parts of naughty women. He had a red face pock marked from a near fatal encounter with smallpox in his youth and a swagger that suited him as a natural leader. Calvert was about the same age as his cousin, a much smaller and bonier man.

Before joining the militia, I did not know Granville Calvert, but knew of him. Everyone in Catawba County knew of Granville Calvert, a local legend - a mix of daring, military accomplishment, and whoring.

As a youngster, Granville quit school and worked his way west as a muleskinner. A teenager in Missouri when the Mexican War began, Calvert joined a volunteer company assigned to General Kearney's army. As a soldier, he served with the victorious army that deposed the Mexican government in Santa Fe and then marched over the Great Western Desert to defeat the Mexican Army in California. Calvert earned field promotion to Lieutenant before he honorably retired from the army. After the war and his wanderlust sated, Granville came home and worked in his cousin's dry goods store.

As a natural born military officer, the war was a godsend for him. He much preferred leading troops than clerking in a store. Although new to command, I knew it was good to have a man of Calvert's experience and ability in the company even if he seemed overly fond of drinking and winching.

"Think we ought to order the men down before one of them gets hurt?" I asked.

"Nah," Wilkins said, "let 'em have their fun. We'll get back to command when we get to Raleigh."

Calvert leaned over to me and said, "They're all thinkin' we'll give the Yankees a good lickin' and be back for next year's plowin'. They're hopin' the affections of the girls won't fade before they get back."

"What do you think?" I asked.

"I think we force a surrender quick or it'll be a long and bloody war."

"Which do you think it will be?"

"This war's about slavery. Abolitionists stirred it up. Average folks in the North don't care any more 'bout the niggers than we do. They won't fight us to free 'em. I think, when they find we can bloody their nose, it'll be over soon."

"I hope you're right."

We sat quietly for several minutes then Calvert said, "They don't know it yet, but many of our boys won't come home alive. They don't understand what it's like linin' up and firin' at an enemy line shootin' back. Henry's right. We ought to let 'em have their fun while there's still fun to be had."

Wilkins cared about the men and, in my opinion and over time, it would make him a good officer. With his experience, leadership, and swagger, I thought Granville Calvert might become a very good officer.

Raleigh, North Carolina,
May – June, 1861
Jim Cobb

Outside Raleigh, I saw many militia companies, fields of tents, a mass of men, and much confusion. The Catawba County militia company was assigned to the 6th North Carolina Brigade as Company B of the 16th Regiment commanded by Colonel William Dorsey Pender. I knew nothing of Colonel Pender but soon learned.

After our assignment, I met with Henry Wilkins, Granville Calvert, and officers from other companies in the regiment. The primary topic of discussion was our newly appointed regimental commander. Officers from Edgecombe County, his home county, sang Pender's praises. I learned he was an experienced Indian fighter and a highly regarded officer. Pender graduated from West Point in 1854 and entered the state militia as a Captain, but quickly progressed to Colonel and command of the 16th Regiment.

As the company uniforms were not completed before our departure, I stayed in my VMI cadet uniform when the company assembled for inspection by Colonel Pender. Pender noticed me, or more accurately my cadet uniform, and called me over to his tent for an interview after the inspection.

I stood nervously before the regimental commander, but Pender quickly put me at ease. "How many years did you study at VMI before joining us, Lieutenant?"

"Three years, sir."

"I know you've trained in drill, firearms, horsemanship, artillery, and military tactics. You'll find these are useful skills in the army."

I gratefully accepted Colonel Pender's recognition of what I had accomplished.

He smiled, winked at me, and said, "I suppose you attended Old Jack's classes."

No cadet ever called Professor Jackson "Old Jack", but I had learned it was a nickname his West Point classmates hung on their serious minded fellow cadet from Western Virginia who seemed, to them, older than his years. Jackson started out last in his class, but, through diligent study and long hours, worked his way up to second when he graduated. His classmates were convinced he would have finished first if he had not run out of time.

I answered, "Yes, Sir" without going on to describe Jackson's dull and uninspiring lectures.

Pender wrote out a promotion to First Lieutenant for me and said, "I am assigning you to serve as my aide."

I got my first promotion after less than two weeks of service and would be an aide to a highly competent and experienced officer, a man I already liked and admired. I expected to learn much from Colonel Pender.

* * *

Dorsey Pender was, himself, soon promoted to command the 6th North Carolina Brigade. His brigade, along with another North Carolina brigade, was ordered to join the Light Division, First Corps of the Army of Northern Virginia commanded by one of the South's brilliant young generals – Ambrose Powell Hill.

Robert E. Lee, who previously commanded the Virginia Militia, now served as military adviser to the Confederate President, Jefferson Davis. He hurriedly organized the Confederate Army from the disparate state and local militias. As I later learned, General Lee had a keen eye for talent and many competent younger and less experienced officers were quickly promoted to higher levels of authority and accountability in the newly created Confederate Army. I was pleased the young officers earmarked for promotion included my new commanding officer, Dorsey Pender.

The Catawba County uniforms finally arrived and I put away my cadet uniform. Pender's Brigade took the railroad to Richmond, joined with the Light Division, and then marched on to Manassas Junction to repel an expected Union march on Richmond from Washington.

From my diary written at Manassas, Virginia,
Sunday, July 21, 1861

I heard from everyone you never forget your first fight. They are right. Wish it were some other day than Sunday, but that is when the Union Army came to engage us.

The battlefield was a series of rolling hills. We fought on a bright, sunlit day where each army had the other clearly in view as the battle began. I saw civilians in carriages camped behind enemy lines as if for an afternoon outing. They brought picnic baskets for refreshment as they watched the first battle of the war. Amazing how lightly the citizens of Washington treated the war, like it would be no more than a field exercise.

I admit I did not know how I would react. Reading about a battle and being in one are two different things. I was disappointed to learn I was terrified. I wanted to be anywhere other than where I was. My mouth dried and I felt my stomach turn and my knees shake as the long line of Union soldiers came into view. I saw myself being killed when the firing started.

When the battle began, General Pender gave me an order to take to one of the regiments. I became confused and wandered not knowing where or wanting to deliver the order. Pender, who stayed close to front lines, rode up and angrily pointed to the where the regiment deployed. Embarrassed, I moved quickly to deliver the order and somehow held on the remainder of the day.

After nearly panicking, thank God, I learned something else about myself. I can control my fear by just doing what Mother taught me. If I focus totally on the task at hand, I can block out the worry and panic by concentrating on what I must do next. I did not lose my fear and apprehension, but worked through it and did my duty.

I watched the massive Union Army slowly approach. Their uniforms, like ours, included militia units with local dress of blue and gray uniforms. If we did not keep them in front of us, it would have been hard to know which were theirs and which ours. The Union troops in the colorful Zouave uniforms, with bright red pants, white shirts, and head bands, made a particularly dazzling display as they led the Union charge. When the cannons fired and muskets spewed out smoke and shot in recurring sheets, soldiers in both armies staggered and fell in waves. The beautiful uniforms became mottled with blood and dirt.

After the battle was joined, the fighting became confused. I was dazed as I rode back and forth with orders from General Pender and replies from the regiment commanders. I saw soldiers stagger, fall, grab their throats, heads, wounded limbs, and moan from their wounds. A cannon ball took off one soldier's leg when it bounced along the ground before hitting him unawares. What I saw had little resemblance to what I read in books and was taught in school. The horror and overwhelming sense of fear cannot be described in writing.

When the Yankees fell back, I went out on the battlefield and pulled a pistol from the stiff fingers of a dead Union officer. I now had a Colt revolver, a much better firearm than I had before. I took his pistol, holster, and a box of ammunition to replace the pistol I brought from home.

The Yankees dropped rifles, cannon, equipment, and supplies we picked up. I wonder if they realized how much arms and supplies they left for us.

When the fighting ended, I was appalled with the sight and smell of dead and wounded men and horses. The field was covered with corpses — husbands, fathers, sons, brothers, and sweethearts — lying grotesquely where they fell. At home, they would have a decent burial with family and friends to mourn their passing. Here they are buried in common graves by indifferent work crews intent on rapidly planting the bodies to reduce the sickening odor of death, a hideous sight I pray to God I never see again.

Chapter 6: Peninsula Campaign

New York Tribune, Lead Article, Special Addition,
Tuesday, July 23, 1861
byline Samuel Payne

The first major land battle of our Civil War ended Sunday, July 21 at Manassas Junction, Virginia. President Lincoln appointed Brigadier General Irvin McDowell to command the Army of Northeastern Virginia. His objective was simple. Take Richmond. McDowell knew his task, but was concerned about his untrained and untried army.

From the beginning, Washington politicians and citizens harassed him to attack the Confederates, remove the threat of their army taking Washington, and end the rebellion. President Lincoln reasoned, "You are green, it is true, but they are green also; you are all green alike."

Against his better judgment, McDowell commenced the campaign. He departed Washington on Tuesday, July 16 with the largest field army yet gathered on the North American continent.

They sought to engage a force of 21,000 Confederates under Brigadier General P G T Beauregard encamped near Manassas Junction, approximately 25 miles from Washington. McDowell planned to attack the numerically inferior enemy army, while Union Major General Robert Patterson's 18,000 man army held down Confederate Brigadier General Joseph E Johnston's 11,000 men in the Shenandoah Valley and prevent them from reinforcing Beauregard.

After a two day march in the hot July sun, the Union army rested. McDowell searched for a way to outflank Beauregard who had drawn up his lines along Bull Run Creek. On July 18, he sent a division under Brigadier General Daniel Tyler to attack the Confederate right (southeast) flank. But Tyler encountered stiff resistance at Blackburn's Ford over Bull Run and made no headway. With his battle plan frustrated, McDowell attacked the Confederate left (northwest) flank instead. He planned to leave one division at the Stone Bridge on the Warrenton Turnpike and send two divisions over Sudley Springs Ford. McDowell expected these divisions to attack the Confederate rear. A sound plan, but McDowell delayed while Johnston's Valley force boarded trains at Piedmont Station and rushed to Manassas Junction. On July 19 and 20, Johnston's reinforcements bolstered Confederate forces along their Bull Run defensive line. But, the Union attack broke through.

On the morning of July 21, divisions under David Hunter and Samuel P. Heintzelman crossed Sudley Springs and attacked the Confederate left. At this point, approximately six thousand Union soldiers confronted Confederate Colonel Nathan Evans reduced brigade of nine hundred men. Evans brigade was reinforced by units from Bernard Bee and Francis Bartow, but the Confederate defense buckled and then collapsed against the numeric superiority of the Union attack. As the Confederates fled, they pulled back to Henry House Hill where Thomas J Jackson's Virginia brigade stood firm. It was the turning point of the battle that initially favored a Union win.

Scattered Confederate units rallied around the Virginia brigade. The fighting continued as Union forces pushed forward up the face of Henry House Hill. Fresh Confederate brigades raced to the fight and turned the tide of battle. McDowell's flanking column was blunted, then crumbled and broke. In the disorder that followed, Confederates scooped up hundreds of Union prisoners. A wagon overturned on a bridge spanning Bull Run Creek inciting panic in the fleeing Union Army. The rout was on in what the soldiers call "the great skedaddle".

Fortunately, Beauregard and Johnston did not pursue the retreat-

ing Union Army. Their combined army was badly disorganized even in victory.

The elite of Washington drove to the battle site to picnic on assorted delicacies and spirits and witness an easy Union victory. When the Union army was driven back, these panicked civilians fled in their carriages and clogged the roads back to Washington. Further confusion ensued when an artillery shell fell on a carriage, blocking the main road north.

In future years, much will be written of this battle and, undoubtedly, the blame for the disastrous result will fall on Irwin McDowell. But, to this reporter, McDowell did the best he could with an army, most particularly an officer corps, totally unprepared to attack an entrenched, dedicated enemy force. General Patterson's failure to hold Johnston's army in the Shenandoah Valley allowed addition of reinforcements to the Confederate defenders at Bull Run Creek which turned the tide of battle.

Union forces were initially victorious until Confederate resistance stiffened and reversed their advance. McDowell devised a sound tactical battle plan. He lacked the trained officers to carry it out. Washington was not captured because the Confederates were equally unprepared. To all intents, the battle at Bull Run Creek was the coming together of two armed mobs where the Confederates were entrenched and had better field commanders.

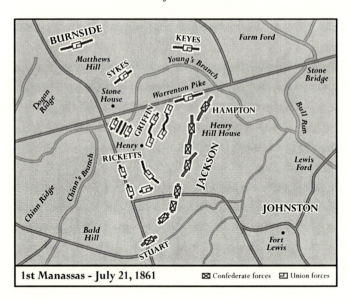

1st Manassas - July 21, 1861 — ⊠ Confederate forces ⊡ Union forces

Manassas Junction, Virginia,
Sunday July 21, 1861
Jim Cobb

"You look like you need this" General Pender said as he poured two glasses of whiskey and handed me one. More than the terror I felt in the battle, I feared the dressing down that awaited me. I knew I had disappointed him by freezing in battle the first day and expected he would dismiss me or worse.

Whiskey was not particularly appealing, but I cherished what might be a reprieve.

When we sat down, he asked, "Were you scared?"

"No sir, I was terrified," I answered honestly as I had nothing to gain in telling him something different than he saw himself.

With a knowing smile, he said, "I remember my first combat and being terrified. But you did well. You kept your head and that's absolutely the best you can do in any battle."

I felt instant and overwhelming relief. He had looked past my poor performance in my first battle. Maybe I belonged in the

Confederate Army after all. General Pender's praise reassured me and resurrected my shaken confidence. The same day, I developed a taste for Kentucky bourbon and associated it, for the remainder of my life, with Dorsey Pender.

He proceeded to explain, in detail, what happened in the recent fighting. I only saw panic and confusion. Pender understood the ebb and flow, the turning points, tactics employed by both armies, and explained them to me. It occurred to me then and many times later that a master in the art and science of war schooled me in a terrible and exacting profession. VMI taught the theory. Pender taught the practice.

Among his many fine command attributes, General Pender was a keen observer of military strategy. I had the privilege of his insight as the Peninsula Campaign unfolded. It also helped that we gained the Northern perspective from newspapers intercepted during the course of the campaign. It pleased me to find several articles written by Sam Payne, New York Tribune reporter, whom I knew and liked from the John Brown hanging.

I compiled a summary of the Peninsula Campaign from what I observed, learned in discussion with General Pender, and later read. It was the beginning of my real education as an officer.

Northeast Virginia,
March 21 – July 1, 1862
Jim Cobb

Following our victory at the battle at Manassas, High Command decided the position could not be held. We pulled back, took a defensive position, fought a few skirmishes and waited. While we waited, the new Union commander, General George McClellan, sailed the Army of the Potomac to the peninsula between the York and James Rivers with the obvious intent to march north to Richmond. He hoped to capture Richmond and quickly end the war.

We were ordered down to reinforce General Magruder in Williamsburg. We finally had enough horses, wagons, and supplies to carry out the order. The Union Army was building up on the coast to drive north and we had to stop them before they threatened Richmond. We set off for Norfolk, hometown of Sissy's parents and where my father studied law.

After we stopped the first day, I went to visit Henry Wilkins, Granville Calvert, and the men of my militia company, friends from Catawba County. As I dismounted at Captain Wilkins' tent, I heard two soldiers loudly talking for my benefit, "Hey, Emmett, see what I see?"

"It's the General's boy. Pretty ain't he."

"Remember when his Lordship was in camp with us?" Henry Wilkins came over and said, "Good to see you, James. Pay no attention to the boys. They're just joshin'."

"I know" and thought back to when we were boys. I did not know the other soldier, but Emmett Shuford shot marbles with me when his father brought corn to our gristmill. I lost track of Emmett when he quit school after the sixth year and felt pleased to find him in the Catawba County Company. I asked Captain Wilkins, "How's the company doing?"

"One killt and two wounded in the fightin'. Five more lost to swamp fever." I knew our casualties were heavy on his mind. Captain Wilkins would have to explain each loss to the dead soldier's kin when he returned, God willing, to his store in Hickory.

Granville Calvert joined us and we talked briefly about the war, home, and mutual acquaintances. Henry missed his wife and family, Granville his assorted female friends, and for me it was Mother and Sissy Morgan. Granville gave me advice I did not appreciate at the time, "Poke her or move on. That girl won't wait the war on you."

As I mounted my horse to leave, Wilkins said, "The boys and I are proud of you. We've been in the war less than a year and one of us already made it to the General's staff."

Granville called out, "Tell the General to issue an order that B Company, 16th Regiment eats first at every mess."

"And I'll tell him the Brigade's best Lieutenant made the request," I called back and rode off.

Granville hollered after me, "Won't do, James. He already picked you as the best Lieutenant."

I knew the Catawba County militia had, by then, fully assimilated into the 6th North Carolina Brigade, Light Division. None of the soldiers asked me to take requests back to the General, at least not in earnest. Boyish expectations of a quick, easy victory had given way to the realities of life as soldiers in a poorly supplied army.

* * *

Each army tested the other's strength in a series of skirmishes along a defensive line established by General Joseph Johnston who succeeded Pierre Beauregard as head of the Confederate Army of Northern Virginia. During this period, I saw the strangest confrontation of the war.

We sent a regiment to extend our line and the Yankees countered with one of theirs. Then we sent out another regiment and they countered. It was as if each waited on the other to get organized before attacking. It went on for nearly an hour.

Just as we prepared to fire, a wagon with a farm family piled up in back came up the road. They seemed unmindful of us and the impending battle. The father looked straight ahead and kept the horses moving up the road. Our soldiers and the Yankees were eager to fight, but no one fired as the wagon moved between us. A pretty teenage girl, probably their daughter, saw young men on both sides of the road and began waving. Almost in unison, they forgot the fight and began cheering and whistling. It seemed to please the girl and her younger brother. After the farm wagon passed, the fighting began. Several volleys were fired. Both sides took casualties and retired.

General Pender did not find the incident amusing. "When did our officers get the idea we wait for the Yankees to deploy before attacking? This will not do. We're further behind in training than I thought."

Fair Oaks, Virginia,
Sunday, June 1, 1862
Jim Cobb

While riding back to General Pender with a report on Federal positions, I saw a Union patrol through a thicket and a possible quick end to my army career, but did not panic. I dismounted and pulled my horse into a clump of trees, reached down, and grabbed a handful of grass to feed her. I stroked her nose and neck, anything to keep the horse from snorting and giving away our position.

I heard the Union Sergeant talk with one of his Corporals. "I wish I knew where the hell the Rebs are. Stumblin' around looking for 'em is drivin' me crazy. We could come up on a brigade before we know it. The idiot Lieutenant don't know his ass from a hole in the ground. Keep the men spread out and tell 'em to get back to me right away if they see any Rebs." The Yankees moved on without looking into the thicket or they would have seen a Reb officer listening to what they said.

I waited until they were out of sight and started to remount when a Union brigade commander and his staff came up to almost where I could reach out and touch them – 4th Corps, 1st Division, 1st Brigade, General John Peck. I stood behind as much cover as I could find but it was not enough. I fell on the ground face down, stayed motionless breathing slowly, and prayed I would not be seen. The Union officers apparently saw me and the horse, but paid no attention. No doubt they had seen many unmounted horses and dead bodies on the field after the earlier fighting.

My horse settled, stood quietly, and nibbled at a grass clump. General Peck stopped and discussed their latest orders with his staff. It was obvious, as I listened, that none of them had a good grasp of what they were expected to do. The orders were confused and, to straighten things out, the General described what he knew of regiment and brigade positions. The battle around Fair Oaks was muddled. We had deployed poorly. I was not surprised to hear uncertainty among the Yankee staff. Their conversation was scattered, but I picked up descriptions of unit positions and relative strengths I added to my earlier field observations.

The irony of listening to Union officers review their orders as I prepared my report to General Pender did not occur to me until later.

After a five minute rest, the Union staff moved on to find their patrols and, maybe, get a better understanding of our deployment. Again, I waited until they were out of sight and then mounted, took off to find General Pender, and give him an expanded field report.

After I gave my report, Pender laughed and said so the nearby regimental commanders and other staff could hear, "Next time, Lieutenant Cobb, you don't need to drop by and listen in on Yankee staff meetings. Just give me your field observations."

* * *

The Army of Northern Virginia fell back under tentative advances of McClellan's army. Daily skirmishes with occasional battles, but no significant victories for either army. After one skirmish, General Pender sent me out to count casualties and determine where the Union troops camped. The Yankees had made a hasty advance and unplanned withdrawal. I found bodies along the retreat route. With no possibility of a counterattack and several hours before I would report, I inspected the dead.

Most were shot in the back as they fled. Some turned to fight and took frontal wounds. The faces of the dead Yankees were mixed – some relaxed, some angry, and others shot up or blown away.

I thought of the senseless slaughter on both sides. The South went to war to defend a decrepit 'way of life'. The North fought to preserve a union with Southern states that no longer wanted to be part of their Union. Slavery would fade away without Northern intervention simply because it was unprofitable. These men did not have to die. Before more lives were lost, wouldn't it make sense to peacefully divide and go separate ways?

I found a jacket and riding cape on a dead Yankee. I could have used them to hide from Union troops earlier. There could and likely would be occasions, in the future, when I might need to pass through enemy lines. The cape and jacket could cover my uniform and trick the Yankees long enough to escape. I heard high minded talk about disguises being ungentlemanly, but thought it inane. We were at war.

If I could fool the Yankees by wearing their uniform and save capture, injury, or worse, I would do it. I promised Mother and Sissy I would do all I could to stay alive.

On the same field, I found another dead Yankee officer with feet approximately the size of mine, something our soldiers sought with every dead or captured Yankee they found. Most of the dead were already stripped of footwear. I removed the boots and a cap from the second corpse to add to my disguise.

* * *

Letters from Mother and Sissy lifted my spirits. Mother's letters gave me details of life on the farm and in Catawba County. She included specifics of where my friends served. Most, like me, were in the Army of Northern Virginia. Some went over the mountains to the western army. I suspected some hid out in the mountains and avoided the war altogether.

Sissy wrote about her life on the Morgan Plantation. She reassured me that she loved and missed me and looked forward to when we would be together again. Her letters brought back memory of the parting kiss and were the source of daydreams when I wanted to escape, briefly, the reality of war. Despite the growing horror and ugliness I witnessed daily, I hung on to the notion of a beautiful fiancé and the Cobb Farm waiting for my return.

* * *

During the long months of inaction and sporadic fighting in the Peninsula Campaign, General Pender concentrated on training. His unwavering standard for the 6th North Carolina Brigade was victory in every engagement with minimum casualties. He expected and got the best from our soldiers. They marched and assembled sharply and deployed swiftly and accurately. Our camp was always organized and clean. Although they frequently grumbled about the extra work, our officers and soldiers appreciated Pender's competence. They even liked him.

Stories floated around camp about Pender fighting the Apache before the war. Though probably exaggerated, the men took them as true. I repeated some of the stories to General Pender. He laughed without bothering to set the record straight.

General Pender often observed drills in progress. He knew the key in defeating the enemy was how rapidly and how accurately his troops could maintain fire on the opposing line. A good, well-disciplined soldier was trained to fire and reload an average of three times per minute. Pender drilled and drilled the brigade until we achieved a four shots per minute average.

On one occasion, Pender gathered officers and sergeants from each company in the Brigade. He dismounted and ordered the sergeants to select their best marksman to load and fire at a post one hundred feet away. Pender took out his watch and timed the fire to determine the average rounds per minute.

When the Sergeant finished, General Pender handed his watch to me and said, "Count the rounds and time me." He removed his coat and stepped out in front of the assembly.

General Pender took a smooth bore musket from the Sergeant who performed earlier. The assembly suppressed laughs when Pender put a handful of balls in his mouth, and then, in rapid succession, poured powder down the musket barrel, spit a ball down the barrel, tamped the musket barrel on the ground to seat the ball, placed a cap in the firing pin seat, and fired.

He even managed to hit the post a few times. In the later rounds, the musket spewed fire from gunpowder that collected along the barrel. When he finished, Pender turned to me and asked, "How'd I do?"

I recorded the time and rounds accurately and quickly answered so all could hear, "General, you got off thirty rounds in four minutes and twenty-seven seconds."

"How many rounds per minute is that?" I knew Pender already knew the answer, but wanted it announced.

I did a quick calculation. "It's about six and six tenths rounds per minute, Sir." General Pender smiled. The rate of fire was over two rounds per minute more than what the selected sergeant was able to get off earlier.

General Pender held up the musket as he turned to the Brigade officers and sergeants and asked, "What do we know about the musket?" No immediate response so the General answered his own question, "It's inaccurate but can be quickly loaded and fired. I just gave you a demonstration of this and remember you were watching a broken down old general who was not that good a shot when he was younger."

The men laughed and Pender added, "I expect you to train our soldiers to do much better. Tell any of them who fall under six six they cannot outshoot the General. That should motivate them to do better."

More laughter and then Pender said, "We've been in many skirmishes and battles where our men are face to face with the enemy at short range. It's not like long range rifle shooting where accuracy counts. The side that gets off the most rounds takes fewer casualties and wins. I want that to be our brigade in every close engagement we fight. What I demonstrated to you is sloppy and unorthodox and cannot be sustained over much more than five minutes. You saw how the gunpowder built up in the barrel. But, 'spit and tamp' loading is effective when the fighting is intense and the enemy close. I want you to train the men in its use, but limit them to twenty rounds of powder for now."

Short, modest, soft spoken, cultivated, pious, and polite, Dorsey Pender looked more like a kindly country parson than an army general. He did not have the swagger of a senior officer. Pender was younger than many of the company officers and sergeants which was one of the reasons they laughed when he described himself as an "old man".

He often worked hands on demonstrations and humor into the training as in the recent rapid musket firing demonstration. General Pender encouraged questions which I considered continuation of the relation I had with my father and mother, then Oliver, and then Colonel Bradshaw. I very much liked serving under General Pender and would have been pleased to finish my army career as his aide. Every day, every minute provided opportunity to learn.

After my initial failure at First Manassas, I worked hard to provide calm, objective, and factual reports of the back and forth of the fighting. It seemed to make a favorable impression on Pender and the regimental commanders. After four month service, Pender recommended me for promotion.

New York Tribune Article,
Thursday, July 6, 1862 byline Samuel Payne

Following Bull Run, President Lincoln placed General George McClellan in command. I am pleased to report he began rebuilding the demoralized Union Army of the Potomac. His sole objective is simple, straight-forward, and the same as for General McDowell earlier - capture the Confederate capital, Richmond, and thereby end the rebellion. In this regard, "Little Mac" has done a splendid job of organizing, drilling, and preparing our army for the coming battles with the Confederates.

But more important than anything else, he has restored the confidence and morale of our army. The men love him and McClellan loves them in return so much that he is reluctant to commit them to battle. President Lincoln and the Cabinet begged, pleaded, ordered, and finally forced McClellan to move against the Confederate Army.

Rather than march directly from Washington to Richmond, a relatively short ninety mile distance, McClellan sailed his massive army of over 100,000 men down Chesapeake Bay and landed at Fort Monroe. McClellan was opposed by a Confederate Army, under General Magruder, about one tenth the size of his Army. Magruder, who had an active interest in the theater before the war, worked hard to entertain and mislead McClellan by cleverly disguising and inflating the size of his overmatched army. He spread out his artillery, fired randomly at Union positions, and marched his troops in a circle as Union observers counted them. The deception worked. McClellan telegraphed Washington with the astonishing news that he was outnumbered and needed 40,000 additional troops.

Finally, with prodding by Secretary of War Stanton and President

Lincoln, the Union Army moved slowly up the Peninsula toward Richmond. Joseph Johnston gave ground grudgingly and sensibly fell back before the superior Union Army and sought advantageous positions to counterattack. The Army of the Potomac advanced steadily until it came within nine miles of Richmond.

At Seven Pines, General Johnston discovered two apparently isolated Union corps below the Chickahominy River and ordered four Confederate columns to attack using three roads. The battle plan was flawed from the outset. The marching orders were verbal and muddled. General Longstreet took his army on a road Johnston intended General D H Hill's troops to use which delayed their joining the battle.

Initially, the Union defenders were driven back, but reinforcements quickly came up. Heavy rains swelled the Chickahominy, but Union relief columns found an intact bridge and crossed unimpeded to the south side of the river.

The Confederate Army's situation became desperate; their defenses stretched thin with Union forces close enough to break through to Richmond. But, then, the South caught a fortunate break in what appeared to be a major setback. Their senior field general, Joseph Johnston, was wounded by a minie ball in the shoulder and had a chest wound in the first day of the Battle at Fair Oaks.

Jefferson Davis passed command to Major General G H Smith with orders to drive back the Union Army menacing Richmond. Smith renewed the attack on Union positions, but was unable to dislodge them.

Desperate for a victory, President Davis wasted no time in replacing General Smith with his trusted military advisor, Robert E Lee. The fate of the Confederacy literally hung in the balance as Lee took command.

McClellan was delighted when he heard the news. He fought Lee in Western Virginia early in the war and got the better of it. McClellan anticipated an easy victory and quick end to the war. Johnston had been cautious and judicious in engaging the Union

Army, but Little Mac was convinced Granny Lee would be easily confused, outmaneuvered, and overwhelmed.

As it has turned out, McClellan was badly mistaken. But, he was not by himself. Many of the Confederate officers and soldiers were disappointed with Lee's appointment. Lee favors trenches and bulwarks and is thought, by some in the Confederate Army, to be a defensive general.

General Lee had a much better understanding of his opponent. He knows McClellan is reluctant to fight and hesitant in following up on whatever advantages come from his better-armed and numerically superior army. When the Union Army landed at Norfolk, one of Lee's staff aides telegraphed that unfortunately McClellan brought 100,000 troops and fortunately he brought himself. It succinctly summarizes what General Lee and the Confederate High Command think of McClellan.

At Fair Oaks, both armies claimed victory. But, in reality, it was a draw even though the Confederates had more casualties. The South will not win with bloody draws. The Union will inevitably win a war of attrition and were positioned very near Richmond. The Confederacy could yield no more ground. An immediate victory was needed and no one understood that fact better than the newly appointed commander of the Army of Northern Virginia.

General Lee gave himself two weeks to gauge the Union Army in the field and then on June 25th began a series of attacks at Oak Grove, then Mechanicsville on the 26th, then Gaines Mill on the 27th, then Garnet's and Giddin's Farms on the 28th, then Savage's Station on the 29th, then Glendale on the 30th, and finally Malvern Hill on July 1st where the Confederates suffered 5,000 casualties.

Only one of these battles can be rightfully counted as a Confederate victory, but, more important, Lee unnerved McClellan and kept him off balance. Convinced his army was opposed by a superior Confederate Army, McClellan retreated back to Washington to regroup leaving President Lincoln and Congress angry and perplexed.

Through audacity, superior generalship, and better morale, the *numerically inferior and poorly supplied Confederate Army turned back a superior Union Army. Sadly, it appears, we are in for a long and bloody war before President Lincoln finds a general to defeat the Rebels.*

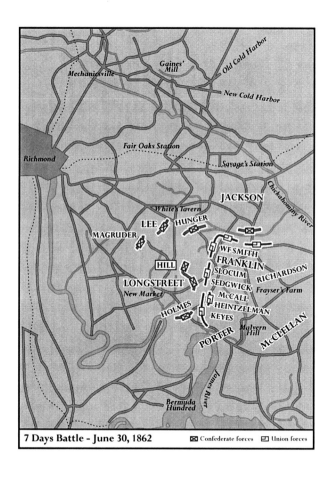

7 Days Battle - June 30, 1862   ☒ Confederate forces   ☐ Union forces

Chapter 7: 1862

Northern Virginia and Maryland,
July – September 18, 1862
Jim Cobb

While writing letters to Mother and Sissy, my mind drifted between catching catfish in the stream that runs through our farm and my last kiss from Sissy. I cultivated these daydreams. The fish always bit and Sissy's kiss led to lovemaking that became more passionate with each recollection. The alternative was dwelling on the daily gore – severed limbs, headless bodies, mangled horse and human flesh – and eventual insanity I had seen in other officers and soldiers.

An attendant interrupted my thoughts when he saluted and announced, "General Pender wants to see you at your earliest convenience." I suspected, by the way the order was worded, it had something to do with the promotion recommendation General Pender had put in for me.

When I arrived, Pender sat in front of his tent reading a book where I often found him when weather permitted. Putting down the book, he motioned me to follow him into the tent, invited me to take a chair, and sat down in the other. Although often in awe of General Pender, I felt comfortable in his presence. He had that affect on his subordinates.

"I have good news." He took an envelope from the table and handed it to me. I removed two shoulder boards.

"You're now a Captain."

"Thank you, Sir. I would not have this promotion without your support and recommendation."

"You've done excellent work since coming over as my aide. I've thought, for some time, you're capable of performing at a higher level and I'm pleased the Promotions Board agrees with me. Congratulations. If you like, I'll pin these on you." Because promotions were often earned in the most dangerous circumstances, it became customary to pin on new insignia immediately. Later, one of the orderlies, a tailor's apprentice before the war, would remove the First Lieutenant insignia and sew back the Captain shoulder boards and collar insignia. For now, General Pender wanted to see me as a Captain. I was not opposed.

"General, there's no one, outside of my mother, whom I would rather have do the honor." I meant it. I was convinced Pender was the finest officer in our army.

As he pinned the bars on my shoulders, he said, "I want to talk with you about your new responsibilities before I pass you on to General Hill."

I thought the promotion would be to General Hill's staff and General Pender confirmed it. In moving over to Division Staff, I sensed a shift in our relation. I would be an aide to General Pender's commanding officer. Pender spoke to me more like a colleague than a subordinate and I treasured that far more than my new shoulder bars.

"A P Hill is an excellent general, one of the best we have. But you'll find he tends to keep things to himself. It's a problem Generals Jackson and Longstreet share. They do not like to give orders until the last minute and, when they do, the orders are sometimes unclear. I've discussed this with General Hill as I'm talking with you now. But it does no good."

"You'll be carrying orders and messages to me and the other brigade commanders. Each message is a magnitude greater than the messages you have carried from me to the regimental commanders. As best you can, make sure communications from

General Hill are as precise and timely as possible. If you have to, ask him to repeat unclear orders and, unless the General tells you otherwise, deliver all messages with urgency. Serve General Hill as you have me and you'll do well on Division Staff."

"Yes, Sir." I felt a rush of pride and could not think of a better response.

General Pender asked me to stand as he said a prayer for my new service. He was more than a mentor to me, more like a loving father or older brother. I left his tent feeling both elated and sad. I would be moving to a new and challenging assignment, but away from my favorite general.

* * *

I felt uneasy in coming over to General A P Hill's staff. I knew them from prior service but becoming part of Division staff would be something different. No one discussed my duties with me when I reported. They treated me like I had been with them all along. I took it as a measure of the respect General Hill and his staff had for General Pender.

No mystery in my promotion. A P Hill considered Dorsey Pender his best brigade commander. When Hill's aide died of pneumonia, he reasoned that Pender's aide would be the best replacement. General Hill relied on whatever Dorsey Pender said and Pender told him Jim Cobb was an excellent aide. When I performed as I had for General Pender, it was what General Hill wanted and expected.

General Hill often discussed strategy and troop deployment with me and his other aides, looking for different viewpoints and he seemed to value mine. He may or may not have known that many of my comments came directly from my continued and frequent discussions with my sponsor with whom Hill often consulted. In effect, General Hill often got Pender's opinion twice.

In battle, commanders most need timely and accurate

information, an area of competence where, by the grace of God and Dorsey Pender, I excelled. After three months of service on Division Staff, General Hill wrote a performance review and showed it to me before passing it on to Corps. It read, "Captain Cobb has demonstrated fine ability to evaluate terrain, observe relative troop strengths, note unit tactics, and return the information to me quickly and accurately. He has learned to ride through contested areas rapidly and avoid capture."

I never saw General Pender's fitness reports on me, but suspected they may have read the same. I had found a career, but a career that could kill me.

I learned well from Dorsey Pender, whose orders were always concise and specific. On occasions when I arrived with orders circumvented by changes in battlefield conditions, I discussed needed revisions with the local commander. With knowledge of the overall plan Pender had for the brigade, the regiment commander and I decided on a revised action which I immediately reported to the General. It worked well.

I recall Gaines Mill in particular. Battle lines became fluid. Unit positions changed completely from our plan. I rode to the 38th North Carolina and found Colonel Hoke wounded and unconscious. I took charge until the adjutant could be found. In the meantime, I ordered the companies into an arched defensive line. I sent Hoke's aide back to General Pender with a message informing him of what happened and recommended the 16th North Carolina swing around our left to drive out the Yankee troops bunched up attacking us.

I was proud to serve in the 6th North Carolina Brigade which functioned efficiently and effectively. We had one of the best service records in the Army of Northern Virginia and I had contributed.

In talking with their staff officers, I learned other Generals gave vague orders, even the written ones. Poor communications led to lost opportunity for victory and needless casualties. General

Hill stressed this point in staff meetings not apparently understanding that he was a frequent offender. In moving to his staff, as General Pender had instructed, I determined to do everything in my power to ensure orders to the brigade commanders were clear and concise and function effectively as I had for General Pender. I was twenty-one years old, the youngest member of General Hill's staff. I felt honored and challenged by my new responsibilities, but not overawed.

New York Tribune Article,
Friday, September 5, 1862 byline Samuel Payne

I look forward to writing an article on the success of our armies in the war in Northern Virginia and regret it will not be now.

Our efforts began favorably when the Confederates pulled back from Manassas and General McClellan led our army to Fort Monroe, Virginia. Confederate attention was drawn to McClellan and the Army of the Potomac leaving the Shenandoah Valley open to Union Armies in Western Virginia. Washington sent three separate armies under Generals Banks, Fremont, and McDowell to capture the Shenandoah Valley and deprive the Confederate Army of its primary food source.

In response, General Lee sent his best field general, Thomas J, now called "Stonewall", Jackson with no more than 15,000 Confederates to contend with three Union armies. Union forces had an over two to one troop advantage, but Jackson took an interior position and defeated them in a rapid series of battles where he demonstrated amazing troop mobility. The Confederates continue to control the Shenandoah Valley.

Our armies should have destroyed Jackson's small army. But they failed to communicate effectively, were defeated singly, and were themselves driven out. Constant and incompetent meddling from Washington hampered flawed Union command throughout.

To rectify the inadequacies of Union command structure, the Lincoln Administration pulled the three departments together to form the Army of Virginia on June 26, 1862. This army was expected to operate in concert with McClellan's Army of the Potomac to crush General Lee and the Confederate Army of Northern Virginia. But, Lincoln made a curious choice to head the new army.

Since the war in the West is going well, Lincoln thought bringing a general from the Western Theater would infuse new fighting spirit to the defeated, demoralized, and newly formed Union Army of Virginia. Unfortunately, he chose John Pope despite a personal dislike and distrust of him.

Pope did as he should and moved the Union Army of Virginia toward Richmond creating a crisis in the Confederate Army. Lee had approximately 80,000 troops to defend the Confederate capital. The opposing Army of the Potomac numbered 90,000 and was in position to operate in concert with the Army of Virginia which had approximately 50,000 troops. Lee knew he must defeat the Army of Virginia before it could effectively link with the Army of the Potomac. As we have come to expect, McClellan hesitated and was inactive as the possibility of coordinating with Pope and jointly defeating the Confederate Army became available.

On July 14, 1862, Pope moved down toward Gordonsville with his full army. General Lee sent Jackson with 12,000 troops to defend. At Jackson's request, Lee sent A P Hill's Division to reinforce bringing Jackson's command up to about 24,000 men. Although the Union Army again had a two to one advantage in troop strength, things went badly for General Pope and the Army of Virginia.

The Army of Virginia advanced slowly and piecemeal. At Cedar Mountain, Jackson saw an opportunity to destroy the first Union troops to arrive, take an interior defensive position, and defeat the remainder of the Union Army. This was how he crushed the Union Army in the Shenandoah Valley earlier. However, Jackson has a passion for secrecy and failed to effectively communicate with his division commanders – Charles Winder, Richard Ewell, and A P

Hill – in time to coordinate the attack. General Banks attacked and drove back Winder's and Ewell's divisions before Hill arrived and rolled up Banks' eastern flank.

Lee learned McClellan had belatedly reacted to Pope's situation and sent reinforcements. He knew the Army of Virginia had to be defeated before reinforcements arrived and he must move quickly. To accomplish this, General Lee depended on the continued mediocrity of the Union command. He was not disappointed.

Lee sent Longstreet's corps to trap Pope at Cedar Mountain. Fortunately, the Confederates were slow in moving into place. Pope captured Jeb Stuart's adjutant, Norman Fitzhugh, learned of Lee's plan, and withdrew in time to avoid being caught.

To offset our good fortune, Confederate cavalry, under command of Fitzhugh Lee, General Lee's nephew, captured Pope's headquarters at Catlett's Station. They took $350,000, food stores, and learned Union reinforcements would arrive in five days and swell Pope's army to 130,000 troops. They also captured Pope's coat and sent it to Richmond where it is displayed. A wag attached a note stating that the coat Pope planned to wear on his triumphal ride into Richmond arrived before him.

Even with our armies closing in from both sides, Lee did not abandon hope of a decisive victory. On August 25, Stuart's cavalry and Jackson's "foot cavalry" left with three days' rations to a position behind Union lines. They reached Salem, 26 miles away, on the first day and destroyed the Federal supply depot at Manassas on the second day after marching another 36 miles. Pope learned Confederates were at his rear, but thought it merely a raiding party.

Pope ordered his divisions to positions situated between Jackson to the north and Longstreet in the south. Had he moved decisively, Pope could have blocked Longstreet while he used his superior numbers to crush Jackson. But Jackson's maneuvers confused Pope and he did not take advantage of his favorable strategic position.

Stonewall Jackson, in his own words, lives by the maxim "always mystify, mislead, and surprise the enemy if possible". Jackson ordered

A P Hill's Division to Centreville and his other division across Bull Run Creek with instruction to join up at Stony Ridge. Pope ineptly attempted to react to Jackson's deployments and was unaware that Longstreet's corps had moved up from the south. Pope thought Jackson's entire corps was at Centreville and ordered his army there. The opposing forces fought a bloody skirmish at Groveton.

Confederate troops ate all they could from Union stores and trains captured at Manassas and destroyed the rest. Pope had no provisions to maintain his army and proceeded to retreat back to Washington. Jackson could have easily and safely stepped aside and let the retreating Union Army pass. Instead, he ordered his badly outnumbered troops to take a defensive position behind a railroad cut at Manassas and block Pope's retreat. He had about 20,000 troops to oppose Pope's army that numbered approximately 62,000 men.

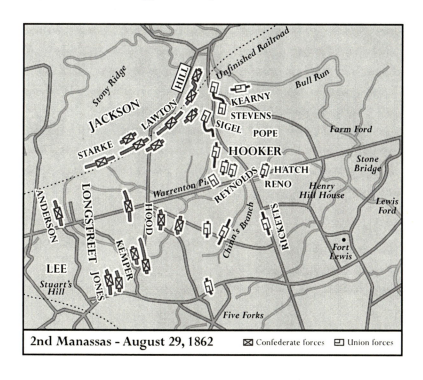

2nd Manassas - August 29, 1862   ⊠ Confederate forces   ⊡ Union forces

111

Given the opportunity to destroy Jackson's army, Pope took the challenge and ordered a series of piecemeal, uncoordinated attacks. Jackson's army repulsed each attack, in turn, and inflicted heavy casualties. After the first day, Jackson fell back from positions taken in the counterattack. Pope misinterpreted this movement as a retreat and ordered a vigorous, all out assault on Confederate positions and came away badly mauled. By now, Pope knew Longstreet's army had moved into place on Jackson's right, but ordered the attack anyway. In the ensuing battle at Manassas, the weakened Federal left wing was crushed between Jackson's and Longstreet's Corps. The Union Army of Virginia was saved from destruction by an effective rearguard action and hasty retreat across Bull Run Creek. Ironically, Union troops staged their holding action at Henry House Ridge where the Confederates had stopped a Union advance in the previous battle at Bull Run Creek. Unlike Beauregard at First Bull Run, Lee vigorously pursued the retreating Union army and caught us at Chantilly Hill on September 1 where we fought another bloody skirmish. The Union Army lost an additional 1,300 troops and two of its brightest young generals. Reinforcements were nearby, but Pope retreated back to the safety of defensive positions around Washington.

Pope will be relieved of command. But, unlike General McDowell earlier, he earned his demotion. Is there a leader among the many Union generals who can cope with Lee and Jackson? So far, no one has emerged.

Groveton, Virginia,
Friday, August 28, 1862
Jim Cobb

After a brief meeting in which he updated us on current conditions, General Hill invited his staff and brigade commanders to share a drink before retiring for the night. The conversation became informal as jokes were told and stories swapped.

General Hill related a story we enjoyed hearing. "Yesterday, our pickets captured a Yankee staff officer while he was scouting our lines. Captain Simon York, a talkative young man, General Banks' aide. He told us General Pope got off to a bad start with his new army. He compared them unfavorably with the army he left in Mississippi. And, in the same address, laid out harsh treatment of Confederate sympathizers in the area under his control which stirred up a hornet nest."

"Captain York went on to say John Fremont resigned rather than serve under Pope and was replaced by Franz Sigler. It appeared the young man, and by extension, General Banks, do not think much of Pope."

He added, "We all know General Lee. I've never heard him say anything bad about any of the Yankee generals except for Pope. I think General Lee actually hates him. Yesterday, I heard him call Pope a miscreant which is about as strong language as General Lee uses."

General Branch, the other North Carolina brigade commander, smiled and replied, "We'll all take pleasure in sending Pope back to his home in Illinois, preferably in a pine box." With that, General Hill offered the final toast.

* * *

Action next day was frantic and fast paced. No time to think, just react and perform. I stayed in constant motion between A P Hill and the rapidly changing front throughout the day. It was the heaviest combat I had experienced as Division aide. Yankee troops seemed to be everywhere. We would drive them back in one sector and see them pop up in another. General Hill wanted to know where all the combatants were and I could not tell him.

During the fighting, I was surprised when one of General Jackson's aides, rode in with a new order. The aide was none other than Bryce Carlton who apparently followed Jackson from VMI and obtained a position on his staff. Carlton sneered when he saw me, but said nothing to indicate he knew me.

General Hill read the order and then motioned me to come over. He handed me the message and asked, "Do you understand this?"

I read the dispatch twice, shook my head, and answered, "No sir".

Hill turned to Bryce Carlton and asked, "Can you tell me what General Jackson wants me to do?"

Carlton repeated the message which was vague about where Jackson wanted General Hill to take the Light Division and when.

General Hill threw up his hands and said, "Major, go back to General Jackson, find out what he wants me to do, and return immediately. The enemy is upon us and we must move together to defeat them."

Carlton hastily explained, "General Banks' army overran all of our positions between the Light Division and General Jackson's headquarters. I could be captured and the Yankees already know too much of our deployment. General Jackson ordered me on to General Ewell. I've already lingered here too long."

A P Hill turned to me and asked, "Captain Cobb, can you take this message back to General Jackson and get it explained?"

"Yes Sir, but, begging the General's pardon, Major Carlton's right. There's possibility of capture. With your permission, I'll ask General Jackson for his orders verbally, memorize them, and bring the message back to you orally."

"Very well, Jim, but repeat the order back to General Jackson and make sure he agrees. While you're there, find out what he wants General Ewell to do. Most likely his orders are as muddled as ours. And get back to me as soon as you can. We will not regain the time that's been lost."

General Hill turned to Bryce Carlton and said, "You will stay with me until Captain Cobb returns".

Carlton started to explain, "General Jackson ordered me to proceed to ..."

General Hill cut him off. "I don't care what your orders are. You will stay with me until I hear back from General Jackson."

As I ran to my tent, I ordered an attendant to saddle a fresh mount. I removed the Union riding cape, jacket, and cap from my locker and left my hat behind in the tent. I rolled up the cape like a blanket, tied it behind my saddle, stuffed the Union cap and jacket in the saddlebag, and rode hatless toward where I thought General Jackson headquartered.

I left camp at a fast pace. Through the trees, I caught sight of a Union detachment. I stopped, put on the Union jacket, cape, and cap, and rode on until the Yankees were out of sight.

At the next clearing, Union sentries stopped me and demanded me to explain "Who are you. Where are you going?" I pulled up the cape tightly to completely encircle my uniform. My heart went up to my throat, but I calmly told the sentries I had a message from the general to troops in the forward area. The sentry asked, "Which general?"

I answered "General Banks" and did my best to imitate Ken Johnson's speech which I practiced after finding the cape. I succeeded at least well enough to deceive these sentries. "If you'll excuse me, the General ordered me to get the message to the brigades as quickly as possible."

The sentry nodded, waved me on, and shouted after me, "What's the message?"

I shouted back over my shoulder, "Fall back!" and smiled as I rode off.

I removed the Union cape and Jacket, reached Confederate lines, and got direction to General Jackson. When I found him, I saluted and told him, "Sir, General Hill did not understand your last command. He ordered me to get a clarification and also statement of your last order to General Ewell which, with your permission, we will take to him."

"Major Carlton killed?" Jackson asked.

"No, Sir. He is with General Hill until I return with your order."

Jackson took a sheet of paper and began writing his order. I interrupted and repeated what I told General Hill earlier. He stopped, looked directly at me, nodded, and said, "General Hill is to move his division to support General Winder's right. Tell him to be careful of Union cavalry circling in behind. Yankees like gnats at a Sunday picnic. Got to swat 'em away before they get thick."

I listened intently.

When Jackson finished, I repeated back, "The Light Division will coordinate with General Winder in support of his right flank, move in concert to drive back General Banks, hold two brigades to protect our rear, and combine field artillery with Winder."

Jackson added, "Take two days provisions. Got the Yankees on the run, we'll keep after them."

I repeated the revised command. General Jackson nodded his head. We repeated the procedure with the order to General Ewell which was shorter.

"Sure you can remember all that, Captain?"

No way would I admit a deficiency to Stonewall Jackson. I answered, "Yes, Sir."

I saw a slight smile as Jackson took up his pencil and made marks on the paper I did not understand. It was code which he explained to me and said, "This'll help you remember".

"Yes, Sir." It appeared we had finished. I added, "General, with your permission, I'll exchange my horse for a fresh mount before returning to General Hill."

The bill of General Jackson's cap nearly covered his legendary blue eyes as he replied, "Very good, Captain Cobb. I'm pleased your fine education at the Institute is being put to good use by

General Hill." I smiled as I saluted, pleased that the general remembered me from all the cadets he taught at VMI.

Jackson mystified me. I remembered the dull, uninspired professor of artillery and the single-minded and effective commander of cadet units at John Brown's hanging and Richmond training. It seemed, to me, Jackson was two men. I was much influenced by my mentor, Dorsey Pender, and Pender did not like Jackson. He thought Jackson a poor leader who drove his men too hard and would eventually break them. But, who could argue with the results Jackson produced? Certainly not the Yankees who had already demonized him.

General Jackson seemed pale, tired, sluggish, and unsteady on his feet during our encounter. I wondered if he might be sick. It was not mid-afternoon drinking. Jackson was a known and severe teetotaler.

On the ride back, I thought of Bryce Carlton and became angry. How many battles will we lose because General Jackson's aides will not stand up to him and insist on clear orders? No excuse for lackadaisical staff work. Soldiers put their lives on the line in every battle. The very least we could do is deliver orders accurately and promptly. Too often brigades or divisions showed up late and spoiled an opportunity to defeat the Yankees.

When I arrived at camp, I ran to General Hill's tent and reported General Jackson's order. General Hill said, "Well done, Jim. I'm putting a commendation in your record. Now give Major Carlton General Jackson's orders to General Ewell."

I took paper and a pencil and wrote the order to General Ewell. I did not need the code Jackson gave me which I did not understand anyway.

General Hill looked over my shoulder as I wrote and commented, "Major Carlton, your performance today earned you a formal censure I'll send along to General Jackson" and then walked away to send couriers with fresh orders to the brigades.

After General Hill left, Carlton walked closely behind me,

snatched the written order from the table, and muttered, "I despise you" and continued toward his horse.

Three years of persecution at VMI taught me to hate Bryce Carlton. But what pushed me over the edge was the recent thought that the cowardly VMI bully was costing Confederate victories and lives by delivering muddled orders. And now the pompous ass walked away as if he had done nothing wrong.

I jumped up and spun him around as he prepared to mount; grabbed his lapel, and pulled his face within inches of mine. I saw the orderlies staring at us and whispered in his ear, "You gutless piece of trash. If I see you after the war, make sure you have a pistol. God may forgive you. I will not." I released Carlton, pushed him toward his horse, and walked away. Carlton seemed shocked, but said nothing and quickly rode away. I hoped the son of a bitch at least got the order through to General Ewell.

My uniform was thoroughly soaked with sweat. I wore a Union jacket and cape for much of the ride to General Jackson and back. It seemed like I spent the day in an oven. The cape saved me from capture, but I hoped, if I ever used it again, it would be in winter. I went back to the staff tent and found, to my surprise, an attendant had brought up a pail of fresh, cool creek water. I peeled off my clothes and indulged in a sponge bath.

That night, as I ate with the staff, General Hill asked me for details of my ride. I told him how I used my disguise to get by Union sentries and pickets. He commented, "Good work. When there's more Yankees than we can whip, we have to outsmart them."

"Yes, Sir. And if Pope and McClellan are the best they've got, we'll have more opportunities," I replied in the same spirit.

In my next letter home, I included the coded note General Jackson scrawled for me. Stonewall Jackson was already a legend in the South. Anything he had touched – handkerchief, spent rifle cartridge, hair allegedly from his head, even hair from his horse – became treasured memorabilia. I thought she might enjoy her own special keepsake of the great general.

*　*　*

Following the fighting at Chantilly, I enjoyed a long and a leisurely meal followed by two drinks of General Pender's fine whiskey. Alex Tarkington, Pender's new aide and one of my friends, joined us. I had difficulty sorting out the back and forth of battles over the past two months and relied on General Pender to tell us what had happened.

Pender leaned back, lit a cigar, and explained, "Taken as a strategic whole, the Peninsula Campaign, the Shenandoah Valley Campaign, and the latest battle at Manassas, the Army of Northern Virginia drove two Union armies back to Washington despite their heavy superiority in numbers and equipment. General Lee has been brilliant.

Second Manassas was a curious victory for us. It duplicated the earlier victory at First Manassas in that the Union Army was again routed and demoralized. The victory was gained with brilliant, but flawed, troop movements by our army and poor intelligence and generalship by the Yankees. Each army had opportunity to destroy the other and failed.

The losses have been horrific. But, by superior generalship, the morale and competence of our men, and the grace of God, we have thrown the Yankees back."

Despite bullets and shells flying around me, I came out of the latest battles unharmed. All the more remarkable because General Hill routinely sent me into the thick of the fighting to deliver messages and bring back information. Like General Pender earlier, he also used me, when needed, as a troubleshooter. At Second Manassas and other battles and skirmishes, I took temporary command of companies, regiments, and even brigades when General Hill wanted them moved quickly and their commanders were killed, seriously injured, or otherwise incapacitated. In performing my duties, I was unscratched. I had been remarkably lucky.

Harper's Ferry, Virginia,
Monday, September 15, 1862
Jim Cobb

After the hectic fighting around Second Manassas, another opportunity quickly came up. General Hill gathered his brigade commanders and staff to discuss a directive.

"We've been ordered to Harper's Ferry. The Yankees left a garrison when we went north into Maryland. General Jackson has them near surrounded. McLaws took the Maryland Heights. General Jackson knows artillery alone won't defeat the Yankees and ordered us to attack their flank on Bolivar Heights. We have an opportunity take the entire garrison with all their equipment and supplies."

In their haste and confusion, the Yankees foolishly left fourteen thousand troops at Harper's Ferry ready to be scooped up. Capture of the Union garrison would free the Shenandoah Valley and provide much needed supplies.

I scouted the area before the Light Division deployed and reported back, "General, we can use the School House Ridge for cover and move the Division on to the Shenandoah River and seal off the Yankees there. It'll be difficult to drag the artillery up the bluffs. I spoke with Colonel Temple. He thinks we can and I agree. We're up to it."

General Hill gave the order and our Division methodically pushed to within a thousand yards of the Union exposed left flank.

On September 15, Union command acknowledged the hopelessness of their position and surrendered. I learned 12,500 Union troops, along with 13,000 arms and 47 artillery pieces were captured. Jackson knew, as well as Lee, Davis, and the Confederate government, the mass of surrendering Yankee soldiers could not be housed, guarded, and fed with the Confederacy's overstrained resources. Jackson offered parole to the Union soldiers on condition they would not resume armed conflict with the Confederacy. They took the pardon and we knew we would see them again. Yankees had no honor.

It would have been a good time to rest except the Light Division was ordered to Sharpsburg, Maryland as soon as possible. The main army was in trouble.

* * *

On the train ride, I left Division Staff and joined the new commander of the 16th Regiment, 6th North Carolina Brigade, Lieutenant Colonel Granville Calvert. Henry Wilkins had been severely injured early in the Peninsula Campaign and succeeded by his adjutant who distinguished himself in subsequent combat. When the regimental commander was killed during the battles preceding Second Manassas, Dorsey Pender promoted Granville Calvert to replace him.

I shook his hand and said, "You old rascal, you've been double promoted to Colonel in less than six months. It's comforting to me and others that the Confederate Army recognizes talent."

"In all modesty, you're right, Jim," Granville replied and told me, "I've waited all my life to lead a regiment and, finally, my time's come."

"How are our boys in Company B doing?" I asked.

Like a proud father Granville replied, "They're the best soldiers any commander ever had the privilege to lead. But, you know what? So are the other companies in my regiment. I'm blessed to have them."

I agreed. The war had honed all our units. It was getting hard to tell one from the other. They all performed well.

Sharpsburg, Maryland,
Wednesday, September 17, 1862
Jim Cobb

The Light Division railed to within nineteen miles of Sharpsburg, marched the rest of the way, and captured Union uniforms along the way.

After repeated assaults, General Burnside, who commanded the Union left wing, finally crossed a bridge over Antietam Creek and drove General Toombs' badly outnumbered Georgians back toward Sharpsburg. If the Union Ninth Corps had forded out of range of our sharpshooters, they would have taken Sharpsburg before we arrived, but they didn't. We slammed into their flank and averted a certain defeat.

The appearance of fresh Confederate troops startled Burnside's troops. They fell back. To add to the confusion, three of our brigades wore fresh Union uniforms into battle. I did not know whether to laugh or cry, but the Yankees held fire until we started shooting at them. The Light Division was, in turn, caught in heavy Union return fire. I had no time or opportunity to take evasive action in riding to the center of action with an urgent order from General Hill.

It happened suddenly. I went down in a fusillade, my horse shot out from under me. I did not feel it at the time, but a bullet creased my scalp above the left ear. I fell unconscious from my horse as blood spurted out from the head wound. When I went down, my dying horse rolled over my left leg and broke it in two places.

In late afternoon, we quit the field but posted sharpshooters to cover our withdrawal and that prevented the Union Army from immediately evacuating its wounded. I remained on the battlefield littered with Union and Confederate dead and injured along with numerous dead and severely crippled horses. I knew our situation before I passed out.

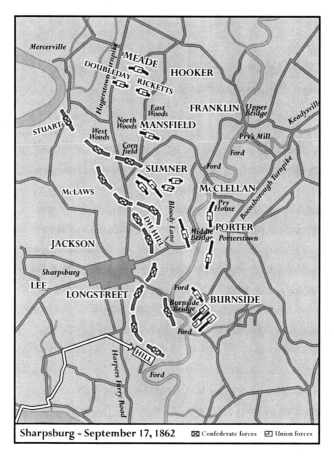

Sharpsburg - September 17, 1862   ⊠ Confederate forces   ⊞ Union forces

Chapter 8: Hospital

Union Hospitals in Maryland and Northern Virginia,
September 18 – November 20, 1862
Jim Cobb

I regained consciousness at dusk and became aware of someone moving slowly among the dead and injured. I slowly realized I would have died on the broken field south of Sharpsburg if my hat had not pressed tightly over my head when I fell. The hatband acted as a tourniquet, slowed the blood flow until it clotted, and finally stopped further bleeding. As my head cleared, I saw a looter callously searching dead bodies and rifling the pockets for valuables. He used a sharpened bayonet to cut off stiffened fingers to remove rings. Apparently to prevent anyone from calling out, he slit the throat of anyone not already dead.

The looter moved down the line of dead and dying men stealing from Confederate and Union alike. Most likely an experienced soldier, he stayed low to avoid notice of sharpshooters.

When he turned his back, I drew my pistol and found it still loaded. After carefully cocking the hammer, I opened my jacket and closed it over my right hand holding the pistol. I knew I would only get one shot. My heart pounding, I put my head down, closed my eyes, took long silent breaths, and waited.

Eventually the looter knelt beside my apparently lifeless body, and started to roll me over. Ignoring sharp pain from my broken leg, I rose quickly and pointed my pistol at his ferret-like face. His eyes widened as I fired. The bullet hit him in the forehead and he fell on top of me. Weak from blood loss and excruciating pain in my leg, I passed out.

* * *

To my great joy and surprise, I awoke the next morning in a Union ambulance. After taking in my new circumstances, I reasoned I was much better off with the Yankee Army. They had much better ambulances and hospitals than ours and, regardless, we had abandoned the field. In removing injured soldiers from the battlefield, they naturally took their own first and must have thought me one of theirs.

The soldier next to me nudged my arm and said, "Thanks, Reb."

"For what?" I asked as I had no idea what he meant.

The soldier spoke in a lowered voice, "He would've killed us all if'n you hadn't shot him."

"Who was he?" I asked.

"One of our'n, a Sergeant. Real mean sumbitch from G Company. Bled all over you. Covered up your reb uniform. Fittin' I guess. If you hadn't killt him most of us wouldn't be ridin' back to the hospital."

Another soldier hollered out, "Shut up! I'm goddamn tired of you two yappin'." I probably saved his life and he cursed me. Typical Yankee.

The Yankees had Moses ambulances designed to carry eighteen - fourteen inside and four on the front seat. On the inside, they planned one, two, or, in an emergency, three men lying down, with one man in a recumbent position, and twelve men seated. This ambulance carried too many - two dozen wounded, five on the floor including me and my new found friend.

Packed as we were, I could not move without disturbing another passenger and being cursed. I remained still and ignored the pain and stench that came with each breath.

When we reached the hospital, the orderlies seemed more concerned with putting wounded soldiers into beds than sorting out Yanks and Rebs. They carried me inside where an orderly glanced at me and yelled at the two attendants, "What's wrong with you dumb sons of bitches. This'un ain't near dead. Go back and get me 'nother who ain't nearly breathin'." The attendants dropped me in a cot and scurried back to the ambulance.

Inside I saw constant activity. Groups of orderlies and surgeons rotated wounded soldiers to and from operating tables. Surgical knives flashed as they cut away the soldiers' uniforms and exposed bare and bloody flesh. The surgeons sliced skin open and used a small handsaw to cut into the soldier's flesh. Wounded men cried out in agony. In my semi-delirium, I did not realize the saw cut through bone. I was only conscious of the back and forth scraping sound.

The indifference to massive suffering both shocked and repulsed me. The Yankee surgeons seemed detached, coldly professional, and oblivious to the suffering surrounding them. For the remainder of their lives, these young men would be without an arm, foot, or leg. Maybe dead if they did not survive the infection that set in after amputation.

The orderlies casually threw bloody disembodied arms and legs, many with shoes attached, on a stack in the corner.

In my later years when I became involved in founding a teaching hospital, I realized the surgeons could not perform if they allowed themselves to be emotionally caught up in the ongoing tragedy of mangled bodies and severed limbs. Too many wounded soldiers and too few of them to consider individual suffering. They had to be aloof to survive the carnage somewhat like we in the field became for the same reason.

During a lull in the surgeries, the orderlies found another cot for me and set about cleaning and stitching my wound and applying a powder of potassium bromide, yellow jasmine, and belladonna alkaloid to reduce infection. After they bandaged my head, one of the orderlies leaned over me and said, "Here Reb, bite down on this." He winked and added, "It might hurt a bit" while handing me a thick leather strap.

Viewing the horror of the operating room, I worried that the surgeons would saw off my leg. Instead it throbbed and I was thankful, only broken. I set the strap between my teeth and clenched tightly. As the orderlies pulled at my leg, working to set the fracture, I passed out. Later, a doctor stopped by, found me breathing and conscious, and left.

When I awoke, I said a silent prayer. That I survived the last twenty-four hours was a series of miracles. Dead men covered the fields around Sharpsburg. I could easily have been one of them and thanked God I was not.

Maybe God did have a plan for me. Beginning with my recovery in the Union field hospital, I began developing a basic, unprovable, and unshakable belief God had a mission for my life. Never before or since has God talked to me directly. But I had seen signs of His presence, including my lying alive in a Union hospital cot after Sharpsburg.

Friday, September 19, 1862
Union Hospital outside Washington, DC
Jim Cobb

I found the convalescent hospital comfortable, possibly someone's home before the war. Walls had been knocked out to form wards with stacked beds and just enough room for an attendant to pass between. Still, it was the first cushioned bed I had since leaving home. The interior had been painted white to provide a bright surrounding for the patients. It did not work. This hospital still looked like a hospital – dreary.

When I healed, I would be taken to a Union prison. Over the next weeks, I received care from the attendants, clean bandages, medication, and defeated an infection-induced fever. I slowly regained my strength and planned an escape.

A severely wounded Confederate officer occupied the adjoining cot. Heavy bandages over splints covered his lower face. He had taken a shot through the jaw. I could not talk with him. Others in the ward, Union soldiers with similar wounds, were fitted with mechanical devices that could be removed and adjusted. It appeared, again, the Yankees took care of their own first and put splints and bandages on the Confederate. An orderly confirmed my guess.

I worked to ingratiate myself with the orderlies, learned their names, and talked with them about their families and sweethearts. Several could not write or wrote poorly so I composed letters for them as well as illiterate soldiers in the ward. They wrote of homesickness, longing for loved ones, and an odd combination of fear, disgust, and pride in their part in the war. Sentiments I understood well.

I watched the orderlies tend my neighbor, another Confederate, and felt pity. It wasn't they were unkind or indifferent, just too busy to give him the care he needed. They fed him through a hole in the mask over his mouth. The orderly spooned liquid and ground food into his mouth but the wounded soldier had difficulty swallowing and frequently gagged.

I volunteered to take over feeding and eventually all of his care. After the first feeding, the wounded Confederate motioned me to come closer. He held out his open left hand and wrote on his palm with his right finger. I understood he wanted a writing pad and brought it to him.

Abel Robertson served as a Lieutenant in the 31st Virginia Regiment under Brigadier General Jubal Early at Sharpsburg. The 31st Virginia was part of the counterattack at the Dunker Church. Abel turned his head to call out an order when a minie ball tore through his left lower jaw and exited through his right upper teeth. The bullet mangled and nearly severed his tongue.

Weakened from blood loss and unable to cry out, he lay for three days among the dead. Civilians hired to pick up and bury the bodies found Abel and dragged him to an open pit where other bodies were laid for mass burial. They discovered he was alive and hailed a passing Union ambulance. Orderlies cleaned his mouth of rotting flesh and maggots while he was unconscious. Then Union surgeons sewed up his tongue and facial wounds and set his jaw.

When Abel finished writing, I asked, "How did you survive?"

He pointed upward.

I found a patient with a rat tail comb and talked him into temporary "loans". Abel used the pointed end to scratch under his cast providing welcome but temporary relief from the sores and rash on his jaw. As his beard grew, so did the discomfort. His recuperation was pure misery. The staff and I were sympathetic but unable to relieve his suffering until his jaw set and the splints and bandages could be removed.

* * *

The hospital was lightly and loosely guarded. After all, who wanted to escape from a hospital during wartime? Escape would be easy. Simply walk off.

Of those who could, wounded soldiers, nearly all Union, got up during the night to relieve themselves in outside latrines. After the third week, I used crutches to walk to the latrines and return. In the sixth week, an orderly removed my splints.

The Yankees routinely took ambulatory prisoners from the convalescent hospital to a Union prison for later exchange. The orderlies asked that I be exempted as I helped them with care of Abel and other patients. But, after a month, the patient load diminished as soldiers died, returned to duty, or went home. They no longer needed my help.

In the ninth week, the orderlies removed Abel Robertson's bandages and splint and took out the stitches from his tongue or what was left of it. I trimmed his beard as close as possible. I used a cloth, soap, and water to give Abel's face a gentle and much needed cleaning, but his face was still too tender for a shave. Afterward, I rubbed ointment on his sores. The jaw was set poorly and it left Abel's lower face pinched and badly distorted.

From a photograph in Abel's few possessions, I saw a handsome young man grouped with others who enlisted in the Winchester, Virginia militia. No more. With his skewed chin he looked like an old man, years before his time.

* * *

During the time I spent in the convalescent hospital, I became friends with Judson Gamble, an orderly and devout Quaker from Ohio. He wanted to serve in the Union Army, but, in keeping with the tenets of his faith, would not bear arms against other men. The Union Army allowed him and other pacifists to serve as orderlies.

God blessed Judson with a cheery, optimistic disposition – exactly what was needed in a ward of men with severed limbs and broken spirits. We had numerous conversation from which I came away impressed with his unshakable, childlike devotion to Christ. If only all were like him, there would be no war.

For my part, I wrote a list of great books for Judson. More than anything, he wanted an education but had no way to pay for it. I convinced him that reading the great books would give him knowledge and understanding, the basis of education. We found a copy of the New York Tribune which included an article by Sam Payne. Judson was impressed I knew Sam and more impressed that Sam's skill as a writer was mostly self-taught.

One day, Judson told me, "You're scheduled for transfer to a prison tomorrow. I heard the Sergeant talkin' with the Lieutenant tonight. They're gatherin' up all the Rebs. I'll miss you. Good luck, Jim."

That night, around midnight, everyone slept including the attendant on duty. I got up and went to the cot of a Union Lieutenant. He was my approximate height and weight and, more importantly, had feet the same size as mine. I took off my clothes and dressed in the Lieutenant's boots and clean uniform, but retained my bloodstained shirt. I thought about a note and settled on leaving my bloodied Confederate uniform as a "good-bye". Not a fair exchange, but it was still war even in the civility of a convalescent hospital.

I went to the latrine, finished, and started limping south. No one awakened and no one stopped me in escaping. And then a soft voice from behind startled me, "Take me with you. I can't stand this place any longer." I turned and saw Abel in uniform. He had followed me from the hospital

I could make it back easier alone, but could not refuse Abel. "Sure," I said, "maybe we can steal some horses along the way." As we walked away, I became increasingly aware of the stiffness and ache in my leg.

After less than an hour, we saw a campfire in the distance and, when we got closer, found a sentry. He had tied his horse to a nearby bush for the night and was fast asleep. It would be simple to steal the horse, blanket, and saddle without disturbing the sentry, but I had a better idea.

After saddling the horse, I went over to the sentry, carefully removed his pistol, woke him, put the pistol in his face, and said, "Pardon, young man, but if you do as you're told, you'll not be harmed."

The sentry woke with a start, but did not panic. I motioned for him to stand up and said, "We want your uniform. Take it off and then your boots. You'll spend the rest of the night in a Confederate uniform." I smiled and added, "An officer's uniform." My humor was lost on the unfortunate Union Private.

The next day he would explain, to his Sergeant why he slept on duty and would do it wearing a gray uniform.

Abel undressed and put on the sentry's uniform. The fit was not good, but good enough at a distance or in dim light. The Union sentry looked at me wide eyed like he thought I would put a bullet in his head. Instead, I motioned him to get dressed in Abel's uniform. Then I told him, "If you remain still, we'll tie you up and gag you. If not, I'll hit you on the head until you're unconscious and you don't want that, do you?" He nodded.

We used shoelaces, the belt from Abel's uniform, and the sentry's handkerchief to tie and gag him. It would not take him long to get loose, but we would soon be lost in the night.

Abel and I doubled on the horse and rode south. After a few miles, we saw another campfire, and this time found a Union patrol camped for the night. They tied their horses between two trees and stacked the saddles nearby. A sentry guarded the horses. A cup dangled idly on his finger. He appeared drowsy, but not yet asleep.

I whispered to Abel, "Stay here. Don't come up until I motion you. If the Yankees catch me, take off."

Abel nodded.

I circled behind the sentry, came up slowly, and hit him over the head. Not hard enough to kill him, but hard enough to knock him out and give him a bad headache the next day. Moving slowly down the line to the last one, I stroked the horse's nose to gentle him and untied the rope. We took a saddle and horse blanket and moved quietly away from the camp. After saddling the horse, we continued our journey south at a faster clip.

We found it easy to spot Union pickets as they kept fires going during the night to warm themselves and their coffee. The sentries we saw also appeared to be asleep. My left leg ached in the cool night air, but I enjoyed freedom from the hospital and opportunity to return to the Light Division.

To evade capture, I used lessons learned as a courier which

meant riding through woods and thickets to be further invisible to the enemy. As the sun came up, we knew we could be seen and questioned. We needed a friendly farmhouse to hide until nightfall.

* * *

After daybreak, in the distance, we saw a farm lad leading six cows from pasture. I turned to Abel and started to tell him we should approach the boy, test him, and, if it went well, he might lead us to a safe home. But, we saw a Union patrol riding up. Abel spoke first, "It may be the Yankees we took the horse from last night."

"Any thoughts on what we tell them?" I asked.

"The Yankees at the hospital talked about a build up around Fredericksburg. We tell them we're reporting to a unit in Fredericksburg?"

"That's it. We are released from the hospital and reporting to General Sedgwick as scouts. We're from West Virginia. We know the area. Sedgwick asked for us as scouts when we were released. We got an early start. Sedgwick's anxious to put us to use."

"Why General Sedgwick?" Abel asked.

"Why not?" I answered. "His corps shows up everywhere the main army moves. Keep riding like we don't notice them."

When the patrol came alongside, the Lieutenant moved over to me. "Where you headed?"

I replied, "Good Morning" and went into the story Abel and I had just concocted.

The Union Lieutenant glared at me and asked, "Where'd you get that horse?"

"I told you. We were released from the hospital and ordered to Fredericksburg. I got my horse the same place you did - the army."

The last statement was true, but I heard a voice from the

rear of the patrol holler out, "He's lying, Lieutenant. That's our horse."

I drew my pistol, aimed it at the Yankee Lieutenant's head, and said, "Order your men to dismount." He hesitated. I pulled the Lieutenant's pistol from his holster, and shouted, "Now!"

The Lieutenant turned back and said, "Dismount boys."

I tossed his pistol to Abel and said, "Help cover ..." when we heard a shot. I took a bullet in the left shoulder. The soldier who fired had a bandage around his head probably the one I hit last night. I fired back, caught him below the neck, and took off with Abel close behind.

We headed toward a grove. As we rode, I shouted, "We'll try to lose them in the woods. Stay low. Our horses are fresher. We'll outrun them."

We heard pistol fire, but the bullets missed. Maybe the Yankees were cavalrymen and did not want to hit the horses or, maybe, simply bad shots. The bullets sailed over our heads and into the ground. But, before we made it to the woods, a bullet hit Abel in his left arm above the elbow. Now both of us were wounded and losing blood.

I saw a rise above a creek on the other side of the grove and yelled, "Follow me."

I rode into the creek behind the rise and dismounted. Abel followed. We kept the horses quiet while the Union patrol raced past.

When they were out of sight, I said, "It won't take them long to stop, reorganize, fan out, and start looking for us. Let's head back and find the farm boy."

We had escaped the Union patrol, but not for long.

Chapter 9: Blaylocks

Blaylock Farm, Fauquier County, Virginia,
November 20 – December 27, 1862
Jim Cobb

We retraced our escape and, again, saw the boy in a pasture with his cows. A raw-boned lad with uncombed hair, barefoot and a shirttail hanging out the back. Could have been me at the same age. He barely looked up and then lowered his head as we approached. Using my practiced Yankee accent, I asked the youngster, "Seen any Rebs hiding in the woods?"

The boy mumbled, "No, but if I did I'd sic 'em on you and the rest of the damn Yankees."

I hoped we had found our 'man'. Speaking normally, I asked, "Do you know where to hide escaped Confederate officers?" I watched carefully for the boy's response. As he slowly looked up, I opened my coat to reveal my bloodstained Confederate shirt.

The boy stood wide-eyed for a moment and then looked at Abel. It was his first good look at Abel and he recoiled before recovering, "Wuz it you two runnin' from the Yankees?"

"Yeah and we're hit," Abel answered and held up his bloody arm. "We need to get bandaged up before moving on."

The boy dropped the rope he held, said, "Follow me."

I asked, "What's your name?"

"Christopher Blaylock. Who're you?"

"I'm Jim Cobb, a Captain in the Confederate Army. This is Lieutenant Abel Robertson, also Confederate Army. We were wounded at Sharpsburg and have been in a Yankee hospital for the past nine weeks. We escaped last night and are headed back to Confederate lines."

Christopher's jaw dropped and his eyes widened. I asked, "Would you like to ride with me?" and lowered my hand. He took it, swung him up behind me, and wished I hadn't. A sharp pain went through my left shoulder, like what I felt with the broken leg.

I asked, "Are your folks at home?"

"Yes, Sir. Me, my ma and pa, and my brother, Andy. He's home healin' up from fightin' Yankees. My other brother, Matthew, is with the Army in Fredericksburg."

"Do you know in which unit Matthew serves?"

Christopher did not respond so I asked, "Who's Matthew's commanding General?"

"Oh, that's General Field."

Our good luck continued. Charles Field was a Brigadier General and commander of the Virginia Brigade. We stumbled on a farm with two sons in the Confederate Army and one of them served in the Light Division.

As we rode to the farmhouse, the Blaylock Farm impressed me. It had obviously been cultivated over many generations. Split rail fences neatly divided the fields. Cattle grazed in another field and, as we approached the farmhouse, I saw pigs and chickens, a large vegetable garden in back, fruit trees of different kinds surrounding the house, and damage from fighting in the area. Portions of the fences were broken down and blown away and some of the fields were torn up.

"Had fighting here?"

"Yes, Sir. The Yankees took our house for their headquarters. We slept in the barn. Made Ma real mad, but nothin' we could do. They left 'fore Andy came home."

Before we reached the farmhouse, the Blaylocks came out on the porch. Christopher jumped off the horse, ran up the porch steps, and excitedly introduced us to his parents. We dismounted and stood by our stolen horses.

The mother, Mary Blaylock, looked at our bloody coats and went back in the house to get sheets to cover and bind the wounds before we came in. I staggered as I stepped up to the porch. Andy Blaylock reached forward, took my right arm, put it over his left shoulder, and helped me inside. He was about my height and weight and strong. He had his right arm in a sling.

John Blaylock took charge. "Christopher, take the horses to the barn and tend 'em. Mary, get Jim and Abel ready for surgery. I'm off to find Doc Burrus." With that he mounted a horse and left.

A wiry little man, John Blaylock seemed decisive and I appreciated it. No telling when a Union patrol might show up looking for us. We needed to get patched and on the move.

Mary Blaylock instructed Andy, "Help the boys take off their coats and shirts. I'll prepare our bed for the surgery."

If not for the seriousness of our condition, it was a comical sight as three men, with one usable arm each, awkwardly took the coats and shirts off two of them.

Andy said, "We're used to patchin' up Reb soldiers, but you two are the first officers."

"I presume you're speaking from first hand experience."

"Yep. Ma'll get your wounds cleaned before Doc Burrus comes."

We knew the procedure.

After Mary Blaylock cleaned Abel's wound with alcohol, she said, "Looks like the bullet passed through, but maybe broke or fractured the bone in your arm."

"Yes, Ma'am. It feels broke. Thanks for cleaning me and your hospitality. It's more than we expected." The Blaylocks must have had trouble understanding him. I did. But none of them let on, not even Christopher.

"Captain Cobb, get up on the bed and make yourself as

comfortable as you can. You're still carryin' a bullet. Doc Burrus'll have to put you under to take it out."

An hour later, John Blaylock returned with a short, gray haired, bearded man who carried a worn leather bag. Doc Burrus wasted no time. He opened his bag, took out a bottle and rag, doused the rag and came over to me on the bed. "Captain Cobb, I'll render you unconscious before operating. Take a deep breath when I put this cloth over your nose."

I instinctively pulled back, but recovered and breathed the noxious fumes and drifted off. I awoke later with a tight bandage around my shoulder, a headache, and a spent bullet on the nightstand. I wanted to thank him, but Doc Burrus had left.

I saw the family and Abel Robertson and Andy Blaylock, with slings around their necks, watching me. John Blaylock said, "The bullet fractured, but did not break, your shoulder bone. Doc Burrus says you should be fit in about six weeks."

I counted myself lucky to be in a friendly home and have a competent surgeon treat me. Looking at them together in a row, the family resemblance was apparent. They all had sandy hair and light blue eyes. Andy was about a half head taller than his father. I thought Christopher would be taller than Andy when he finished growing. They all looked at me intently as if they really cared.

John Blaylock grinned. "I have a jug of our best whisky. If you like, take a drink. It'll help you sleep better."

Abel answered for us, "Thank you, Mister Blaylock. It's been a hard day. A good night sleep is welcome."

Andy brought out a corked jug and short glasses and poured drinks for everyone including his mother. I took a sip. It tasted much like raw alcohol. But, John Blaylock was right. I needed something to take the edge off the ache in my leg and left shoulder. After two drinks, the family left Abel and me in the bedroom.

* * *

I awoke rested the next morning. The home brew whisky did its work. My shoulder still hurt, I felt hungry, but the headache was gone. Abel had already gotten up and left.

Andy looked in and asked, "How about breakfast, Captain Cobb?"

I smiled. "Most hospitable of you. I'll join you in the kitchen."

Andy anticipated my next question and said, "Outhouse's behind the back door. Be careful of our dog. He don't know you and Abel. You can use my razor and comb on the back porch to freshen up."

Andy and Abel were seated when I reached the kitchen table. John and Christopher had left earlier to start their chores.

Mary looked out from the kitchen and asked, "I have eggs, ham, and cornpone. What would you like?"

Mary Blaylock was slightly plump with a pleasant face, an appropriate matronly presence. I was immediately drawn to her. Both of my grandmothers died before I was born, but I imagined that at least my Grandmother Cobb must have been something like her.

She had thin lips, light brown hair beginning to turn gray, and light blue eyes that rested above pink cheeks. She wore a stained apron, but kept her house neat and clean. I felt comforted in the way she fussed over Abel and me while preparing the breakfast and earlier tending to our wounds.

She brought three plates and sat them in front of Andy, Abel, and me. Rather than digging in as she expected, I pushed my plate to the side and pulled Abel's plate over to me. I held down the ham with my fork while Abel used his knife to carve it into small pieces.

She asked, "What're you boys doin'?"

I looked up and answered, "Abel's mouth's still tender. He doesn't have many back teeth left to chew."

Mary Blaylock picked up Abel's plate and said, "Eat yours,

Captain Cobb. I'll grind Lieutenant Robertson's food for him."
She retuned shortly with Abel's plate heaped with finely minced
ham, egg, and cornpone.

Andy finished eating, pushed back from the table, and began
his story. "I joined a militia company assigned to defend the
Gosport Naval Yard in Portsmouth. All of us wuz green as grass,
but, for reasons best known to themselves, the officers picked me
to be a Sergeant. I didn't mind. I'd rather give than take orders."

"I heard we raised a sunk ship, the Merrimack, and plated
it with iron. I didn't believe the stories until I saw it, one hell
of a battleship. The Virginia – that's what we called it after it
wuz fitted - sailed down the James River and sank a bunch of
Yankee ships. Next day the Yankees showed up with a little iron
clad cracker box and fought the Virginia to a draw. Bad timin',
real bad. I know the Virginia could've sunk all the whole Yankee
Navy if that damn little cracker box hadn't showed up."

"As it wuz, the Yankees went after the Gosport Naval Yard
and eventually drove us out. Too many of 'em to beat back. We
scuttled the Virginia in the river. I nearly cried when they done it
and wuzn't by myself."

Andy leaned forward and his eyes glazed as he continued his
story. He had started calmly and became animated as he talked.

"In one scrap, I took a shot in the leg and 'nother in the
arm. Neither wuz serious. An orderly bandaged me up. Captain
gave me orders to take a message to command up river and then
told me to go home, recuperate, and return when I wuz well. At
the time, he did not know and I did not know the Yankees had
overrun Fauquier County."

"I dropped off the message and rode back to our farm. I wuz
near home when a Yankee patrol caught me. They took my rifle
and a pistol I carried in a side holster. They didn't look in the
sling. If they had, they would've found a small revolver I took off
a dead Yankee."

"They wanted to send me back to a holdin' area and then to

a prison. Life might've been easier if I'd just gone along. I'd be swapped by now, but I wuz nearly home. I waited 'til it wuz just the Yankee Sergeant, a Corporal, a Private, and me. The Sergeant had a horse. I pulled out the pistol and shot him and then the Corporal. I jumped on the horse and took off. Didn't have time for the Private and he got off a shot that caught me in the shoulder."

"I don't know how it wuz when you went down, but my shoulder hurt like old billy hell. I could feel the broke bones rub together. I didn't think I'd last until I made it home. The folks tell me I passed out at the front door. Thank God, they wuz awake. Dad and Christopher carried me inside. I don't remember any of it, even comin' home."

Andy's face was red by now. He punched the air and thumped the table to make points as he talked. Abel looked at me with raised eyebrows. I knew what he thought, but could not discuss it in front of Andy. Andy worked himself into a lather for no obvious reason. I looked for an opportunity to slow him down, maybe back off from the anger he generated.

"Dad rode off in the middle of night to find Doc Burrus and bring him back to take care of me. In the meantime, Ma used alcohol to clean the wound like she dun for you. Doc Burrus came with his bag and did surgery on me in the bedroom. He set the bones and, with Dad's help, put my arm and shoulder in a splint. That's what I remember - a big, ugly splint on my left arm when I woke up. It hurt, but at least I wuz home."

"Doc Burrus took the bullet out of my leg and bandaged it. The bullet to the arm passed through without lodgin'. He bandaged it too."

I asked, "Is Doctor Burrus trustworthy?"

"Absolutely. He has two sons in the Confederate Army. One of 'em served with me in the Coastal Militia."

"Your arm appears fine now. How long did it take to mend?" Abel asked.

"Longer than I wanted. Doc Burrus had to go back in and reset the bones after they knitted."

Abel winced and said, "That must've hurt." As I listened to Andy's story, I wondered if it might be possible to reset Abel's jaw in the future.

"Yeah. But it wuz that or a bad shoulder for the rest of my life. As it is, it hurts on cold nights, but it'll be good as new when I take off the sling and get back to killin' Yankees. It took a half-year to heal. I wuz lucky. Doc Burrus's better than the surgeons we had in the army."

Our diversion seemed to work. Andy had become self-absorbed, but now reacted to us. He asked, "How 'bout you?"

"I hate to say it, but the Yankees did good work on my leg. With time, I'll be fine. They did the best they could with Abel's jaw."

"After the war, maybe I can buy new teeth" Abel kidded. Andy and I looked at him and laughed politely, but it wasn't funny.

With a little small talk and kidding, Andy seemed to change to a different man, like what he was before he got worked up in telling us his war experiences. He looked at me admiringly and said, "You came away with a great head scar."

Without thinking, I rubbed the left side of my head.

"You got a good one there, Captain. Should turn some purty heads." Andy grinned and I knew what he meant.

"I haven't thought much about it, but you're likely right. It damned near killed me. If I had had my druthers, I would've passed on it."

* * *

After retiring to our bedroom, Abel and I talked into the night. Abel sat in the one chair in the room while I put on a nightshirt and climbed into bed. He said, "I like the Blaylocks, but Andy puzzles me. He isn't any more shot up than you or I, but seems to have a rage to get at the Yankees while just sitting and talking about them."

I nodded in agreement and commented, "You and I would just as soon walk away if the Yankees would leave us alone. But, I don't know how I would react if Yankees had occupied my farm."

"Andy's anger with the Yankees aside, I have noted the two of you are much alike."

"What?" With his partial tongue, Abel did not speak clearly. I thought I had misunderstood him.

"To start with, you look alike. Light brown hair, blue eyes, about the same height and weight. You are educated and he is not, but both of you are smart. One of the things I like about you is your ability to take in all the facts and come up with a reasoned conclusion. I see the same in Andy, except I think he is more impulsive. You both seem to be honorable, moral men. But, he's more talkative than you. You want to hang back until you size up a situation where I think he is more inclined to jump in."

"Interesting observations, Professor Robertson" I said, "But, yeah, we sure as hell don't think alike. Andy's dangerous, hopefully just to the Yankees."

* * *

The Blaylocks seemed decent, hard working, kind people. What I imagined all the South was like. Seemed like a good place to be restored before we went back to the war. I asked Abel, "What if they ask us to stay, do you want to?"

"Sure. We're not much use to the army with lame arms and my shot up face. But, what makes you think they want us to stay?"

"They're shorthanded. Whatever help they had must have taken off. You saw the fields and the fences. Lot of repair work before spring planting."

"What can two one-armed men do?" Abel asked.

"More than what they have now. I am just saying if they ask, let's stay until we're ready to go back to the army."

"We'd have to put on civilian clothes and hide every time we see a Yankee rider. If we go back to the army now, they'd want to stick us in the hospital or put us in supply duty. I'd rather stay here until we're healed." Abel had a good grasp of our situation.

After breakfast John Blaylock leaned back in his chair and lit a pipe. He enjoyed one of the few pleasures left to Virginians in the war – tobacco. Earlier, I told him, I served on staff with the Light Division where his son served in the Virginia Brigade. He obviously had something on his mind as he looked at me and puffed. "How's the war goin'? We ain't had letters from Matthew since the Yankees overran the county."

"In the hospital, I overheard the Yankees talking about Sharpsburg which they call Antietam. They think they won a major victory."

"What do you think?" John asked.

"From what I saw, it was a bloody draw. We took a lot of casualties and so did they. We left and I suppose the Yankees decided it made them winners. But, I hope we don't fight any more draws like Sharpsburg. We won't have an army left."

Abel interjected, "Amen. We have to find some other way to whip the Yankees. They'll always put more soldiers on the field than we can muster."

John asked, "What else did you hear in the hospital?"

"Lincoln replaced McClellan with Ambrose Burnside."

"And what does General Hill and the other generals think of Burnside?" John asked.

"He's an incompetent."

John Blaylock slapped his knee, laughed heartily, and said, "That's the best news I've heard in months."

He puffed on his pipe for about a minute and then asked Abel and me, "Would you boys like to stay on with us 'til you're healed? The Yankees're gatherin' around Fredericksburg. They'll still be there when you're able to rejoin our army."

I looked to Abel who nodded and responded, "Thank you, Mister Blaylock. Your offer's most welcome. But, we don't want to be around eating Missus Blaylock's good food and do nothing for our keep. Whatever we can do to help, we will."

John Blaylock seemed pleased when he answered, "Maybe you and Abel can work with Andy mendin' fences while me and Christopher take care of the chores. But, whatever you're doin' at the time, best hide if you see Yankees. We don't want 'em pokin' around."

* * *

That morning, Abel and I worked at shucking seed corn. One held the cob while the other scraped off the kernels. It did not take long to get blisters on our good hands. In the afternoon, we went on to working with Andy in splitting logs for firewood and repair of the fences. One held the logs while the other two split and sawed it.

We worked dawn to dusk. Over several weeks, we finished shucking the seed corn, cut and stacked firewood for the winter, and made fence repairs.

At supper, John Blaylock commented, "For one armed men, you've done well."

"Yeah, I'm havin' fun orderin' two officers around." Andy grinned impishly.

"Andy, you be nice to Jim and Abel. They're good boys," Mary scolded from the kitchen.

Andy looked at her in mock indignation. "Give your son some credit. I boss 'em without 'em knowin' it."

Truth was Andy took pleasure in ordering us and correcting whatever mistakes he saw us make. I became tired of him as did Abel. But our arms had not healed and we regained our strength with steady work and good food. Abel worked on improving his pronunciation with the partial tongue left from his injury. I practiced with him during the day, constant repetition of consonant and vowel sounds. He gradually got better.

Thinking they might be needed later, Mary washed, rewashed, and carefully mended the stolen blue uniforms. She got out most of the bloodstains and hid them under a board in the storeroom should Yankee soldiers return.

In late December the splints and slings came off, an event not as significant as it could have been. From about the third week on, each of us used the injured arm increasingly in our work. However, John Blaylock decided it would serve for a celebration. He pulled out glasses and his best 'shine we sipped in the front room. We discussed return to the Confederate Army.

Since all Confederate units needed replacements, I suggested, "Why not report to the Light Division? Better yet, the 6th North Carolina Brigade. You won't do better. General Pender's the best officer in the army. He looks after his men."

"Sounds good to me, but you know Andy and I are both Virginians," Abel pointed out.

"I know and don't care. Neither does General Pender. There's been so many casualties and replacements no one much minds anymore who fights in what brigades."

"I'll go along. Who'd keep you two out of trouble if I'm not there," Andy teased.

I felt pleased. I would return from the dead and bring Abel with me. Good, too, to get Andy back to being a Sergeant in the army rather than our commander at the Blaylock Farm.

Chapter 10: Mosby

Blaylock Farm, Fauquier County, Virginia,
December 27, 1862 – March 21, 1863
Jim Cobb

While planning our return, we heard riders approaching. We saw two men, one in a Confederate officer's uniform and the other under an ostrich plumed hat and a gray cape with an inner lining that appeared bright red in the fading sunlight.

"Who are they? Maybe the Yankees learned you're hidin' here," Mary cried out. She had already seen too many them in her home.

Andy looked out the window, laughed, and hugged his mother to reassure her. "Do you think the Yankees would send out a man in costume to arrest us?"

But, as a precaution, each of us got his pistol while Mary took Christopher to a back room.

After a knock on the door a voice called out, "I'm Major John Mosby, Confederate Army looking for John Blaylock."

John Blaylock opened the door and invited them in. Mosby was a slight, wiry, nattily dressed man. His dress, carriage, and piercing blue eyes suggested decisiveness and intelligence.

Mosby removed his hat and introduced his aide, Tyler Jennings, and got to the reason for his visit. "I have a commission from General Lee to create an army behind enemy lines. We'll do what we can to disrupt their communications, steal provisions, and generally harass the Yankees. I need men in Fauquier County to provide information. Can you help us, Mister Blaylock?"

I had been staring at Mosby since he walked in and asked, "Were you with Stuart's Cavalry?

"Yes. Who are you, Sir?"

I stepped forward to shake his hand and replied, "Captain Jim Cobb, Aide to A P Hill. I recall seeing you at Second Manassas."

Mosby nodded and replied, "I remember the face if not the name. How'd you find your way here?"

I nodded toward Abel. "Lieutenant Robertson and I were wounded at Sharpsburg, escaped, had a scrape with the Yankees, and were taken in by the Blaylocks while we mended. We were planning our return when you and Lieutenant Jennings rode up."

Mosby clapped his hands. "Sorry about your misfortune, but God or the fates put you in position to help me get my organization started. I need men like you, officers and soldiers recuperating, maybe some freebooters. We won't take slackers."

Looking at John Blaylock, he said, "But what I need most is information. I was told John Blaylock is the man to see in Fauquier County. Can you help me?"

"What information will you need?" John asked.

Lieutenant Jennings answered, "We need to know where the Yankees are, troop strength, their movements, things like that." Everyone, including Jennings, looked to Mosby who nodded.

"My mission's to bedevil the Yankees in all areas they occupy in Northern Virginia," Mosby said. "We'll hit them with small raiding parties at times and places they won't expect us. We'll never have more than twenty or thirty men on a raid and may confront the Yankees at the same time in different locations. We can't do it without timely and accurate information."

"How will you finance this operation?" Abel asked.

Mosby seemed surprised by Abel's question, but quickly replied, "General Lee expects us to support ourselves, but he assured me the Confederate government will buy whatever arms, horses, and equipment we take from the Yankees." Abel may have worried that they would live off the civilians. With the Yankees stealing from them, which army would they support? A good question, but, from what Mosby said, that would not happen.

"How can we help you?" Andy asked.

"I want to start with something special, something that will get their attention, let the Yankees know they're not safe anywhere. I'm hoping Mister Blaylock can suggest our first strike in Fauquier County."

John Blaylock grinned slyly and said, "The Yankees have a payroll wagon they bring in weekly. They pay their soldiers Saturday afternoon. Not smart. Most of 'em are liquored up by Saturday night. They'll be mad as hornets when their pay's not there."

Mosby pounded a fist into the palm of his other hand. "That's it. Hit them where it hurts most and, at the same time, capture Union money. Perfect." He turned to me and said, "Captain Cobb, you know what's needed - dates, times, and routes. Can you get the information we need to plan a strike? May I count on you?"

Before I could answer, John Blaylock spoke up, "Where can we contact you? I want to discuss your offer with the boys."

Mosby appeared disappointed, but looked at John Blaylock and said, "We'll be at the Parnell Farm for the next two days. You understand no one besides us needs to know this."

John Blaylock responded, "Major Mosby, I'll see you at Parnell's place tomorrow."

After we served them with polite talk, cake, and the Blaylock's remaining coffee, Mosby and Tyler Jennings left.

John Blaylock turned to his "boys". "Who's this dandy? Comes in and says General Lee ordered him to organize an army behind Yankee lines. Jim, you seem to know him."

What Stuart proposed appealed to me. Independent

command behind Union lines with mostly Confederate sympathizers. "Stuart used Mosby as a scout. He led a raiding party behind Union lines before Second Manassas and captured supplies for us. I remember Stuart telling General Hill he was a good one. You saw the way he dresses. I'm guessing Stuart would like to take the war to the Yankees, but can't because he leads our cavalry. So he did the next best thing – appointed one of his officers, the one most like himself, to lead this group."

Abel added, "Before the war, I attended the University of Virginia in Charlottesville. Mosby's a legend there. He shot another student and was expelled. I heard he got a parole and studied for the law with the attorney who prosecuted him. If I remember correctly, he had a practice in Bristol before enlisting. I have no doubt this man is the same John Mosby."

John Blaylock smiled and rubbed his hands together, "This is excitin'. Instead of watchin' Yankees ride around like they own us, we can take the war to 'em. If you boys agree, I'll ride over to Parnell's place and tell Mosby we're in. Put off rejoinin' the army a few months. I think we can do more for the Cause here."

Abel said something he had mentioned to me earlier. "I don't know if it'll help Major Mosby, but back home I worked as a telegrapher and got pretty good at it. I could listen to incoming messages and learn the tapping style of the telegrapher. It's called his 'voice'. For the hell of it, I'd confuse them and send back an answer in the same voice. Dad heard about it and made me stop. But, I'm thinking we could tap into Yankee telegraph lines, learn the voices of their telegraphers, and send along made up messages."

John rocked back and forth in excitement. "That's good, Abel. Real good. I'll pass it along to Mosby when I see him." Turning to Andy and me, John said, "I'll tell him you'll scout the Warrenton Road and the Yankee payroll wagon for a robbery."

* * *

The next morning, while we ate, Lieutenant Jennings rode in. We invited him inside and offered breakfast. He declined, stood beside the kitchen table, and asked, "Have you made your decision?"

John Blaylock answered, "I'll set up a network of loyal men and women to keep eyes on the Yankees and what they're doin'. Tell Mosby Andy, Jim, and Abel will serve with him for two or three months until they rejoin the army."

Jennings broke into a wide grin. "Delighted to have you with us, Sir. Begging your pardon, Mister Blaylock, Major Mosby asked that you, Captain Cobb, Lieutenant Robertson, and Sergeant Blaylock accompany me for a meeting. He wants to discuss your suggestion from last night."

We followed Jennings back to Mosby's base. During the ride, I talked with him. Jennings also served in the cavalry and knew Pete Morgan. I learned Mosby brought nine men with him and was intent on building an army of over three hundred raiders. He started an intelligence network and added seasoned officers and soldiers where he found them to carry out his mission.

Mosby made temporary camp in the woods near the Parnell Farm eight miles from the Blaylock Farm. We passed a sentry who smiled, saluted, and called out, "Major Mosby's waitin' for you."

Mosby stepped forward and shook hands with each man as he dismounted. I was last and Mosby commented, "We would've given Pope a good licking at Gordonsville if Norman Fitzhugh hadn't got himself captured."

I wondered whether Mosby made apology for the blunder that cost a decisive victory or was simply establishing common ground for conversation. I decided to move on to the more positive results, "We got them at Second Manassas and Chantilly on their way back to Washington. But you're right; it could've been better. Abel and I've been out since Sharpsburg. How's the war going?"

"You and Lieutenant Robertson saw what I saw at Sharpsburg. Another fight like that and we won't have an army left. Last month, we gave 'em a good licking at Fredericksburg. With God's grace, the Yankees will count their dead and go home. Until then, we'll nip at their heels."

By now, John, Andy, and Abel gathered with me around Mosby who got to why he had invited us to meet. "I'm asking you to write a report. Tell me when the payroll wagon runs, how many escorts accompany it, how fast it travels, and where best to take it. I'll send Lieutenant Jennings for the report a week from now."

John Blaylock told him, "The boys've been restless, ready to get back to the fightin'. This'll give 'em somethin' to do. As you know all our names, I won't put them in the report in case Lieutenant Jennings is captured like Stuart's aide at Gordonsville."

Mosby laughed. "I heard you were a good man before I came last night. I'm looking forward to working with you."

John nodded graciously and joked with Mosby with the grace of a Planter. Could have passed as a Planter except for the way he dressed and talked. "Thank you, Major. If you're willin', I'll make another suggestion."

"By all means. You've done well so far."

Following closely what Abel told him last night, John said, "Union command has telegraph lines throughout the county. We can tap into their lines, intercept orders, and send out some of our own."

Mosby listened and nodded in agreement as John made the suggestion. "We've done it on Stuart's raids." He commented, "But I don't have a telegraph key or a telegrapher."

John answered, "The Yankees commandeered the telegraph office in town. I suggest we make it an early raid. The telegrapher you need is closer than you think."

"Your son?" Mosby asked.

"No. Lieutenant Robertson wuz a telegrapher in Winchester 'fore the war. I suspect he's good at it. I can vouch for the time he spent with us. You're getting' a good man."

For Abel, the opportunity to work and finish the war with Mosby would be a godsend, something I suspected his adoptive father understood. He knew Abel did not want to return to duty and endure the stares and questions about his disfigured face and slurred speech. Maybe, just maybe, in contraband taken from the Yankees, he could find false teeth and at least eat normally again.

Abel had given up on having a wife, children, and a normal life after the war. But, for now, he could fill a vital role in the new army Major Mosby was forming and worry about his problems later.

Mosby removed his hat and bowed to John Blaylock. "I'm beginning to think General Lee made a mistake in giving me this command. With you, there's a better man in place. As of now, Lieutenant Robertson is my staff aide responsible for disrupting Yankee communications. Tomorrow, I'll send four men into town to rob the telegraph office and bring back a key."

"Make it day after tomorrow," John suggested. "I'll get word to Zeke Fleming and let him know you're comin'. He'll make sure you get a good key and throw in some batteries."

"This Fleming reliable?"

"Yes. His sons serve in Longstreet's Corps. He lied to the Yankees to keep his job and nobody has yet set them straight. Just make sure your men make it look real."

Before we returned to the Blaylock Farm, Abel shook hands with John, Andy, and me. He said, "Before you leave I want to tell you again how much I appreciate your patching me up, hiding me, and all the good meals Missus Blaylock fed me."

He turned to me, tears rolling down his face, and said, "I would not be alive without you."

I put my arm around him and whispered, "God saved you before you ever got to the field hospital. You have a second chance at life. I know you'll make the most of it. I don't know where your path will take you, but I know we'll be proud of you."

Abel regained his composure, but barely.

Thereafter, Andy and I saw Abel infrequently. Mosby held him out of most raids and used him only when he had opportunity to tap into the telegraph lines and mislead the Yankees. Mosby considered him too valuable to risk to a chance shot or capture.

* * *

On our return to the Blaylock Farm, John took Andy and me to the kitchen table and spread out a map of Fauquier County.

"The Yankees send the payroll wagon out weekly from Washington. By the time the wagon gets here, it's early night. They want to hide the shipment from us. Station yourselves here and here." John pointed to the map as he spoke. "You'll be about ten miles apart. Note the time when the payroll wagon passes and we'll know about how fast it moves. Count the escorts and compare your totals later. Should be the same. No one has said anything about escorts droppin' off along the way."

"Do you have any thoughts on where to take the payroll?" Andy asked.

John pointed to a turn in the Warrenton Road. "Here. There's heavy woods on each side. Easy to conceal our men and capture the payroll before the Yankees know what hit 'em. We can come at 'em from both sides at the same time as the wagon slows down to make the turn."

"Sounds good to me," I said. "When does the payroll wagon run?"

"Friday night."

The next day, Andy and I rode over to the suggested intercept point. It was perfect.

"Match up the raiders with the escorts and fall on them before they panic. The Yankees'll be alert for common highway robbers, not an organized group with equal numbers," I commented.

Friday evening, we timed the wagon, counted the escorts, and returned. The number of escorts was the same – seventeen including the driver, no additions or subtractions along the way.

John Blaylock asked my advice on how to write his report to Mosby. It was simple who, what, when, and where that anyone could understand, most particularly a brilliant officer like Mosby. Lieutenant Jennings came by Monday morning to pick up the report. He said Mosby had changed his base of operations. No one asked where.

* * *

Two days later, Clifford Ramsey came in late afternoon and identified himself as a "Mosby Ranger". Andy said, "Good name. We're Rangers. I suspect the Yankees'll have other names for us," grinned and added, "to hell with 'em."

Ramsey was talkative, but careful not to reveal where Mosby stayed. He told us the Rangers now numbered twenty four, including Captain Cobb and Sergeant Blaylock. Enough to carry out the payroll robbery.

Ramsey returned to the Blaylock Farm on Friday, January 16 at six in the evening and announced, "We'll take the Yankee payroll tonight. Meet outside the tavern at the Warrenton Road and Saylor's Creek. Be there before ten." He rode off to gather other Rangers for the raid.

As our group huddled in the woods waiting for the expected Union payroll shipment, I thought about what I could learn from Mosby and working with him. My left leg ached in the night chill as I waited. The Blaylocks were right. I needed more time before I healed completely.

Mosby came over to talk. I asked, "How did the idea of a partisan army in Northern Virginia begin?"

"General Pope was my inspiration" he said naming the one Yankee general I knew he hated. "Among other stupid things he did, he was quoted in the press as saying the Union Army would always look forward. I read it and thought it an invitation to steal his supplies in the rear. I brought it to the attention of General Stuart who took the idea to Lee. Sure enough, the Yankee supply lines were weakly defended. The raid was successful. Later, they decided to establish a separate command for me in the occupied areas of Northern Virginia, but I got no officers, other than my aide, men, supplies, or anything else. I am creating this command as I go along. Thanks to you and Sergeant Blaylock, we'll get their attention tonight." Mosby smiled as he thought on the planned theft.

As the time for the payroll wagon arrival approached, Mosby ordered us into position and absolute silence. The arrival time came and passed. We waited and the Union payroll wagon did not appear. Mosby was upset and sent Andy and me to learn what happened.

It did not take long to find the problem. The wagon was two miles up the road with a broken wheel. Yankee soldiers gathered around cursing while trying to fix it. They made little progress. It appeared they needed a new wheel and axle and that would likely take the remainder of the night. We returned to Mosby and reported what we found. We could have taken the payroll where the wagon broke down, but he called off the raid.

On the next scheduled trip, Friday, January 23, at the wooded turn in the road, a "ghost army", including Andy and me, overwhelmed the escorts without a shot fired. We treated Union troops kindly and with respect, but took their payroll, side arms, and valuables and slipped back the way we came.

Mosby and John Blaylock were pleased. The payroll theft created the expected furor in the Union Army. Patrols went out daily looking for us. It weakened their defense of depots, supply trains, and other points of attack for the next several weeks.

For the following two months, Andy and I went out on raids, sometimes together, sometimes separately. The raids were dangerous, but also exciting and fun. Each was a new adventure. Most often, we captured Union supply trains or raided their depots. We stored our plunder in barns of friendly farms, including the Blaylock's, and took it back at night under Ranger escort to the Confederate Army. Yankee officers who slept in commandeered homes of Confederate sympathizers had uninvited late night visitors. Our successes included payroll theft, cutting telegraph lines in support of Confederate operations, intercept of Union communications, and even capture of a Union general's personal wardrobe.

Mosby became a major distraction to the occupying army. In particular, Abel established his worth. The Yankees brought in new telegraphers. It did not throw off their tormentor. Abel quickly learned to mimic the voices of the replacements.

Gillison Farm, Fauquier County, Virginia
Thursday, February 26, 1863,
Jim Cobb

Toward the end of our time with Mosby, the Yankees nearly captured the entire raiding party. The Ranger Army became an intolerable irritant and an order came down to destroy it. Soon thereafter, we were betrayed.

Mosby waited to the last instant to order us to the Gillison Farm for a raid on a nearby Union supply depot. We assembled as ordered at the appointed time and place. Twenty-six Rangers, including Andy and me, gathered for the raid. Depot raids had become routine. We spent time talking and joking with the others while waiting for the order to move out.

Unknown to Mosby and the rest of us, notice of the planned raid was forwarded to the local Union cavalry post.

As an established precaution, Mosby sent scouts out to look for Federals that might be in the area. Fortunately, one of them saw Union cavalry surrounding the farm and raced back shouting, "The Yankees circled us". A Union detachment of approximately one hundred twenty cavalry surrounded the farm and closed in to bag the raiding party which they knew included Mosby. As we had been instructed, the Rangers took off in twenty-six different directions.

Pistol shots rang out around the perimeter. I rode directly toward six oncoming Union cavalrymen. I feinted right, got them to turn in the same direction, veered left, and sped by the Union troopers on my right. By the time the Yankees turned to follow, I had too much lead to be caught. I heard their cursing and the pistol fire, but the bullets hit harmlessly in the branches above my head.

After escaping, I heard more gunfire and knew Union cavalry had caught up with some of our boys. I worried about Andy and circled back toward the Gillison Farm. I carefully stayed concealed in the woods when I heard or suspected Union patrols. It took most of the night.

About three in the morning, I looked into a clearing and my heart sank. Three Yankee troopers had Andy tied and on the ground kicking and beating him. Nearby, I saw a wounded trooper motionless, maybe dead. I suspected Andy may have shot him. A fourth Yankee appeared to be fashioning a noose.

Four to one, but they did not see me. I had a fully loaded Colt six shot Model 1860 44 caliber revolver and a short barrel shotgun which I took from Union prisoners.

Andy rolled away from them and tried to stand up. All but

the one working on the noose moved toward him providing the diversion I needed.

In the dim light, they did not recognize that a Ranger rode toward them. With my left hand, I pointed the shotgun at the detached Yankee and knocked him down with a blast to the chest. I dropped the shotgun and grabbed the reins while aiming my pistol at the Yankee to the right. He jumped to the side, but I hit him in the shoulder. The trooper on my left pointed his pistol at me. He got off a quick shot that missed, but I startled him. My next shot hit him in the chest and he dropped.

The remaining trooper looked stunned as I rode to where he stood near Andy. I clubbed him on the head and he dropped in a heap. I jumped off my horse and used a bayonet I carried to cut the rope that tied Andy.

Andy pulled a pistol from the trooper I clubbed and, without hesitation, shot him in the head.

I shouted, "No, Andy, we don't have time or reason for that."

He ignored me and shot each of the other Yankees in the head. I had not killed any of them except maybe the first, but Andy did. He appeared deranged as he climbed on one of the Yankees' horses and shouted, "Let's go."

I wanted to chew him out but did not have time. In his state of mind, he would not listen anyway. Andy cost us time and needlessly murdered men we did not have to kill. Worse, he delayed our retreat from a confrontation I knew would draw other Union troopers. I retrieved the shotgun and we took off.

Andy said nothing as we rode back. I figured it best if I just let him calm down. We reached the Blaylock Farm and explained what had happened. Other than his bruises and cuts to his face and arms, I would not have guessed Andy had been in a shootout and nearly hanged. He seemed calm and rational in talking with his family.

I saved my lecture and never gave it. Controlled anger is good in combat, but not rampage. When you fight with a unit, like a platoon, you have to worry about the others. I wondered how Andy would fit in the 6th North Carolina. We went back to the bedrooms and slept.

Later, I thought about what happened and decided I might have done what Andy did if I had been beaten and nearly hanged by the men I killed, but, probably not. It was the first time I saw him go off on Yankees.

* * *

At the next raid with Mosby, we learned that, miraculously, only three Rangers had been killed, five wounded, and two captured following the near disaster.

With John Blaylock's help, Mosby retraced the order to assemble at the farm, in terms of who knew what and when, and identified the spy. The next week, Andy, Clifford Ramsey, and I pulled him out of bed.

He was a stableman, Purvis Green, who learned Mosby would need fresh horses for a raid. He pressed the stable owner for details and took the information to the Union Provost office. After we got him out back, he seemed contrite and knew his fate.

Andy led our party to an oak tree. As we prepared to hang him, he pleaded, "I know I dun wrong. Don't kill me. I'm sorry. I learnt my lesson."

Andy answered, "Too late to be sorry. Rangers were killed, captured, and wounded because you sold us out. Could've caught Mosby. It's treason and you'll hang for it."

"Can't you get it over quick and shoot me instead?" He pleaded.

"No. The Yankees might hear the shots. Say your prayers. When you're finished, we'll hang you."

Purvis Green dropped to his knees and began a long, mournful prayer intended to evoke sympathy from God if not those of us on the ground.

Ramsey brought a rope and used it to fashion a noose that we tossed over a tree limb as the prayer droned on. Finally, Andy yanked him up, tied his hands behind his back, placed the noose over his neck, and, with my help, mounted him on a horse. Ramsey pulled the rope tight and tied it around the tree. Andy slapped the horse that ran out from under the condemned man. His feet flailed and eventually stopped. We rode off leaving the traitor hanging as a reminder to others who might be tempted to sell out.

Later, Andy told me, "I hated having to hang Purvis. Not a bad kid, just got greedy."

I shook my head. "We shoot traitors in the army. Same here." I thought it ironic Andy had sympathy for Purvis Green, who sold us out, but not Yankee soldiers he killed who did their duty, as he would have, and put on blue uniforms.

* * *

In future raids, Mosby became even more circumspect. All of the raids in which we participated were dangerous, but the near entrapment at the Gillison Farm was the only time we came close to capture or injury.

I rode with Andy and the Mosby's Rangers from early January to late March 1863. My leg strengthened. The Union orderlies did good work. I could walk and even run normally without limping or feeling pain. After getting over the initial soreness, my shoulder came along well as if I had never taken a bullet.

I enjoyed the thrill of riding nights behind enemy lines and used my time as a Ranger to study John Mosby and absorb as much of his operation as I could.

While repairing a fence, Andy and I took time off to eat lunch and talk.

Andy brought up the subject first. "Mosby's amazin'. He does what we're taught all our lives. Plan carefully and execute the plan. But he does it better than anyone I've known and never asks from us what he won't do himself."

I replied, "For the Rangers, everything's done in secret. It has to be. And, from what we've seen, Mosby's good at it."

"Yeah, but we keep learning the same things," Andy observed. "The raids succeed when we get good information, plan the raid well, and carry it out according to plan. We fail when there's a breakdown in any one area."

Andy said what I had been thinking. I could only agree. "The other part is the more we do it, the better we become."

I paused and said, "We've learned about all we can from Mosby. It's time to move on. The Light Division needs us."

Blaylock Farm, Fauquier County, Virginia
Saturday, March 21, 1863,
Jim Cobb

Andy and I spent our last day at the farm celebrating Christopher's eleventh birthday. We had no money to spare for presents but Christopher was as thrilled with the Union bayonet I gave him as if he had a wrapped and expensive gift. Andy and I surprised Mary and John with gifts of valuables taken from Union captives.

Mary Blaylock baked two of the family's remaining chickens and added dressing, sweet potatoes, and peas. She passed me the wings, my favorite piece. I enjoyed the meal and appreciated being included as a member of the Blaylock family.

I told the family my leg had healed and it was time I went back to my duties in the army. Andy told them he would go back with me. I preferred traveling alone, but felt I owed it to Andy to bring him with me when I reported. I took Mary's hand

and thanked her for making my time with the Blaylock family special. I said, "I've been away from home over two years. It has been very nice being part of your family."

John Blaylock commented, "I think it's a good time for both you boys to move on. The Yankees'll keep on tryin' to break into our organization. Someone will talk and the Yankees will hang everyone they find to make an example. It's better we keep movin' Rangers in and out so no one's around too long."

Before Andy and I mounted two horses taken from the Yankees and left for Confederate lines, John Blaylock handed Andy a map and directions on where to reach the nearest Confederate troops. As he shook hands with me, John said, "Give our regards to Matthew and tell him we pray for him." Mary Blaylock hugged me and Andy and gave us a kiss on the cheek. Christopher had tears in his eyes when he said goodbye. He loved his brother and even seemed to like me, the "Yankee Lieutenant" he found wandering in their pasture.

Andy's militia company had disbanded. It freed him to serve with me. I knew the Light Division would welcome him. But, better if he served in a different brigade than his brother. Better yet that he serve with my old brigade, the 6th North Carolina, and General Pender.

Poole Farm, Fredericksburg County, Virginia
Sunday, March 22, 1863,
Jim Cobb

With food from the Blaylocks and coins taken from Union captives, we left to make our way back at night using the route John Blaylock laid out earlier. We traveled through the night and came near Confederate lines at daybreak two days later. We searched out a safe house identified on the map John Blaylock provided - a farmhouse owned by Jarvis Poole, a leading Virginia secessionist.

Andy rapped on the door which was partially opened by a half-awake young man. He appeared to be about the same age as Andy and I, but larger with dark hair and dark eyes. He did not seem pleased to see us.

"Who are you? What do you want?" he demanded.

"We're Confederate soldiers on our way back to the fightin'," Andy answered. "We rode with John Mosby. This house wuz identified as a safe house. May we spend the day in your barn and move on tonight?"

The young man opened the door and allowed Andy and me to enter. Andy said, "If you could provide food we'll pay you."

The young man answered, "Take your horses into the barn. I'll send out food for you after a while."

Andy gave him a few coins to reimburse for what would be used to prepare the meal for us. We left to bed down in the barn for the day.

After unsaddling the horses and putting them into stalls, we climbed up to the hayloft to get needed rest. Later, a young woman, probably wife of the man who opened the door, came to the barn with biscuits and a slice of ham for us to eat. She had a thin, sickly appearance and seemed upset and nervous. Andy tried to engage her in conversation, but she seemed anxious to leave. He asked her about Sanford Poole. The young woman explained, "My father-in-law died and my husband, Jarvis Poole, is now owner of our farm" and left.

"Peculiar people. Very peculiar. The husband acts like we came to rob them. The wife seems afraid of us. They're unfriendly at what's supposed to be a safe house." I was anxious about our hosts. So was Andy.

As we ate, I asked Andy, "Do you think the son shares his father's loyalties?" With a mouth full of biscuit, Andy shook his head and kept eating.

Later, Jarvis Poole entered the barn, hitched a wagon, rode off, and said nothing to either of us. He stopped in front of the house and his wife climbed up to the seat beside him. After they left, we looked at each other with raised eyebrows.

Andy said, "I don't like this. They may've gone off to find Yankees to arrest us. Do you think we should leave?"

"They might be off to church for all we know. Unpleasant people, but the Mosby organization thinks they're loyal. Besides, we're near Confederate lines. The roads and woods are full of Yankees. I don't know where else we could hide."

"All right, but if we stay here, we need to keep the horses saddled and loaded. Might have to take off in a hurry." Andy resaddled his horse as he spoke.

"It's the sensible thing to do," I said. "We don't both need to stay up. You take the first turn in the loft. I'll wake you mid-afternoon to stand guard until night and we can get out of here."

Andy nodded and said, "In case a Yankee patrol shows up, we'll take off like Rangers – in different directions. But we need to pick a place to meet after we get through Union lines."

He pulled out the map. I saw a crossroads directly behind where John Blaylock indicated Confederate troops were positioned. I pointed to the intersection on the map and said, "Here."

Andy put the map in my saddlebag and muttered, "I knew the area better than you".

After we saddled the horses and loaded the saddlebags, Andy went up to the hayloft to nap, but did not remove his pistol. I took the first watch. I wanted to appear calm for Andy, but felt nervous and apprehensive. I would sleep better in the afternoon and evening if all went well.

Mid-morning, what we feared happened. From a crack in the barn door, I saw Jarvis Poole and his wife riding to the house leading six mounted Union troops. I shouted, "Andy", pushed open the barn door, jumped on my horse, and raced out to the left, away from the approaching Yankees.

Andy followed, out the door to the right.

In response, the Union patrol split. Three pursued me and three chased Andy. After riding several miles, I lost my pursuers by hiding in a thicket as they raced by. I held my pistol at the ready in case the Yankees heard the horse snort or traced the tracks into the thicket. But they noisily rode by, heard nothing, and saw nothing.

When the Union pursuit was out of sight, I doubled back toward the Poole farmhouse hiding in the woods and moving several times. On one occasion, I rode slowly through a field while scanning the ground as a local farmer laying out a plan for a fence. With a Union saddle and boots, I avoided Union soldiers passing by including the three who chased me earlier. I hid in the woods until night before going back to the farmhouse.

We were betrayed at what the Mosby organization considered a safe house. I did not like the idea of creating a young widow, but there could be other escaped Confederates, like Andy and I, who would be sold out. The traitor had to be eliminated as the spy I helped Andy dispatch earlier. My sympathies were to other possible betrayed Confederates, not Jarvis Poole and his scarecrow wife.

I began thinking of how to kill him and decided to enter the house after nightfall and shoot him in bed if need be. While waiting, another and better opportunity came up. I saw Poole walk from the farmhouse to the barn carrying a lantern with the apparent intent to tend the animals. He appeared relaxed and likely thought the Rebs were killed or captured or otherwise gone away if he thought about us at all. I quietly followed him into the barn and closed the barn door startling Poole who recognized me. He grabbed a pitchfork and started toward me shouting, "Get out!"

I shot him in the chest before he took three steps. He fell alternately cursing and begging for his life, "You stinkin' Reb. Don't kill me. The Yanks wouldn't hurt you. Just swap you for one of theirs." He stopped and started coughing blood.

I stood over him and said, "You dishonored your father and betrayed Virginia" and shot Poole through the head. I started walking toward the barn door when the wife entered. She saw her dead husband bleeding on the floor, dropped to the ground, and wept hysterically. I noted something we missed earlier. She was pregnant.

* * *

The remainder of my escape went peacefully until the very end. Challenged by a Union sentry, I hunkered down in the saddle, spurred my horse, and raced toward a Confederate camp visible in the full moon. The Union sentry fired a shot and missed. I had been out of effective rifle range from when he raised his rifle. By the time he reloaded, I disappeared into the woods.

Confederate sentries saw what happened and did not fire as I approached their position. After brief questioning, the sentries welcomed me with a cup of heated wood bark and chicory flavored water, Confederate coffee.

Feeling the cold of the night, I thanked the sentries, drank the "coffee" offered, and pulled out my map. I asked, "Do you know where I can find General Hill?"

One of the sentries replied, "Sorry, Captain. Not certain, but I think he may be over yonder" pointing back behind his left shoulder. "I heerd the Light Division camped there."

On the map, I pointed to the crossroads, and asked, "Am I about there?"

"Yes, Sir. Just over the rise."

"Thank you for the chicory and directions. Good to be back with the army," I said.

The sentry, a pleasant young man, laughed and replied, "Won't take long for army food to ruin that, but good to have you back."

I rode over to the crossroads. I knew my friend, Andy, was

a skilled rider and crack shot, but, nevertheless, worried he may have been captured or shot before he could reach Confederate lines. No time to think when the Yankee patrol showed up. I should have let Andy take the route away from them.

I camped and waited.

Chapter 11: Chancellorsville

Fredericksburg, Virginia,
Friday March 28, 1863
Jim Cobb

Mid-morning, I saw Andy riding up to the crossroads and shouted, "That you, Andy?"

Andy spotted me and shouted back, "Well, Jim, it ain't your best girl", rode over to me, jumped down, and hugged me.

Andy seemed particularly pleased I went back to the farm and settled with the turncoat. "Did you kill the wife?" he asked.

"No, she was pregnant.

"Nest of traitors, Jim. Should have cleaned 'em all out."

"I don't know where war should end. Poole's scrawny wife was with him in turning us over to the Yankees. Guilty of treason as he was, but we have to draw the line somewhere. I can't make war on women and children, particularly unborn children."

Andy shrugged his shoulders.

"You haven't said anything since you got here? What happened? I was worried about you."

Andy gave me one of his sly grins and replied, "I got away."

"That's all you got to say?" I asked. I really did not feel like playing mental games after staying up most of the night worrying about him.

Andy sat down on a log which I knew meant a long story. He wanted to tell me but did not want to volunteer the details. He began "After separatin' from you, I spurred my horse and raced to the woods behind the barn with the Yankees yellin' and cussin' behind me, then gunfire. They had an angle on me and closed fast. I went into the woods, ducked under a branch, turned, and got off a shot at the lead Yankee. He slumped over, slowed down and pulled up. I pushed my horse as fast as I could, then it appeared the Yankees had stopped chasin' me.

"After shooting one of 'em, I knew they'd comb the area for me. If they caught me, they'd kill me. I took off toward a crick, crossed over, dismounted, and walked slow lookin' right and left for Yankees. I wanted them to think me a farmer searchin' for livestock. Got caught up in lookin' and failed to see a picket behind bushes on the other side of the crick."

'Halt. Identify yourself', he called out.

"It startled me but I recovered quick, smiled at him like I hadn't done nothin', and walked toward him. 'Hey, Yank', I said. 'Seen any loose pigs or cows? Mine got out last night and I've been lookin' all over for 'em.'

"He kept his rifle pointed at me the whole time. "Nope. If I seen 'em our cook would be carvin' 'em up now."

'And, of course, your quartermaster would pay me for 'em,' I joshed back.

"I got him laughin'. He knew as well as I did Yankees didn't pay for nothin they took."

"I waded across the crick pullin' my horse behind me. The Yankee picket lowered his rifle. As I came close, he asked, 'Why ain't you out fightin' us, Reb?'

"I raised my hands and replied, 'You're talkin' to the wrong man. I want no part of secesh, just look after my farm, pigs, cows, kids, and old lady. I'd take it as a favor if you Yanks moved your war somewheres else.'

"The picket put his rifle barrel at his side with the stock on the ground like he wuz relaxed. 'My folks have a place like this back in Indiana. Onct we whip the Rebs, I'm goin' back to tendin' pigs, cows and such,' he allowed."

"I moved over beside him and offered a plug of tobacco. As he reached out, I looked to see if anyone watched and there weren't. I pulled out my pistol and hit him on the head. Fearin' more Yankees could show up, I lifted the picket over my horse, led the horse into the woods, and quickly undressed him. I took off my shirt, pants, and boots and placed them in the saddlebags and put on his uniform and boots. The fit was close enough. I dragged him behind a clump of bushes and rammed the bayonet on his rifle through his heart."

Another senseless killing. I told Andy, "You could have thrown a blanket over him and left. The kid was just doin' his job. Didn't deserve to die for trusting you when he shouldn't have."

Andy shrugged his shoulders and said, "One less Yankee bastard to kill later. If you're through with your sermon, I'll tell you the rest of the story."

I nodded knowing Andy was in no mood for a lecture.

"I rode out as a Union Private and worked my way toward Confederate lines. When hailed, I used a West Virginia accent to ask if they had seen an escaped Reb in civilian clothes to see if maybe they had seen or caught you. That night, I rode over to Confederate lines in an area where I saw no Yankees."

"I changed back into civilian clothes. When I came on Confederate sentries, I introduced myself and told them how I happened to be in the area after dark."

"Since comin' into the army and meetin' soldiers from Virginia and other states, I wuz told I speak with a Tidewater accent. To me, it's just how folks talk, but after sayin' a few words, the sentries had no doubts about me. I stayed up late and entertained them with tales of ridin' with Mosby."

More than anything else, Mosby, John Hunt Morgan, and the other Confederate partisan leaders uplifted Confederate morale. I knew the soldiers took pleasure in hearing Andy give a first hand account of taking it to the Yankees and getting revenge for what they had done in the occupied areas of the South.

"I slept in their camp and rode off in early mornin' to find you after thankin' my hosts for the breakfast and 'coffee' they shared."

I felt thankful to have Andy back with me and came away even more impressed with his resourcefulness.

* * *

From soldiers we passed along the way, we got directions to the Light Division and A P Hill's tent. We arrived around mid-day and found General Hill and his wife, Dolly, entertaining a group of staff and line officers inside the General's spacious tent. They apparently took advantage of the lull in fighting to celebrate something, maybe a birthday. General Hill frequently organized informal get-togethers for his senior officers, particularly when Dolly Hill was available to serve as hostess.

Lieutenant Titus Palmer, a Division Staff aide and my friend, stood on duty outside and recognized me. I introduced Andy before Palmer hugged me.

He said, "I had to make sure you weren't a ghost." Palmer asked Andy, "If you would, Sergeant Blaylock, wait here while I take Jim inside. They'll be as shocked and pleased as I am to see him alive and well."

My sudden appearance startled General Hill and the Division officers. General Hill looked at me wide-eyed and nearly dropped his cup. When he recovered, he said, "Jim, I'm amazed, absolutely amazed. We saw you go down at Sharpsburg and were convinced you were dead. I'm pleased you proved us wrong. How were you able to survive?"

I briefly recounted what happened at Sharpsburg. Later, as I shook hands with the officers, General Pender said, "Come by and see me after you're settled."

Dolly Hill asked, "Captain Cobb, how did you come by

that scar on the side of your head? Was it from your wound at Sharpsburg?"

"Yes, Ma'am. I was lucky to survive. An inch deeper and I would not be standing here. I was fortunate the Yankees took me to their hospital. Strange, but I'm glad the Yankees captured me. They even made it easy for me to escape."

Dolly Hill shook her head, took the General's arm, and said to me, "You saw first hand how the Yankees take care of their wounded. It's shameful we cannot do as well for our men." Dolly Hill was an outspoken critic of our post-surgical care that she often brought to the General's attention and anyone else who would listen. I realized I had just given her witness to the superiority of Union care, but glad I did. Our care of the wounded was deplorable.

I was not surprised to find Dolly Hill with her husband near the front. More than most senior officers' wives, she liked to spend as much time as possible with her husband. She married A P Hill shortly before the war began and was very much in love with him. Others criticized General Hill for keeping his wife with him during the fighting, but he ignored them. She was a favorite with the officers and men of the Light Division. We all loved her.

General Hill asked, "Ready to return to duty?"

"Yes, sir, I'm fit and rested."

"We're under command of General Jackson again. Been here since before Fredericksburg still trying to contain the Yankee Army. We hoped they had enough, but they didn't back off. We've got more work to do."

How did Jackson, the dull, pious, and uninspired VMI instructor became the darling of the South and terror of the North? Jackson's staff considered him at least half mad, that he drove his troops too hard, and carried and carefully studied large and detailed maps of the local terrain. Everyone, and most particularly the Yankees, knew he was absolutely brilliant in devising and implementing winning strategy and tactics.

Jackson believed God ordered his battles and willed his victories. His officers and men served as instruments God placed in his hands to defeat the Yankees. Indifferent to the welfare of his subordinates and disliked for it, Jackson, nevertheless, had the devotion of his troops. They fought hard for him for one simple reason. He won battles.

I excused myself and returned with Andy. I explained how Andy and the Blaylock family took care of Abel Robertson and me as we recovered after the encounter with the Union patrol. Knowing it would create an opportunity for Andy to make a favorable impression on the Light Division officers, I recounted our initial meeting with John Mosby and Tyler Jennings and brought Andy into the conversation.

Everyone at the party remembered John Mosby favorably from his earlier service with Stuart's Cavalry. They heard rumors and stories and seemed delighted to get a first hand account of Mosby's operation.

Andy handled himself well. I felt proud of him, a Sergeant talking with the generals as if he belonged. Taking no chance of disclosing his role in the Mosby organization, neither of us mentioned John Blaylock's position in the Mosby organization. But, from their questions, they seemed to know Andy was not just another Mosby Ranger.

I told General and Dolly Hill, "I had opportunity to talk with Major Mosby on several occasions. I told him I would return to the Light Division and he asked that I convey his regards to you and Missus Hill."

Dolly Hill, in particular, seemed flattered. "What a gallant and dashing officer he is. His wife must be as proud of him as I am of you, dear" she gushed.

Hill patted her hand and said, "He's colorful all right. From what Captain Cobb and Sergeant Blaylock told us, he's off to a good start. We'll put the supplies he captures to good use, as you know, what he's doing is good for morale."

Standing next to them, I overheard and commented, "Yes, sir. He's already taken five hundred rifles, twenty thousand ammunition rounds, hundred twenty horses, and over thirty thousand in Yankee coin and currency." My numbers were current. John Blaylock kept us updated throughout the time we served as Mosby Rangers.

"Most impressive, Jim. We need all he can bring us." He grinned and said, "I wonder if the Yankees have figured how much of their supplies ends up with our army."

"General, as you may recall my mentioning, Andy's brother, Matthew, is a sergeant in the Virginia Brigade. I am thinking, if General Pender is agreeable, Andy might serve in the 6th North Carolina."

"Good thought, Jim," General Hill replied, "but he can't serve in those clothes. I want the two of you to see the Quartermaster and get new uniforms."

Dolly Hill listened, smiled sweetly, and said, "Disregard that order Captain Cobb. General Hill has a field uniform he never wears. I think it would be appropriate if we alter it to fit a favored aide who has miraculously returned to us."

She turned to General Hill and scolded him, "You don't need it. You insist on wearing that ridiculous red shirt and civilian coat in battle. You won't wear a second uniform. I think Captain Cobb can put it to better use." Her comments drew laughter from General Hill and a chuckle from the officers in attendance.

General Hill went along and said, "Jim, we better do as Missus Hill says. See her for your uniform."

I stiffened for a salute and turned to Dolly Hill to deliver it. She nodded to acknowledge which brought on additional laughter.

We left the General's spacious tent in good humor. Our reception could not have been gone better. But I saw one of the generals, Charles Field, commander of the Virginia Brigade, follow us out. He stopped us and said, "Sergeant Blaylock, I regret to tell you that your brother, Matthew, was killed yesterday. We thought the field had been cleared of Yankee sharp shooters and then a lone, stray bullet took him down. He was a Regimental First Sergeant, maybe the best soldier in my brigade. Matthew Blaylock was highly regarded and is sorely missed by all who served with him including myself. I'm very sorry for loss of your brother, a fine soldier and good man."

Fighting back tears, Andy replied, "General, with your permission, I'd like to take my brother's place."

"Where have you served previously?" General Field asked.

"I wuz Sergeant in a coastal militia unit disbanded several months ago, Sir. Since then, as you heard, I rode with John Mosby while I recuperated from wounds I got defendin' the Gosport Shipyard."

"I'm honored to have Matthew Blaylock's brother and a Mosby Ranger join us. After you pick up a uniform and rifle from the Quartermaster, see my adjutant for an assignment. I'll talk to him and tell him who you are. Sergeant Blaylock, all I ask is that you be as good a soldier as your brother and that's asking a lot."

Andy straightened to attention, saluted, and said, "Sir, I'll do my very best."

After General Field went back in to join the party, I stood awkwardly with Andy. I could not think of anything appropriate to say and finally told him, "Andy, I'm so sorry for you and the family."

Andy nodded, shook my hand, and we parted for the night.

The immortality of youth had passed. Not so much my own near death experience, or even Abel Robertson's miraculous recovery, it was the death of Matthew Blaylock that brought it home. I never knew the older brother, but felt like a member of the Blaylock family and mourned his loss. I knew the family would be devastated and felt badly for them and Andy. War was glory, adventure, honor, gallantry, and all the things that stir the imagination of young men, but, ultimately it is tragedy as in the recent, untimely death of Sergeant Matthew Blaylock. I had no illusions about war since experiencing it close up at First Manassas. Matthew Blaylock's death added to my mounting hurt and sadness.

* * *

I spent the night with the Division staff and went by for my fitting the next day in the General's tent. Dolly Hill had moved in furniture and a rug to give her home at the front a parlor look. A colored servant brought cookies and real tea with lemon and sugar. Dolly Hill questioned me at length about the Union hospitals. She was sweet and sincere. I thought the idea farfetched, but hoped she might be able to do something about our atrocious field hospitals.

Like a seamstress, she measured me before I left. I picked up my new uniform the next day. It fit perfectly. I took good-natured kidding for the next week. I later learned Dolly Hill did the alteration and sewing herself.

In my new uniform, I rode over to where the 6th North Carolina Brigade quartered and found General Pender speaking with Colonel James Conner, 22nd North Carolina Regiment Commander. I dismounted and waited for the General at his tent. Pender motioned me to follow him inside.

Known as a pious man, General Pender nevertheless enjoyed an occasional nip of Kentucky bourbon that he shared with me on my visits. He handed me a drink and said, "Jim, It's good to find you alive, well, and among the living" and, he noted, "outfitted in General Hill's second uniform."

"I often think back on everything that happened and consider my escape a miracle also. I enjoyed my time with Mosby and the Blaylocks, but it's good to be back."

Pender smiled at me as I talked like a son to a father even though he was only nine years older. He said, "If you have time, I'll fill you in on the war since you've been absent."

"General, if you would, tell me about Fredericksburg."

Gracious as always, he smiled and proceeded to analyze the great victory. "The Union Army initially advanced on our right flank which the Light Division held. After we drove them back, they repeatedly and foolishly attacked our fortified position on Marye's Heights where we had ample artillery and ammunition."

"Early on, we learned how to pass rifles back for reloading and forward for firing and used it to great advantage. We laid down rapid, accurate, and withering fire on the Yankees. Marye's Heights was covered with Union dead. Later Union troops used their bodies as protection from our fire."

Pender paused as he described the painful scene and added, "It was gruesome. But our boys made the best of it. They helped themselves to boots and shoes from the dead Yankees. So many, they threw them in a pile. Turns out the Yankees make shoes and boots that fit either foot. It simplified the sorting."

"Jim, I cannot comprehend the incompetence of General Burnside. A frontal attack could not succeed. Our rifles covered the field and devastated whatever the Yankees threw at us. But, General Burnside kept ordering more attacks. I can imagine no Confederate general that incompetent and reckless in squandering the lives of brave men and continue in command." Pender shook his head in disgust.

I appreciated Pender's observations and comments. This time I thought he spoke from the heart rather than the detached logic he normally discussed battles. I replied, "General, once again, it appears we whipped a numerically superior Union Army."

Pender corrected me. "No, we humbled, not destroyed them.

As you saw, they're still here threatening Fredericksburg despite the licking we gave them."

* * *

The next night, I found Andy and invited him back to my tent. "We've got unfinished business."

We drank the whiskey John Blaylock included in our provisions. It helped ease the pain we felt. I had a brother to replace - the one who ran off to sea - and Andy lost a brother he replaced in the Light Division. Without expressing our feelings, each knew he had a brother in the other. We simply drank. After a while, Andy broke down and cried.

"Jim, it wuz awful. Just a little wood cross over his grave. Somebody scrawled his name on it. Only way I could pick his grave out the others. They all talk about him now, but he'll be forgotten 'fore the war's over. If I do nothin' else, I'll get his bones back to our farm."

I knew too well how Andy felt. I tried not looking at graves. The hard reality of this war was that I, and everyone else I knew in uniform, could easily be in a grave. It seemed luck or fate or maybe, I hoped, unknowable Divine Will. I did not want to die and I would not shirk my responsibilities. I wanted to live and depended on God to keep me from harm.

I fell back into my responsibilities as if I had never left, but different for Andy. No one knew him when he showed up unexpectedly with Captain Cobb. But they all knew his brother. Word spread and Andy was deeply touched by comments of the officers and soldiers who offered condolences to him and the Blaylock family.

Initially, he served as a staff orderly for the brigade. Two weeks later, when a platoon Sergeant became ill and incapacitated, the company commander assigned Andy to lead his platoon. Two Corporals in line for Sergeant stripes resented having an outsider placed over them. Andy ignored them and went about running the platoon and earning the respect of his men and the company officers. He had a continuing high standard – the pledge he made to General Field – and worked toward it throughout the war.

* * *

I appeared to be dead or captured at Sharpsburg, but Titus Palmer was not certain and retained the unopened letters on the chance I may have somehow survived. For the same reason, I was not reported on the casualty list. With great pleasure and satisfaction, Palmer turned over the letters to me when I returned.

I wrote return letters to Mother and Sissy, but, first, pondered what to say. I read their letters, three from Mother and two from Sissy, several times. In their letters, they scolded me for not responding. It gave me the option of simply apologizing, making up a face-saving story about the past five months, and carrying on. But Mother would know I lied.

I finally settled on an abridged version of the missing months. After capture at Sharpsburg, I escaped after nine weeks, and stayed with the Blaylocks behind enemy lines until I could safely return. I concealed other details from Mother. I wrote an expanded letter to Sissy and put both letters in the outgoing mail on the first day of my return. I heard back from Mother with the earliest return mail, but did not receive a return letter from Sissy.

Sunday, April 26, 1863
New York Tribune Article
byline Samuel Payne

As commander of the Army of the Potomac, General Ambrose Burnside was headstrong, incompetent, and, ultimately disastrous for the Union Army at Fredericksburg. Following an examination of the disaster, President Lincoln and his chief of staff, General Halleck, replaced Burnside with "Fighting Joe" Hooker who has a known weakness for loose women. We hope he will make good on the nickname the soldiers have given him.

Lincoln had considerable reservations about the appointment, but the supply of competent generals capable of leading the Army of the Potomac is apparently meager. Our best generals are in the West, but, after the calamity of John Pope's command, no more of them have been brought over to the Army of the Potomac. We are apparently limited to shuffling our corps commanders to find a general capable of contending with Robert E Lee.

"Fighting Joe" Hooker is not without bravado. He promised President Lincoln he will bag General Lee and the whole Reb Army. Besides, he is popular with the soldiers; they like and admire his fighting spirit.

Hooker commands a still formidable army of over 100,000 troops along the Rappahannock River in Northern Virginia. The Confederate Army has about half that number. The opposing armies have fought a series of skirmishes as each probes the other's position and strength.

The two armies settled into a long stalemate that lasted through most of April. To break the stalemate and catch General Lee by surprise, Hooker left Sedgwick's division in place across the river from Fredericksburg to occupy the Confederate Army while Hooker, with the main body of Union troops, moved west and then south across the Rappahannock River and its tributary, the Rapidan River. The Union Army maneuvered to a position seventeen miles west of Fredericksburg.

However, Hooker did not surprise the Confederates who had pickets positioned along the river and quickly learned of his deployment. Lee left a portion of his army under Jubal Early to defend Fredericksburg and sent troops out to meet the Federals head on. The Union Army split into two groups to push the Confederates back to Fredericksburg. With superior numbers, the Union Army

slowly moved forward until Hooker ordered them back into The
Wilderness.

His army encountered stiffer resistance than anticipated. But,
mainly he had an inspiration and decided to take a defensive position in a heavily wooded area. In one bold strategic move, he expects
to force the Confederates to attack him and inflict heavy casualties
on them as the Confederates had earlier done to the Union Army
on Marye's Heights at Fredericksburg. It is a curious strategy. If the
Confederates do not attack, Hooker must move on Fredericksburg or
deeper into the Confederate interior. Either move is risky.

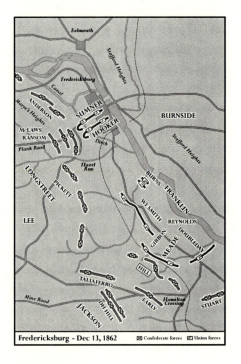

Fredericksburg - Dec 13, 1862   ⊠ Confederate forces   ⊡ Union forces

Fredericksburg, Virginia,
Thursday, April 30, 1863
Jim Cobb

The Light Division was engaged across from the center of the
Union line far too strong to be defeated or pushed back. Since

the decisive victory in Fredericksburg, we were consumed with determining where the massive Union Army might strike again. Then the Yankees came from the west along the river and the Light Division went out to confront them. But the Union Army withdrew, leaving me and others puzzled.

General Hill came back from a meeting with Generals Lee and Jackson. I noted he seemed unusually animated and suspected something exciting was afoot. He ordered me to gather the staff and the Brigade generals.

General Hill announced, "The Yankees' withdrawal presents us with an opportunity to destroy them. Our scouts discovered that General Hooker's headquarters is positioned well behind Union lines, at Chancellorsville. Any of you been there?"

Hill answered his own question, "A farmhouse and general store."

He continued, "They expect us to come at them from here. We will turn the tables on them. General Lee decided to flank Union lines through The Wilderness, strike behind them at Hooker's headquarters, and push the Union Army back to the river and destroy it."

Hill's announcement stunned us. Dorsey Pender started to speak, but was cut off by General Field who asked, "General Hill, do I understand you correctly? We will divide our army, send a strike force behind the Yankees, and attack them from the rear."

General Hill nodded and replied, "Yes."

Field spoke what we all thought. "Pardon, General, but this is madness. The Yankees outnumber us two to one. We divided our army once. General Lee will divide it again. Every cadet at the Academy knows you never divide your army in facing an army with superior numbers."

General Hill rapped the table with his fist to emphasize what he said next, "General Field, you answered your own question. The Yankees have us badly outnumbered. What is insane is fighting them on their terms. Hitting them at Chancellorsville is our one chance at victory and we will take it. Tell no one what I just told you. We must have absolute secrecy. But, prepare the Division for a long march. We will be third in line on the strike force."

As A P Hill's Chief of Staff, I attended the planning meeting with General Lee and his top generals. Lee and Jackson sat apart on hardtack boxes beside a campfire. The attending staff heard them calmly discuss Lee's plan to defeat the Union Army. No reason to hide anything from the respective attending staffs. Then and later, I realized military history was made that night. More than anything else, General Lee's calm demeanor and the fierce determination in General Jackson's eyes impressed and inspired me. The outcome of the pending battle remained in doubt, but I knew I was in the presence of greatness.

* * *

We held position opposite the Union Army at Chancellorsville with only 14,000 troops as Jackson's corps moved around the Union lines but, because of the dense woods, the Federals were unaware of the actual troop strength of the Confederate Army facing them. On the sweep around the Union right flank, General Jackson took approximately 28,000 Confederate troops, including the Light Division, on a long trek along footpaths through thick woods. The march started in the early morning and took most of the day before we were positioned and ready to strike.

For most of the time, we hid from Union observers. When they saw us, we were headed south and Hooker assumed it was a Confederate retreat to Gordonsville. I later learned Union headquarters ignored scattered and alarmed reports of Confederate troop movements in the woods around their right flank.

General Jackson ordered absolute silence. I worried the snorting of the horses, that could not be ordered, and movement along the extended trail might give away our position. Somehow Jackson's determination came down to each soldier in his command. I saw it in their eyes and clenched jaws. They were ready to finish the victory at Fredericksburg and destroy the Union Army. No Union forces hindered our long march and a good thing they didn't. Our strike force was strung out along most of the twenty six miles. Even a weak Union response would have wrecked our plan.

The Light Division engaged after the other divisions began the attack at 5:20 pm. Our troops raced toward and through Union lines. From the beginning, we routed and rolled up the Union Army. I had never seen the Yankees in such disarray.

I saw terror and bewilderment in the hanged heads and slow shuffle of the stream of disheveled and broken captives moving back to hastily established holding areas. They were promised victory and were now inexplicably overwhelmed by the same raggedy army that humiliated them earlier at Fredericksburg. The aura of Confederate invincibility now permeated both armies.

A shell fell on the porch of the house Hooker used as headquarters. It stunned him and he gave confused and conflicting orders throughout the conflict. The battle soon degenerated into a series of isolated engagements as individual Union commanders, with confused or no direction from higher command, fought desperately to save their units from being overrun and annihilated. The Confederate army suffered much higher casualties than at Fredericksburg, but, overall, we thoroughly defeated the Union Army.

In pursuit of the fleeing Yankees, our lead divisions became entangled and disorganized. I saw precious time lost as our troops went through Union supplies, captured and guarded prisoners, and rested with retreating Union troops in sight. As did all the senior staff, I felt frustrated with fading sunlight and annihilation of the Army of the Potomac within grasp.

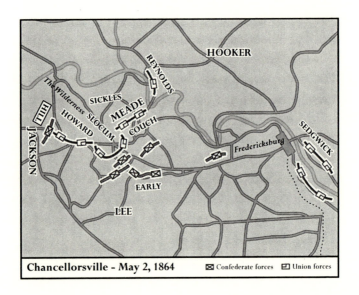

Chancellorsville - May 2, 1864   ⊠ Confederate forces   ⊡ Union forces

As always, Jackson's objective was not to defeat the Union Army, but destroy it. He sought to push the Union Army back to the Rappahannock River and annihilate it there. Jackson ordered the Light Division to continue the attack. But, it was late in the evening and General Hill feared dissipation of our brigades if the attack continued into the night. The Yankees fought desperately and, like General Hill, I saw possibility of a counterattack that would reverse the gains of the day.

General Hill sent me with an order to the brigade commanders to halt and set up defensive positions for the night. The 6th North Carolina Brigade was my last stop and I found time to talk with Dorsey Pender. As usual, General Pender explained clearly what happened and why. He ended by saying, "I'll be honest, when we started, I doubted we could succeed, but, no question, we have routed the Yankees. Our victory is partial at this point. I agree with General Hill. We must pause, regroup, get the troops fed, and finish them tomorrow."

Like other officers and soldiers in the Division, I counted myself lucky and began to rethink my earlier pessimism about actually winning the war. Morale was very high. All Confederate officers and soldiers I saw were very tired but seemed charged by the prospect of destroying the Yankee Army.

My morale went higher when I saw Andy, with his platoon, leading a large group of Union prisoners to the rear. Each of us saw what he wanted – the other alive and well after the heavy, hectic fighting – and waved in passing.

With Lee, Jackson, Longstreet, Stuart, Hill, Pender, and our other splendid generals, we were invincible regardless of the ever increasing numerical and material superiority of the Union Army. I thought on what General Pender said, "We took our greatest gamble and won our most memorable victory." Maybe Jackson and the ministers were right - God willed a Confederate victory.

In later years, I retained vivid memory of a soldier who laughed as he chased after the retreating Yankees. In a sing song voice, I heard him say, to whomever might be listening, "Oh happy, happy day, we'll run the Yankees back home with Old Stonewall leadin' the way."

* * *

Euphoria of the stunning victory quickly diminished when disturbing news filtered through our camps. Confederate soldiers, in a forward position, accidentally wounded General Jackson as he pursued the retreating Union Army.

Eager to finish off the Yankees, Jackson and his aides went out in front of Confederate lines to observe disposition of Union troops. When he returned, his party was mistaken for Union cavalry. To make matters worse, soldiers of a North Carolina Brigade shot General Jackson and his aides.

At first, the surgeons did not consider Jackson's wounds serious, but one week later he died of pneumonia. We later learned that, in his delirium before death, Jackson called out "Order A P Hill to prepare for action! Pass the infantry to the front.

Tell Major Hawks ..." The great general passed out and did not finish the sentence. He later awoke briefly and uttered, "Let us cross over the river and rest under the shade of the trees." Then Stonewall Jackson, the South's best hope for victory, died peacefully in bed.

A P Hill was also wounded at Chancellorsville, but his injury was not severe. With both Generals Jackson and Hill down, General Lee turned over field command to Jeb Stuart who continued the attack and performed effectively as corps commander. Stunned and completely defeated, the Union Army reeled back.

General Pender filled in as Light Division Commander which put me back working directly for him, something I enjoyed very much even in the hectic follow up to our great victory. I had another pleasant experience in the short time Stuart commanded Second Corps. In coordinating with Stuart's staff, I saw Pete Morgan several times. We had little time to talk, but it felt good to see him alive and well and flush with victory as we all were.

I longed for the war's end so I could return to the Morgan Plantation to claim Sissy and hopefully take her to a post on the expanded Confederate frontier, maybe West Texas or California if we sustained the momentum from Chancellorsville.

*   *   *

Following our tragic loss of Stonewall Jackson, General Lee divided the Army of Northern Virginia into three corps. General Longstreet retained command of First Corps. Lee appointed General Ewell to lead Second Corps including Jackson's former command. A P Hill took command of a newly formed Third Corps.

Initially assigned to 1st Corps, A P Hill squabbled with General Longstreet. General Lee moved A P Hill and the Light Division over to 2nd Corps where Hill feuded with General Jackson. In the Union Army, Hill would have been demoted or cashiered. In the Army of Northern Virginia, General Lee tolerated his cantankerous insubordination. Lee needed Hill and used him effectively to seal a victory or reverse a defeat. Lee must have reasoned that, if A P Hill could not take orders from a corps commander, he should be a corps commander.

With General Lee's concurrence, General Hill promoted Dorsey Pender to Major General and command of the Light Division in the Third Corps.

I went from aide to a company, regiment, brigade, division, and now a corps commander in two short and intense years. Young officers who demonstrated talent rose quickly in both armies, but my career as a staff officer was exceptional. A promotion in rank came with the latest advancement in responsibility. At age twenty-two, I was now a Major in the Confederate Army. I felt much older.

* * *

On learning of his promotion, I went by to congratulate General Pender. He invited me in for another of our talks. After we were seated, he asked, "Well, Jim, you think our promotions worthy of a sip of whiskey?"

"Yes, Sir." I still did not care for the rot gut shine that passed for whisky in our camps, but I developed a taste for Pender's fine Kentucky bourbon. We usually drank it straight, sometimes with a bit of water if more drinks seemed probable.

As Pender poured us each a drink with spring water, I asked, "We stunned the Yankees at Chancellorsville. What's next?"

Pender leaned forward and said, "One thing we've learned of General Lee is he's not reluctant to take the strategic initiative. That's what he's doing now."

"I didn't know he had left camp."

"General Lee went to Jefferson Davis and the War Cabinet and will recommend taking the Army of Northern Virginia north and attack the Union Army on its home ground. He sees opportunity to further humble the Yankees and bring recognition for us from Britain and France."

"Do you think General Lee will convince Davis?" I asked.

"Jefferson Davis can be obstinate, but he understands strategy. I'm sure he sees the same picture as General Lee. We'll move north and soon."

I thought on what General Pender told me and commented, "We have to cross Maryland to get at the Yankees. Maryland's a border state leaning Union. We got no support when we went there earlier. Will we have to defend our supply lines?"

Pender shook his head. "Don't think so. Those in Maryland who would attack us are already in the Union Army."

"Heard anything of Joe Hooker?" I asked.

"He'll go the way of McClellan, Burnside, and Pope. But, of course, the Yankees never do anything expediently. They'll do a study and conclude Hooker is incompetent and then relieve him of command."

"Any thought on who comes next?" I had no idea who would be next in line to face us, but thought General Pender might. He had a better grasp of strategy than General Hill who now reported directly to General Lee.

Pender smiled as he thought of the Union's predicament. "The smart thing would be to bring over Grant, Sherman, or Thomas from the West. But, the Yankees are not smart. They'll do what they've always done – pull up one of the corps commanders and hope for the best. I'm guessing it's George Meade's turn."

"Hate to ask, but which one's Meade?"

"You'll know him if you ever see him. He both resembles and acts like a snapping turtle."

Chapter 12: Furlough

Cobb Farm, Newton, North Carolina and
Morgan Plantation, Brownsburg, Virginia,
June 1863
Jim Cobb

General Hill returned to active duty in late May and came back mentally and physically restored. Throughout his brilliant career, he reveled in his role as General Lee's gamecock and a favored son of Richmond society. Usually I enjoyed working in the reflection of his fame, but I had recently revisited my roots – serving as aide to Dorsey Pender. Return to serving General Hill created a restlessness I did not understand at the time. And, unfortunately, my discontent came out in performance.

General Hill sent me out to gather the division commanders for a routine meeting. After a listless ride back, he called me aside for a talk. "I'm accustomed to a lively chief of staff. Lately, I haven't seen much of him. You look fine, but something's wrong."

I snapped out of my lethargy and apologized, "General, I'm fine. I've disappointed you. I'll do better from now on."

"No, that's not it. Your performance has always been good, but you're out of sorts and I'm concerned. I think I know your problem." General Hill had the habit of stroking his beard as he thought which is what he did now. He asked, "When's the last time you were away from the army? The time you spent in a Yankee hospital and riding with Mosby doesn't count."

"General, you needn't worry about me. I'll be fine," I assured him.

General Hill seemed both stern and concerned when replied, "Major Cobb, as indispensable as you think you are, I am ordering you to take a two week leave. It'll improve your outlook and put the spring back in your step."

I started to protest, but General Hill raised his hand, as he had many times in staff meetings, to cut off further discussion.

I had protected my position as Hill's Chief of Staff, but I appreciated his insisting I take a furlough. I had not seen Mother, the farm, nor Sissy since leaving with the Catawba County Militia two years earlier. I knew they were anxious about me following my six month lapse in correspondence. The best way to reassure them would be to show up healthy and whole.

So he would not worry or wonder where his friend went, I rode over to the Virginia Brigade, found Andy, and told him of the furlough. Andy agreed, "It'll do you good. Look me up when you return. Meanwhile, I'll try to keep the Division going."

* * *

After packing and saying goodbye to Titus Palmer, I caught a ride on a supply wagon to the depot and boarded a train to Charlotte. On the train and at the frequent stops along the way, I saw only very young and old men. A hundred pounds of bacon bought a year's relief from the draft, but I met no one wealthy enough to buy his way out of service. Slaveholders with more than twenty slaves were exempt and hated for it by the soldiers. I heard several say, "Rich man's war, poor man's fight." Enthusiasm for the war waned with the length and frequency of the casualty lists posted outside the newspaper offices after each major battle.

Soon after deboarding the train, I rented a horse at a nearby livery stable to ride up to Newton. The liveryman, who appeared to be in his mid-twenties, had lost his left arm past the elbow. As he adeptly saddled the horse with his good hand, the liveryman engaged me in a conversation.

"What outfit are you with Major?" he asked.

"I am an aide to General A P Hill with the Third Corps." The liveryman looked puzzled so I explained. "After Jackson died, General Lee divided the army into three corps. He appointed General Ewell to command Second Corps and General Hill to the Third Corps."

"No one can replace Stonewall Jackson," the liveryman commented. "Ewell's a good general, but he's not fit to command a corps."

The feisty little man seemed sure of himself. He appeared to be knowledgeable or opinionated, maybe both. I asked, "Who would you have picked if you were General Lee?"

Without hesitation, he answered, "Jubal Early. He's the closest we got to General Jackson's boldness and he's damn near as crazy."

I laughed. This ex-soldier knew more than most. "I'm Jim Cobb from Newton. What's your name, Sir?"

The liveryman finished cinching the saddle, stood at attention, gave a salute with his good hand, and said, "Brian McGee, formerly a Corporal in the Stonewall Brigade."

"How'd you lose your arm?" I asked.

"Second Manassas. Thought I could save it, but gangrene set in. The surgeon had no choice. When the army released me, my uncle, who owns this stable, gave me a job workin' with him." McGee paused and asked, "How's it goin' for us?"

Mostly I replied to questions about the war with a standard optimistic answer, but not this time. "After Chancellorsville, I wish I could tell everyone we're winning the war, but there are even more Yankees in the field than you saw and they're better armed and trained every time we fight them. We whipped them good at Second Manassas, Fredericksburg, and again at Chancellorsville, and took a beating at Sharpsburg. The war's not over until the

Yankees quit. We had our best chance at Chancellorsville, but when General Jackson went down, we lost it."

I unconsciously ran my hand across my left temple and watched Corporal McGee's expression change. He seemed to follow what I said as someone who understood the real meaning of battlefield victories and defeats. I mounted the rented horse, reached down, shook his hand, and said, "I have a two week furlough and will return the horse next week. Thank you, Corporal McGee, and all the others who have sacrificed so much".

Corporal McGee looked at me pensively as if with a question I could not answer. He may have considered loss of his arm acceptable payment for an honorable escape from the war. I would.

* * *

On the ride home, I reflected on what happened since leaving. Talking with Corporal McGee reminded me I was one of the fortunate returning alive with my limbs intact. As I came nearer, I felt a growing sense of homesickness, a feeling I suppressed for over two years. This is where I belonged, not on the battlefields of a war that seemed to have no end.

From the parlor window, Mother saw me and ran out the front door. I dismounted and raced to meet her. I hugged her tightly. Nothing felt better, not even my last embrace with Sissy. I was finally home and alive. Mother cried as I wrapped my arms tightly around her.

She saw the scar and asked, "James, how did you get that?"

"It's nothing, Mother. I rode through the woods and ran into a low-lying branch. It's my reminder to be more careful." I laughed.

She looked at me sternly and started to scold when Oliver came up and shook my hand vigorously. Looking at my shoulder and collar insignia, he commented, "Mister James, you now a Major."

Mother stepped back, took a longer look at me, and asked, "James, you are a Major. Why didn't you write your mother?"

"My apologies. It happened recently when General Hill was promoted to Corps Command. I should have written you earlier." Mother nodded in agreement. I spent my first four days home visiting with family and friends and relaxing as Mother and Hannah fussed over me. Both thought I had lost weight and worked to, as Hannah said, "put meat on your bones".

I went to Hickory to pay respects to Henry Wilkins who had been severely wounded during the Peninsula Campaign and returned to his dry goods store for the remainder of the war. I saw him outside the store and he nearly dropped the crutches in his hurry to shake hands and give me a hug. "Damn. Already a Major. Tell me about Chancellorsville."

We went inside and sat in chairs in a waiting area he kept for the men while their women shopped in his store. I glanced into the store area and saw mostly empty shelves. The war treated honest retailers as poorly as their customers.

I described at length what happened since he'd left, updating him on the Light Division and, particularly, 16th North Carolina, Company B, his former command. I learned that letters from Granville Calvert kept him informed, but Wilkins hung on every detail I gave him.

I finished in telling him of the Army of Northern Virginia reorganization and my promotion to Major.

"I must've done somethin' right," Wilkins commented. "Granville commanded the company better than I ever could and now he's got the regiment. And you. It took less than a week for your promotion to Regimental staff and then Brigade, Division, and now Corps. Sorry a company commander as I wuz, ain't many Captains had subordinates that's done better."

I squeezed Wilkins' shoulder gently. "Captain. You were a good officer. One of our best."

Wilkins shook his head. "No. I knew first day Granville and you were better officers than I'd ever be."

"Being a good officer is looking after your men, carrying out orders, and staying calm when all hell breaks loose. You did that well. In my opinion, and General Pender's, you were one of our best officers."

Wilkins' eyes misted as he took my hand with both of his "Thank you, Jim. That means more to me than you'll ever know."

After parting comments and mutual pats on the back, I mounted the rented horse and rode home. What I told him was mostly true. But, Granville Calvert was a much better officer. In the end, though, and the true measure of Henry Wilkins, he did the best he could and was worthy of commendation.

* * *

I took a fishing pole to the stream and caught perch, brim, and catfish for supper. Another day, I went with a hunting rifle to the woods, but found no rabbits or squirrels to shoot and bring home and did not care. I enjoyed riding through the woods and fields without being fired upon.

After a long, leisurely ride over the farm and into the nearby woods, I felt relaxed and content for the first time since leaving home for the war. I unsaddled, watered, and fed the rented horse and began brushing the horse with long strokes down from the back.

Suddenly my knees buckled and my hands shook. I tried to stop the trembling, but could not. At first, I continued grooming the horse, but finally gave up and sat down. I continued shaking despite my best efforts to stop. It became more violent. I crossed my arms and lowered my head to cover my face. A deep undefined terror and fear gripped me. Was I going insane?

At the depth of my fear, I looked up and saw Oliver watching from a distance. He stood there waiting to help. When our eyes met, Oliver hurried over to me, sat down, and asked, "Are you all right?"

As I trembled, I assured him I felt fine. He knew better. "James, I nose sumtin' bad troublin' you fierce. Want to talk 'bout it?"

After my father died, Oliver was the older male I went to for advice before I entered VMI and became close to Colonel Bradshaw. Oliver was uneducated, but wise from a lifetime of hard work and service to our family. He was, more than anything, a good friend. I did not want to express my concern to Mother and distress her, but felt I could be open with Oliver and benefit from his advice.

"War's worse than I ever thought possible. No one not there could believe the slaughter. Dead and mangled bodies pile up in every battle, more than can be buried before they decompose and stink. It's a smell you never forget. The worse part is, after a while, dead bodies are treated like things. No one remembers or cares they were once young men with mothers, wives, sweethearts, and children. Now they're nothing but rotting corpses. The soldiers go over the dead bodies and take anything they want." As I talked, I saw the love and concern in Oliver's face and felt my fear dissipate as I unloaded my feelings.

I pointed to my head and said, "You see the scar over my ear. I came close to being one of the dead, rotting bodies at Sharpsburg. The question at the back of my mind always is 'why was I spared?' I'd like to think it's God's will, but I've seen better men go down in every battle. I just don't know. Life's cheap on the battlefield. It may be my time coming up and I worry what it'll do to Mother."

Oliver said nothing at first, but put his arms around me. Finally, he said, "James, I wish I cud take de hurt from you, but I can't. You've seen more'n any man should in one life. I loves your family more'n you'll ever know. I promise you as long as I'm able and de udder Negroes on dis farm are able, your mother'll never suffer from nuttin' but the loss of her son and we both know that would be powful."

The terror passed. Oliver's words calmed me as I knew they would. I told him, "I don't want Mother to know any of what we discussed."

"She nose widout us tellin' her."

In my letters home and conversation with Mother, I omitted details of my service including being severely wounded and near dead at Sharpsburg. I felt giving her particulars of the danger and horror I faced as an officer in the Army of Northern Virginia would needlessly worry her. I would either be killed, maimed, or return home intact. No purpose served in distressing her about what might happen.

* * *

The war drained the Piedmont of young men. At first local militias turned away volunteers because they could not provide arms and uniforms for them as when the initial Catawba County militia company was formed. Later, volunteers from the Piedmont joined the 49th North Carolina Brigade that had a distinguished unit record at, of course, the cost of heavy casualties.

Toward the end of the week, as my time at home came to an end, conversations with Mother turned serious. At my request, Mother laid out the account books. I could see our situation had diminished if the receipts in Confederate currency were discounted, which Mother had done, but it was not yet critical.

With Mother's and Oliver's able management, the farm produced bountiful crops Mother sold to the army knowing full well Confederate currency could become worthless. With the only gristmill in the area, she could have held out for barter or hard cash as a few of the mean spirited neighbors had done, but that was not Mother. She was a patriot and definitely not mean-spirited. She knew the sacrifice her son and other mothers' sons made and did all she could to support the Confederacy even though she and I had reservations before North Carolina joined.

We had enough cash to pay for seed, equipment, and other outside purchases for another year, maybe two. She told me she had difficulty finding sellers who would accept Confederate currency or barter for payment. Increasingly she dipped into our diminishing reserve of US coins to pay bills.

Mother said, "We're talking about the farm. We should bring Oliver into the conversation. Go out and see if you can find him."

Serious discussion of farm operations was something we did many times before I went off to war. I felt both nostalgic and comfortable as did, apparently, Oliver and Mother. Oliver started, "I heerd 'bout a cottonseed from Gawjah wid a long strand blossom. Yankees use it to make bettah cloth. We make moe ifn we plant de new seed."

We questioned him about growing the new cotton, but Oliver reassured us. "It'll grow jes fine in de fields as de old cotton. We plant it and rotate it jes like we always dun."

I asked how we could get more Union currency for our crops and Oliver told us of a thriving, but illegal, trade with Yankee millers who paid top dollar to keep their mills working. Like most Confederates, I pretended it did not exist. Oliver insisted they would pay more for the long strand cotton and we should participate. Mother and I agreed. We might as well profit from what the Yankees would get elsewhere.

Mother marked the ledger book to set aside US coins to buy long-strand seed for next year's planting.

"James, you have sat with the Generals and listened to them talk. How do you see the war going?"

I thought of my transformation from junior partner in the Cobb Farm to Third Corps Chief of Staff and replied, "I'm cautiously optimistic and, at the same time, concerned we may lose the war despite our recent run of victories. The war's going badly in the West and the Yankees have captured all our major ports except Wilmington. The Army of Northern Virginia will have to win the war if it can be won."

"The war has to end sometime and lumber will come back. Should the Yankees win, there'll likely be occupation troops in the area and our farm can supply them with food. If we win, it'll be more difficult. Even in victory, the Confederacy will have little cash to buy anything."

Mother smiled. "Thanks to you two I feel better. Regardless how the war goes, the long staple cotton will sell. After the war, we can sell openly to the Yankee mills. No matter what happens, the Cobb Farm's mostly self-sufficient. We require little from the outside to survive."

We agreed the farm would "hunker down" and be ready to expand mill output following the war. It calmed me to concentrate on the farm and, for the time being, not worry about the war. I wanted to stay. The thought of desertion crossed my mind. However, I knew I would have to live with dishonor the rest of my life and could not do it.

Leaving was difficult, but I took comfort with the belief Mother and the farm would survive and eventually prosper even if I were killed or severely injured.

* * *

I returned the rented horse when promised to Brian McGee and took a train to Western Virginia as far as it would go. I changed trains in Roanoke and left it in Lexington. I walked and hitched rides to the Morgan Plantation. I learned that travelers willingly gave rides to Confederate soldiers especially officers.

As in Charlotte, I saw the differences from what I remembered before the war. Most notably, no young men. Youngsters, old men, and women worked jobs young men did before the war. The Yankees had been driven out of the Shenandoah Valley, but they left scars and everyone knew they would return before the war ended.

I noted farms and plantations around Brownsburg fared poorly. Some were abandoned, others run down. Union cavalry raided the Shenandoah Valley and took food and cattle. Many slaves ran away to Union lines. The Yankees torched some farms and plantations and damaged others. Although their plantation was likely in disrepair, I suspected the Morgans would work hard to keep up appearances.

I rode to Brownsburg beside a Morgan neighbor who offered a ride I gladly accepted. He looked surprised when I told him I was engaged to Sissy. I explained, "Well, not officially, but we had an understanding before I went off to war."

I had not written earlier, figuring I would likely arrive before the letter.

Missy greeted me at the front door. She wore a working dress and seemed surprised and embarrassed, but pleased I came for a visit. She excused herself to get into something more presentable and alert the family I had arrived.

I was taken by Missy's appearance. She had blossomed. No longer the scrawny, developing teenager I remembered from my cadet days.

I sat in the parlor in field uniform until the Morgans came in to greet me. After talking with the family about the war and the edited version of my service, I sat down to a simple meal with them. I later learned, from Missy, it was the only meat they had eaten in a week. During conversation over the dining table, I learned Pete had been promoted. By his parents' account Pete commanded an outstanding cavalry company. I spoke of the brief encounters I had with him which pleased them. Apparently Pete wasn't much for writing. They appreciated having a first hand account from someone who had seen him recently.

To ensure their only son and heir to the Morgan Plantation would be properly tended, the Morgans sent the family footman,

Scipio, with him as a personal attendant. None of the Morgans, except Missy later, described it as such, but I knew they sent Scipio so Pete would not be outclassed by the Blue Bloods in Stuart's cavalry.

I remembered Pete often laughed at his mother's pretensions, but readily accepted the good things that came with it. Though not an intellectual or deep thinker, he was good company and a good friend. I saw him in passing at Second Manassas and Chancellorsville, but we only had time to speak briefly before moving on.

As the family and I moved to the parlor for more conversation, William Morgan looked at me and nodded his head toward the front door. "Ladies, if you'll excuse us, I have some things I want to discuss with Jim. We'll return shortly." I followed Captain Morgan out to the front porch.

Captain Morgan got to the point quickly. "Jim, I appreciate your not discussin' details of the war with Margaret and the girls, but I know from talkin' with Peter it's been horrible for you and the others. As General Hill's aide, you have a position to see the war more clearly than any of us. How is the war goin'?"

I saw concern in the face of my future father-in-law and a man I respected. He asked an honest, heartfelt question I had to answer in kind. "The Yankees have thrown everything they have at us and we pushed them back. Our generals have been brilliant, but you know we lost General Jackson at Chancellorsville and were badly mauled at Sharpsburg. In thinking back over our victories, I believe the reason for our success has been the incredible incompetence of the Yankee generals. Not the regimental, brigade, and division commanders, but their corps and army commanders have been awful. I know, from reports from the West, putting on a Union uniform does not make you stupid. We must force the Yankees to surrender soon before they find competent leadership or it's over for us. The Yankees keep bringing in reserves and we're running out."

Later, Sissy and I sat alone in the parlor to talk and the conversation became strained. Reality had set in. I tried to take her hand, but Sissy pulled away. Not knowing what else to say, I spoke frankly with her, as I had with her father earlier, about the war. Not what she wanted to hear.

"If the Yankees win," she commented, "our home will be lost along with all our hopes. You cannot protect me. You and our army, including my brother, are off fighting somewhere else."

"You see this?" I pointed to my scar. "I nearly died for the Confederacy. Tell me. I don't know what more I can do to protect you."

Sissy looked at me contemptuously and did not answer. Her silence and cold demeanor hurt.

I asked, "Have you forgotten what we promised?" She looked at me dumbly so I continued. "After the war, we will marry and I'll take you with me to my first posting."

"If the Yankees win the war," she coldly replied, "they'll not want you in their army no matter how highly you're placed in our army. If we win the war, where would we go and be away from poverty and misery?"

"Whatever else the Cobb Farm will always be there. It's bigger than your plantation. We will go there and be happy."

"And be a farmer's wife?" Sissy looked at me as if I had lost my mind. "I have decided not to marry you."

I expected a warm reception from my fiancé and got blunt rejection. The South fought for its right to be a separate country. Pete and I risked our lives every day. Sissy did not care. She only thought of herself and how the war affected her.

So there would be no doubt later, I asked, "You're telling me there's no future for us. Is that right?"

Sissy nodded her head.

I jumped up and turned to leave, but remembered my manners. I sought out and separately thanked Margaret and William Morgan for their hospitality.

William Morgan said, "I'm sorry you're leaving so soon, Jim. I'll have one of the slaves drive you to the train station. I know you're needed back with the army. Before you go I have gifts for you."

We went to his study where the Captain took two cigars from a desk drawer and a bottle of bourbon from a shelf. He handed them to me and said, "Smoke the cigars at your leisure, but save this bottle to celebrate final victory over the Yankees."

One of the lessons I learned from the war was to gracefully accept gifts when offered. I said, "When I see Pete again, I'll share these with him. If not, I'll find someone worthy to help me celebrate. Thank you, Sir."

Missy overheard and offered to accompany me on the ride back to the Lexington train station. The Morgan driver came to the front door. I helped Missy into the coach and got in behind her.

I did not feel like talking. We sat in silence. Finally, she said, "You're unhappy and I think I know why. Do you want to talk about it?"

I smiled through my inner pain and told her, "We are in a life and death struggle, literally, and all your sister thinks about is herself. Our promise to marry meant nothing to her. I've been a fool."

Missy took my hand and said, "I love my sister and I think you do also. I wish, for both your sakes, she would think things through instead of reacting to what she sees as here and now."

"She discussed it with your mother didn't she?" I asked and was near certain she had.

Missy nodded. "Mother's genuinely fond of you and I know Father likes you. But, as you suspected, Mother learned your family is considered odd in North Carolina. Never mind she learned the Cobb Farm is bigger than our plantation. In her mind, the Cobbs are Piedmont farmers and we're plantation owners. She told Sissy she can do better. Father knows nothing of this and I only learned after the fact. You're far too good a man to be treated as you have by my sister and mother."

In a misguided attempt to reassure her, I smiled, squeezed Missy's hand, and said, "In the end, it may not matter. An inch closer, the bullet that took me down at Sharpsburg would've killed me. I'll likely be dead before the war's over."

Missy began sobbing. I offered a handkerchief but she shook her head and kept sobbing. Eventually she lifted her head and said, "Please, Jim, don't ever say that again. Don't even think it. I don't know what I'd do if I lost you."

Missy reached across the coach seat and held my hand tightly until we reached the train station. I felt sorry for myself, but took comfort in her support and concern. I saw a tear form and slowly descend her cheek and regretted being morbid with her.

I reached up and, with a handkerchief, wiped the tear from her cheek. I said, "Please excuse me, Missy. Maybe, with God's blessing, I will return and resume our friendship. You, Pete, and your family are dear to me" and, after a pause, added "even Sissy. I didn't intend to distress you. I felt sorry for myself and made you sad. That's inexcusable and I apologize."

Missy did not respond, but smiled and moved closer to me.

The train to Richmond arrived and I departed. As I boarded, Missy reached up and kissed me on the cheek. I appreciated her kindness, but it made me sadder knowing it was Missy and not her sister who saw me return to the war. Especially as I noted she had grown to look like her sister, but with darker hair.

* * *

I sat next to Silas Young, a Captain and company commander in Field's Virginia Brigade of the Light Division. We struck up a conversation. I lit one of Captain Morgan's cigars and gave the other to Silas to smoke with me.

As I looked around the railroad coach, I saw many returning

soldiers like Silas and me. All were gaunt. But, more distressing, so were the civilians. I imagined the war being fought by all in the South and wondered again if winning could be worth the massive suffering.

Silas said, "While you were gone, orders came down to march north. We'll take the war to the Yankees."

"I'm not surprised. General Pender told me Lee went to Richmond for approval."

"I'm not on Corps staff like you, but I think this decides the war. We win in Pennsylvania or it's over for us. I hate to leave my company. It's strange how they become family. But I have a wife who's expecting our first child. I had to see her when the opportunity came up. I can't wait for the war to end and we can be a family again. It's what keeps me going."

I listened enviously. I knew Silas had no idea I had been betrayed by my intended and did not tell him. I simply shook his hand and gave him heartfelt good wishes when we parted.

I caught up with the corps in Maryland. Since leaving to join the Catawba County Militia, I thought often about Sissy and our life together following the war. I realized it was a vain hope, but it had helped me endure the war. The hope was gone. I understood I had overrated Sissy and my relation with her, but, nevertheless, the loss of her affection hurt. I regretted stopping by the Morgan Plantation.

Chapter 13: Gettysburg

Maryland, Southern Pennsylvania, and Northern Virginia
June 1863 – April 1864
Jim Cobb

The earlier foray into Maryland disappointed General Lee, but, with momentum gained from our stunning victory at Chancellorsville, he hoped the march to Pennsylvania would tilt sentiment in Maryland to the Confederacy. He ordered us to be polite and courteous to all the citizens. He even encouraged the men to sing the state song, "Maryland, My Maryland" as they marched.

> *The despot's heel is on thy shore, Maryland!*
> *His torch is at thy temple door, Maryland*
> *Avenge the patriotic gore*
> *That flecked the streets of Baltimore,*
> *And be the battle queen of yore,*
> *Maryland! My Maryland!*

Our soldiers quickly learned the words when they understood the "despot" mentioned in the verse was President Lincoln and the "patriotic gore" expressed outrage at the news of Union troops putting down secessionist riots in Baltimore.

For other than a few obvious Southern sympathizers, it did not work. I saw mostly fear and resentment in the eyes of the citizens we passed. The Army of Northern Virginia was an invading, not a liberating, army in Maryland.

I thought it unfortunate Maryland had not thrown in with the Confederacy. Verdant, rolling hills with neatly arranged farms, corn fields, and cow pastures, Maryland could have provided food and where we most needed it. Instead, I haggled with farmers who insisted on Union money for payment of foodstuff and got Confederate scrip.

On the march north, General Hill seemed uncharacteristically short with his division commanders and staff. Not rude or brusque, but terse and self-absorbed. Finally, I asked, "Sir, you seem changed since I returned. Is there anything troubling you?"

He was absorbed in a status report as I stood before him. He looked up. "Can't talk about it now," he said and went back to reading the report. General Lee traveled with Third Corps and that was a source of concern, but I sensed General Hill's anxiety ran deeper.

The divisions became strung out during the march. Hill ordered me to ride back and instruct the divisions to close ranks. In carrying the message, I saw Dorsey Pender at the head of the Light Division. He looked splendid atop his favorite horse, a black stallion. His professional, confident demeanor permeated the division. Pender was popular with the troops who recognized, as I did, that he was a better general than their former commander, A P Hill.

Pender motioned me to come along side. He had not seen me for several weeks and asked that I fill him in on what I had done since we were last together. I briefly described my visit home and rejoining Third Corps in Maryland. Then I asked, "General Pender, something's bothering General Hill. Do you know what might be troubling him?"

"We don't know where the enemy is and no one knows where Jeb Stuart and the cavalry are. General Lee sent out scouts to find him, but no information has come back yet. We're marching blind."

"Do we know anything?"

"We know the Yankees are looking for us as we look for them. General Longstreet sent out spies, but nothing has come back from them either. I'm concerned, as is General Hill, and General Lee for that matter, that we'll stumble into a major battle before we are ready."

* * *

Third Corps marched toward Chambersburg, Pennsylvania, a rendezvous point where General Lee would pull together the Army of Northern Virginia for the grand assault. General Hill sent Captain Palmer and me on to the next destination, Hagerstown, Maryland, to buy provisions and coordinate movement of the brigades through town. His orders were simple, "Keep them moving and keep an eye out for Yankee patrols and bushwhackers."

With a company from the Georgia Brigade, I informed city officials that large numbers of Confederate troops would pass through, but have no time to linger. The merchants were unhappy with the interruption in commerce by a large raggedy army of dirty, hungry, and underpaid Reb soldiers. They were particularly upset with taking scrip for payment, but such is war. Our advance party cleared the streets of wagons and carriages. Titus and I waited near the courthouse, which still flew the Union flag, to direct traffic if needed.

To our relief, Third Corps moved easily through Hagerstown. Townspeople gathered along the main street to watch the procession – watch, not support. Off to the side, I saw a Confederate Colonel dismount and talk with a Jewish peddler. He snatched the yarmulke off the head of the startled peddler, remounted, swung his horse around, placed his hat on the peddler, and rode down the line showing off his new headpiece. I rode over to reprimand him, discovered it was my friend Granville Calvert, and joined in the laughter. Granville waved to me as he passed.

As I expected, Calvert came back to return the peddler's yarmulke and reclaim his hat. Palmer joined me and sarcastically observed, "That's a fine example the Colonel set for the men."

I laughed, "Yeah, I wish we had a hundred more like him." Granville wanted to lighten the mood of our troops who must have felt tense marching through hostile territory. Our men had training and discipline. Morale was the critical issue Granville addressed.

Gettysburg, Pennsylvania,
Wednesday, July 1, 1863
Jim Cobb

General Heth sent two of his brigades into Gettysburg. They encountered stiff resistance. I did not anticipate a major battle at Gettysburg. No one did. General Hill sent me to investigate the fighting. We thought Gettysburg would be lightly defended by Pennsylvania militia easily swept away at first appearance of the Confederate Army. I talked with General Heth and his staff, surveyed the town and Union deployment, and rode back to make my report.

"General, as you thought, it's not militia. Judging from the carbines they use, it appears we have dismounted cavalry in support of regular army, the 71st Pennsylvania. Probably Buford's cavalry we tangled with at Fairfield. The Union Iron Brigade may be involved. I suggest we send more troops in to drive the Yankees out before they reinforce the town and take the high ground."

"What did you see in town?" General Hill asked.

"Two intersecting roads. If this is where we take on the Yankees, we'll have difficulty getting the army through the town.

We need the high ground for observation and to position the artillery. There's a telegraph office in town. We don't know where the Union Army is, but it is most certainly moving rapidly to Gettysburg."

That night, General Hill slammed the table with his fist and cursed. I had only seen him that angry once before. "Damn it, Jim. We wasted opportunity. With our help, Second Corps pushed the Union Army from Gettysburg but failed to drive them from the hills. Jackson would have stayed after them until we had the high ground, but he can't command Second Corps from the grave. The Yankees will reinforce their position tonight and we'll pay hell getting them out."

From the Diary of Jim Cobb,
Friday, July 3, 1863

I have never seen morale this low. The men are stunned. After Chancellorsville, we considered ourselves invincible and now two straight days of defeat. The Yankees are entrenched in the hills and we cannot drive them out. Ewell failed to take the high ground the first day before all the Union Army gathered.

Second day, we came close. But, improbably, a Union regimental commander, Colonel Joshua Lawrence Chamberlain, performed an unorthodox, 'swinging gate' bayonet charge to prevent us from flanking and rolling up the Union Army from Little Round Top.

General Longstreet pleaded with General Lee to pull out of Gettysburg, flank the Federals, stay between the Union Army and Washington, and defy them to attack - sound strategy. After Fredericksburg, no one should need convincing of the tactical advantage in fighting defensively from a protected position. But I'm continually amazed how the generals on both sides order attacks in close formation. They use the tactics of Napoleon and smooth bore muskets and think in terms of bayonet charges that rarely occur in battle yesterday being an exception.

Defenders with rifles behind cover shoot at the exposed soldiers attacking them before they are close enough to effectively return fire. But, to the men, holding your place in line and marching forward is the test of courage and self-worth. It is insane, but routine with soldiers on both sides. Give any of them a choice and he would much rather take cover and fire at the enemy marching toward him. This is the advantage Longstreet wants, but General Lee is unaccountably stubborn. He is determined the strategic battle will be won here.

Since General Lee took command, our army has consistently defeated numerically superior Union armies. In his mind, we are unbeatable. Never mind Second Corps failed to take the high ground on the first day or First Corps failed to turn the Union flank on the second day, we will break the weakened Union center and crush the Union Army on the third day, tomorrow. I fear the worst.

I think back to my discussions with Colonel Bradshaw and his predictions of how the war might unfold. Initial victories over a massive and poorly led Union Army and then a sharp change in fortune as Union material strength and resolve stiffened. A chance encounter at Gettysburg may become the turning point of a war ultimately decided by massive Union superiority in manpower and resources.

Gettysburg, Pennsylvania,
July 2, 1863
Jim Cobb

Third Corps Staff were billeted to the home of Paul and Gertrude Hoffman. I later learned Paul Hoffman taught history and rhetoric at Pennsylvania College. They left a Mennonite community in Eastern Pennsylvania when Paul accepted the teaching position in Gettysburg.

With my fellow officers, orderlies, and our baggage in tow,

I knocked on the front door. Paul Hoffman stepped out on the porch.

"Sir, I am Major Jim Cobb. This is Captain Titus Palmer and Lieutenant Tracy Simpson. We are staff officers of Third Corps, Army of Northern Virginia. Your home has been requisitioned to house us for the duration of the occupation."

I wanted to continue, but Hoffman interrupted. He demanded, "What gives you Rebels the right to destroy the homes of decent citizens of the country you disgrace by your rebellion?"

"You, Sir, are ignorant," I replied. I'd wanted to tell that to all Yankees and particularly a college professor. "We are under standing orders not to harm any private property or citizen of Pennsylvania. Had you seen the barbarity of your troops at Fredericksburg, the wanton vandalism of our homes, you would appreciate the decency and restraint of General Lee's orders. As things stand, you have no choice. We will take what accommodations you can provide and leave you with payment for the food we are served."

I took it for what it was. Professor Hoffman was the man of his house. He had to show his wife and children he could defend them, but he was helpless to prevent our occupation of his home. He reluctantly opened the door and we walked in. Gertrude Hoffman stood inside with a tight hold on her children who huddled closely behind her skirt and peeked out at the strange men in gray uniforms. The orderlies brought in our change of clothing and toiletries, placed them in the assigned bedrooms, and left with us for a staff meeting.

Understandably hostile and resentful at being forced to feed and house enemy officers, the Hoffmans gradually became interested in us. First, as ordered, we conducted ourselves as gentlemen and paid for our food and lodging. Even though we compensated them in virtually worthless scrip, they seemed to appreciate the gesture. In turn, we welcomed having a bed and home cooked food.

Second, in supper conversation the first night, I told the Hoffmans my mother was Moravian. I had learned some German words and Moravian customs from her and talked knowledgably with the Hoffmans about their ancestry and religion. The subject turned to other topics such as the war, VMI, the Cobb Farm, Professor Bradshaw, and my former roommate from Carlisle who likely served in the Union Army near Gettysburg.

I asked, "How many history professors have the opportunity to witness a major battle and, at the same time, house enemy staff officers? In the future, you will lecture, not from reference books, but from direct observation."

Paul Hoffman grinned as if it were the first time the thought had occurred to him.

The Hoffman children, two girls and a boy, five to eight years old, were taken with us in particular the younger girl, five year old Matilda, who never took her eyes off me. I motioned her to come over.

She wore a blue lace dress with pantaloons. She had light brown hair drawn into two braids tied with yellow ribbons, an angelic round face, and blue eyes. She asked, "Do you know Stonewall?"

I nodded solemnly and replied, "Yes, I do. He was a general in our army." I thought that would satisfy her curiosity.

"Does he take away children who misbehave?"

From the corner of my eye, I saw her mother watching us anxiously. "Yes, we got a report each day from the mothers and Stonewall rode out and took away naughty children for punishment."

She nodded, walked back to her mother, and kept staring at me.

Later, Gertrude Hoffman thanked me. "I am so scared the children will be harmed by all the rifle and cannon fire. I keep them in the house, away from the windows. They are fascinated by all the activity and too young to understand the horror. They want to get outside and play and can't. Thank you for your answer about Stonewall. It is a fiction I tell them to keep them inside and out of harm's way."

On the second night, Tracy Simpson impulsively put the young son on his back and proceeded to "gallop" through the Hoffman home. Of course, the girls wanted to play "horse" as well. I put Matilda on my back and Titus took the older daughter. We chased Simpson and his "rider" through the entertainment room and up and down the stairs.

Paul Hoffman laughed with the horseplay as his wife stood wide-eyed waiting for a vase to come down or favored chair smashed. Miraculously, we did not break anything.

Thereafter, to my delight and dismay of her parents, Matilda fixated on me, followed me around the house, and hung on my every word. Before leaving in the morning, I heard Paul Hoffman tell his wife, "If she has to hero worship an officer, can't he at least be one of ours?"

Our army converted Pennsylvania College and other buildings in town to hospitals. The slaughter in the battles outside Gettysburg became horrific and the hospitals soon overflowed. The second morning, as I passed through town, I saw objects thrown out of windows. Curious, I rode over to where the "objects" landed and wished I hadn't, human limbs – severed arms and legs.

As I approached, I heard the cries and moans of a soldier in an 'operating room' – "please, please don't take my leg" – and guessed the surgeons ran short of chloroform again. I remembered my experience in the Union hospital after Sharpsburg and nearly vomited before I recovered and joined General Hill at a staff meeting.

Gettysburg, Pennsylvania,
Friday, July 3, 1863
Jim Cobb

At General Hill's side, I observed the futile artillery bombardment of the Union's weakened center. General Lee ordered two Third Corps brigades to standby should Pickett's Division require reinforcement. For over an hour, we pounded the Union center to soften it for the attack, but our shells mostly passed harmlessly over entrenched Union troops. The delayed fuses did not work well. Shells that landed on target did little damage and provided rubble for concealment of the defenders. The firing stopped and I felt sick in my stomach knowing what would ensue.

General Hill muttered, "This is madness. They'll be slaughtered as soon as they get within range of the Yankee rifles."

Every soldier on both sides knew the long march over the open field would end in disaster. Unfortunately, everyone was right.

As the brave soldiers they were, Pickett's Division marched resolutely into concentrated Union rifle and canister fire and fell en masse. All the Confederate observers, including me, stood horrified as we watched the slaughter. Soldiers and their officers fell in waves as they were raked by enemy rifle and canister fire from the front and sides. I hoped and prayed they would fall back before more were killed. But, instead, they marched onward. Some crossed over the rock wall the Yankees put up and were killed or captured there. More than half of the Division were dead or seriously injured before they slowly withdrew with no hope of victory, there never was.

As the remnants staggered back, I heard Union defenders chant, in unison, "Fredericksburg, Fredericksburg, Fredericksburg ..." They waited over seven months to get revenge and got it, Friday, July 3, 1863, at Gettysburg. Third Corps support brigades were not ordered in when Pickett's Division returned.

General Lee, brilliant before and after Gettysburg, had a fatal judgment lapse at Gettysburg. This time the hastily gathered Union Army dug in and won a hard fought, bloody victory in the decisive battle in the East. The Union Army fought on home soil and were determined not to lose to the Rebel Army that had repeatedly humiliated them in Virginia.

For the first time, I saw something in the eyes of our soldiers I had never seen before – defeat. Hope of victory disappeared with the smoke drifting from the ghastly field where Pickett's men lay crying out in agony.

We lost the war at Gettysburg.

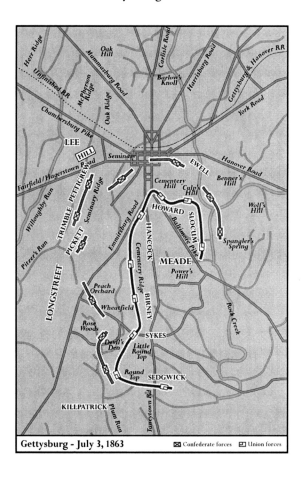

Gettysburg - July 3, 1863   ⊠ Confederate forces ⊡ Union forces

General Lee witnessed the outcome at Gettysburg and issued an order to the Corps commanders – retreat. General Hill called a staff meeting and we planned our withdrawal. I stayed behind with the Virginia Brigade to provide cover should Union troops pursue as we feared they might. Certainly General Lee would have pursued the Army of the Potomac with the intent to destroy it if the situation were reversed.

We left hastily, but thanked the Hoffmans for their hospitality. Paul Hoffman pulled me to one side and said, "I'm glad your army was defeated and you're turning back, but I want to thank you, Captain Palmer, and Lieutenant Simpson for your conduct in our home. I wish you the best in the future."

I shook his hand and replied, "I don't believe we can recover from this defeat. I don't know how much longer this miserable war will last, but I see the end coming and we will, again, be one nation."

"For all our sakes, I hope you're right. God be with you, Major Cobb," Hoffman said.

Matilda peeked around her mother's skirt and waved to me as I rode away. I waved back thinking if I ever had a daughter I wanted one like Matilda.

Ostensibly to report on Union troop movements, I lingered as Third Corps left Gettysburg. I saw thousands of unburied Confederates rotting in fields around Gettysburg. The Army of Northern Virginia had no time or opportunity to bury them, but, still, the idea of retreating from the sacrifice of brave, loyal men troubled me. I rode to the battlefields not yet occupied by Union troops and said prayers for our fallen soldiers.

I was surprised and saddened to find the familiar face of Captain Silas Young among the nameless dead. If not for the bullet through his forehead, he appeared to be resting on his back in an open field. I did not know the other dead and focused my grief on the single casualty from the thousands who fell at

Gettysburg. With tears in my eyes, I stopped, dismounted, and took his watch, wallet, ring, and other valuables which, somehow, had not been stripped. I found a spade and fashioned a shallow grave for Silas Young and buried him. I wanted to stay and give all the Confederate dead decent burials, but a lifetime would not be enough.

I thought again of the cruelty and futility of the war as I rode back to General Field and the Virginia Brigade staff. I stayed to serve as an observer - estimate the size and speed of Union pursuit and get back to General Hill. But my thoughts were with Silas Young. Why did he have to die? A good man with a pregnant wife and prospects for a happy, productive life. Why did any of them have to die? More than anything, vain, sectional pride played out horribly. I knew my grief multiplied many times over with mothers and fathers who lost sons; girls who lost sweethearts; children without fathers; men who would, for the rest of their lives, walk on stumps or make do without an arm; countless unborn children who would not have the opportunity for life; and otherwise uninjured survivors whose minds would forever be twisted by what they saw and experienced in battle.

Union troops never came. I had nothing to report and left with the Virginia Brigade to rejoin the Light Division and Third Corps.

* * *

General Meade's reluctance to follow up on his costly victory was the only reason the Army of Northern Virginia survived. We read President Lincoln was displeased the Confederate Army escaped, but understood the Union Army was also badly mauled with 25% casualties following the battles at Gettysburg. The Army of the Potomac recouped while we slipped back into Virginia. Our retreat was orderly, not frantic, giving me time to check on our deployment and report back to General Hill.

After making my first report, I sought out Titus Palmer. I needed an audience to talk through my concerns following the recent catastrophe. We went back to our tent, closed the flaps, and pulled out cracker boxes to rest our saddle sore butts. I saw no reason to hold onto the bourbon bottle Captain Morgan gave me to celebrate a Confederate victory and poured us both a generous glass.

"Morale's lower than I've ever seen it," I told him. "It's the kind of depression that only comes after everyone was convinced we couldn't lose. Our invincible army was defeated."

Palmer nodded. I spoke the obvious, but he understood I needed to unwind and simply listened to me.

Third Corps was not involved in the heavy fighting First and Second Corps endured at Gettysburg. When I mentioned it, Palmer replied, "General Lee will see we get caught up. We'll beat the Yankees yet."

In my estimation, I saw a quick end to the war and argued, "The Yankees always have more men and more and better equipment and supplies. Now they have the scent of victory. I don't know what will stop them from annihilating us."

"We still have the best generals, officers, and soldiers," he pointed out.

I knew it was not enough to win a war clearly going the Yankees' way, but did not argue the point. Instead, I brought out what I really wanted to discuss with him. "I'm thinking of applying for a command, a company or regiment, when we get back to Virginia."

"Why in the world do you want to put yourself more in the line of fire? You're doing a good job as Chief of Staff. General Hill relies on you. Who would replace you if you take regimental command?" Palmer asked. Palmer was guileless, one of the qualities I liked in him.

I pointed a finger at him. "You will. Don't tell me it hasn't crossed your mind. You're ready to take over Corps staff. You know it. I know it. General Hill knows it. You filled in capably while I was out after Sharpsburg. Besides he needs a Chief of Staff who actually believes we can win the war."

Palmer leaned back and took another shot of whiskey. Like me he was tired, but we always enjoyed a stimulating discussion. "If I'm to take over staff command, it's time to speak frankly," he said. "What do you really think of A P Hill?"

"I admire him. He was a highly competent, courageous, tenacious, and aggressive field general with the Light Division, but he's not showing well as a corps commander. Not a matter of courage or competence. His orders are as well thought out and appropriate as ever and he still looks out for his officers and men."

Palmer sat and listened. He did not argue with me so I kept on. It was the first time I talked honestly with anyone about General Hill and who better than Captain Titus Palmer, my probable successor?

"However, he's easily offended and much too conscious of his position as a favorite son in Richmond. He suffers from a recurring illness, many think is gonorrhea, which frequently takes him out of service. That and the wounds he gets coming up close to the fighting require him to give up command too often. Hard to lead when you're not there much of the time."

"Both Lee and Jackson relied on him and he never disappointed. But he has vexed General Lee in his petty feuds with both Jackson and Longstreet over imagined slights. As his aide, I am sometimes embarrassed by his behavior. You will be too."

I figured Palmer knew all I did about General Hill, but I wanted to make sure. He nodded as I spoke and did not dispute anything I said. Instead he added, "I heard rumors he was something of a lady's man before he married. May have picked up a 'social disease' at home while he was at West Point."

Hard to keep secrets in a close knit staff, but I thought I was the only one who heard the story. "Yeah, you probably heard about when he attended West Point. Seems he competed with George McClellan for the affections of a young lady named Nell. McClellan won out. May be the only time he beat us at anything."

"Things work out," Palmer commented. "The General did well. Dolly Hill's a good one. I doubt McClelland's wife could bring more gentility and grace."

Little I could add. After altering the General's uniform for me, Dolly Hill would always be one of my favorite people.

"I think your reservations about General Hill are that he's not Dorsey Pender," Palmer correctly observed.

I never told Titus Palmer how I felt about General Pender, but he somehow knew.

We finished the bottle while discussing the generals and the defeat. It gradually devolved to lamenting lost loves. I became intoxicated and woke up hung over the next morning, but reasoned if loss of a war and Morgan's beautiful daughter did not justify getting drunk, nothing would.

* * *

Few of the 16th North Carolina Company B, my original company from Catawba County, remained. Most of them were killed or injured in the many battles they fought or died of diseases rampant in the camps. New faces filled my old company, many from other areas. I did not know most of them.

I went over to regimental headquarters and spotted the indestructible Granville Calvert as he ended a brief meeting with his staff and company commanders. He extended his rough, scarred hand, and said, "Good to see you James."

I replied, "It looks as if you've done well, Colonel. Saw you entertaining the boys at Hagerstown. Remember?"

Calvert laughed. "Don't let the rank fool you. I'm still the same ornery cuss you knew in Hickory."

I smiled. It was good to be back with a friend from Catawba County, particularly one with all his limbs and in reasonably good health. I told him, "I spent time with Henry Wilkins when I was home on furlough in June."

"Yeah, he mentioned it in his last letter. Did him a lot of good to see you. From what he writes, he's walking around on crutches and back to running the store. He'll stay there until this miserable war ends."

"How're you doing?" I asked.

"I'm still in one piece and count myself lucky, but the war's hard on me and the boys. Not near enough whisky or women. The rations are sorrier as we go along. I think they fight hard for a victory so they can get at the Yankees' stores and shoes. We never should've gone to war and I think you knew that on the train up to Raleigh."

I agreed but pointed out, "I had strong suspicions, but didn't know the war would go poorly. It's not over yet. The newspapers we intercept tell us the war's unpopular in the North. Maybe the Yankees will get tired of the bloodletting and give up without us having to actually destroy their army."

Calvert cocked his head, looked at me with disbelief and a half grin, and responded, "Not likely. The Yankee soldiers we face are tougher every time we fight. I don't see 'em givin' up. Maybe the politicians, but the soldiers won't stand by and let the politicians take away their victory."

I did not answer. Could not. Granville spoke the truth. Hope for victory was illusory.

After small talk and reminiscences, I got up, shook his hand, and said, "If we survive this, I'll look for you at the Wilkins General Store. We'll take Henry to the nearest saloon. First round's on me."

Calvert shook my hand again before I left and replied, "It's good to see you again James, but the first round's on me."

Northern Virginia
Monday, July 20, 1863
Jim Cobb

On our return to Virginia, General Hill rode over and told me, "I just received sad news. General Pender died at home yesterday."

The news stunned me. I felt like I had taken a hard blow to the stomach and became temporarily speechless. I knew Pender suffered a leg wound at Gettysburg, but his injury was not considered serious. A later report indicated surgeons amputated his leg and sent him home to recuperate. Others lost limbs and went on. John Hood lost two limbs and kept on. It was part of the horrid routine we lived with in the war. I had crowded the possibility of Pender dying from my mind and went on busily with my duties. Now the awful truth I did not want to accept.

General Hill added, "General Lee is most grieved. He asked me earlier about promoting General Pender to Second Corps command. I gave him a strong endorsement, but it wasn't needed. General Lee had high opinion of him with or without my endorsement. I think of all the officers in the Division you best understood and appreciated his contribution."

"Yes, Sir, he was the best, the very best," I responded as I choked back tears. I appreciated General Hill seeking me out, but wanted to be alone.

I excused myself and rode off to collect my thoughts. General Hill understood too well. He also grieved the loss of his best division commander.

New York Tribune Article,
Friday, October 16, 1863
byline Samuel Payne

As expected, President Lincoln appointed Ulysses S Grant Lieutenant General and head of all Union forces in the war. He is the first field general to command our armies in both the East and West. Grant appointed his able subordinate General William T Sherman to lead the Army of Tennessee while he concentrates on the Army of the Potomac.

He is a welcome fresh face in the cavalcade of generals who have passed through command of the Army of the Potomac. Grant is top general not because he looks the part, but because he earned the opportunity with a succession of victories in the West. In General Lee and the Army of Northern Virginia, he will meet his ultimate test and we can only pray he succeeds where the others failed.

After Gettysburg, it is increasingly apparent the Confederacy can be defeated but only after more bloodshed. Appropriately, Grant has become known as "Butcher Grant" in the press because of the heavy casualties inflicted on the Army of the Potomac even as the Confederate Army is being destroyed. We, the Union citizens, must bear the ultimate cost of victory in the lives of our sons.

Northern Virginia
November 1863,
Jim Cobb

When the Light Division settled into a defensive position for the anticipated Union onslaught, I sought out Andy Blaylock for a private conversation.

"Andy, I'm thinking about requesting a transfer to a line command."

Andy did not seem particularly surprised. "Staff not danger-ous enough for you?" he asked.

"That's not it. Nearly everything I know about the war and being an officer I learned from Dorsey Pender. He died from wounds he got at Gettysburg. I like working for General Hill, but the war's worn him down. I can see it in his eyes and the hesitation he has in giving orders. It's time to move on. I've been thinking for some time about applying for a regiment or company command."

Andy knew how highly I regarded General Pender and gave me a sympathetic nod when I mention his name. Then to lighten the mood he said, "If you get a command, ask them to transfer me in as First Sergeant. I'd like to work with you again. Had fun and did some good ridin' with Mosby, didn't we?"

"Thanks Andy. I am thinking the same thing." In fact, it was why I came to see him.

Northern Virginia
April - May, 1864,
Jim Cobb

General Hill's recurring illness incapacitated him again. Jubal Early temporarily replaced him as head of Third Corps.

General Lee had confidence in Early and used him frequently as a troubleshooter, some complained troublemaker. Later, General Early also relieved General Ewell as Second Corps Commander when he became incapacitated.

General Early aggressively attacked the Yankees; even more than General Hill, but never foolishly. Other officers considered him eccentric, self-absorbed, opinionated, and difficult. But I liked the feisty old general and admired his intelligence and ability to get results with limited troops and supplies.

Early brought his staff with him. With little constructive work I could do, I waited with others on General Hill's staff until General Hill was well enough to resume command.

I decided it would be a good time to put in my request for transfer. Facing General Hill and coming up with a reason, other than the real reason, would be painful. I respected A P Hill too much to lie to him. Better if I submitted the request to General Early.

I approached Early's Chief of Staff, Major Henry Douglas, and asked for a meeting with the General. Douglas was much like Early – rough and profane. I was not surprised. Most of the generals tended to surround themselves with aides like themselves. I thought it reasonable. The generals did not need personality clashes to add to their concerns.

If I were still a Captain, the aide would have denied me, but penciled me in for a short meeting in the afternoon. After a brief exchange of pleasantries with General Early, I went directly to the reason I came. "I request transfer to command a line unit."

"Major Cobb, before I decide on your request, I need to know your reasons for wanting the transfer."

I had rehearsed what I would say to this question and told General Early, "We've lost many line officers in the recent fighting. I believe I can better serve Third Corps as a regimental or company commander."

Early nodded in agreement and replied, "I have no objection in assigning you to regimental command, but do you really want to leave your position as General Hill's Chief of Staff? General Hill regards you highly."

I had a prepared answer for this question too. "I have the highest regard for General Hill. As you know, he's been a stalwart. General Jackson and General Lee have relied on him. But, there are several officers on General Hill's staff who can perform my duties. I'm concerned that too many junior and inexperienced officers will be elevated to company and regimental command to fill the vacancies."

"I agree. Your request is granted. I'll work out a regimental command for you next week."

I thanked General Early, saluted, and left knowing I would be reassigned soon.

* * *

When General Early called me in for official appointment as Regimental Commander, he said, "Major Cobb, your regiment is assigned to the Georgia Brigade of the Light Division. But, you will be available to Third Corps for special assignments from me and General Hill when he returns. Have you thought of a unit designation for your regiment?"

"Sir, I first want to thank you for the assignment. I know I will receive officers and soldiers from all of Third Corps maybe all of the army, but I request we be designated the 78th North Carolina. That number was somehow skipped in earlier regimental designations."

General Early submitted a promotion for me to Lieutenant Colonel, but I never received it. Maybe the promotion was lost or not approved. I never knew and did not care. I could have insisted on the promotion when General Hill returned, but I took perverse pleasure in commanding the regiment as a Major. The regimental officers and men seemed to appreciate the quirk of fate as well. Besides, the difference in pay came in increasingly worthless Confederate currency. I served because I could not honorably quit, not for rank or pay.

Upon taking command, I arranged transfer of Sergeant Andy Blaylock to my newly created regiment. Andy's commanding officer protested and refused to release him. I insisted I needed a seasoned sergeant with Andy's leadership ability to serve as the Regimental First Sergeant and train the young recruits and new officers brought in to supplement the regiment. I prevailed in the dispute that went back to General Early for resolution. The arguments I used were all valid reasons to transfer Andy Blaylock to the new regiment, but the real reason was I wanted him with me in my new command.

When A P Hill returned to the Third Corps, Titus Palmer told me Hill was disappointed to learn I would no longer be his

Chief of Staff. But he agreed. Transferring me to a line command was a good decision. I was most valuable to him when the army went on the offensive and battle lines fluid. It was when General Hill most needed immediate and accurate information to make quick decisions. There was another reason Hill agreed with my transfer nobody wanted to discuss or recognize. Years of combat and disease had worn down Lee's gamecock. He lacked his earlier fire and taste for battle.

Our reality was that we lost ability to carry out offensive operations after Gettysburg. The strategic initiative had passed to the Union Army. Their superiority in numbers and supplies coupled with our losses at Gettysburg were too great for us to go on the offensive again. Even if we could, the ring around Richmond tightened leaving us little room and opportunity for maneuver. We could and did inflict heavy losses on the Union Army in defensive battles. But, the only lingering hope for victory was the Union would become weary of the bloodletting and finally give in. Under the circumstances, General Hill agreed I was more valuable to the Corps as a regiment commander.

New York Tribune Article,
Sunday, May 8, 1864
byline Samuel Payne

In heavy fighting in The Wilderness, the thick woods General Jackson used to hide his flanking movement before Chancellorsville, both armies were heavily bled. But the Union can provide replacements and the Confederacy cannot. Unfortunately, it is our overall strategy for winning the war – outlast the Rebels.

Fighting in The Wilderness has been particularly difficult and brutal. The dense woods hides troop movements until the enemy comes well within rifle range. Many surprise fights and skirmishes occur as opposing armed units stumble on to each other. There is much hand-to-hand fighting with spades and rifles used as clubs when the bullets are spent. It is war at the basest level.

Lincoln finally found his general in U S (dubbed "Unconditional Surrender" by the others in the press) Grant. Grant is not a brilliant general, but he has an iron will and an indomitable stubborn streak. He retained Meade as head of the Army of the Potomac. But, Grant moves with and, to a large degree, will direct strategy of the Army of the Potomac until war's end.

Lee defeated other Union generals who turned back to Washington to lick their wounds before taking another run at Richmond. Not Grant. Grant absorbs losses that daunted earlier Union generals and keeps coming. Lee cannot defeat Grant simply because Grant will not stay beaten.

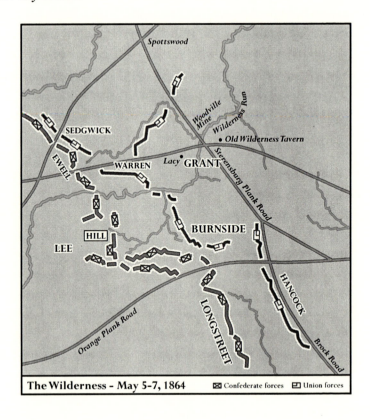

The Wilderness - May 5-7, 1864   ⊠ Confederate forces ⊡ Union forces

Chapter 14: Cold Harbor

Northern Virginia,
May – September, 1864
Jim Cobb

General Early ignored convention in creating the new regiment. Deserving officers usually progressed to regimental command by demonstrating courage and competence in command of a company. It is how my friend Granville Calvert earned command of the 16th North Carolina. But, for the newly formed 78th North Carolina, General Early appointed a high ranking Corps staff officer who had not previously led a company or even a platoon – me. Concerned with weakening overall strength in Third Corps, Early assigned a few officers and soldiers from many regiments and companies across the Corps along with new recruits and hospital releases to the 78th North Carolina.

The incoming officers and soldiers knew me by reputation, that I was General Hill's Chief of Staff. Rumors floated around about Sergeant Blaylock and me riding with John Mosby. But what they heard was something different than competence as a line officer. Outward appearances suggested Early picked an inexperienced favorite to command the new regiment. The leadership ability of their new commander was, at best, uncertain to the officers and men assigned to the new regiment.

From my fitness reports, Early read that I had demonstrated ability to adapt tactics to actual battle field circumstances. He took this and envisioned the 78th North Carolina as a quick strike unit to halt incursion of Union penetration of Confederate lines. He knew, from recent engagements, the Yankees concentrated on perceived weak sectors to break our lines and then roll up and trap Confederate units positioned on the wings. Early wanted the new regiment held in reserve until Union intentions were clear and then strike hard to halt or roll back the incursion.

General Early favored offensive operations and, even as Grant forced the Army of Northern Virginia into a defensive posture, saw the new regiment as an opportunity to retain at least a semblance of offensive capability. He wanted us available anywhere to lead or support a counterattack when opportunity arose.

The Wilderness, Virginia,
Friday, May 6, 1864
Jim Cobb

Heavy fighting continued as my new regiment assembled. I spoke with each company commander as he reported. On their recommendation, I appointed my aide, an able young lieutenant, Lloyd Graham, a recent George Washington College student who quit school to join the army. He had performed well in one of the companies.

I sent Graham to find Sergeant Andy Blaylock and bring him to my tent. Andy entered, gave a proper salute which I returned and then grabbed him by the shoulders and hugged him.

I asked, "What do you think?"

Andy took a seat and asked a pertinent question, "What the hell have you got us into?"

I sat on a hard tack box facing Andy. "We're a quick strike regiment. Yankees poke a hole in our lines. We drive 'em back, seal the breach, maybe capture some."

Andy arched an eyebrow and gave me a half grin.

"I know you're thinking General Early sampled barley corn when he came up with this scheme."

"He's been known to imbibe," Andy commented repeating a rumor that floated around camp.

"No, but I think he sees things the way he wants to see them. Early wants to stick a finger in a leak. You, me, anyone who spent time in our army know there's too damn many Yankees, too many incursions. We'll end up going to the first one."

Andy rocked forward on his box. "You wouldn't believe what they're saying about you and the new regiment."

"Head off what you can."

"They don't know you," Andy explained. "You need to show 'em you can command the regiment. It'll take time, but you're up to it."

I got up and started pacing. Andy had a good point, what had I gotten us into? "I know I am, but, keep me informed if you see any problems. Butcher Grant won't give us time to whip this regiment into shape before we're in the fight."

"I'll do what I can." Three years in the army taught me that the men respected their sergeants far more than their officers. I knew Andy would turn the men faster than I could.

"I'll make it easier for you to do that," I replied and called in Lloyd Graham. I ordered him to assemble the company commanders for a short meeting. Andy got up to leave. I told him to stay.

When the company commanders arrived, I announced, "Gentlemen, we have many new, recently promoted sergeants and corporals to lead our platoons. We need a seasoned sergeant to train them. I am appointing the best, most qualified man I know, Sergeant Andy Blaylock, to serve as our Regimental First Sergeant." I turned to Andy and added, "He's been with us in the Light Division, Virginia Brigade since Chancellorsville. He took the place of his brother, Matthew, who served as First Sergeant until he died after Fredericksburg. Lot of talent and tradition in the Blaylock family."

I did not gather the regimental officers for approval, but to inform them of my decision. At the same time, I wanted to explain who he was to those who may not know him.

I went on to clarify our mission as directed by General Early and found the interest missing in earlier talks with them. I concluded in telling them, "Unfortunately we have no time to meld the veterans and recruits into a cohesive unit before we'll be ordered into battle."

After I dismissed them, I overheard two of the company commanders talking outside.

Captain Claude James, retained from the original regiment, spoke with Captain Owen Ferguson who came over from the Virginia Brigade. I later learned they were cousins and experienced and cautious officers. The overly brave, glory-seekers were mostly dead. I was honored to have company commanders, like James and Ferguson, who would not squander the lives of brave men.

James said, "No surprise Major Cobb appointed his fellow Mosby Ranger to First Sergeant."

Ferguson replied, "Yeah, but Sergeant Blaylock is a good one. We used him in my old regiment to train the new sergeants. Did a good job for us. He'll do well here too."

James asked, "What d'ya think about the regiment?"

Ferguson answered, "Could be interestin'. We have a chance to catch the Yankees with their pants down. Ready to trap us when we hit 'em unawares."

* * *

In our first engagement, General Thomas ordered the regiment out to stop a Union incursion in The Wilderness. I held back Captain Will Boggs and Company D in reserve should the

Yankees break through our extended defensive line. I did not know any of the Captains well, but Boggs seemed the pick of the litter, a possible regimental adjutant commander. I wanted to test him early.

As the battle progressed, I observed troop movements through a field glass and discussed what I saw with Lieutenant Graham, "We can't see into the woods, but we can learn a lot about what the Yankees are doing by watching how our troops react. From what I see, they're trying to tie us down across the line and circle one or two companies to break through on the right."

Graham was eager to learn. He reminded me of me as a green Lieutenant for what seemed ages ago. Even looked like me somewhat but a bit shorter and frail. We had Lexington in common and talked about it in the off hours. Maybe, like me, he could take leadership lessons from the war with him if he survived.

After a pause, I added, "From what he saw of our troop movements, General Pender often knew what was in my report before I gave it."

As we watched the fighting, a runner came up from behind and announced himself.

"Major Cobb, Sir, Captain Ferguson requests you commit the reserve company to the far right where the Yankees are gatherin' to attack."

"Very good, Corporal. Return and tell Captain Ferguson I am ordering Company D to reinforce him. He will be there shortly after you give Captain Ferguson my reply." No point in writing the order as both Captain Ferguson's request and my answer were simple and direct and time short.

I asked Captain Boggs, who stood close, "Did you hear what I told the runner?"

"Yes, Sir."

"Clear about what to do?" I asked.

"Yes, Sir."

"Coordinate with Captain Ferguson when you get there. Don't let the Yankees slip around us. Get going and good luck."

After they left, I put my field glass on the right side of the line to observe deployment of the reinforcements. It appeared the Yankees had doubled up on their left for an imminent attack. I motioned Lloyd Graham over to a table where I spread out a detailed map of the area. Suddenly, Graham went down with a bullet in his hip.

Another bullet passed under my hand and struck the map. I heard the volley, turned, and saw black powder smoke in the thick woods. A Union detachment had somehow circled around our position, came upon the regimental camp, and found an opportunity to kill or capture me and the regimental staff when the last company left.

I flipped the table on its side, dragged Lloyd Graham behind it, and pulled my pistol from a side holster. Several bullets slammed into the table but did not penetrate the thick pine slab top. I looked over the table and saw a Union private running toward me with a bayonet aimed at my head.

I shot the Union soldier below the neck. He stumbled and fell in front of the table. I reached over the table and picked up his rifle. The attendants, not hit in the initial volley, fired into the Union wave as they advanced. I parried the bayonet of the next Yankee soldier and caught him in the stomach with the rifle butt. I knelt, aimed my pistol, and shot another in the chest.

As I turned, I glimpsed another bluecoat, felt his bayonet rip through my left sleeve, and fell backward as the young soldier slammed into me. I grabbed his shirt as we fell and rolled over him. Still holding the pistol, I slammed it over his head, creating a deep gash and heavy blood flow.

I remembered that a bleeding Yankee hid me at Sharpsburg and pulled the unconscious soldier over on top of me. Blood covered arms and hands – both his and mine.

With Lieutenant Graham down and me apparently dead

under a bleeding Union soldier, the others Yankee soldiers raced by. The attendants formed a defensive circle in the middle of the camp. I lay motionless under the unconscious Yankee soldier and watched Union soldiers bayonet the attendants and bludgeon them with rifle butts. Despite determined resistance, the Yankees were about to overrun our defensive perimeter. All of us would have been killed or captured if two platoons from the reserve company had not made a timely return.

I saw a Union Private point a bayonet at me. Before he could make a thrust, his knees buckled. A fraction of a second later, I heard the report of a volley and then the Rebel Yell as our soldiers set on the Union squad with a ferocity I had not seen before. They quickly circled the Yankees, cut off retreat into the woods, and killed and captured all of them.

I pulled out from under the Union soldier and took stock. Graham had lost blood. I folded a kerchief I took from one of the dead Yankees, put it on Graham's hip wound, and said, "Lloyd, press down on this. We'll get you to a surgeon soon."

Graham smiled weakly, put his hand on the kerchief, and said, "I'll be all right, Major."

My arm continued to bleed so I took another kerchief and pressed it on my arm. We lost most of the attendants. The others were being treated by the rescue party.

In the brief fight, I killed two Union privates, wounded another, and stunned a corporal who was taken prisoner.

Andy came over, took off his scarf, and wrapped my arm. "This should take care of you until we get you to a surgeon. You had a close call."

"Too close. They about had us. How many did we lose?"

"'Pears they killed nine of our boys, three from the platoons, and wounded six. About thirty Yankees altogether. Rough count, it appears we got 'em all. Their fightin' days are over."

"None captured?" I asked.

"Just the one you knocked out. Couldn't hold off the boys

from them that wanted to surrender." I noted Andy had a half grin when he answered. I doubted he did anything to restrain the slaughter. He likely led them in killing the Yankees who wanted to surrender.

I shook my head. Pointing at the dead soldiers lying near by, I said, "None of them can be more than twenty years old. Where does it end? How many young men, ours and theirs, have been cut down in their prime? I killed them, but I don't hate them. They did their duty same as we would in their place."

"I don't give a damn for dead Yankees," Andy said, "but I'm glad it's them and not you we'll bury. I'll get a wagon and take you and the other wounded to the field hospital."

* * *

Orderlies tended my arm wound. The surgeon told me, "Deep cut, Major. Give yourself a week before you do anything with that arm lest you open up the bleeding again."

"Wish I could," I told him, "but General Early just organized a regiment for me. No way I can stand down now."

The surgeon shook his head and said, "Keep a tight sling on it. Don't do any lifting until the stitches are removed."

I checked on Lloyd Graham who was still unconscious after the surgeon cut the bullet out of his hip. I left with Andy and several attendants the surgeons patched up to rejoin the Regiment.

An attendant, David Beck, took my coat, the one Dolly Hill tailored for me, and used lye soap to take out most of the blood stain before it set. Private Beck soaked the coat three times. He skillfully sewed up the tear and repaired the coat almost as good as new when he finished.

"You did fine work. Thank you." I handed him one of the Union dollar coins I took during my rides with Mosby.

"Thank you, Sir. Nobody ever paid me that much when I 'prenticed in the tailor shop back home," he said.

"Yes, and you probably never worked as hard to restore a coat. I roughed it up pretty good before you got to it."

After supper, I found Captain Boggs and said, "Thank you, Will. If you hadn't sent Andy back with two platoons, I'd have more to worry about than a cut shoulder."

Boggs shook his head and answered, "Andy Blaylock. You picked a good one for First Sergeant. He heard the firing, took off on a dead run back to camp, and hollered for the two trailing platoons to follow. It's what I would've ordered if I had time, but there wasn't any time. You'd be dead if Sergeant Blaylock had waited for my order."

* * *

Following the heavy, bloody, and inconclusive fighting in The Wilderness, the Union Army did not pull back and regroup as earlier Yankee armies had. They marched southwest. Everyone, and most particularly the Union soldiers, knew they had a different commanding general. Grant kept his primary objective, our army, continually engaged. He understood what earlier Union commanders failed to grasp - if he wore down our army, Richmond would fall.

As the Union Army crossed two roads leading directly into Richmond, Grant saw an opportunity to make a rapid thrust to the Confederate capital and force a decisive battle. The roads came together at an oddly named crossroad, Cold Harbor, only eleven miles from Richmond. It immediately became the Army of the Potomac's prime objective. General Lee ordered defense of Cold Harbor, but our exhausted troops arrived piecemeal and were driven out. They dropped back toward Richmond to form a defensive position against the Union attack sure to follow.

A P Hill returned to command and positioned the Georgia Brigade, including the 78th North Carolina, in the Third Corps' defensive line. We came down from defending the Anna River ten miles north and were the last Confederate troops to arrive. Third Corps took position on the right flank of the long Confederate defensive line. We dug in for the impending battle.

We received a godsend when the Army of the Potomac delayed one day to organize a massive frontal attack. At the time we did not know why, but later learned General Meade moved Hancock's Second Corps across the entire Union line to form the left flank for the upcoming assault. We used the extra thirty-six hours to dig deep zigzag trenches and built up breastworks where topography favored us. We placed head logs over the trenches and breastworks leaving a slit for protected rifle fire at the approaching Union troops with only a narrow opening for return fire.

Union troops had to advance in the open against our protected defensive line. They had little or no likelihood of winning and high probability of being killed or wounded.

* * *

Weather during the fighting around Cold Harbor had been exceptionally dry, but it rained the night before the attack and gave welcome relief to the soldiers in both armies. I left my tent and took advantage of the pause to enjoy the cool air. As I rode behind the defensive works, I heard a familiar voice taunting the Yankees. "Hey Yank, does your mother know you came down here to die?"

A leather-lunged Yankee soldier, heard above the catcalls, replied, "Go to hell, Reb. Come tomorrow and I'll ram my bayonet down your cotton mouth."

Andy grinned. As intended, he had gotten to the Yankees. He yelled, "Be sure to pin names and letters to your uniforms so your folks and sweethearts will know you died here."

"Shut your stinkin' mouth Reb. After we run over you and the rest of the goddamn Secesh Army, we're goin' on to Richmond and do your mothers, wives, sweethearts, and the other whores." An immediate cheer rose from the Union lines following the response of their self-appointed spokesman. I had to admit he had a fine Irish lilt that somehow elevated his vulgar words.

Andy waited for the cheering to die down and then added, "I'll post your letter" which triggered cheers from our lines. More insults were exchanged, but Andy withdrew from the verbal combat. He had achieved his purpose. When the Yankees were angry, they were often careless. Andy was content to nurture seeds of fear and doubt in their minds.

"What're we in for tomorrow?" Andy asked. He knew I had been up the Confederate line observing deployment and the Union troop placement.

"The only way they can succeed is to throw more troops at us than we have bullets. It'll be a turkey shoot."

"You heard their bluster. But, I bet they're scared" Andy said.

"They'd have to be a lot greener and dumber than I think they are. Everyone knows they have no chance except Grant and Meade. If they just rode up and took a good look, like I did, they'd know better than order an attack."

"They would if they wuz General Lee or Stonewall Jackson, but they ain't," Andy accurately observed.

Cold Harbor, Virginia,
Friday, June 3, 1864
Jim Cobb

In preparation for a morning attack, we took an early breakfast and fell in position before sunup. I stayed with Captain James and A Company behind Confederate lines to stop any incursion in our sector. I waited briefly and then heard a cannon barrage, followed by mortar fire, which mostly missed our lines and finally the hurrah of the massive Union Army line as they climbed from their trenches. The troops of Hancock's Second Corps formed a huge blue wave that surged toward us. We held fire until the Union troops came within range then, like rolling thunder, spewed recurring sheets of deadly rifle fire joined with mortar shells on the oncoming bluecoats.

I admired the valor and determination of the Union soldiers as they attempted to overwhelm our lines. They staggered, fell, dropped in waves, and kept coming.

As the battle proceeded, I scanned the Union attack and then stopped to watch an unusual incident. A young color bearer, normally the first to go down, somehow made it all the way to our trenches. Badly wounded and staggering under the weight of the flag he carried, the young man refused to stop or fall down. If he had looked back, he would have seen no one following him. Many of his company had been cut down in a steady procession. The others fled back to the trenches they left. He stood alone and dazed directly in front of the enemy.

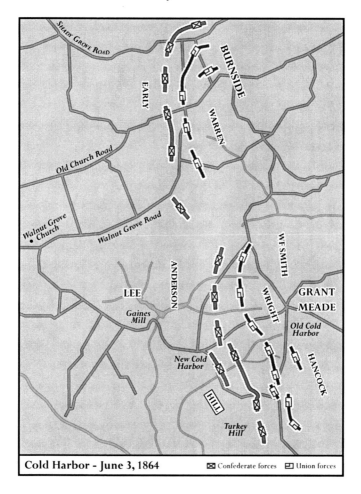

Cold Harbor - June 3, 1864   ⊠ Confederate forces   ⊡ Union forces

Then another miracle occurred. One of our soldiers leaped up and threw the helpless color bearer over the head log before jumping back into the trench. Either Union soldiers within range saw it as an act of mercy or did not want to risk hitting their man, but no one fired at the exposed Confederate soldier during the rescue.

*   *   *

Union forces breached our lines in another sector. Reinforcements quickly sealed the incursion. The Union assault ended in total defeat with over seven thousand Union dead and less than two thousand Confederate losses. General Meade did not immediately recognize the calamity that befell his army and ordered more attacks on our line. Union Corps commanders, veterans of Fredericksburg, ignored this order.

Union casualties covered the field, many with names and letters pinned or sewn to their uniforms, some moaning pitifully. A particularly bitter and painful loss for the Union Army as most of the dead were veteran and proven soldiers; many were Fredericksburg survivors and made the hopeless attack anyway.

Since taking leadership of the Union Army, Grant ended the practice of ceasefire following battles. He had to petition General Lee for a truce to evacuate the wounded at Cold Harbor, an admission of defeat. Grant waited two days to do it; probably ate on him to ask a favor of General Lee. While he stewed, wounded and dying Union soldiers lay on the battlefield for over three days where nearly all of them died. Without a truce, Union corpsmen were unable to come out and tend to the wounded. Even our soldiers felt sympathy for the misery of the fallen enemy.

I sent Jeremy Tuttle, my aide, with orders to "Gather up as many canteens and bandages as you can. Take two platoons. Go out and do what you can for the wounded."

As Tuttle prepared to leave, I stood in the trench and waved a white flag for the Union sharpshooters and handed the flag to him. As an afterthought, I said, "Lieutenant, have the men gather the letters they find and bring them back. We'll put them someplace safe where the Yankees will find them when we pull out." I remembered Sharpsburg and the possibility of looters coming out at night and taking the letters for the money that might be tucked in them.

When he returned, Tuttle handed me the letters found on the dead Yankees. I casually went through the thick bundle and suddenly stopped. My hand trembled as I held one of the letters.

Tuttle noted my reaction and came over. "Anything wrong, Sir?"

"This letter was written by Ken Johnson. He roomed with Pete Morgan and me at college." I looked up and asked, "Do you know where you found his letter?"

Tuttle shook his head. "No telling, Sir. Lot of dead Yankees. We took letters off all we found."

I left the letters in my tent, took the white flag, and went out on the battlefield to search for Ken's body. With increasing difficulty, I wiped tears from my eyes as I rolled over one bluecoat after another looking for Ken's face. I searched for more than an hour, but failed to find him. In a perverse way, I considered it a blessing. I never knew if he died by fire from my regiment.

When I returned to my tent, I opened Ken's letter. The distinctive left-handed chicken scratch left no doubt he wrote the letter. I became overwhelmed with grief and memories of studying with Ken, playing cards, visiting the Morgan Plantation, commiserating on our lives as Outcasts, suffering Bryce Carlton, staying awake through Professor Jackson's dull lectures, and on and on. I struggled to read through the tears in my eyes.
Ken wrote:

Dear Mother and Father,

As I view the field for tomorrow's battle, it appears our position is hopeless. We are ordered to attack the Rebels who have taken a strong position I fear cannot be defeated. I expect to die tomorrow along with many of the brave men I command. They will obey my order to attack as I will obey Colonel Brooks' orders. The men know and I know we cannot succeed.

I should have done this sooner, but ask your forgiveness for the many times I failed you. As I contemplate the end of my life, I realize the only lasting value is love as God loves each of us. I am certain you love me deeply as I love you. I know you will miss me and regret I will no longer be able to be embraced by my mother or talk with my father and be uplifted.

When you receive this letter you will know I died on a battlefield near Cold Harbor, Virginia. Please tell Maxwell, Jr and Susan I always loved them despite my childish protests to the contrary. I will miss them and pray they have full and successful lives and know the peace of Christ as I do now.

I ask a favor. Please tell Olivia Holmes I will not be able to fulfill the plans we had and tell her, for me, I will love her always even from the grave.

As the end nears, I realize my life is what I have made it. There is no time left to amend anything and I pray that God, in His mercy and the sacrifice or our Lord Jesus Christ, will accept me as I am.

Your loving son,
Kenneth

I recalled Ken's father was a Congregational minister and likely experienced in consoling grieving parents and loved ones. This time it would be Ken's parents who would need comfort when they received the heartbreaking news of their son's death. I never met Ken's parents, but felt great sorrow for them, Ken's brother and sister, and Olivia Holmes.

Ken wrote the letter knowing he would die at Cold Harbor. He left the trench with certainty he would give his life for causes to which he was devoted – union, freedom and equality for the Negroes.

With each reading, the horror of war became more personal and immediate. The "enemy" was my good friend and college roommate. A moral, thoughtful, and spiritual man, I always thought Ken was destined to become a pastor like his father – marry his congregants, baptize their children, say good words over them at their funerals, and inspire them with kind, thoughtful, scripture-based sermons. I saw no justice, no sanity in his untimely death on a killing field outside Cold Harbor. The war became unbearably cruel.

Reading Ken Johnson's letter released a flood of sorrow... for Dorsey Pender, the officer I most admired and respected... for General Jackson whose death effectively ended Confederate hope for victory... for the loss of hope to marry and settle down with the beautiful Sissy Morgan should I survive the war... for Silas Young who loved his wife and unborn child and died at Gettysburg ... for Lloyd Graham who died too young in The Wilderness ...and now for Ken Johnson, my roommate and good friend.

Each man with whom I served or commanded and died in the war marched by, in turn, through my mind, a seemingly endless line. It was more than I could bear.

I held Ken's letter and sobbed. Later, after composing myself, I wrote a condolence note. Everything I considered writing seemed shallow and empty particularly as it came from an officer in the army that had killed their son. Finally, I simply wrote of my sorrow on the passing of a good man and good friend, attached it to Ken's letter, and resealed the envelope.

I needed to do something and left my tent to seek out General Thomas. I asked if I could deliver the letters to Union lines. He asked my reasons and I gave them.

Appalled with the slaughter himself, General Thomas agreed, "Permission granted."

I took the letters, mounted my horse, and prepared to ride to the nearest Union troops when Andy stopped me. He handed me the white flag and said, "Here, take this. We don't want Yankee sharp shooters thinkin' you're crazy."

As I neared Union lines, I saw sadness and bitter resignation in the eyes of the Yankee soldiers. I singled out a Captain from among the officers and soldiers who stood watching me and extended the bundle of letters to him.

The Union Captain saluted as he took the letters and said, "Thank you, Major, for your kindness in bringing them to us and helping our boys earlier."

I returned the salute and impulsively reached down, took the captain's hand, and said, "The top letter is from Captain Kenneth Johnson, 53rd Pennsylvania. He was my friend and former classmate. One of the best men I've ever known. Please see that his letter is delivered ... and all of them. I'm sorry for the loss of so many fine men and regret this sorrowful war ever began."

The Union Captain looked up with a sad face and said, "We also have a high regard for Captain Johnson." I realized then I had stumbled on the remnants of the 53rd Pennsylvania regiment.

I turned slowly and rode back to camp. I did not share in the satisfaction of a stunning and overwhelming victory at Cold Harbor.

* * *

Following Gettysburg, Confederate troop strength steadily eroded from casualties, desertion, and disease. Some communities lost all or nearly all of their young men, sometimes in the same battle. By now, the original Catawba County company was nearly gone.

As a regimental commander, I received orders to shoot deserters if captured. But I figured it was something each man had to decide for himself. The war was lost; I would not be the conscious of others but, to me, it was a matter of personal honor. I managed to "look the other way" whenever I suspected a deserter or desertion in progress and was never reprimanded for it.

One day, as I rode out of camp, I saw a distraught, unarmed soldier who appeared to be walking away. I stopped him and asked, "Are you lost?"

He looked up shamefaced and replied, "Sir, I cannot go on.

If you must shoot me, I would rather die here and now than continue in the war."

On the chance I could salvage his pride and talk him out of desertion, I asked, "Do you know the men in your platoon and are you loyal to them?"

"Yes, Sir", he replied.

"By leaving, do you understand you're letting down every man in your platoon? It's something you will live with for the rest of your life. Do you really want that?"

The soldier, without looking at me, replied, "No sir, I guess not."

"I suggest you return to your platoon now before anyone knows you left." The soldier turned around, walked back to camp, and deserted the next month.

* * *

As the war progressed, our situation became increasingly desperate. Rations, supplies, ammunition, uniforms, medicines, blankets, everything became scarce. I detached Andy and a group of sharpshooters from all the companies to bring in game when we had opportunity. Sometimes, the "game" was cows and pigs from neighboring farms or rations from unfortunate Yankees who drifted too close to where Andy and his party scouted. Andy arranged barter with the Union troops, but found it increasingly difficult to come up with anything of value to trade as even our tobacco rations were meager.

I appreciated what the foragers brought in and did not ask questions. I suspected they ambushed Yankee patrols and took whatever they had of value. I killed Yankees because I had to. Andy killed them because he wanted to. I knew that riding with the Mosby Rangers. However, I never lost sight of my primary concern - keeping my men alive - and Andy's foragers helped.

With what the foragers brought in, we at least kept the

regiment fed. But it pained me to see shoeless soldiers and those with ill-fitting uniforms and tattered boots taken from corpses and prisoners. Months of seeing and smelling dead and mutilated bodies inured me to death and dying, but not to soldiers and civilians living in wretched conditions. I led an increasingly ragged, decimated, and ill-equipped regiment.

Despite the paucity of supplies, I doggedly followed the lessons and example of Dorsey Pender. I insisted our camp be kept clean and orderly. My standing order was not well received by the soldiers who were often tired, underfed, and resentful of regulations to dress up the camp particularly as we moved frequently. Other regimental commanders relented on maintaining an orderly camp. But Pender taught me order, cleanliness, and discipline ran together and saved lives. These were my primary goals for the regiment – do our duty and save as many lives as possible.

After partaking of what little the army provided and the sharpshooters brought in, the men settled around campfires, mended their uniforms and equipment as best they could, teased one another, and told stories. After posting sentries, we retired for the night - often to the strains of a sad song from an informal group of regimental musicians. In the morning, the soldiers ate corn meal fried in bacon fat. They used rancid bacon for the grease and ate the bacon when it was used up.

The men most prized a dead Yankee with feet about the same size as their own. The Yankees generally had good boots and shoes and we did not. Fredericksburg provided a welcome source of footwear, but these boots and shoes were worn out by the time I took command of the regiment.

* * *

When we could, I took Andy with me to Sunday church services. We visited local churches and, after the service ended, asked if any of the congregation could spare bandages, socks, food, anything for the regiment. Andy did his part by looking sad and telling funny stories that amused the congregations, particularly the ladies. It helped improve our haul. But I did not push hard for donations. The circumstances of many of the congregation were as bad as or worse than what my men endured.

I enjoyed the diversion of the Sunday services and visiting the different denominations. Andy did not always speak with the best grammar, but little got by him. I thought him profound when, one Sunday after we heard an impassioned sermon at a Baptist church, Andy said, "They all take great stock in their differences. What makes 'em better than the other churches? The services sure are much the same."

One Sunday, I sent Andy with Lieutenant Tuttle to seek collection at a nearby Catholic church and spent the morning riding to the home of Captain Silas Young's widow. I heard, from an officer in Young's regiment, she had moved back with her parents in a neighboring town. I rode there to find her.

The family had returned from church, eaten dinner, and sat on the porch when I arrived. I introduced myself and accepted their invitation to join them, drink lemonade, and talk.

I described my memories of Captain Young and our long conversation on the train ride from Lexington. I told the widow, "What I remember most from my talk with Silas is how much he loved you and how he anticipated the birth of your child."

I took out the envelope I carried from Gettysburg. It contained Silas's watch, ring, wallet, and two medals he had earned for meritorious service. I said, "I want his son or daughter to have a reminder of Silas" and handed the envelope to his widow.

A capricious thought crossed my mind. What if, after the war, I returned to help raise the unborn child? The widow was pretty and her family nice. Reality quickly set in. No assurance I would survive to help raise any child.

Since Sharpsburg, I developed a basic, evolving belief that

God had given me a mission. I did not know what the mission was but hoped God would preserve me until I did. However, the recurring death, near death, and brutality of war eroded my faith. I believed I would survive the war and then often doubted my certainty.

Karen Young asked me, "Major Cobb, did Silas get a Christian burial?"

"Yes. I buried him and said a prayer before covering him. His body's in Pennsylvania. You'll see him in heaven."

Tears streaked her pretty face as she kissed me on the cheek. It felt good to have a female kiss me even in sad circumstances.

The family thanked me before I excused myself to return to the regiment. Throughout, I was struck by how lovely and, at the same time, how sad Silas' widow, Karen, was – a recurring thought in future months.

Northern Virginia
Sunday, July 3, 1864
Jim Cobb

Retired army Major, Albert Ross, and his widowed daughter, Carolyn Jamison invited Andy and me for dinner after we made our appeal following church service at an Episcopal Church. The daughter was attractive, but I knew there would be no romantic opportunity from this chance meeting. She was a Southern lady and carried herself with grace and dignity as I imagined her mother, the Major's wife, had before she died. She appeared very elegant and pretty. Carolyn Jamison wore black and maintained a polite, but sad demeanor throughout our visit. She mourned her dead husband and brother and worried about another brother in Union prison.

She did not need the complication of a brief romance with a

lonesome Confederate officer sitting in her parlor. I thought of Sissy Morgan and winced. When would I stop thinking of her?

Albert Ross fought in the Mexican War where his left leg was shattered and never properly healed. Barely able to walk, even with a cane, he volunteered repeatedly for service in the Confederate Army and was turned down each time.

Major Ross knew many of the commanding generals in both armies from his service in the Mexican War. He told interesting stories of the march from the Rio Grande down into Northern Mexico and the Battle of Buena Vista.

He thought our army was soft and told stories of army life in the Mexican War. He spoke of long marches, extended guard duty, and Mexican irregulars attacking them along the way. But they were fed well from what the army supplied and they confiscated. Sounded pretty good to Andy and me. We smiled and nodded as he talked.

We learned that his commander, Zachary Taylor, was a third cousin once removed of our commander, Robert E Lee. Major Ross was not impressed with General Lee.

"Zachary Taylor, now there's a general for you. Toughest man in the army. Any man who said a word agin' him would hang. We were scared to death of him. Every one of us from the lowest Private up."

Andy mentioned we had served with Mosby and he confused us with Texas Rangers he served with. "Old Rough and Ready used the Rangers for scouting and support cavalry. Fine horseman, absolutely fearless. But, I never saw more brutal men. They thought nothing of pillaging a village, raping the women, and then shoot Mexicans just to have something to do. Their behavior became too much even for General Taylor. He sent them back after the Battle at Buena Vista. That's where I broke my leg. But, it wasn't all bad. I went home and got to recuperate with my family."

Carolyn reached over and squeezed her father's hand as his

eyes moistened. Major Ross cleared his throat and asked, "How's the war going for us?"

I confined my comments to Cold Harbor and our decreasingly fewer victories. Andy followed my lead.

Late afternoon, when we got up to excuse ourselves and leave, Major Ross asked Carolyn to bring out the bottle of brandy for a parting drink. We shared in the toast to a Confederate victory and left with the coat, ham, corn meal, and the remaining brandy the Major kindly offered.

Carolyn accompanied us to our wagon. In parting, she squeezed my hand and thanked me for my restrained comments about the war. "I know the sacrifice you and your men are making and the dire circumstances of our army. With a son and son-in-law killed at Gettysburg and another son in Yankee prison, Father has few pleasures in his life. His mind is slipping. Your words were comforting to him. Thank you and Sergeant Blaylock."

Our visit was a pleasant respite and reminder of the gentility that once typified the South.

Chapter 15: Petersburg

New York Tribune Article,
Sunday, July 10, 1864
Byline Samuel Payne

General Grant promised President Lincoln he would do what no earlier Union field commander has done — stay after the Army of Northern Virginia until he destroyed them. In that regard, he has not disappointed. After failing to defeat the Confederate Army in the series of battles in The Wilderness and the disastrous assault at Cold Harbor, General Grant has continued to engage the Rebel Army.

After contending with Lee in The Wilderness, Grant came to a hard understanding of what General Meade told him when he took command of the Army of the Potomac, "You are no longer opposed by Bragg and Pemberton." General Lee has outguessed Grant at each battle and defeated or turned back Union attacks in each encounter. No matter, Grant is determined to destroy the Confederate Army and slug it out for as long as necessary. He decided to cross the James River, take Petersburg, and cut Richmond's primary supply line from the south. But, first Grant made a feint toward Richmond. Lee took the bluff and pulled back most of his army to defend the Confederate capital.

On June 15, approximately 10,000 Union troops of the XVII Corps, under command of Major General William F "Baldy" Smith, attacked Petersburg which the Confederates defended with a garrison of approximately 4,000 troops under command of General Pierre Beauregard, the first commander of the Army of Northern Virginia.

Beauregard established the Dimmock Line, a series of fortified positions to defend the city. Union forces penetrated the Confederate defenses but were unable to overcome stiff resistance and take the city. Beauregard did a masterful job of disguising the size of his forces by setting false campfires and showing Quaker cannons. He was able to halt the attack outside Petersburg at dusk. Grant wanted XVII Corps to continue the attack during the night, but Smith was spent and waited until morning of the next day to resume the assault, a costly mistake.

During the night, the Confederates reinforced the garrison and the opportunity to quickly take Petersburg vanished. Over the following weeks, the assault has degenerated into a siege. Both sides have settled into trenches and are lobbing shells at each other. For now, it appears to be an endless stalemate.

Outside Petersburg, Virginia,
Sunday July 17, 1864
Jim Cobb

I hurried to meet with General Thomas after receiving an urgent summons and found him sitting at a desk outside his tent. I walked up and saluted. "Major Cobb, reporting as ordered."

Thomas returned my salute and motioned me to sit down facing him. "I have orders for you. We need to discuss them."

I welcomed a new assignment. After a week of inactivity, I needed something to keep the regiment's morale up.

"You are temporarily assigned to General Mahone. He's asked for reinforcement. I can't spare more of the brigade and decided to send your regiment to help out."

"Sir, do you know how long we'll be with Mahone's division?"

"No, as you know he's responsible for Elliot's Salient. We've heard digging. If they try another assault, it's likely they'll attack there."

Everyone knew about the Salient, sticking out into Union lines inviting an attack. Rumors of Yankee sappers circulated through camp. "Have we dropped any shafts to intercept Yankee digging?" I asked.

"Two or three, but we haven't found anything. Still, Mahone's nervous and rightfully so. You'll be used in the counterattack if it comes to that."

General Thomas was himself harried. Relentless Union pressure kept all of the generals awake at night and tense. Like standing at a dike waiting for the water on the other side to break through. Where? When? What strength? No one slept well.

"Leave now," he said, "and report to General Mahone. He's expecting you."

I ordered the regiment out and began our temporary assignment. The 78th North Carolina was not assigned to any of the brigades in Mahone's Division. I reported directly to General Mahone. Over the next week, I learned the reason for the assignment. Mahone was not confident in his staff and used me, unofficially, to scout enemy positions, submit recommendations on deployment of the division, and, confidentially, give my evaluations of the brigade and regimental commanders.

I carried out my assignment without alarming Mahone's officers. They tolerated me and probably thought the General took a liking to me.

I followed Union deployment, carefully noting the apparent shift of Ninth Corps troops toward Elliot's Salient. Nothing unusual about the Yankees moving their troops about, but this seemed odd for reasons I could not explain clearly to General Mahone. I took a late night walk to clear my mind and do some undisturbed thinking. I came up to the front line and was stopped by a sentry.

"Halt. Who goes there?"

"Major Jim Cobb, 78th North Carolina. I'm taking a walk."

As I came closer to the campfire, the sentry recognized me and apologized, "Sorry Major, I didn't see you too good in the dark." I had taken occasional walks to Elliot's Salient. He had seen me before.

"Don't apologize, Private. You're doing your job and doing it well. Seen anything interesting tonight?"

"No, Sir. Nothin' partiklar, but the Yankees're up to somethin'."

"What've you seen?" I asked.

"You know how the cooks always work well out of rifle range? Well, so do the Yankees. But, for the past few weeks, they keep comin' closer. They ain't cookin' with them fires."

"What do you think, Private?"

"Don't know what they're doin', but they're up to no good. Look'a there just inside their line. See the died down fire? They didn't get it all the way banked at sunset."

I looked to where he pointed. Sure enough. "You're right, Private. I can just make it out. By the way, what's your name?"

"Jacob Taylor, 18th South Carolina, Company C, Sir."

"You boys are really sticking out here in the Yankees' face."

Private Taylor was a man not a boy like most Privates, maybe late joining, maybe demoted. But he seemed knowledgeable. "Yes, sir, we're surely in harm's way. We heerd the Yankees got a nigger division to come after us and told the niggers not to take no prisoners."

I heard the same rumor, but did not believe it. Likely something to get the boys riled. "I don't know Private Taylor. The Yankees haven't included me in their staff meetings, but I doubt they told the Negro troops to do anything different than the white troops. You know General Lee's trying to get Negro troops to fight for us."

Taylor shook his head as if he did not want to accept what

I told him. "No, sir. I ain't heerd that. But, jist the same, I don't plan on takin' no nigger prisoners if'n it comes to that."

I wished him a good night and walked back to my tent. On the way, I thought about what the sentry told me. Unlikely the Yankees could dig to Cemetery Ridge. Too far. But, what were those fires? I settled into my cot, but woke up early morning and could not go back to sleep with the same question on my mind. I lit a lamp and reread one of Mother's letters to get my mind off Yankee tunneling.

Petersburg, Virginia,
Saturday, July 30, 1864
Jim Cobb

The ground shook and roared, and then a rolling crashing sound. I looked at my watch. 4:45 A M. I ran out of my tent, and looked in the direction of the explosion. A cloud of white smoke and dust slowly drifted away which, even in the early morning blackness, revealed a huge hole in the ground and most of Cemetery Ridge blown away. The acrid smell of the black powder was unmistakable.

The explosion aroused everyone in camp. I ordered the regiment to assemble. As they dressed and fell in, I gathered the officers. "It appears the Yankees started an assault by mining Cemetery Ridge. General Mahone may order us to move up after the Yankees play their hand. Stay in camp and stay alert." I sent Jeremy Tuttle to standby at General Mahone's headquarters.

After a few minutes, Tuttle ran back. "Major Cobb, General Mahone says to join him immediately. Put the adjutant in charge and prepare the regiment to come up if needed."

"Find Captain Boggs and bring him to me."

Tuttle took off and came back with Boggs. After trading salutes, I said, "Will, I'll be working staff for General Mahone.

Keep the men ready, but I don't know for what. If we stop the Yankees at Cemetery Ridge, Mahone may order us in for the counterattack. If they break through, we'll be needed in making a defensive line. I'll get back to you as soon as I know anything."

I left to join General Mahone. When I found him, Mahone seemed agitated, looking to counterattack, but unsure how many troops to commit and where. Union activity puzzled him. They blew away much of Cemetery Ridge and then did nothing. Was the explosion a feint and the real attack elsewhere? He had to know before moving troops to the giant hole.

I liked Mahone, a banty rooster similar to A P Hill in the early years. Outside of Jubal Early, maybe the best field general left in the Army of Northern Virginia.

"Jim, get down there now. I've never seen anything like this. Big explosion. You'd think they would come at us with everything they've got, but they do nothing. See if you can figure out what the Yankees are up to and get back to me right away."

I took off running to the hole and found two of the four cannons in Captain Pegram's battery blown away. Rifles, tents, ammunition boxes, mangled bodies, body parts, all in bloody piles. I used my field glass to observe Union lines. Early morning and hazy, but what I saw puzzled me. Union troops milled around. They appeared leaderless and drifting. Maybe they could rush to the front of the hole, scale the sides, and pour over Cemetery Ridge or what was left of it. Smarter if they just went around the hole and attacked our flanks. Either way, we needed to bring up more troops to the lip of the hole. But, as I continued watching Union deployment, I noted Union troops in the crater had no ladders, no scaling equipment. If they entered the hole, they would be ducks in a barrel. The horror would shift to them. I ran back to General Mahone to make my report.

Mahone interrupted me. "This is the major assault. They're just going about it badly. I'll order all the troops to the hole and flanks and counterattack when the Yankees quit funneling in more troops and their artillery lets up."

To make sure he understood what I told him, "Sir, strange as it seems Yankee command is running troops into the hole with no way to get at us. We can sit on the lip and shoot them. No need to counterattack until they start to pull out."

"Keep your regiment just back from the center of our line and be alert for a breakout. With luck this'll turn into another Cold Harbor. Stay with me 'til this plays out."

I went back and found Will Boggs. Without me telling him, he had moved the regiment and posted sentries along the line to watch for Union incursions. The regiment was in good hands. I returned to General Mahone at the forward lip of the hole.

The fighting continued until noon. Union artillery pounded us before their casualties started coming back. No chance of a Union breakthrough although they made momentary advances on the flanks before being pushed back. Mostly the Yankee soldiers rushed to the forward lip of the hole to escape our fire. We called up mortars and used them to lob shells into the mass of frantic bluecoats. Soon Yankee dead were two and three deep in the hole. Then Mahone ordered our troops in for the counterattack.

I watched and became concerned. "General, they're shooting Negro prisoners. We're firing on Union orderlies who helped our wounded earlier."

His eye fixed to a field glass, General Mahone did not look at me when he replied, "God himself could not call them off. It's war."

I watched as Virginia troops of Mahone's Division bayoneted and shot captured black soldiers. I even saw Union troops turn their fire on the Negro troops who entered the giant hole. Many of the black soldiers were escaped slaves. It could be Henry or Hannibal slaughtered and betrayed. Shameful conduct from both armies.

I had seen enough. "General, with your permission, I'll rejoin my regiment."

"Good work, Jim." General Mahone clapped me on the back. "You're released. Give my regards to Generals Hill and Thomas when you see them."

I walked slowly back from the hole, past the mortars, and artillery pieces brought up to inflict canister shot on the Yankees caught in the hole. They blasted away as I passed. I saw the regiment as I got past the artillery battery with First Sergeant Blaylock in front.

Andy called out, "Good to see you alive and well for another day."

I needed to talk to someone and who better than Andy? "It's incredible. We can't beat the Yankees, but they're doing their damndest to beat themselves. Think Cold Harbor was bungled? You won't believe what's going on in the hole they blasted this morning. Like they dug themselves a giant grave."

I did not expect Andy would be sympathetic to the Yankees' plight. He did not say it but I knew, for Andy, the more dead Yankees the better.

"How big's the hole?" he asked.

"Huge. Maybe a hundred to a hundred fifty feet across and thirty to forty feet deep. Damn near vaporized Pegram's Battery and the 18th and 24th South Carolina. With more men we could break out and trap the Yankee troops on the flanks. But, as it is, we're shooting them like sheep in a pen."

Petersburg, Virginia
Sunday, July 31, 1864
Jim Cobb

On the day following the attack at the Crater, I witnessed a surprising and welcome act of civility in the brutal siege of Petersburg.

The generals agreed on a truce so each side could remove their dead and wounded. Union and Confederate bands performed during the truce, politely taking turns playing to appreciative soldiers on both sides. All of us felt nostalgic, some even wept openly, thinking back to gentler, kinder times. After listening to the Union band play the mournful *Camping Tonight,* Captain Boggs, who stood by me, asked, "Think the Yankees would trade tunes with us?"

After being repulsed in the direct attack on Petersburg and with fresh memories of horrendous losses in The Wilderness and Cold Harbor, Grant decided to cut transportation lines into Petersburg, surround the city, and starve out the defenders. The Union line moved relentlessly left or to the west to envelop and isolate Richmond. General Lee simply did not have enough men to stop the Union advance and Grant knew it, but the Petersburg Siege went on until the last days of the war.

Third Corps had primary responsibility for holding our right flank, but we had a hopeless assignment. Union troops attacked in overwhelming numbers and kept advancing. They took the Weldon Railroad line in part and finally in cutting off our rail supplies to Richmond from the south. On September 25, 1864, they attacked our defenders at the Peebles Farm with the objective of cutting the Boydton Plank Road from the southwest. The battle lasted four days.

Army of the Potomac, Ninth Corps Headquarters,
Petersburg, Virginia,
Tuesday, August 2, 1864
Sam Payne

I greeted the officers I knew from prior interviews and smiled at the others. Much easier to gain cooperation if you are pleasant, a lesson I learned early in my career. But, Ninth Corps headquarters was as I expected, glum. General Burnside was always a good interview. Loquacious, good humored, and a man who understood and appreciated good publicity. Not today. His army career was over. He knew it and was uncharacteristically brusque.

A tall man with a stout body and open, pleasant face, Burnside stood out among the dour, whiskered Union generals. Before the war, he had been an industrialist and politician. He seemed to know everyone and remembered names including mine. Normally a meticulous dresser and sensitive to his appearance, he appeared disheveled and indifferent. Stubble grew down from his legendary side whiskers, his uniform rumpled and stained as if he slept in it the night before.

Before I could say anything, Burnside told me, "Don't have the time or inclination to talk with the press today."

"General, I know how disappointed you are. It's understandable. But our readers have great interest in what happened in the recent assault. With your permission, I'll interview your officers to get the story."

What Burnside would tell me would be self-serving babble Union generals spouted after a defeat. I reported what he said after Fredericksburg and wished I hadn't. The same story showed up in the other papers and did little to inform our readers. The real story would come from his subordinates. Luckily, Burnside cooperated.

"Start with Henry Pleasants, 48th Pennsylvania. If anyone performed well, it was Pleasants." Despite his many failings as a senior general, Ambrose Burnside was an honest man.

"Thank you, General. The mining of Cemetery Ridge was extraordinary. It's a good story and separate from the assault. I'll go look for him now."

"No. Stay here. I'll send one of the staff to bring him."

Burnside motioned an aide. "Lieutenant, go to Second Division, First Brigade, find Lieutenant Colonel Henry Pleasants of the 48th Pennsylvania, and bring him here. Tell him the New York Tribune wants an interview."

Burnside seemed to relax. I considered interviewing him despite the earlier turndown, but, no. Burnside sorted through his papers, not looking up and not answering the occasional questions I directed to him. I gave up and waited for Pleasants.

I had interviewed Pleasants earlier and liked him. An unusual man, Welsh born coal mining engineer, good humored and talkative, unlike most engineers I had met. Pleasants was unique in another way – a Union officer who actually demonstrated initiative in an army prone to bureaucratic shuffling and evasion of accountability.

Accompanied by the young lieutenant sent to fetch him, Henry Pleasants entered Burnside's tent, came to attention, and saluted smartly. Burnside scarcely looked up, half-heartedly returned the salute, nodded to me, and said, "Mister Payne of the New York Tribune, here, wants to interview you."

I jumped in and said, "General, with your permission, I'll take Colonel Pleasants outside for the interview so our talk will not disturb you."

Burnside waved his hand toward the tent opening. Outside and away from the General, I stopped and turned to Pleasants, "Thanks for coming, Henry. Mining of Cemetery Ridge is all the talk in New York. You and your men did well."

"Yeah, but I wish, God I wish the assault had gone better." Earnestness replaced the good humor I saw in him when he came.

"It's what I want to discuss with you, Colonel, what happened in the mining and the assault."

"Thanks for the promotion. It's still Lieutenant Colonel and maybe not that after the inquiry on the assault."

"Never." I disagreed strongly. "I don't know all the details, but from what I do know, your work and the work of your men was the only bright spot of the day. I urge you to talk with me frankly. I'll credit to hearsay or an unidentified source anything that might hurt you with the higher ups."

Surprisingly, Pleasants took me up on my offer. What he would say could get him drummed out of the army, but he did not seem to care. "Like everyone else, I just want the damned war over and us home. On the way over, I thought how nice it would be to dig tunnels, black powder coal seams, and not worry about politics, backbiting, and Rebs shooting at me."

"If you would, start at the beginning." I shared his sentiment. The war had gone on much too long with far too many broken lives.

"You've been with us long enough to know morale's up when we're on the move and down when we're tied up attacking the Rebs in fortified positions. The assault on Petersburg was bungled and here we are doing just that, trying to get at them through the redoubts and redans. I was eating canned beef and beans with the men when I overheard one of them say, 'With enough powder we can dig under that ridge and blow it to hell'. I stopped eating and started thinking. It was so obvious, I wondered why I hadn't thought of it earlier. Before the war, we dug longer shafts to get out coal."

"Yes, but I was told there's never been a military tunnel over four hundred feet." I remembered that fact from one of my classes at VMI.

"Maybe, but, in all modesty, they did not have the 48th Pennsylvania and me. We did not know it could not be done."

I had my notebook out taking down everything he said. Our readers would eat it up. "It could not have been easy. Tell me what you had to do to get the charge in place. It's these details our readers want to know."

I had Pleasants and knew it. I would ask him to talk about his favorite subject – how to dig a tunnel and set a charge. Pleasants face lit up and he launched into a detailed description I knew would be front page material. I had presumed a short interview and did better than expected – a separate article to run with The Crater story. And best, I saw no other reporters coming around for the same story. I looked around and saw two ammunition boxes, turned them over, and invited Pleasants to sit with me.

Pleasants extended his legs, pulled out a cigar, lit it, leaned forward, and continued, "First, I had to get approval. It was easier than I thought. I went up the ladder as I should – brigade, then General Potter, and then General Burnside. Burnside actually seemed enthusiastic about it. I understand Burnside took it to Meade and Grant and they were lukewarm. But we saw little of them while we dug the tunnel."

"You say Burnside was enthusiastic?" I wanted to draw out Pleasants. Since the assault failed, there would be denial up and down the approval process. I might head it off with an early factual account.

"I came away thinking Burnside saw it as redemption for his career which you know has been spotty. It was his chance to put a big lick on the Rebs and maybe take away some from what happened at Fredericksburg if that's possible."

"Give me details of the tunnel." The tunnel was the key to the explosion, crater, and later battle. The only thing that went right in the calamity. Our readers, maybe historians, would want to read the first full interview given by Henry Pleasants.

"It's what we call a gallery. Five hundred and eleven feet from where we started to where we stopped and then another seventy five feet laterally to spread the charge under the ridge."

"How much charge did you set in?"

"Four tons. I asked for twice that, but four tons was all I got. Could have obliterated the ridge and all the Rebs defending it if I had what I wanted. You saw what did happen." If you could read frustration, it was on Pleasants' face.

"Yes, unfortunately. If you would, let's go back to the tunnel, sorry, the gallery."

"Can't dig without a transit. I found a theodolite which the Engineers loaned me for the project."

"Theodolite? They were considered ancient when I took an engineering course ten years ago."

"Yeah." Pleasants grinned, revealing tobacco stained teeth. "But we finished the tunnel exactly where we planned. I had to get out occasionally and take measurements with it. I'm glad the Reb sharp shooters didn't find me. Came close a few times."

"How'd you do it? It's the question everyone's asking."

"We had to do plenty of improvising. We straightened army spades to make mining picks and converted cracker boxes to make handbarrows." Pleasants acted out his description graphically straightening the spades and forming the handbarrows. "I found a bridge and sawmill to provide timber for the shoring. Hit a seam of clay that slowed down digging, but we pushed on. Toward the end I had every man in the regiment working in the gallery."

"Tunnels over four hundred feet are impossible. The air at the end of the tunnel gets too stale for the diggers to work."

Pleasants nodded. I think I surprised him by knowing something about tunneling. "That was our biggest worry, getting fresh air to the men. We dug an auxiliary shaft and vented it with fires along the way. The warm air pulled out stale air in the gallery and kept a fresh flow coming. I worried most about the fires. Kept getting closer to Reb lines. We disguised them as cook fires and fooled the Rebs long enough to complete the digging."

"Tell me about setting the charge. I understand it was delayed." One of The Crater survivors mentioned a delay.

"We brought the powder up in twenty five pound bags, loaded it into the lateral shafts, ran a fuse from each side to a splice, and ran the fuse back to the gallery opening. I lit the fuse, waited and timed the fuse for an explosion at three in the morning. As you know, it did not go off."

"Why?"

"What else? Sorry fuse. When it didn't go off, I had two volunteers, Lieutenant Jacob Douty and Sergeant Harry Reese, go in. They found the break, respliced the fuse, and relit it around 4:30. Barely made it out before the powder went off. Brave lads. I put them both in for commendation. When the charge went off, I looked at my watch. It read 4:44 am. We had done it. Regardless of what happened later, I am proud of the 48th and what we accomplished."

I could only agree. The real story is what happened later. I asked, "Henry, I know this is sensitive. But, I want to hear it from you. You were there. What happened after the explosion?"

Pleasants shook his head in disgust. "Disaster, pure utter disaster. We could not have fouled it up more if we tried. I am so damned angry I have a hard time talking about it now. Nothing went right. Burnside decided to let the Fourth Division, the Negro division, lead the charge. A good decision. They were fresh and good soldiers. Burnside put our best general, Edward Ferrero, in command of Fourth Division. They trained over a month to lead the assault. The other divisions were supposed to come in after, sweep around the flanks, and drive the Rebs out of Petersburg and maybe end the war. Should have worked."

"Why didn't it work?"

"The day before the attack, Meade ordered Burnside not to use the Fourth as lead division. Burnside appealed to General Grant and was denied so Butcher Grant had a hand in the failure too." Pleasants spat to the side. I thought he would throw down his cigar in disgust. He looked at the cigar and thought better of doing it. Might have if it were shorter.

"Why did they pull the Fourth Division?"

"I don't know this for sure, but I suspect General Grant protected his back side. If the assault went wrong, he didn't want an inquiry board saying the battle was lost because he used nigger troops. It's what's wrong with this war. The generals are more worried about covering their asses when things go wrong than whipping the Rebs. Our men look across to the other side, see how few they are and how poorly they're supplied, and wonder why we can't defeat them. Many of our boys are uneducated and some can't read, but they know they're out here dying for dumb, stupid reasons like the latest fiasco. We worked hard to blow away the main Reb defense and then watched as they cut us down like cattle in what one of our men called the 'horrid pit'. General Burnside will be relieved of command and maybe rightfully so for what he did, but, it was Meade and Grant who ruined the assault. You watch. There'll be no mention of their part in the debacle. They'll simply point out they weren't much for it at the beginning. Of course, if we had succeeded, it would have been their idea."

I wanted to let Pleasants vent, but had to get him back to the story. "What happened after the Fourth Division was pulled out of lead?"

"We have competent generals in the Ninth Corps. Even without training, our boys would've followed General Potter in and I guarantee you we would not have gone in without ladders and ropes to get at the Rebs. But, no, Burnside, for reasons best known to himself, had the division commanders draw straws to take the lead. If there was any doubt we would fail, it was settled when First Division, General James F Ledlie won the honor."

Pleasants did not explain, but, in 9th Corps, Ledlie was a well known drunk, incompetent, and coward.

"Only in the Union Army could he be a general" Pleasants said. "Sure enough, when the attack began, Ledlie wasn't there. I learned he was back in the trenches drinking the surgeon's rum. Just as well. He's not worth a damn as a field commander. Our boys poured into the horrid pit they should have gone around. No way to get at the Rebs who threw everything they had at us. You can't imagine how I felt when we dragged our dead and wounded out of the same pit they worked so hard make."

"Unfortunately, I do understand. But, when we sort out responsibility, your part was brilliant."

Chapter 16: Missy

Morgan Plantation, Brownsburg, Virginia,
September 27-28, 1864
Missy Morgan

It did not begin as the worst day of my life. The Yankees passed through Brownsburg, but did not linger. They pursued our tattered army which took yet another defensive stand somewhere to the southeast. It wasn't that I had lost interest in the war, but I worked from early morning to late night to help maintain the Plantation. I had no time or energy left to worry about anything other than survival.

Most of our slaves left with approach of the Yankee Army earlier in the war. They knew of the Emancipation Proclamation and that they would be free when they entered territory controlled by Union forces. I know they thought my father a good master and I also understood the opportunity to be free of any owner was the dream of nearly every slave. Only a few of the house slaves, including our cook, Sara, and her husband, Jacob, and six families of field slaves stayed on, partially in loyalty to us and partially, I suspect, because they feared the uncertainty of life apart from the Morgan Plantation. Not nearly enough workers to maintain the fields let alone the house. Starting in the spring, we fell back on expanding the vegetable garden and chicken flock and tending the Plantation animals to ensure enough food until the miserable war ended.

I worked with Sara in the kitchen. I did not enjoy kitchen

work, but preparing meals for the remaining slaves and us was more than Sara could do by herself. We started at 4 in the morning to prepare breakfast, served another meal at noon, and supper when the field hands quit work for the day. I had little time for anything except work and sleep, a fresh perspective on the life of a slave.

On that day, which started like so many others since the war began, I awoke before dawn, put on my working dress, and went to Sissy's room. As usual, I found her sound asleep. I shook Sissy to get her moving.

"Leave me alone!" she whined.

I picked up underclothing and a work dress from where Sissy dropped them and tossed them at her. "Maybe it escaped your notice, but the slaves ran off when the Yankees came. There's no one left but us to do the work."

"Why do you have to be so mean?" Sissy pulled a pillow over her head. "You can't expect me to work like a slave."

Acting as the older sibling, which infuriated her, I replied, "Oh yes I can. Get moving. You've got ten minutes before breakfast is ready. After you gather the eggs and feed the chickens, you're to do laundry. I'll help when I'm finished in the kitchen. Now get dressed." I hurried out the door to the kitchen.

Half way down the stairs, I stopped and ran back upstairs to Sissy's room. She was half-dressed, lying across the bed. I yelled, "Get out of bed this instant!" and returned to the kitchen to help Sara prepare breakfast.

As she did the day before and the day before that, Sissy went through the motions of getting dressed and then crawled back under the covers. I deliberately waited until after we served breakfast and cleaned up before going back for her. This time, I stayed with Sissy until she finished dressing and pulled her out the front door to start morning chores.

* * *

Sissy brought the laundry inside for sorting. I joined her in the entertainment room. Around mid-day, without warning, the front door flew open. Three men in blue uniforms burst into our house. Sissy shrieked in horror. I stood frozen and saw other blue-coated men moving through our home and outside. I thought, at best, they were foragers for a Union regiment. At worst, bummers, Union and Confederate deserters, who preyed on civilians in occupied areas of the South.

I pointed toward the smokehouse and said, "There's meat in the back. I'll go with you to the kitchen to remove the food we have in the house. There's nothing more of value for you here."

A Corporal with dirty blond hair and stained teeth grinned and said, "A fine house like this has silverware and we'll take it." Then he leered at me. "I ain't been horizontal with a woman since this here campaign started, least ways nuthin' as purty as you two."

Sissy gasped, clutched at her neck and nearly swooned.

"Why don't you show us where you hid the family jewels 'fore we tear up the house lookin' for 'em?" he suggested.

I'd heard the stories. I knew they were capable of carrying out their threat.

Sissy screamed as the Corporal grabbed her around the waist and pawed her breasts.

"All right!" I shouted. "I'll show you where the silver and jewelry are but you must promise to leave my sister and me alone."

The Corporal told me, "Sure, honey, just show us where the food and valuables are and we'll be off to the next place." He released Sissy who dropped to the floor where she lay sobbing hysterically. I showed him to the kitchen hoping and praying they would be satisfied with stealing from us.

I found Sara looking defiantly at a rifle thrust in her face. A Union Sergeant demanded she bring out all of the food and Sara had refused.

"It's all right, Sara," I said, trying to keep my voice from trembling. "We'll feed these men and give them our food and valuables. They promise to leave and not torch the house and outbuildings."

I said this to test whether the Sergeant knew what had been promised and gauge his reaction. He seemed indifferent but put down his rifle. "We'll clean out the smokehouse. Feed us and turn over what you've got hid and we'll be on our way," he said.

My anxiety eased. The Sergeant seemed more professional and intent on getting his disgusting job done. Maybe it was a foraging party after all.

I asked, "How many of you are there?"

"Eight." Perhaps noting there were no older people around, he asked "Where's the rest of your family?"

"My brother's in the war and my parents went to town. They'll be back this afternoon." They would not return before dark, but I hoped giving the Yankee Sergeant an earlier time might cause them to leave sooner. He did not seem to care. No point in omitting Peter. His photograph, in uniform, appeared in several places in the house.

I said, "With your permission, Sara and I will prepare smoked ham, green beans, and cornbread. It will be ready in about an hour. If you'll excuse me, I'll tend to my sister and return shortly."

"That's fine." The Sergeant said as he glared at Sara.

I went back to the front room and found Sissy curled up in a ball and sobbing softly. I knelt beside her and whispered, "Sissy, we will survive this. You need to be strong. Go back to your room, lock the door, and stay there. Do not come out until the Yankees leave." I watched until she disappeared into her bedroom and heard the latch click.

As we prepared the food, I whispered to Sara, "Make a big meal for everyone. They'll be taking it all anyway, let's fix everything in the pantry. Maybe they'll let us eat too, at least the field hands. It may be the last time any of us eat well for awhile."

Sara looked up and whispered, "You don b'lieve dem lyin' Yankees does you?"

"We have no choice. They'll take everything we have whether we help or not. I hope to save the plantation and us. There's nothing else we can do."

Sara looked at me in disbelief. I sensed her concern for me and her anxiety, but no fear. "Missy, honey, stay away from dem men. Don't trust 'em."

We wanted the Yankees gone. I tried to ignore the filthy, crude bummers who leered at me as I worked, but the look on their faces made my skin crawl. I learned the 23rd Psalm as a child and kept repeating the verse over and over in my head. I dreaded what I feared was coming and silently prayed I would find strength to endure it if I could not avoid it entirely.

* * *

The bummers ate hurriedly and sloppily, grabbing food and then wiping dirty hands on their pants and the tablecloth. One of them farted and the others laughed loudly. They cursed and told dirty stories, I think with the intent to embarrass me. Pigs.

Following the meal, the Sergeant ordered two of the men to the smokehouse to finish cleaning it out. He looked at Sara and said, "We'll take the stores you put in the pantry and the stuff you tried to hide while you thought we wuzn't lookin'."

Sara protested, "You'll leave us wid nuddin' to eat. We'll starve."

"Shut up, nigger." He slapped her across the face and shouted, "You stayed with the white trash when you could've left. You can starve with 'em too. I don't give a damn."

Sara stood defiantly while holding a hand to her cheek. "You got what you came for. Now git!"

He laughed and turned to me. "Show the boys where the valuables is hid and we'll be off to the neighbors."

I moved slowly toward my parents' bedroom. I knew the disgusting Corporal and his two lackeys had more on their minds than taking the family valuables. I took a letter opener from Father's desk and pried up one of the floorboards enough to get a grip. I removed it and the two adjoining boards covering the family silverware, Mother's jewelry, a gold watch, and family rings.

The bummers stuffed the silverware and silver plates into pillowcases they used for bags. They put the jewelry and watch in their pockets. I prayed they were distracted as I edged toward the bedroom door. One of the Privates kicked it shut.

The Corporal looked up and said, "Where you goin', sweet thang?"

I stammered, "Please do as you promised. You have what you came for." From the evil grin on his face, I knew they hadn't.

The Corporal walked toward me. "I don't remember makin' no promises. Do you boys?" They laughed.

"I go first. Which of you wants seconds?" he asked.

My head spun. I would rather die than submit to these animals. But I knew resisting would only get me beaten as well as raped. I screamed, "Get away from me!"

The Corporal threw me onto the bed and ripped off my blouse. "Looka' here, looka' here!" he exclaimed while fondling my breasts. I tried to run away but could not break his grip. I wept as he raised my skirt.

One of the Privates said, "Corporal, this ain't right. I want no part of it."

The Corporal snarled, "Get your chicken ass outa here and stay out. We don't need no mama's boy spoilin' our fun." He left and closed the door behind him.

The Corporal laughed and I cried as he tore off my clothes. I lay on the bed and used my arms to cover my bare breasts. In quick order, the Corporal took off his shirt, dropped his pants and drawers, and jumped on top of me. I felt the weight of his body, closed my eyes, and hoped to die.

He did not bother to take off his boots. He rammed his knee up between my legs to separate them. I felt a sharp pain as if I had been stabbed. He thrust repeatedly. Blood ran down my legs on to the bed sheet.

The Corporal tried to kiss me but I turned my head, one more humiliation I would not tolerate. From the corner of my eye, I saw that the other Private undress and eagerly wait his turn, erection ready. If I could have killed myself right then, I would have.

The Corporal got up and wiped himself on the bed sheet now covered with blood and semen stain as I lay on the bed moaning. My insides were on fire. Even with my pain, I was furious. For an instant, rage overcame pain and humiliation. I swung my arm in an arc and scratched the loathsome Corporal across the face. He pulled back and slapped me hard on the left cheek nearly knocking me unconscious. As he pressed the cover against his bleeding face, he said, "Quite the little wildcat, ain't ya" and moved aside for the Private.

I was nauseous and numb from the blow across my face. No matter. The Private jumped on me instantly. He pinned my arms to the bed and began. I was nearly unconscious as I said a silent prayer for Sissy. The childish Private obviously enjoyed himself and laughed when he finished.

They did not care how badly they had hurt and humiliated me. I pulled the cover up and forced myself to watch the two bummers dress. Apparently, they forgot Sissy and I felt thankful. I knew no decent man would ever want me. But, husband or no husband, if I ever saw either of those pigs again, I would kill him. War or not what they did was unforgivable.

* * *

I heard them go downstairs bragging to the other bummers about their haul and the virgin they deflowered. I sobbed. They took the pillowcases filled with the family silverware, all our food in the house and smokehouse, a wagon and horses from the barn, and left. I have never felt as shamed and helpless as I did then.

From her bedroom, Sissy listened and imagined the worst. I knew she felt guilty for staying in her room as I was raped, but she knew as I did, if she came out, she too would have been raped. When the bummers left, Sissy raced to our parents' bedroom and seemed shocked by what she saw. The bed and sheets were blood-soaked and in disarray. I lay in bed sobbing uncontrollably. I had been violated in the worst possible way. Sissy saw the welt on my face begin to swell and turn red.

She ran to the stairwell and called down. "Sara, come here quickly."

Sara ran up to the bedroom and gasped. She lay down beside me, put her arms around me, and said, "Missy, honey, let it all out. Dey's gone and can't hurt you no mo'."

I cried and worked to let my anger and fear subside. I babbled to Sara and Sissy, "They promised they would leave if I helped.... It hurts, it hurts, I'll die ... Can you ever forgive me? ... They wanted Sissy, I'm glad she escaped ..."

Sissy cried along with me.

Sara said, "I's want to stay wid you 'til yo ma and pa come. But dere's sumtin' weze gotta do and we gotta do it now."

She got up and began gently talking with me. "Missy, honey, youse a strong willed chile. You needs alls de strength youse got. What dem Yankees done wuz evil and wicked. De first ting we do is git de devil seed out'n you. Den we get dem Yankees. I knows where dey camp."

I pulled myself up and nodded.

Sara said, "Wait here, chile, and I's bring what's needed."

Sara left and Sissy came over, sat on the bed, held my hand, and stroked my hair.

When Sara returned, she carried a pail with a tube coming from the bottom. I recognized it and thought it fitting - clean out my insides as my bowels had been cleaned with enemas. Sara had another pail with a mix of warm water, vinegar, and salts slave women used to eliminate the possibility of an unwanted pregnancy.

Sissy and Sara gently escorted me into the water closet attached to our parents' bedroom. I laid down on towels and spread my legs as Sara directed. Sara took a cloth and cleaned me softly and thoroughly. She gently inserted the tube into me and released the cleansing fluid. The tube hurt, but I realized its necessity and was eager to get it done. I did not cry out even though the procedure hurt. I took as much of the fluid as I could, got up, and sat over the chamber pot while Sara and Sissy cleaned the floor.

Sara said, "Empty all's you can, chile. It'll take out de devil seed 'foe it take root."

I looked up and said, "Please bring me a tall glass of cool water. It may take a while. But, make another. I'll do it again. I want no possibility of a bastard from those pigs."

Sissy brought a pitcher of water from the cistern and a glass. I forced myself to drink a full glass. The added pressure helped me void. They repeated the procedure, took me to my bedroom, and slipped me into a nightdress. When I was comfortably in bed, Sara and Sissy got up to let me rest. Before they left, I asked, "Did you say you knew where the Yankees would spend the night?"

Sara replied, "Sissy and Ise gwin' to git yo father. I 'spect dem Yankees'll have company. I wuz nuddin' to dem sose dey talk like I wudn't dere. I heard 'em talk 'bout campin' by de creek on de back side of de south field sose dey could move on de Cawltons in de mawnin'. Ifn no one'll go wid Mistuh William, I'll be dere with a rifle."

"Tell him I'll go with him," I said.

Sissy quickly spoke up, "You've been through hell. Sara and I'll handle things from here."

I persisted, "One of the Yankees does not deserve to die. I'll be needed to identify him. But, more than anything I want to see the two who raped me dead. No matter how much it hurts, I'll be there. Tell Jacob to go out in two hours and make sure the Yankees are camped where you think they'll be. Tell Jacob to be careful, but ask him to find out if they post sentries and where."

* * *

Sissy and Sara took a rickety field wagon, the only conveyance left, and went to Brownsburg to find our parents. They had gone to Lexington to sign a new will and withdraw our money from the bank before the Yankees confiscated accounts. On the way back, they planned to stop in Brownsburg and buy what they could at the general store. Sissy decided to look for them in reverse order starting at the Brownsburg store.

I waited anxiously for their return. I knew my father would stop at nothing to find and punish the bummers. I filled my mind with revenge which helped cover the pain I felt.

I nodded off and heard a knock on the door. Mother came in, dropped to her knees, and sobbed. Father watched for awhile and finally said, "Margaret, compose yourself. Be quiet. I need to speak with Missy."

Mother got up and sat in a chair as Father and I talked. She continued to quietly whimper. I ignored her.

"Sissy and I went to the Vestry Committee meeting at church. We told them what happened. To a man, they will be with me tonight when I track down the bummers."

"Vestry Committee still meeting while the Yankees occupy us?" I asked.

"They're stubborn. Everyone of 'em has a son or nephew in our army. Glad we found 'em before they adjourned."

"How do you plan to catch the bummers?" I sat up and pushed my back against the headboard so I could look at Father while we talked.

He sat down on the edge of the bed and took my hand. "They camped where Sara thought. Jacob says they did not post sentries. We should be able to bag all of them. We will gather around midnight. Ones we don't shoot, we'll hang."

"Father, I want justice. One of the three who came with me to your room refused to go along with the rape." Father squeezed my hand, winced, and looked away to hide his rage. "I will go with you."

"No, Missy, what we will do to those bastards ain't fit for women to see."

"Neither was what they did to me." I snapped back. "If nothing else you'll need me to pick out the innocent man."

Father leaned toward me and stroked my cheek. "You're my little girl. It pains me terrible what happened. Why wasn't I here to protect you? You are most precious to me. I cannot add to your pain."

I looked him directly in the eye. "I am going with you. My pain is not seeing those pigs dead."

He nodded. I think he understood. He would not deny me what I most wanted.

* * *

That night, the Vestry Committee men came in separately. Some brought neighbors also heavily armed and intent on killing the bummers who raided our Plantation. In total, twenty-two men, more than enough to capture eight Yankee bummers. If it had been theft of the food, most would have considered it a consequence of the war going badly for Virginia. But my rape galvanized them. No Yankee would molest a Southern lady and live.

Father asked Jacob to repeat his report to the group. Jacob

said, "Mistuh William, gen'lmen, de Yankees camped where Sara said. It's on Mistuh Mogan's map. I wait 'til dey made camp. No sentries. Ise made sure dey didn' see me."

One of the men, Wade Timmons, a former army officer, commented, "These are freebooters. They don't have soldiers' discipline."

Instead of leaving, Jacob lingered and asked, "Mistuh William, if I might, I wants to 'company you and de gen'lmen."

"Yes. You have a score to settle with them too." Father knew the Yankee Sergeant had slapped Sara.

The capture would be simple. Father took out his map and drew a circle around where the bummer's camped. Each man picked a position on the circle. They agreed to converge on the camp simultaneously at early dawn. Any bummer who resisted arrest would be shot, no questions asked, no quarter given.

Before the assembly, he made a surprising announcement. "Missy will go with us. She asked to see the two who attacked her killed or hanged. I'll not deny her. But, her face is swollen and she's still unsteady on her feet. We've prepared a stretcher and I'd appreciate your help in carryin' her to the camp."

Before they set out, I walked stiffly and unsteadily downstairs supported by Sissy and Mother on each side. Tears came to the eyes of several of the men as I took a seat in the front room.

Reverend Cuthbert sat down beside me, took my hand, and said, "I know vengeance is poor compensation for what you've suffered. Jesus said to forgive our enemies, but there is no jury in the South that would not convict and hang these men. Decent people in the North would do the same. They will be punished."

Cuthbert got up and each man came to me singly and paid respects. Some took my hand and squeezed it. I smiled weakly and thanked each. All the years of prejudice against our family seemed to evaporate that night. I had been violated and these men seemed intent to avenge my honor. I felt overwhelming gratitude to all of them and especially Jacob and my father.

* * *

When the grandfather clock chimed two in the morning, I stretched out on the stretcher and was gently carried out the front door. The men took turns carrying me; men who scarcely noticed me in church earlier. The party moved slowly and carefully by foot so as not to alert the bummers. Two hours later we found their camp and, in another thirty minutes, surrounded them. The men waited patiently.

At daybreak, Father stood up and walked slowly toward the bummers' camp. He carried his shotgun, cocked and loaded. The others converged and closed a circle.

A wagon filled with food and the silverware taken from our Plantation sat beside the camp. Shackled horses stood beside the wagon. Captured chickens cackled, but, other than that, no other sound gave away our approach.

Father found the Sergeant snoring on a cot. The other bummers slept on bedrolls. Their campfire had long since died out. Father grabbed the side of the cot, lifted it, and rolled the Sergeant to the ground. He woke up cursing, but immediately quieted when he saw two shotguns pointed at his head.

The men roused the other bummers. Even in partial light, they knew what was in store for them. Several soiled their pants.

Our vigilantes looked to Father for leadership and he obliged. He ordered the bummers to stand in a line and asked two men to bring me up for a close view. My left eye nearly closed, I got up from the stretcher and walked slowly to Father's side. He asked me, "Which two violated you?"

I did not know their names. I did not want to know their names but remembered their faces too well. Without hesitation, I pointed to the Corporal and Private who raped me. "Him and him." Nothing in my life, aside from marrying and the birth of my children, has given me more pleasure than singling out those two pigs. I would see the bastards die, hours from when they raped me.

Father walked directly toward the Corporal who foolishly became defiant. "You ain't hangin' me. When our soldiers catch you, it'll be you Rebs swingin' on a rope."

The Sergeant interceded. "You understand we are a foraging party from the Union Army. If you release us, the soldiers who raped your daughter will be disciplined when we return."

Father said nothing, but motioned the bummers on each side of the Corporal to move away. He walked back five paces, turned, and raised his shotgun. By now the Corporal had rethought his earlier stand and began pleading, "Hold on now. We meant nothin' by it. If I'd knowed ..."

Father's aim was true. The Corporal's body flew back from the impact of the shotgun blast and slammed to earth. The near headless body lay on the ground bleeding profusely. His legs kicked briefly and then the body lay still. I rejoiced.

Neither Father nor I nor any of the men who came with us blinked. But, two of the bummers became nauseous and threw up.

Father looked harshly at the Sergeant and said, "I heard about your discipline at my home. You've seen ours. Foragers. You're filthy, disgustin' bummers."

The Private who took "seconds" fell on his knees and began pleading. "Please don't kill me. We wuz just havin' fun. I didn't want to do it. The Corporal made me. Most of the girls like it. I didn't know your daughter would be upset. We do it all the time and nothin' like this ever happened."

Father let him ramble, but stopped him at that point and asked, "Who else here has had fun with the girls in the homes you visited?"

Either too frightened or too stupid to know where Father was headed with the question, the Private turned around and pointed to two other Privates. They looked at him in anger and disgust, but did not dare to speak up.

Father appeared calm when he asked me, "Which of these men refused to violate you?" I pointed to another Private and said, "That man." Fortunately, he was not identified as one of the other two Privates who had raped women. I returned to the stretcher but propped my head up to watch with my good eye as Father sorted through the remaining bummers.

He addressed the men who came with us. "This is not a court of law. We came here to obtain justice not vengeance. We have three here who raped Southern women. They're not fit to live." The two Privates implicated earlier began to protest until Father waved his shotgun at them.

Father continued, "We have a Sergeant who either did not know what his men were doin' or did not care. Either way, he swings with 'em." He looked around at the men. Heads nodded and several verbally agreed the Sergeant and three of his Privates would be hanged including the one that earlier raped me who cried uncontrollably.

Father addressed the remaining three bummers. "We are starvin' and you took food from us. It's an evil and mean thing to do. But, this war's mean and evil. We'll turn you over to the nearest Confederate Army. What they do with you, I don't know and don't care. We'll tell them you're bummers, but, to our knowledge, had enough decency to not violate our women when others did."

He turned to the condemned men and said, "You can sit here and wait your punishment or you can help the other three dig your graves. If you help, we have paper and pen you can use to write your kin. We will post the letters, maybe they'll get to your folks. If any of you want to make confession to the Lord before we hang you, Reverend Cuthbert here, will pray with you. But, either way, you'll hang for what you've done."

The Sergeant and two of the condemned Privates took Father's offer and helped dig the graves. The other Private, the one who raped me, sat and whimpered. Sorry gutless, little bastard. I thought I hated the Corporal most until I saw him snivel and plead for his miserable life.

Reverend Cuthbert talked with the other three condemned men. Each repented and asked that Cuthbert pray for his soul which he was pleased to do. They wrote their letters and included mailing addresses.

Father backed the wagon up under a study oak branch. Jacob fashioned nooses on four ropes, threw the nooses over the branch, tied the loose ends to a nearby tree trunk, and evened out the spacing. We stood the condemned bummers along the length of the wagon bed, hands tied behind their backs, nooses fitted over their necks, and the ropes tightened around their necks.

Assured he had everything ready for the hanging, Father looked at the condemned men and asked if there were any final comments. After a pause, the Sergeant spoke up, "It's too late, but I'm sorry for what happened to your daughter and ask your forgiveness."

"It's my daughter from whom you should seek forgiveness," Father told him.

The Sergeant turned to me. I looked at him, saw him slapping Sara, shook my head, and said, "No."

With that, the horses moved forward and the four bummers dropped off the back of the wagon one by one, about two feet, before the ropes became taut. The short fall did not break their necks, so they choked to death. It took over four minutes before the kicking, gurgling, and twitching stopped.

We took down the bodies and buried them in the freshly dug graves. Some of the men rode the bummers' horses. Others sat in the wagon with me on the return trip. The captured bummers walked beside the wagon back to our house where we fed them with the recaptured food.

One of our men thought a Confederate regiment was stationed ten miles to the east. Father took six of the party and the prisoners with him in the wagon and delivered them to the first Confederate officer he found, but they refused to take them. He drove another mile where he found a Colonel who took the prisoners after Father explained what happened.

* * *

Tired and emotionally drained from the past two days, I ate an early supper and went to bed,, hoping for a long, uninterrupted sleep. But I could not drive the terrible memories from my mind. After a few minutes, I heard a soft rap on my bedroom door.

"Come in," I said.

Sissy walked slowly to me, kissed me on the forehead and sat down beside my bed. "I feel terrible about what happened." She paused, took a breath, and continued, "I grew up yesterday and regret it was at your expense."

"No. There's nothing you could have done," I reassured her. "The only good was that they took so much interest in me they forgot about you."

Sissy sobbed. "I know. But, I had to come by to talk with you. You told Sara and me no decent man would ever want you. You're wrong. As bad as things were yesterday and as you think they are, you've earned a good future and you'll have it."

"Thanks, Sis. One of us needs to believe that. But, you may be the only one who really understood what I meant. Jim Cobb will never ask me to marry him." I considered it a certainty and the part of the horrible incident that most depressed me.

Sissy turned my depression around when she said, "You don't know him as well as you think."

"What do you mean?"

"I mean he's a big enough and honorable enough man to

understand you are a courageous young woman who was cruelly victimized."

"Do you really think so?" I desperately wanted to believe her.

"We both know he's the man you are meant to marry."

I stammered, "Hope you're right about him and hope he survives."

Two weeks following my ordeal, Sara handed me a mix of herbs and told me to swallow it with a glass of water. She said, "If somehow our cleanins' missed de devil seed, dis poshun'll take it out." I considered it "insurance" against unwanted pregnancy and readily swallowed the foul tasting brew.

Chapter 17: Fort Delaware

Petersburg, Virginia and Fort Delaware, Pennsylvania,
September 27, 1864 – March 1865
Jim Cobb

General Thomas summoned the Regimental commanders and staff for a brief meeting. We knew what he would say. The Union Army moved relentlessly west. A schoolboy could guess what they would do next and we were powerless to stop them. One by one they cut all lines into Petersburg. The Boydton Plank Road was next.

He told us, "We've been ordered to the Peebles Farm. We can expect the Yankees to attack in a force much larger than we can muster. I don't have to tell you if we lose the road, the Yankees will cut off all supplies to Petersburg and Richmond from the South. General Hill's depending on us. We'll be with the 6th North Carolina. Look for 'em on your right. Position yourselves to protect your flanks and be ready to help out if the next regiment is overrun. The Yankees will try to break off and surround any of us they can." No questions. General Thomas dismissed us but called me back.

"I want you on the far left. We expect the Yankees will use the creek that runs beside your position to hit us hardest. If they take out your regiment, they can roll up the brigade and have a clear shot at the road. Don't let it happen."

I reconnoitered the area earlier and mentally pictured our

deployment. I told General Thomas, "I'll form a tight line and keep two companies ready to counter if they come around us." General Thomas nodded. "Very good, Jim. Good luck."

Peebles Farm outside Petersburg, Virginia,
Friday, September 30, 1864
Jim Cobb

Little left to indicate it was once a farm. The Peebles family sold off their stock and left before the siege. I suspected they knew their farm, like so many in Virginia, would become a battlefield where they would be intruders on their own property.

I took the 78th North Carolina to the far left of our line and passed Colonel Granville Calvert and his regiment on our right. The 16th North Carolina and Granville would be there to support us. We waved in passing. No one I would rather have at my side and, if prior action along the Weldon railway was an indicator, we were in for a fight.

Granville pumped his fist. I caught his meaning. He was pleased to see us on his flank.

We did not wait long. Before I could get my companies placed, the Yankees opened an artillery barrage. From the rear, General Hill returned fire with the few cannon we had left. The artillery duel stopped and the infantry came in force. The battle was on.

Since Gettysburg, since Grant effectively took command of the Army of the Potomac, I noted a difference in the Union troops. Before, they stopped and regrouped when they ran into heavy fire. Now they kept coming.

I knew offensive tactics and what I saw the Union troops doing disheartened me. They concentrated on their right flank with the obvious intent of overrunning my regiment and making an immediate dash to Boydton Plank Road as General Thomas warned. No room to maneuver or take evasive action. We could only hunker down and catch what the Yankees threw at us. Little by little, the regiments separated. I knew what they were doing and was unable to stop it. The Yankees would isolate and overrun us and then roll up the regiments to our right.

Efforts of the 6th North Carolina to reinforce us were repulsed by heavy and concentrated fire. We had no alternative to digging in for the next Union assault. I ordered additional trenches and stationed the companies to repulse flank attacks. The defensive perimeter formed an entrenched 'U'. I knew the brigade was within rifle range and could keep the Yankees from surrounding us and attacking from the back side during the day.

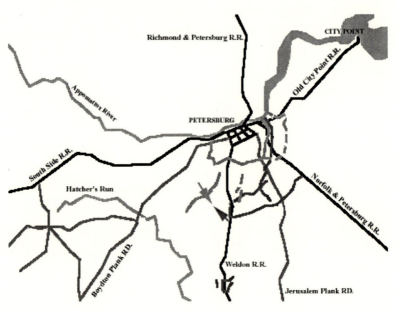

From the heavy fighting on my right, I knew my friend, neighbor, and former senior officer, Colonel Granville Calvert, led the relief force. It was also apparent they ran into the same murderous fire that kept my regiment from linking with them.

I saw the brigade pull back and wondered if Calvert argued to continue the attack. But pulling back was the right thing to do. My regiment was lost. Nothing could be gained in sacrificing more of the brigade to rescue us. The counterattack broke off at nightfall.

* * *

As I walked around the defensive perimeter, turning over possible plans of attack in my mind, I found Andy talking with the sentries. I motioned him over to where we could talk privately. "Andy, I've got something I need to discuss."

"What is it?" he asked.

"Around two in the morning, when it's darkest, we'll send the men out behind the hedges to the 16th North Carolina. If they stay low and keep quiet, the Yankees won't see them. We'll gradually collapse out through to the brigade. I'll leave last. We'll reform over the rise down the creek."

Andy shook his head. "Like the Captain on a sinking ship? Good thought, but it won't work." I started to defend my idea, but Andy continued, "You may have noticed there's a near full moon out. The Yankees wait for us to try somethin' like what you suggest."

I wanted to argue but Andy stopped me and said, "Watch. I'll demonstrate."

He removed the ramrod from his Enfield rifle and put his cap on the end. He crawled to the bulwark and lifted the cap just above the top rung. Pop, pop, pop and the cap flew to the ground with a bullet hole across the top.

Andy picked up the cap. "Damn. I won't have anything to wear at review. But you get the idea. Yankee sharpshooters are waiting for us to come out."

I dug my toe in the dirt. Andy was right. "Let me ask you something else and this is your friend and fellow Ranger asking. Is honor worth dying here at the Peebles Farm when we both know the war's lost?"

Andy offered an alternative. "We can just retreat when the Yankees attack."

"No, they'll attack across the line. It's what they want."

I needed a plan and nothing came to mind. "Our leaving opens the left flank to the Yankees. Pour in enough troops and they capture the whole brigade. It's the one thing we can't do. We have to at least stall them and give the brigade time to fall back, tighten the line, and fill our place."

Andy put a hand on my shoulder and said, "Sorry, I can't be more help. It's a tough decision. Whatever you decide, we'll follow. But, speaking personally, I'd rather live than die. Even if it's Yankee prison."

I stayed up through the night and finally decided the only honorable option was to simply dig in and fight as hard and long as possible when they attacked. I thought back to how Ken Johnson must have felt before Cold Harbor. It was now my turn. Good chance we would all be killed. So much for God's plan for me.

Peebles Farm outside Petersburg, Virginia,
Saturday, October 1, 1864
Jim Cobb

At daybreak, as if an answer to an unstated prayer, a Union Lieutenant, carrying a white flag, approached and called out for the Confederate commander. I felt relieved. The Yankees would offer surrender before attacking. The regiment's situation was untenable. I knew it and they knew it. We had no hope of relief and no possibility of breaking through the Union forces that now surrounded us.

The brigade had pulled back during the night. By repulsing the Union attack, we had prevented roll up and capture of the brigade, my old brigade, the 6th North Carolina. I felt good about that if not about the hopeless position of my regiment.

As he approached, I noted the Union lieutenant was about my age. I went out to meet him.

"I am Major Jim Cobb, 78th North Carolina Regiment."

The Union Lieutenant rendered a smart salute. "I am Lieutenant Robert Jordan, Aide to Colonel Philip Skidmore, 60th Ohio. The Colonel invites you to a parley and ordered me to accompany you. We will be under white flag."

I stepped out and followed Lieutenant Jordan through the skirmish line to a group of Union officers standing outside of rifle range. I saw loathing in the eyes of the soldiers we passed. One of them spat tobacco juice on my boots as I walked by. Another made a show of coming after me until Lieutenant Jordan stopped him and put him on report. Thereafter, I looked straight ahead and did not make eye contact with any more of them.

Jordan seemed calm and professional in carrying out his duties. He wore a spotless, pressed uniform, something we never saw in a combat area. He spoke in a clipped, precise manner suggesting he might have been a college student or graduate before going to war. But, whatever his past, he had a much brighter future than the regiment and I.

I stopped in front of a group of Yankee officers with Colonel Skidmore standing in the middle. He gave me a cursory salute, which I returned. Skidmore was more what I expected. He wore a crumpled, dirty blue uniform, had a thick reddish beard streaked with tobacco stains, and looked to be a tough, battle-hardened field commander. Foregoing polite opening small talk, he curtly asked, "Prepared to surrender your regiment, Major?"

"What are your terms?" I asked.

"No terms. Unconditional surrender."

I wanted to string out the parley as long as possible and decided to test the Colonel. "We both know my situation's hopeless, but I'll point out two facts. First, we have enough supplies to last us a week." I hoped he believed the lie. "Second, as you can see, we're firmly entrenched including the back side during the night. Begging the Colonel's pardon, but, many more of your men than mine will go down if you attack us."

Skidmore spat tobacco juice to the side and said, "I don't need to attack you. We have enough cannon to stand back and blow your regiment to hell."

I knew the Colonel could carry out his threat. I counted four field pieces in the artillery battery behind Union lines. I put on my best poker face and countered, "We've faced worse and survived. Tying up cannon to blast us will slow you down from chasing the rest of our army, capturing General Lee…." I stopped and acted nervous, like I had said something I shouldn't.

Colonel Skidmore took the bait. "General Lee? Is he behind your lines?"

I quickly answered, "No, I meant General Hill. He's always out front with the troops."

"Well, how about it? Will you fight us and die or surrender?" Colonel Skidmore glared at me with an obvious intent to intimidate. "One way or the other, we'll destroy you and your regiment if you resist."

I also lied about taking worse shelling than the Colonel threatened to inflict, but I knew by a brief tic on his face that I touched a sore spot with the second point. I guessed he was under orders to vigorously pursue our retreating troops. I bravely and, as it turned out, foolishly responded, "Our men might prefer a quick end here than starvation, disease, and a slow death in Yankee prison."

Colonel Skidmore exploded, "Damn you and the whole goddamn Confederacy. You have my terms. If you want to fight, we'll oblige you."

After watching him react, I calmly requested, "Colonel, I'd appreciate a thirty minute cessation to speak to the regiment."

Skidmore calmed down and agreed.

As we walked back, Lieutenant Jordan said, "Major, there are some things you need to know. Colonel Skidmore's younger brother was captured by your army outside of Chattanooga and sent to one of your prisons. He died there as did many of our boys. Photographs and survivors are coming back from your camps. Don't expect sympathy from the Colonel for you or your men. Our prisons are bad, but they're better and more humane than yours." Unfortunately, he spoke the truth, but, nevertheless, I knew it would be horrible for us in Yankee prison.

With a heavy heart I returned to my regiment. I told Lieutenant Tuttle, "We have a thirty minute truce. Gather the regiment." As the officers and men assembled around me, I saw a tired, sullen, but proud look in their eyes. I knew what I must do and knew it would be difficult.

I spoke slowly and plainly, "I fear we've come to the end of the line. Our situation's hopeless. The Yankees have us outnumbered and cut off. Our choices are simple – stand and fight and likely die here or surrender and spend the rest of the war in Yankee prison. All our lives depend on this decision. What are your thoughts? At this point, I am not concerned with rank." I figured it would go better with the men if I discussed surrender with them rather than simply capitulating to Colonel Skidmore's demand.

A long and awkward silence followed. Finally, Andy spoke. "Major Cobb, you've gotten us out of tight places before. We've served too long under your command to question your choice. Whatever you decide, we'll follow."

I looked out over the regiment and asked, "Is that what the rest of you think?"

Heads nodded. I turned slowly to walk back to the Union lines and heard one soldier mutter, "Fine time to turn yeller now." I ignored the comment, but understood how the soldier felt. Once more I was indebted to my friend, Andy Blaylock. He had made the surrender easier.

I called for Tuttle and ordered, "Get over to Colonel Calvert. Tell him we will surrender. Stay with the 16th North Carolina. You've done your duty and been a good aide. Thank you." I looked away as Jeremy broke down and cried. He did not want to leave the regiment. A brave and loyal young man, but I knew he would not survive Yankee prison.

I waved a white cloth and motioned for Lieutenant Jordan to come out. I told him, "Please ask the Colonel for another thirty minutes. The men are still discussing surrender."

Jordan went back, gave Colonel Skidmore my message, came back, and announced, "Colonel is not pleased with the delay, but grants your request for thirty more minutes."

I went back to camp, told the men to look like they were talking to one another, and spoke with my adjutant, Captain Boggs. I told him what I was doing and he laughed. "More we stall, the more time our boys have to reform and trench."

After thirty minutes, I went back and gave Jordan a similar story. But this time Colonel Skidmore came back with his aide. I expected a chewing out and got it. "God damn you. What kind of army do you Rebs run? You give me an answer now or I order an immediate attack."

I acted offended, but gave Skidmore the answer he wanted. He stomped off and I discussed surrender details with Lieutenant Jordan. I returned and gave the order and told them to drag out the surrender.

They came out from protected positions and slowly laid down their rifles, side arms, and regimental and company standards in an orderly pile. Their uniforms were in tatters. They were gaunt and dirty. But, to a man, each held his head high. I felt proud of them, magnificent even in surrender. Unlike me, they glared back at and jawed with the Yankee soldiers who gathered to watch the surrender.

Colonel Skidmore ordered out two companies to escort us to a holding area behind Union lines. I noted, when the Union regiment pulled out, that we outnumbered the Yankee troops guarding us. But I did not surrender to have our men fight armed Yankees barehanded.

Union soldiers herded our regiment into a guarded pen. We found a few stragglers from the Brigade, but the "big haul" was our regiment. In a counterattack during the Weldon Railway encounters, Third Corps took over two thousand Union prisoners. At the time, I wondered how they felt. Now I knew.

* * *

In late afternoon, Lieutenant Jordan ordered me removed from the holding area so we could talk privately. He said, "Colonel Skidmore requests the pleasure of your company at supper tonight. He would like to talk with you more."

We both smiled, knowing why Skidmore extended the invitation. I replied, "Inform the Colonel I am pleased to accept his invitation after my men are provided extra rations and blankets for our trip north."

"Thank you, Major Cobb. I will relay your message to the Colonel." We exchanged salutes. Jordan rode off to find Colonel Skidmore and I returned to the holding area.

An hour later, a supply wagon loaded with rations and blankets arrived. The driver called down to the guards, "This here's for the Rebs. I'm to take the Reb Major back with me."

The guards unloaded the wagon. I put Captain Boggs in charge of distribution and sat next to the driver on the ride back to Union camp. Two Privates sat in back to guard me and mostly horse played with each other.

Lieutenant Jordan escorted me to Colonel Skidmore's tent where I found the Colonel and another officer, Major Martin, waiting. I had never seen a more decorated tent, not even tents of Corps Commanders in our army or General Lee's tent. Formal dining table, chairs, rug, I was amazed. Orderlies brought in a fine meal of roast, scalloped potatoes, and green beans served on porcelain plates with silverware and napkins. Colonel Skidmore poured red wine for everyone starting with the guest of honor, me.

I thoroughly enjoyed the fine meal knowing it would be my last for a long time and ate heartily. Turned out, Lieutenant Jordan was a recent graduate of Oberlin College. His father was bank president in Gallipolis, Ohio where the 60th Ohio mustered out for service in the Shenandoah Campaign. Major Martin was what I assumed – Ninth Corps Chief of Staff. If Ninth Corps had a spymaster it would be Martin and I knew why he was with us.

From when I first saw Skidmore, I thought I had seen him before but could not come up with when and where. Skidmore looked at me during the meal and I sensed he studied me for the same reason. Finally, Skidmore smiled in an "I've got it" moment. "Major Cobb, you served on General Hill's staff at Harper's Ferry."

I nodded, "Yes, sir, I did", but it still did not come to me.

"Two years ago, I was your prisoner." Skidmore grinned. He obviously enjoyed the role reversal.

I thought, that's it. "You were with the Union Army we captured at Harper's Ferry right before Sharpsburg. I remember vaguely. Sorry, sir, but there were a lot of you at the time. Didn't you promise not to take up arms against the Confederacy? If I remember, it was a condition for your parole."

Skidmore turned red as if ready to explode. I watched as he settled down to his earlier calm. I enjoyed his discomfort.

After swapping stories of our careers since the earlier meeting, Skidmore passed around cigars and poured me a drink of Kentucky bourbon. He leaned forward, gracious as he was gruff earlier, and said, "Major Cobb, you are obviously an intelligent man. You know as well as we the South cannot win this war, but many more lives, yours and ours, will be lost before you're defeated. You have an opportunity to do a major service to both armies. You can effectively end the war now."

I feigned surprise. Skidmore continued, "General Lee is the heart and soul of the Army of Northern Virginia. If he were captured, your army would quickly surrender. Do you agree?"

I innocently asked, "Yes, Sir. But what has that to do with me?"

Skidmore's face lit up. "I talked with Major Martin earlier. We can put together a strike force, dress them in captured Confederate uniforms, and seize General Lee. But, we need someone to lead the strike force. Someone familiar who will not alert the men around General Lee."

"You need me to find General Lee and help get the strike force in close enough to capture him."

"Exactly."

As if pondering Skidmore's offer, I took a long sip of bourbon, puffed my cigar, and leaned back. All eyes were on me as I replied, "Two flaws in your plan, Colonel. First, I don't know where to find General Lee. Second, I would not betray him if I did know."

Skidmore's expression quickly turned to anger. "You lying son-of-a-bitch. I heard you. Lieutenant Jordan heard you say 'capture Lee'."

I nodded. "And I quickly corrected myself and said 'Hill'. I am not leading any disguised Yankees to capture General Hill either."

Skidmore jumped to his feet. He yelled at Jordan, "Get him out of here. Get him out of my sight."

I calmly stood up, bowed to Skidmore and Major Martin, and said, "Gentlemen, thank you for a most gracious meal and stimulating conversation. But, if you will excuse me, I must rejoin my men at the accommodations you graciously provided us." Skidmore fumed, but I saw the flicker of a smile on Martin's face. I followed Jordan out of the tent toward the wagon.

Out of earshot from the tent and before we reached the wagon, Jordan burst out laughing. "Major, congratulations, you really made a fool of the Colonel."

I chuckled. "Was it that obvious?"

"To me and Major Martin, but not to Colonel Skidmore. Before you got there, he worked an hour trying to convince Martin you would go along with his crazy scheme. Damned if you didn't get blankets and extra rations for your regiment and a fine meal for yourself."

"He's hot tempered, but I suspect he's a good field officer for you," I observed. Skidmore seemed like some of our better field commanders. Headstrong, full of himself, but put him on an objective and he would get it done.

Jordan agreed. "He is, but an outsized self-opinion you won't believe. He had himself President of the United States or at least General of the Army. The man who captured General Lee." Jordan started laughing again.

* * *

Next day, Union soldiers marched us to a train on a newly con-structed spur and locked us in boxcars for an uncomfortable ride to Pennsylvania. The train stopped twice and surly guards opened each boxcar separately. Our men, under guard, were allowed to relieve themselves in the woods and handed rations as they re-turned to the boxcars. I ordered them not to, but several boys could not hold on and pissed on the boxcar sides. Soon the whole boxcar smelled like an outhouse. We sat on straw. I suspected the same boxcars carried cattle earlier. Based on how we were transported, my low expectations of Union prison dimmed.

I considered making an escape, but quickly discarded the idea. As the senior officer, I needed to stay with the men.

Finally the train stopped, the side doors opened, and I, along with one third of the prisoners, jumped down and marched about a mile to Fort Delaware near Wilmington, Delaware and forty miles south of Philadelphia.

As the departing prisoners assembled, I made a quick survey. Captain Boggs remained with the train and I was pleased. The regimental officers would need a leader in prison and Boggs, my adjutant, was a good one. For the men, Andy came with us to Fort Delaware.

The train took the remaining prisoners to Union prisons farther north for the duration of the war. Before leaving the train, I gathered the remaining company commanders together and told them, "Take care of the men. The Yankees will likely separate us, but tend to the weakest as best you can. The Yankees don't care if we live or die. We must look after our own. Our responsibility is down to a single issue – survival. We must save as many of our own as we can." At about the same time, Andy had a similar talk with the regimental sergeants.

Fort Delaware, Pennsylvania,
Tuesday, October 4, 1864
Jim Cobb

On arrival at Fort Delaware, the guards examined each prisoner and confiscated every possession brought in – money, Bibles, photographs, clothing, toiletries, and the blankets and extra rations we got before leaving.

First week, the new prisoners assembled in the yard for an address by the camp commandant. He spoke with a thick accent. Many of our officers did not understand most of what he said. Schoepf advised us to make our stay pleasanter by cooperating. He seemed gracious, but, at the same time pompous and insecure.

If anything, Yankee prison was worse than we had imagined. Located on Pea Patch Island in the middle of the Delaware

River, Fort Delaware was already crowded before we arrived. The Yankees housed prisoners in crudely constructed, fence-enclosed barracks in an eight acre compound about five hundred yards northwest of the fort. A double line of plank fences divided the compound into two camps – one for the officers and one for the enlisted men. A parapet for the guards sat atop the fence. Schoepf allowed no communication between the two camps which added to our isolation and misery. Andy and I could not see or communicate with each other.

Each camp held ten rows of barracks divided into divisions under one roof. A division was nineteen by sixty feet and had a narrow passage between three tiered bunks on either side and housed from four hundred to nine hundred men. We were allowed one blanket or one overcoat, not both.

Following reports of conditions in Confederate prisons, Union prison bureaucracy determined the amount of food necessary to sustain life and made sure no Confederate prisoner got more. Fresh food could only be purchased from sellers in the prison and a few outside Southern sympathizers. Since the guards took all our money coming in, we had nothing to buy fresh food except what came by mail which occasionally escaped confiscation.

Rain barrels caught run off water from the roof. When it rained, we had fresh water. When it did not rain, we drank putrid water, swarming with wiggletails and white worms, from the Delaware River. We ate small portions of barely tolerable barley bread, hard crackers, and miscellaneous meat scraps. Occasionally, the Yankees "treated" us to a thin, tasteless corn soup.

Malnutrition was our common lot, all the more cruel because we saw abundant crops growing in the fields around Fort Delaware. Prisoners sent out on work details pilfered produce and brought it back under their shirts – brief and appreciated supplement to prison rations. However, as officers, we did not have the lowly field work or opportunity to steal produce.

I shared a small area of the division with seven other officers. Blankets became scarce so prisoners doubled up on cold nights to preserve body heat. I had never slept that close to anyone before or after, until I married when I found I much preferred closeness of the scented female body.

I considered the guards loathsome for reasons that were part circumstantial and part deliberate Union policy. In Confederate prisons, I heard the guards were old men and youngsters, unfit to serve in the army because of age. The Union guards did not serve in the army because they were morons, slackers, incompetents, and otherwise unfit for combat duty. Regular Union soldiers looked down on them for good reason. The guards, in turn, took out their resentment on the prisoners, particularly enemy officers, in petty and cruel ways.

Albin F Schoepf, the Hungarian émigré and one of the Union's socialist generals, commanded Fort Delaware. Caught up with fear of conspiracies and escapes, he organized flying squads of guards to conduct random raids in the prison compound. It was also an opportunity to confiscate anything they had not earlier taken. Schoepf even planted spies to discover emerging conspiracies. They were easily detected and shunned.

* * *

As officers and gentlemen, my group decided we could best use our time in prison by improving our minds. We took turns teaching in areas where each had expertise. Surprisingly, despite the grim circumstances, I learned much useful information, especially from James McCracken, a Lieutenant Colonel from Georgia, who had been a practicing attorney before entering the army. For my turn, I taught sawmill and gristmill operations, a welcome diversion. Thinking about the mills took my mind off the daily misery, hunger, and tedium of prison.

In my youth, I particularly enjoyed working in the mills. Our gristmill was built by my great-grandfather, Benjamin Cobb, in 1783. He constructed a three story wooden building for receiving, storing, and grinding the grain. He put in two-foot square foundations that he hewed with a broad ax. The mill had mortised beams pinned with hard wooden pegs. Square nails held the whip sawed lumber walls to the frame – a primitive structure, but solidly built. It showed little deterioration by the time I came along to delight in its internal workings.

Benjamin Cobb took justifiable pride in the large grinding stones formed in a New Hampshire quarry and shipped down the Appalachian Trail to the mill. Each stone weighed 1,400 pounds and, over time, became worn smooth. Our gristmill produced the finest flour, corn meal, and barley meal in the Western Carolinas.

My grandfather, Elisha Cobb, added the sawmill in 1797. It was also a wooden frame structure built with mortised beams, wooden pegs, and square nails. Both mills used overshot water-wheels for power. He attached a cam to the wheel shaft in the saw mill to create the up and down motion of the reciprocal saw.

The mills provided ground meal and lumber for the farm. Over time, neighbors brought grain and logs to our mills for processing which we performed for a fee. One of my tasks, as a youngster, was sharpening the saw blades with a whetstone.

Cobb Farm slaves operated the mills. In thinking back on what they taught me, I became even more impressed. Thanks to my mother, their children were literate and knew sums, but not the slaves who taught me mill operations. But somehow they could accurately draw and explain inner workings of the mills to their eager young pupil.

I took great pride and pleasure in describing the family mills and then explaining how they operated to my sometimes bored audience of fellow officers. It occurred to me, as I prepared the talks, that the mill operations were the part of the Cobb Farm

I most enjoyed, maybe the direction for my career if I survived Yankee prison.

Disease ravaged Fort Delaware, but my group was spared for most of our stay. Captain Virgil Grimes, 4th Alabama, had studied medicine and insisted we keep the area as clean as possible. His sister sent soap, one of the few amenities to reach our group. We joked that the guards did not steal the soap because they also tired of the stench. Not funny and probably true.

* * *

We learned to go barefoot and roll up our pant legs when we went out for occasional walks on the muck and swill that passed for the prison yard. Guards kept careful eye on us and amused themselves by taking shots at those who came close to the edges of the yard, the dead line. Sometimes they "accidentally" hit a prisoner.

While visiting on the courtyard, I met another interesting group – political prisoners. During the war, the Union government suspended rules of habeas corpus. Any individual suspected of treasonous behavior could be imprisoned and held without indictment. Their treatment was relatively better, but still terrible.

I saw a civilian prisoner sitting alone, an older man. He wore a heavy wool overcoat that none of the Confederate prisoners had and smoked a pipe. I thought he seemed lonely as he blankly looked over the dreary expanse of the yard. I approached him to strike up a conversation.

"Hello, Sir," I said, holding out my hand. "I'm Jim Cobb from Newton, North Carolina."

"Julius Snyder," he replied as he shook my hand.

"I notice you're dressed differently from us and probably not a Confederate. Pardon my asking, but how did you come to enjoy the pleasures of Fort Delaware?"

As intended, it brought a smile. "My story will probably amuse you and the other Rebs. I'm a county judge from Chambersburg, Pennsylvania."

"You're right. I thought judges sent others to prison, not themselves."

"I did too. In early July, the sheriff brought in two local men for trial as deserters. I threw out the case because there was no proof they had sworn into the army and, if there was, the proper jurisdiction was an army court. I thought nothing more of it until the next week when an Army detachment came into court, arrested, handcuffed, and marched me off to a military camp. I ended up here with you Rebs. No trial, no hearing, just prison until the war is over."

I was puzzled. "Seems odd. Were you somehow involved in promoting the Confederate cause?"

"No." Snyder shook his head. "Copperhead sentiment in the county, but I wasn't part of it. I'm a Democrat and have political enemies in state government and apparently in the Army. They wanted to make a high profile arrest and use me as an example. They even alerted the newspaper to send over a reporter."

I offered to introduce Judge Snyder to other officers, but he declined. No longer a fervent Union supporter, he was not a Confederate sympathizer either.

During one of our gatherings on the yard, I came across a young Lieutenant, Sydney Ross, from the 9th Virginia Regiment of Garnett's Brigade in Pickett's Division. He was captured at Gettysburg and taken to Fort Delaware over fifteen months earlier. In a sense, he was fortunate. I saw the charge to the stone fence. Nearly all of his regiment went down in the battle that decided the war. Sydney explained that a Union soldier clubbed him on the head and left him for dead. He awoke as a prisoner.

As he talked about his home and family, I realized he was the son of Major Ross and brother of Carolyn Jamison. In turn, Sydney Ross seemed pleased to learn I had met his father and sister. He liked talking with someone who knew his family and had visited in his home. I liked the young lieutenant, but had other motives in cultivating him as a friend.

As often as we came together, I made a point to seek out Sydney Ross for conversation. We exchanged addresses and agreed to meet after the war. I began to think of the beautiful Carolyn Jamison and let my mind drift back to the soft kiss she gave me on my departure from the Ross home. Maybe, after the war, her mourning would pass and there would be opportunity to court her. These were some of the few pleasant thoughts I carefully nursed during captivity.

Chapter 18: Christmas 1864

Fort Delaware, Pennsylvania,
Sunday, December 25, 1864
From my diary

Another cold, miserable, forgettable night. Captain Dowd has not mastered the art of spooning. Understandable. He is the new man. Took the place of Captain Grisham who died mid-month. Grisham could turn and roll with the group, but it is something you do without thinking. At first, the rolling of the men on each side wakes you, interrupts your sleep and, after you doze off, it starts again when they roll the other way. That is Dowd and, to make it worse, his body odor is particularly bad and he snores. He will lose weight eating prison slop, snore less, and start smelling like the rest of us. Then someone else will die and we will start over with a new man.

Christmas celebrates the birth of the Christ child and the promise of salvation from a wicked and despoiled earth. A time of hope and joy in prospect of better times to come. Not this Christmas, only misery to come. Even dodging Yankee bullets is better than eating their putrid food, drinking the foul water, and waiting for a disease that makes you vomit your guts out as you die. It is terrible when your best hope is defeat, surrender, and leaving Fort Delaware alive.

A woman would be nice, not that I know for sure. But sleeping with a soft, clean, perfumed woman has to be better than spooning with dirty, smelly men. But, it is that or freezing to death. We don't have near enough blankets to keep us warm. Come spring, we can get back to the rickety, bug ridden bunk beds.

Little to distinguish today from any other day since we came here. We wanted to swap gifts, but hard to swap when no one has anything. I would gladly give away some of the Yankee dollars I took riding with Mosby, but the cretin guards took everything. If I ever see any of the sons of bitches after the war, I will shoot them on sight. Not a worthy thought for Christmas day.

Today is cold and wet, but I will take off my shoes and wade around in the yard until my feet freeze. At least outside I can see the sky and life outside prison. It is a world I hope someday to rejoin.

I try not to think about women, but it is impossible. At the most improbable times, thoughts of Sissy or Carolyn Jamison or Karen Young pop into mind. I should have better control of my thoughts, but I don't. Sissy is gone and I can see now that she and I do not belong together, never did. I pity the man she marries and finds he married her mother. Still her kiss when I went off to war lingers. A reminder that emotion rules reason. Never was any romance with Carolyn Jamison or Karen Young except in my fantasy, but still nice to think of them.

* * *

I put on my boots to go out on the yard hoping, maybe, the ground was firm enough they wouldn't stick in the ooze. Too cold to stay out without covering my feet. Had to do something to ease the funk of Christmas in Fort Delaware.

I needed conversation and looked around for someone to talk to, someone who might brighten my spirit, and saw Syd Ross standing off by himself. Talking with Syd brought back memories of his sister and that would be pleasant.

I approached and greeted him. "Merry Christmas, Syd. Mind if I join you?"

Syd looked up and smiled. "Hi, Jim. Glad you came along. I'm standing here feeling sorry for myself."

I rubbed my hands together and stamped my feet to warm

myself. "Easy to do. I've been here three months and am sick of it. You've been here since Gettysburg. It has to be worse for you."

"Yeah, but what can I do? Self-pity doesn't help much."

I heard what Syd said, but sensed he had something more on his mind. "Afraid I'm not much help either, but sometimes sharing misery lightens the load."

Syd nodded.

"Anything in particular troubling you?" I asked.

Syd bit his lip and answered, "Hard not to think about home."

"From what I saw and heard, you have a wonderful home and family. Does thinking about not being there make you particularly sad?"

Syd lowered his eyes and muttered, "There's more to it than that."

Not wanting to intrude, I looked off to the farmhouses beyond the barricade and saw what I thought might be merrymaking. Farm families coming together to celebrate Christmas like Mother, Oliver, and the Negroes were doing at the Cobb Farm. After a few minutes, I became uncomfortable, but sensed Syd wanted to say more and had difficulty doing it.

Finally he said, "Jim, I'll tell you something I've never told anyone." He added in a half-whisper, "I'm a bastard. It's my family and then it's not. I feel empty when I think of them."

Startled, I told him, "This is crazy. I talked with your father and sister. Neither described you as anything but son and brother. You are a Ross and those good people are your family."

Syd shook his head. "No, the Major's not my father and Carolyn's my half-sister."

It occurred to me that Syd was very young, maybe eighteen or nineteen, maybe conceived while Major Ross was with the army in Mexico. I had not thought about it before, but he favored Carolyn much more than the Major. Syd was thin bordering on frail and pale. I remembered Albert Ross as short, stout, and swarthy. Nevertheless, I asked, "Why do you think you're a bastard?"

"When I was ten years old, I got into a fight with my older brother and he blurted it out. My mother died when I was an infant so I went crying to my father. He was furious when I told him what Todd said. He calmed down and told the whole story in terms a ten year old could understand. He pulled me over to him, put his arms around me, and said, 'Forget what you heard today. You are my son and that will not change.' But, I never forgot what Todd said and that I'm a bastard."

I started thinking and acting like an older brother and not a senior officer. What could I say to Syd to ease his hurt? I started with factual observations. "You talk as if you're ashamed. You did not pick your parents. You had no responsibility for your birth."

Syd shuffled his feet. Maybe it was the cold, but more likely nervousness. "I know, but it doesn't change the fact that I'm a bastard."

I took a different tack and told him, "It's Christmas, the day we celebrate the birth of Jesus Christ, son of God, savior of the world. Did you ever stop to think about the details of His birth?"

"What do you mean?" Syd asked.

Recalling what I learned in Sunday school lessons, I replied, "Jesus was born to a woman who conceived him before she married. He, too, was a bastard in the same sense you say you are. But, like you, he had a mother who loved him and a father who treated him as a son. From all we read they were a strong, loving family and baby Jesus went on to do great and wondrous things to the glory of God."

"So, being a bastard makes me like Jesus?"

"No, but it sure doesn't stop you from being his follower. We both know bastards in the figurative sense who'll have difficulty explaining themselves to Jesus. But, not my friend, Syd Ross."

I doubted my words helped much, but hoped they would. Syd was a fine young man deserving a good future without carrying a burden that was not his.

Syd said, "Still, don't repeat what I told you."

"Your secret's safe, but hold your head up. Once we get out of here, you've got a good life waiting."

"Let's hope we walk out."

In the background, we heard a surprising and pleasant sound – Christmas carols played by a band the Commandant brought in to impress visiting dignitaries. It had a startling effect on the prisoners standing in the yard. First silence, then several began to openly cry, no doubt thinking back to happier times. Syd's expression changed probably more from the music than my attempt to bolster his spirits.

My thoughts went across to the soldier's prison. Andy and the soldiers of the 78th North Carolina Regiment heard the same beautiful music. It was a link by which I mentally reached out to each of them with a "Merry Christmas" for their well being. And then I heard singing, the soldiers sang the melodies of the music the band played. Then the officers on the yard joined in so that the whole of Fort Delaware became alive with Christmas carols. The singing was off key and delayed, but nevertheless unified all the prisoners in songs of hope and praise.

* * *

My spirits rose with feelings of goodwill, extending even to the pompous Hungarian who provided the band. As I became caught up in the singing and spiritual fellowship, I heard a familiar voice call from behind me, "Mistuh, Jim. It's me, Scipio. I's got a message fo' you suh."

I spun around and, sure enough, it was the Morgan family footman standing behind me with a wide grin on his face. I grabbed Scipio's hand with both of mine and shook it. "What in the world are you doing here?"

"I's tendin' Mistuh Petah. The Yankees dun caught him and sent him heah. He's still bad hurt and needs me."

"Scipio, you're a free man in Pennsylvania. You don't have to be here."

"I nose, but he needs me and dere's uttah officahs needs tendin'."

"You mean you followed Pete into this hellhole to look after him?"

"Yassuh."

"Could you take me to him?"

"Yassuh, but 'fo we go, I's got a lettah from Miss Missy. She learnt you'se heah an askt me to bring her lettah wid me."

Scipio reached into his shirt and pulled out a crumpled enveloped letter. Probably hid it in his shoe to get it past the guards. I smiled, took the envelope, and opened it. It read

Dearest Jim,

I know my first prayer is answered in your reading this. You are alive. You talked about dying when we were together last and your safety has been on my mind since.

I met an officer from the Light Division who told me what happened to you and your regiment at Petersburg. He was badly wounded and home probably for the remainder of the war. He spoke highly of you and the courage of your regiment in holding off the Union Army as the Brigade pulled back. I know it is terrible for you in prison and, as I am sure Scipio told you, Pete has come to join you and the others at Fort Delaware. I pray for all of you.

Please, Jim, when you are released, come see me before you go home. There are things I must tell you. Until then, please keep the promise you made when we last talked. Stay alive.

Your loving friend,

Missy

I put down the letter and noticed Scipio watching me.

"Very nice of Missy to think of me and write this letter. She was always a good friend."

"Pahdon, Mistuh Jim", Scipio said, "she mo' n dat. She loves you and needs you wid her."

I was puzzled. "I could always talk with Missy and enjoyed being with her, but she's just a girl, Pete's kid sister."

"No, suh. She's grow'd and a fine lady. She needs you."

"Needs me? Missy's a pretty and smart girl. She'll have her pick of the young men left after the war."

"Yassuh, but she gotta leave home. She needs you."

"Scipio, there's something you're not telling me. What is it?"

"Yassuh." Scipio looked down and shuffled his feet. "Miss Missy wuz tack't by Yankee bummers. Mos' shameful ting de Yankees dun in de wah. Cap'n caught 'em and hung 'em. But dere's no goin' back on whas dun. Miss Missy tole Sara you de only man she knows who'd look past what happen and take her away sose de talk won' hurt her."

I was stunned. The thought of Missy raped sickened me. Bad enough our men fought and died in miserable conditions, but thinking of our women violated tore my insides. Especially, raping my sweet, innocent, intelligent little sister. I was pleased Captain Morgan tracked down the bummers so Pete and I would not have to do it after the war. I promised, "Thank you, Scipio. If I do nothing else, I will see Missy after we get out of here."

Syd Ross heard everything. I turned to him and said, "Sometimes I wonder why we went to war. Remember how we treated Yankee civilians in Pennsylvania? And they think nothing of sending out filthy, lowlife bummers to pillage us. Missy, your sister, my mother, no woman in the South is safe from them."

It was Syd's turn to console me. "Sorry about your friend, Jim. But, it's a reminder no matter how bad we have it, there are others that have it worse. The best revenge we can take after the war is to live well and that's what I wish for you."

"And you too, Syd. Merry Christmas."

I turned back to Scipio and said, "At a time when I felt forgotten and alone, my Christmas gift came with you. I don't wish Fort Delaware on anyone, but having you and Pete to talk with will make prison easier. If you would, take me to him."

* * *

The sight of Pete on a filthy cot shocked and saddened me. Nearly unrecognizable under a scraggly beard and in a badly soiled and crumpled uniform, Pete got up when he saw me. He had a noticeable limp as he staggered toward me. His eyes misted as he worked to hold back his tears.

"Near miracle finding you and Scipio on Christmas Day," I said. "I'm sorry for everyone here except the bastard guards. I wish you weren't here, but, God, it's good to see you."

Pete hugged me. "I'm sure Scipio told you, I'm not here by choice. Seeing your friendly face is the best thing that's happened to me since I went down at Opequon Creek. Sit down. Let's talk. We've got a lot of catching up to do."

Pete ignored Scipio, but I motioned for him join us. Scipio pulled up a cracker box and sat to the side. I told Pete, "I was shocked when I saw Scipio. Then he explained he was looking after you. He brought me a letter from Missy. We both owe him a lot."

Pete waved a hand in Scipio's direction and said, "When we got here, the Yankee guard said he did not care if the little nigger wanted to throw away his life". Pete laughed. I felt embarrassed for Scipio who sat nearby and smiled as Pete talked about him as if he weren't there.

To change the subject, I asked, "What happened at Opequon Creek?"

"General Early did all anyone could do to hold the Shenandoah, but the Yankees had us outnumbered two or three to one. They got pretty good using what we taught them early in the war. Sound familiar? Sheridan pushed us back toward Martinsburg. We fought a big battle there. I went down when we fought their cavalry at Opequon Creek. My company hid in the woods until the Yankees crossed and then we hit them on the other side. I remember leading the charge and then waking up in a Yankee field hospital."

Pete grimaced as he said, "Grapeshot caught my leg and took down my horse. I must've hit my head on the ground.

The surgeon was ready to cut the leg off. Would've done it except Scipio pleaded with him. I think he was one of those New England Abolitionist nigger lovers. I asked him not to cut it off and he ignored me. Scipio asked and he backs off. Shows you what the Yankees think of us. Sometimes I wish he had cut it off. Been nothing but trouble. Can you imagine me riding around the plantation with a wood leg?"

"I can imagine worse," I told him, and I could. "I left a Yankee hospital with a handsome young man who had half his face shot off at Sharpsburg. It's like my friend Syd Ross just said, 'anytime you think you have it bad, there's always someone that had it worse'. Right now, I'm counting my blessings. You should too. You're blessed Scipio stuck with you."

Pete laughed. "Damn, you never change. Still the Reverend Cobb." Pete smiled so I took a mock punch at him as we had done as cadets.

Pete turned serious for a moment and told me, "I think the only reason the surgeon did not amputate my leg was Scipio promised to attend me. The orderlies showed him how to change dressings and apply the powder. Somehow, I've survived with my leg and I'm thankful. Scipio also tended Yankees and some Confederates which helped keep him around to tend me. When I was well enough to leave, they sent me here."

I gave Pete a short account of Peebles Farm and my journey north. Pete wanted more details and I picked up the story from when we last saw each other at Gettysburg. "In thinking back, I've been blessed too. I'd be pushing up flowers in The Wilderness if my friend and First Sergeant, Andy Blaylock, had not looked out for me. We've got to survive to repay our guardian angels."

I asked, "Did Scipio tell you what happened to Missy?"

Pete nodded. "I nearly went crazy when I heard about it. If Father hadn't caught those sons of bitches and hung them, I'd be out tracking down and shooting bummers. Ruined my little sister for life."

I shook my head. "She's not ruined. Missy was a victim. She has nothing to be shamed of. She's still the pretty, smart girl we know."

"No. She's changed. She's a woman now. Hard to think of her that way, but she is. Scipio tells me she's worked hard to keep the plantation going. We were all kids before the war. I can't blame you for going after Sissy, but if you're inclined to marry my sister, make it Missy."

I thought briefly on what Pete said. Hard to tell when he was serious and when he wasn't. Maybe he felt responsible for Missy, something he did not do before the war. "In her letter, she asked me to visit after the war. God willing I survive this place, I'll come by before I go home. I have a hard time thinking of her as a woman. In my mind, she's still the smart girl who thought like an adult. She's a sweet, sensible girl, but Scipio tells me she wants to leave the plantation, leave the area. Maybe I can help her get a new start. We'll talk about it when I get there."

Pete looked at me earnestly and said, "Jim, just keep an open mind. Tell her what you told me about her rape. You know I'm not the brightest penny in the drawer, but I know you two belong together. You think alike. Talking with you is like talking to her."

After the initial excitement in seeing me, Pete began to fade. I put my hand on his shoulder and bid him farewell, "I'll be by to see you as often as I can. Come see me when you can."

Pete smiled and closed his eyes. I motioned Scipio to follow me. When we were outside, I took Scipio to my division and introduced him to the other officers. They, too, were surprised to find a newly freed slave in Fort Delaware.

* * *

He remained weak from his wound, but Pete gradually gained strength. With Scipio's and my help, he was able to take increasingly longer visits to the yard, where I introduced him to Sydney Ross and others I knew. Pete had writing paper, pen, and ink and bribed one of the guards to post letters without going to the censor where most letters were simply thrown away. Through Pete and Scipio, I finally sent a letter to Mother with the news her son was in Yankee prison and alive. I sent another letter to Missy, thanked her for her letter, and told her I would come by the Morgan Plantation on my way home after the war.

From Scipio, I learned Margaret Morgan asked some of her Union guests to intervene on behalf of her son which explained how Scipio had accompanied Pete to prison and the writing materials, much appreciated favors. She worked hard to get Pete a parole but futilely. General Grant denied all paroles and prisoner exchanges since taking command of the Union Army.

Chapter 19: Sissy

Morgan Plantation, Brownsburg, Virginia
December 1864 - February 1865,
Missy Morgan

I awoke early in the morning to a loud pounding on our front door. Since the incident with the bummers, I kept a loaded pistol on the lamp stand. I grabbed it, put on a night coat, and went out to the stairs. I saw Father ahead of me and fell in behind. Before answering the knock at the front door, Father turned back and said, "Stay behind the stair wall while I go to the door."

Joseph, our houseman, had left with his wife and children when the Union Army first invaded the Shenandoah Valley leaving Father the only man in the main house. I knew he had the same thought I did. It might be more bummers even though, like the earlier group, they would more likely break down the door and shoot anyone who attempted to stop them. Bummers – Yankee and Confederate deserters alike - nothing but common thieves who fed on misery, the absolute scum of the earth. Father hated them particularly after they had violated me and robbed our home. Father held a pistol in his other hand and opened the door. I steeled myself to back him up.

As the door opened, I peeked around the wall and saw a Union Lieutenant standing beside a burly sergeant. Father opened the door wider and I saw mounted cavalrymen in front of the porch.

The Lieutenant announced, "Your home will billet our Colonel and the officers of our cavalry battalion."

Little pissant Yankee Lieutenant commandeering our home.

My blood boiled. I looked at him, a pale, thin young man with feminine features. The sort Peter and his friends beat up after school. Father took the news better.

More relieved than angry, he seemed to breathe easier. They were not bummers, not even foragers. If they chose to house their officers and camp on our plantation, they would not burn it down as they had neighboring plantations, at least not until they left. He quietly slipped the pistol into his coat pocket.

The Yankee officer asked, "How many bedrooms do you have in the main house?"

"Eight."

"We'll take all of them."

Father bristled with indignation as he told the Lieutenant, "I'll sleep in the barn or the slave quarters, but I will not move my wife and daughters out of our home to accommodate Yankee officers."

The Lieutenant sneered. "I hold you in contempt, you and the rest of the slaveholders. But, the Colonel ordered us to be considerate."

He turned his back, apparently settled on a compromise, and turned back. "We don't make war on women. Take the largest bedroom for yourself, your wife, and daughters. We'll take the others."

I have always been proud of my father, never more than then. He had nothing but command presence to back off the Yankee Lieutenant and did it. It would be difficult and uncomfortable, but housing Yankees was small compared to the misery of our current condition. Mother, Sissy, and I would have to make the best of it. We would need Pearl to wash and change linen in the rooms, including hers, the Yankees would occupy. She could stay with Sara and Jacob for the duration.

"When will you occupy our home?" Father asked.

"Soon. Our Colonel is holding a staff meeting down the road and will arrive shortly with the battalion. We'll put our men in tents on the yard. Get your things moved now."

The Lieutenant turned smartly on his heels and left with the Sergeant following.

As he walked back to the stairs, Father muttered, "The damn Yankees will steal everything the slaves did not take earlier. I don't really care, little left anyway. We're safe for now. We'll worry about what to do next when they leave."

He put his arm around me, lifted my chin, looked me in the eye, smiled, and said, "We will find a way. Right now, we have to deal with Yankee officers. I know I can count on you."

We went back upstairs and put on our work clothes. When Father told Mother and Sissy what the Union Lieutenant said, Sissy sobbed and starzted carrying on as if our world had ended. Mother, initially flustered, saw opportunity in our misfortune. She said, "Peter's in a Union hospital. Maybe, just maybe, we can charm the Union Colonel and have favors done for him."

Father patted her on the arm and said, "Thank you dear. That's putting the best face on our situation."

I left to gather Sissy's and my things to move into our parents' bedroom.

*   *   *

We ate a hurried breakfast and, at eight in the morning, heard a gentle knock on the door and saw the same officious Lieutenant standing beside a handsome young Yankee Colonel. Tall with striking green eyes, he had an angular face, dark hair, and whiskers that came down to his chin. Without the blue uniform, I might have been attracted to him.

The Colonel spoke first. "My name is Jonathan Hamilton Curtis, Colonel and commander of a cavalry battalion. My aide informed you that your home will be used to house our officers until further notice. I apologize for the inconvenience to your family, but it is a necessity of this war I hope and pray will end soon."

The sight of blue uniforms terrified me, but I found the young Colonel's demeanor and words reassuring.

Father addressed the Colonel, "If you agree, my wife will show your aide the rooms and water closets. While they are doin' that, I'd like to discuss housin' of your men and horses."

Colonel Curtis told the Lieutenant to accompany Missus Morgan. She lost no time in applying her charm as they toured the house, treating the officious Lieutenant as an honored guest rather than a loathsome Yankee invader.

Sissy and I watched Father speak with the young Union Colonel who shyly turned his eyes when he saw us looking at him.

Sissy whispered, "Cute isn't he?"

"How can you possibly be attracted to him? Did it escape your notice that Yankee officers will occupy our home?" I whispered back.

Sissy stared at the Yankee Colonel and said with her eyes fixed on him, "Look at him. Handsome face, strong jaw, even the whiskers are nice. I'll wager he's lonesome away from home all these years."

I wanted to throttle her, but held my temper as the Colonel and Father continued their conversation.

"Our food and grain are about gone," Father told him.

Colonel Curtis assured him, "Mister Morgan, I understand and appreciate your circumstances. Food and supplies will be brought in for the battalion. We will leave you with adequate food and supplies when we move out."

We could barely feed ourselves let alone Yankee soldiers. So far only words, but I felt relieved to hear them.

Father replied, "Thank you, Colonel, come with me and I'll introduce my daughters."

Colonel Jonathan Hamilton Curtis looked at us and, by the look in his eyes, I could tell he was smitten with Sissy. I was sure she saw the same thing. Father introduced me first. I smiled, he smiled, and we shook hands. Father then introduced Sissy and Colonel Curtis became befuddled. Temporarily tongue-tied, he stammered, "I'm very pleased to meet you but regret the circumstances." I began to warm to him. He was nothing like his pompous aide. I thought him charming and his initial shyness endearing.

Colonel Curtis left to address his battalion assembled on our front lawn. Father went upstairs leaving us to talk.

"He won't be here long. I must move him along fast," Sissy said.

Her bluntness startled me.

"What's come over you? You just met a Yankee Colonel and already you're intent on catching him."

Sissy looked toward the door where Colonel Curtis had just gone out and replied, "You saw how he looked at me. This one's ready to be caught."

"A Yankee Colonel." Sissy motioned for me to lower my voice. In a quieter tone, I continued, "He's been out there fighting Peter, Jim, all our men. How can you even consider marrying him?"

Sissy dismissed my objection. "Fate dropped him in my lap. He's handsome. He's intelligent. He's terribly lonesome. You watch. We'll find he's wealthy. What's not to like?"

Exasperated, I could only respond, "He's a Yankee. Want to ruin our family forever?"

Sissy arched her eyebrows and responded, "Ruin what? Every farm and plantation in the Valley is destroyed. If we don't get money, everything we have will be gone."

I started to argue, but stopped and shook my head. Arguing

with Sissy when she had made up her mind was futile and, unfortunately, what Sissy said was true. But how could she be so cold-blooded and calculating with something that should be loving and kind?

Sissy said, "I am counting on you and Mother to help."

I sighed and nodded my head.

* * *

Colonel Curtis took a quick ride around the plantation with his aide and Father. Father told me he saw the devastation and apparently felt sorry for us. "The war was not your fault, but here it was on your plantation - destructive, wasteful, and cruel." He could have been speaking about every farm and plantation in the Valley and it was his army that caused the destruction. But, Father thought he seemed genuinely concerned about our welfare.

While he rode beside Father, Colonel Curtis asked, "When the war's over, how much do you estimate it'll cost to bring the plantation back to where it was before the war?"

He surprised Father with the question but Father gave the Colonel a dollar estimate. When he told me about the conversation with Colonel Curtis, Father asked, "Why would a Yankee Colonel be concerned with how much to fix our place?"

"I think the handsome young Colonel may want to marry our Sissy. Maybe paying to restore the plantation would be a way for him to win your blessing. I am guessing he has the money to do it."

Father shook his head in disgust. "Sissy marrying a Yankee. Can we sink any lower?"

"If you deny them, Sissy may run off with him when they move out regardless of what you, Mother, or I think." I let my warning sink in and asked, "Why not get money from the Yankee Colonel to do what they'll do anyway? Want me to suggest it to Sissy?"

Father took a long time in replying, "We live in desperate times. Maybe it's best she marries the Yankee. Don't be hard on your sister. She sees an opportunity to get out. I cannot fault her for that."

I took Father's reply as approval and thought on the quirk of fate. Before the war, our conversation would have been impossible to contemplate. The idea of Sissy selling herself to a Yankee was repugnant. But the more I thought of her marrying Jonathan, the more I liked the idea. When the war mercifully ended, the local swains who buzzed around her would be mostly dead, wounded, or impoverished. The notion of either of us marrying a wealthy Planter was hollow. And, here by fate, was a handsome, intelligent, polite, wealthy, and lovesick Yankee Colonel. I could think of no good reason she should not pursue Jonathan. Besides, I wanted her gone if Jim ever returned to us.

I later made the suggestion to Sissy. She took it well, maybe too well. She said, "If he's to win me from Father, he needs to pay."

In talking with the Yankee officers, I picked up comments about Jonathan Curtis and liked what I heard.

General Sheridan sent Colonel Curtis' battalion to the Morgan Plantation for rest. They fought hard in the recent battles with Jubal Early's cavalry and took many casualties. Sheridan wanted Colonel Curtis and his troops fresh for the coming final assault on Richmond. Brownsburg was mostly pacified. The battalion had little to do other than make occasional appearances in the county.

Jonathan Curtis was one of Sheridan's favorite officers. According to his fitness report, Union command considered him exceptionally brave, dependable, and resourceful in battle even if he reluctantly obeyed orders to torch Rebel homes and farms. Earlier in the year, our cavalry surrounded Jonathan's battalion, but he fought his way back to Union lines with most of his men.

He had received several meritorious citations and medals for bravery. But, deep down, his officers told me he hated the war.

* * *

With the best of everything we could muster, Mother, Sara, Sissy, and I prepared an evening meal for Colonel Curtis, his staff, company commanders, and the family. Mother brought out, from hiding, our finest plates, glasses, and silverware to serve our guests. It had the intended effect. We impressed the Yankee officers who appreciated eating a fine meal with the Morgan Family instead of the usual army field rations.

At supper, Mother and Sissy worked to draw out the Colonel on his family and service record. We learned Jonathan Curtis was a native of Lowell, Massachusetts, where his family had made a fortune in textile manufacture. He graduated from Tufts College. Jonathan served as President of the family company before the war and would again when he returned. He had no brothers and sisters. His father took over management of the company after Jonathan enlisted and was anxious to resume pursuit of his hobbies and philanthropic interests.

Jonathan Curtis told us he and his family were Universalist free-thinkers. We had mixed reaction to this bit of information. Father winced thinking about his daughter marrying into an atheist family. I had read articles and books by New England free thinkers and became more fascinated with our guest. Mother was indifferent as long as the money part held up. I don't think Sissy knew or cared about Jonathan's religious beliefs.

Colonel Curtis asked about Peter and VMI. Father answered the Colonel's questions but withheld details he thought the Yankees should not know. His caution was wasted. The Union Army had little need of information about our army that was all but finished. But concealing selected items made him feel better about talking with the Yankee officers.

I smiled when Father told Jonathan that a family friend had served as A P Hill's Chief of Staff. Jonathan commented, "He must be a fine officer." From then on, he could do no wrong.

One of the Yankee Captains noticed the piano in the entertainment room and asked if anyone played. Mother allowed that she and her daughters played on occasion. He pleaded with her and was joined by other officers in requesting a tune, a song, anything musical. Mother demurred, but, when Colonel Curtis joined in the request, she relented.

Turning to Sissy, she said, "Take your sister to accompany and sing a song for our guests." Sissy stood up and motioned me to follow her. As we walked to the piano, the Yankee officers called out requests which I ignored.

I whispered, "Let's give them one they'll really enjoy." I sat down on the piano bench and started playing the *Bonnie Blue Flag*. Sissy stood beside me, stunned. She gulped and began singing the verses which began

We are a band of brothers and native to the soil,
Fighting for the property we gained by honest toil;
And when our rights were threatened,
the cry rose near and far,
Hurrah for the Bonnie Blue Flag that bears a single star!

Hurrah! Hurrah! For Southern rights hurrah!
Hurrah for the Bonnie Blue Flag that bears a single star.

To our amazement, the Yankee officers applauded, whistled, and sang along with her. It was also one of their favorites. They liked the tune written by a New York songwriter before the war. When we finished *Bonnie Blue Flag*, the Yankee officers requested *Dixie*, also one of their favorites, and I accommodated them.

The party gathered around the piano with Mother, the Colonel, Sissy, and me in the center of an impromptu circle. The

Yankee officers seemed to enjoy themselves in our company. I suspected they were lonesome for wives, mothers, and sweethearts, and tired of the horror and misery of the war. Colonel Curtis stood beside Sissy and joined her in singing a ballad. He had a fine tenor voice. His officers applauded and they sang several more duets to the delight of the party.

The following evening, Colonel Curtis asked Father if he could take Sissy on a ride around the plantation. Father accompanied them and Jonathan was a perfect gentleman. Sissy and the Colonel came together each evening thereafter. Mother considerately withdrew from the parlor so the young people could talk alone. By degrees, their conversations turned serious and more romantic.

I knew all this because Sissy came to our bedroom each night after Colonel Curtis left. Blue uniform or not, Jonathan Curtis was a good man. I saw much of Jim Cobb in him – handsome, kind, and intelligent.

* * *

While Yankee officers stayed in our home, we had a welcome visitor. Scipio returned, brought news, and picked up what he could to take back. We knew Peter had been wounded, captured, and taken to a Union hospital, but little beyond that and appreciated the opportunity to learn more.

He told us the Yankees took Peter to their hospital, where Scipio found him. The surgeons wanted to cut off his leg before gangrene set in, but Scipio begged them not to do it. Scipio changed Peter's bandages frequently, drained and washed the wound, and applied an acidic solution that ate away dead and diseased flesh from the wound. It worked. The infection was defeated, although Peter's leg remained stiff and sore when Scipio left for home. The Yankees would send Peter to Fort Delaware Prison when he was able to walk.

I had met a young man at church. He had returned from Petersburg. A thoughtful young Lieutenant whose army years were over. He had one leg and showed scars from what must have been a horrible injury. He served in the Virginia Brigade of the Light Division. I asked him about Jim and the 78th North Carolina. He told me they were captured at Peebles Farm after delaying a Union assault on the 6th North Carolina Brigade. He thought they had been taken to Fort Delaware.

My spirits soared. Peter and Jim in the same prison. Maybe, Lord willing, they would both survive and return to me.

Scipio had to get back before Peter went to Yankee prison. He returned home and spent two nights with his wife, Pearl. They married when Peter brought Scipio home on a furlough early last year.

Sissy mentioned what happened to her brother to Colonel Curtis. As expected, Colonel Curtis volunteered to do what he could for Peter. He began by signing a pass for Scipio to help get him get through Union lines and back to the hospital and gave Scipio extra money to take to Peter. He also wrote a letter to General Sheridan explaining our circumstances and requested the General do what he could for Peter Morgan in the Union hospital. It was all he could do for Peter and we appreciated his efforts to help.

* * *

On the tenth day, Jonathan received orders to take his battalion east the next day. Now would be his only chance to wed the beautiful young lady who had become the light of his life. Jonathan proposed to Sissy that night.

Both a gentleman and romantic, he got down on one knee to make his plea. "Sissy, darling, you have only known me a short time. And I know I'm an officer in the army that wasted your home and captured your brother, but if you can find it in your heart to marry me, you'll make me the happiest man on earth. Please say 'yes'. I love you very much."

"Colonel Curtis, I do love you, but I don't know how I could possibly leave my family in our dire circumstances."

Sissy's reply had the intended effect.

Jonathan quickly added, "Your father told me it will require fifteen thousand dollars to restore the Morgan Plantation to its former magnificence. It would be my pleasure to give him that amount of money after we are married."

For reasons known only to her, Sissy decided to tease and test her love struck suitor. "You mean fifteen thousand dollars to my father to purchase his older daughter?"

Jonathan became flustered and stammered, "No, no. We'll be one family. It's my privilege and pleasure to help in a time of need."

Sissy leaned over, kissed him on the cheek, and said, "I know, dear. We will be very appreciative of your help. It will be most difficult for my family and the plantation after the war. The money you promise will allow us to survive."

"Does that mean you'll marry me?" he asked.

Sissy smiled and said, "Yes, silly, I'll marry you."

Jonathan jumped up and suggested that he and Sissy immediately talk with Mother and Father. They found them in the parlor. Father cautioned them about jumping into a marriage much too soon. Mother pretended to be surprised.

Later, Sissy told Father of Jonathan's offer and he nearly wept. "I've been worried sick since the war began. Thanks to you and Colonel Hamilton, we will keep our home."

Sissy hugged him and said, "Father, I really do love Jonathan. Yankee or not, he's a near perfect man."

Father agreed. "Yes, I've come to like him too. But, I dread thinking of the backlash we'll get."

* * *

It was difficult to tell who was happier – Jonathan or my parents. After breakfast, Jonathan handed Sissy two hundred dollars in Union coin and said, "If you could plan this wedding for the earliest date in February, I'll ask the General for that day off. To simplify things, I'll bring my staff in dress uniform and have them serve as attendants. I regret I won't be available to help with the planning."

"It will be easier if we marry here in our home. I will speak with Reverend Cuthbert for the earliest date available. How can I get a message to you?"

Jonathan must have anticipated her question and replied, "I'll send a courier one week from today. Will you have the wedding date set by then?"

Mother answered, "Yes."

Afterward, we sat in the parlor where Sissy and Jonathan talked about their life together. As they should be, the two lovers were completely engrossed in each other and barely noticed or cared I was in the room with them.

He told her, "The war will be over before summer. The Confederate Army has fought bravely and skillfully, but each day I see reduction in their numbers and supplies. More lives will be lost, but the war is definitely winding down."

"What will we do until the war ends?" Sissy asked.

"I've thought about it even before you accepted my proposal." Jonathan took a kiss from Sissy. They giggled and he presented his plan. "After the wedding, we won't have an opportunity for a proper honeymoon. I'd like to send you to Lowell to stay with my parents and away from the war. It'll give you a chance to get to know them and become adjusted to your new home."

Because she had put all her thought and energy into catching him, Sissy had given her future life in the North little thought. Somehow, the subject of where she would live never came up in our nightly conversations. As it dawned on her that she would be living among Yankees and without the support of her husband for several months, reality set in. But, she kept smiling and replied, "That will be fine, dear." Sissy did not want to stay with us after she married either.

Jonathan looked at her and vowed, "We will have the best ever honeymoon once I muster out of the army. Where would you like to go?"

Sissy had not given that much thought either. She had heard of Niagara Falls, but imagined it would be cold, wet, and full of Yankees. She finally said, "Paris, France."

Jonathan laughed and said, "Someday, but, I can't take that much time away from my duties at the company when I return from the war."

Sissy began to pout before Jonathan said, "What if we go half way this time, to Bermuda?" Sissy did not know where Bermuda was but figured it must be half way to Paris. She cooed to her intended, "Anywhere with you will be wonderful, Darling."

"I apologize for not having an engagement ring for you," Jonathan told her. "I will send a letter to Mother today and ask her to buy a diamond engagement ring and wedding rings for us. If I remember correctly, her hand is about the same size as yours. I'll ask her to buy rings for you that fit her finger. We can have them adjusted by a jeweler later if needed."

Sissy nodded in agreement and unconsciously held out her left hand and examined the ring finger. Jonathan continued, "Mother and Father will be upset that we'll have the wedding without them. But, under the circumstances, they could be exposed to Confederate fire in getting here. I hope they understand."

Sissy reassured him, "I'm sure they will" not knowing if they would or would not.

Midmorning, the battalion left for reassignment.

* * *

Jonathan made good on his promise to Father. He left more food stores and grain than before the battalion came. Sissy and Mother met with Reverend Cuthbert and settled on a date in mid-February for the wedding. Banns for the wedding were posted the next Sunday. Sissy had friends in the congregation who were pleased for her, but fell away from attending the wedding when they learned she would marry a Yankee officer.

Marrying a daughter to a Yankee was absolutely the worst thing any Southern family could do, but the Morgans had a low social standing regardless of what we did or did not do. Sissy marrying a Yankee Colonel was repugnant, but did not surprise anyone in the community.

A courier came the next week and Sissy handed him a note. She made him promise not to read it before delivering the note to Colonel Curtis and added some sweet thoughts to the note. I learned from one of the staff officers that the courier read it on the ride back and had a laugh at the Colonel's expense.

Three weeks later a package came addressed to Sissy. Inside she found an engagement ring and two wedding rings. The engagement ring was exquisite and fit perfectly. Sissy knew, at least, her future mother-in-law had good taste.

Jonathan sent daily letters that included little about the war, but we knew things were going well for the Yankees. Union cavalry roamed unopposed as the remnant of our army fell back to defend Richmond. We had long since had our fill of war. Sissy just wanted the war over so she could join her husband and get the Morgan Plantation back on its feet.

Finally the wedding day came and Colonel Curtis rode in with his staff in their resplendent blue dress uniforms.

None of the neighbors attended. Even the earlier incident with the bummers had not brought the community acceptance we worked years to achieve. I served as Maid of Honor and Colonel Curtis' Adjutant was Best Man. A brusque, short-tempered Yankee, I hated him more for his blue uniform than anything else. During the ceremony, my mind wandered and I imagined Jim Cobb standing beside me. I did not know where Jim was or even if he were alive, but said a silent prayer as Sissy and Jonathan exchanged vows.

The newlyweds walked under crossed swords of the battalion officers. They left in a decorated carriage, but simply took an hour ride and returned to gather Sissy's clothing and accessories for her trip to Lowell. After the men loaded the luggage, Sissy said a tearful goodbye to Father, Mother, and me and, oblivious to the fact she would be living in enemy territory, promised to write when she got to Lowell. Jonathan shook hands with Father and received family kisses from Mother and me and then the newlyweds rode off for Lexington.

Jonathan took Sissy to the train station and waited with her until the train departed. Sissy gave him a passionate kiss, knowing she would not see him again for months.

* * *

For Sissy, everything finally sank in on the long train ride to Boston. She loved her new husband and worried he might be killed or injured before the war ended. She wanted desperately to leave the misery of home, but, at the same time, dreaded living in the North.

She was the wife of a Yankee textile owner, not a Southern plantation owner as she had always imagined. Sissy would live with Yankees. Other than Jonathan, she considered Yankees to be rude and inconsiderate. Certainly the passengers on the train did not change her thinking. Sissy cried when she thought of her plight. In Pennsylvania, a kindly older lady came over to comfort her, but Sissy shooed her away. Knowing Sissy, she enjoyed her cry.

Her new in-laws, Edgar and Cynthia Curtis, met her at the Boston train station. Sissy did her best to impress them, but her efforts fell short. Jonathan's parents were offended by being excluded from his wedding and took out their displeasure on the siren that lured Jonathan from marrying a nice, prim New England girl as they had intended. In addition, as a fervent abolitionist, Edgar Curtis resented that his son had married a slave owner's daughter.

Sissy spent most of her time in her room sulking and writing letters. It is how I learned what had happened to her after she left us. She was finally liberated when Jonathan returned from the war on Friday, May 5, 1865. They left immediately for Boston Harbor and a long, overdue honeymoon in Bermuda.

To my surprise, we got regular letters from Sissy during the last months of the war. Union mail service, including service to occupied areas, was much better than ours.

* * *

After the wedding, I felt depressed. My sister had married well and escaped the misery of the war. Life would be better when the war finally ended. The family plantation would be restored. But, my circumstances would never change as long as I stayed in the Shenandoah Valley. Everyone in our community knew I had been raped by Yankee bummers. They were kind and understanding to me, but I knew they would never forget and the shame would follow me all my life. No quality man would want to marry me. Some of the Yankee officers tried to flirt with me, but I could not see past the blue uniforms that terrified me. Like Sissy, I had to find a way to honorably leave.

I would not give up my longstanding dream. Desperate times required desperate measures. On the night Sissy left, I sat in her room and wrote a letter to Jim Cobb and addressed it to the Fort Delaware Prison where I sent letters to Peter. Peter wrote that incoming letters were routinely discarded by the guards. I doubted my letter would find its way to Jim and regretted I had not added it to the letter I sent back with Scipio earlier, but I sent it anyway. Any chance was better than no chance.

I wrote:

Dearest Jim,

I pray you are well when you read this letter and will not consider me forward in writing you.

I realize your feelings for me are as a caring older brother for an awkward and opinionated younger sister. It is how you have known and treated me. I have always treasured our friendship. But, Jim, I am now a woman and have loved you since the first day I met you.

It is unbecoming for a young woman to declare her love to a man without any encouragement on his part. I suspect you are uncomfortable as you read this as you have never shown any romantic interest in me.

Please think about me and the life we might have together when you are free. I know I was intended to be your wife. Please come by the Morgan Plantation, perhaps with Peter, on your return home. I dearly want to see you even if you cannot find it in your heart to consider me in a romantic way.

I wait to hear from you.

Your loving friend,

Missy

I did not get a reply.

Chapter 20: Surrender

Horace Greeley's Office, New York Tribune, New York City,
Monday, April 3, 1865
Sam Payne

"The South's defeated, Mister Payne. It's all over except the details. I spoke with General Grant earlier. He wants to take one of
our reporters into Richmond with him. He asked for you."

As usual, Greeley spoke with authority, as someone who held
unelected national office and created news as well as published it.
After five and a half years of reporting the war and its prelude, I
was accustomed to Greeley's pontifications. I welcomed them as
major assignments usually followed.

In keeping with his social station, Greeley kept a box of pre-
mium Cuban cigars on his desk he shared with dignitaries and, on
occasion, a reporter or editor he invited to his inner sanctum.

"The war's not over yet," I commented while taking one of
Greeley's cigars.

"Last wire from Grant's headquarters indicates the Confederate
Army is packing up to abandon Richmond. They will flee west.
Grant sent out cavalry and light infantry to intercept them and
force the final battle. Lee has no more cards to play. The Army
of Northern Virginia will soon be finished. I want you there to
report it."

I smiled. "And why not? I was in Charleston at the beginning."

"I still think it fortunate you got out of there to bring the story." Greeley puffed twice on his cigar, arched his eyebrows, and asked, "Remind me. How'd you do it?"

I told him the story before, but, apparently, he had forgotten. "We printed business cards for the fictitious Albemarle Examiner. I spoke Virginian while I was in South Carolina and passed out the cards freely. I had a couple of close scrapes, but talked my way out of them. Remember Edmund Ruffin?" Greeley shook his head.

"He's the crazy, old Virginia secessionist who fired the first shot and started the war. He knew me from when I interviewed him after the John Brown hanging. He wanted to expose me, but I convinced him, over drinks, that the South would join and the North back down when they learned how determined South Carolina was to protect itself. But, I had to get back to New York to report the story to the nation. He agreed and kept his mouth shut."

"Did he really fire the first shot?" Greeley asked. The man had a passion for the truth even on trivial matters.

"No," I admitted. "Lieutenant Henry S Farley commanded a battery of two mortars on James Island and fired the first shot but Ruffin did fire a shot at Fort Sumter later that morning."

Greeley smiled and pointed his cigar at me. "You've been a clever reporter on more than one occasion, Mister Payne."

"Technically, the war's not over when Grant finally traps what's left of Lee's army. Johnston has a larger army in North Carolina and the Rebs have smaller armies scattered in the West." I picked up my cigar from the ashtray on Greeley's desk, took a puff, and waited for his response.

"The Army of Northern Virginia is the heart and soul of the Confederacy. When Lee surrenders, the war's over for all intents and purposes. We'll see the other Southern armies fall quickly. Our readers will take the final defeat of the Army of Northern Virginia as end of the war. They will want the details."

"It may not go down that easily," I pointed out. "That the

South still has an army is a miracle in itself. The Confederate soldiers left are there for honor or because they hate us, probably both. Good chance some of them will go off into the woods and mountains and continue as a partisan army."

Greeley agreed and pointed out, "That's absolutely the worst outcome. How Grant, Sherman, and Thomas handle the surrender is critical. It's these details I'm counting on you to gather and report to our readers."

New York Tribune Article,
Sunday, April 16, 1865,
byline Samuel Payne

The destruction of Richmond is beyond description. All the citizens who could flee the city left before the Confederate Army abandoned it. All supplies they could not take were burned. Poor whites as well as Negroes came out to greet Union troops as liberators, not conquerors. Gratifying to those who want the South humbled. Sad for we who remember Richmond as a beautiful, gracious tree-lined city. No more. Richmond is totally ruined and able to exist only because of supplies and services provided by the occupying army.

The tattered Confederate Army, a desperate remnant of the once proud Army of Northern Virginia, retreated west seeking to join with Johnston's army in North Carolina. Sheridan's cavalry caught them near Amelia Court House effectively eliminating any hope for escape. General Lee recognized the impossibility of continuing the conflict and sent a messenger to Union headquarters on Sunday, April 9. Lee requested and was granted a ceasefire to discuss surrender. A meeting place suggested by Lee's staff, McLean's farmhouse near Appomattox Courthouse, and time, 1:30 pm, Wednesday, April 12 were agreed for signing the surrender paper. General Lee and his staff came at the appointed time. General Grant arrived late and disheveled.

Appearances were that the haggard Grant would surrender to the courtly Lee.

Grant offered generous terms, too generous for the Radical Republicans in Congress and the President's Cabinet, but the terms offered and accepted nonetheless. On pledge to cease rebellion to the Federal government, Grant paroled all Confederate officers and soldiers and allowed them to return home. General Lee asked that his men keep the horses and mules for spring planting. Grant agreed and included it in the terms of surrender. Confederate officers were allowed to keep their side arms. In an act of much appreciated humanity, General Grant ordered rations for his former enemies, the first decent meal they had in months.

General Lee assigned General John Bankhead Magruder to formally surrender Confederate arms. Joshua Lawrence Chamberlain, perhaps the Union Army's most valiant general, commanded the detachment that received the surrender. After months of privation and disease, the Confederate Army resembled little more than sickly scarecrows, but proud even in defeat. They marched in step, backs erect, heads high and laid their arms and standards before their former bitter enemies. General Chamberlain ordered a cheer from the Union troops for the Confederates which seemed sincerely rendered.

The surrender terms and dignity of the surrender ceremony defused sentiment for continuation of fighting among the Confederate soldiers and partisans. General Lee did his part by urging Southerners to accept defeat and move forward with reconciliation. Congressional action to try General Lee for treason stopped when General Grant denounced it.

On Wednesday, April 19, Confederate General Joseph Johnston met with U S General William T Sherman at Greensboro, North Carolina to discuss surrender. Johnston's army began dissolving when news of Lee's surrender spread but still held over 30,000 Confederate troops at war with the United States. Sherman surprised Johnston and many Southerners by offering terms even more generous than Grant gave Lee at Appomattox Courthouse. Secretary of War Stanton, and the Radical Republicans who now control our government immediately repudiated Sherman's offer. General Sherman prevailed but only after threatening to resign if his offer to General Johnston was not endorsed.

Despite the assassination of President Lincoln, continued fighting in the west, and a Congress and Administration hell bent on punishing the South, there is hope for final, peaceful resolution of the terrible war that bled our nation over the past four years. If it does come about, and we pray it will, the peace, in large measure, will be due to the wisdom and restraint of our generals. They could have pursued vengeance and retribution, but chose the path of reconciliation laid out by President Lincoln before his untimely death.

Home of Professor William Allen, Lexington, Virginia,
Monday, May 8, 1865
Sam Payne

"Sam, have you and Mary decided on a name for my next grandchild?"

We sat facing each other, sipping bourbon I brought with me. I planned to leave several bottles as I know he enjoyed bourbon more than the rotgut he had been drinking recently. I sent letters to Professor Allen during the war, but I had not seen him in four years.

He reminded me of my father. Good man. Similar sense of humor, but, of course, the Professor was much better educated. I could always sharpen my thinking in discussions with him. Mary worried about him and I missed him.

"Considering the timing of the birth, we think 'Victor' for a boy and 'Victoria' if the baby's a girl."

"Good choice I suppose," he commented.

Professor Allen had been depressed since the war ended. He knew why the South lost and was thankful we were alive and well, but had difficulty accepting the loss. I knew he would come around and we needed him with us.

"It's time you come to visit. Thad's heard us talk about you and he keeps asking when he'll see Grandpa. Bring Sukie. Ever since I came, she's peppered me with questions about New York, Mary, and Thad. She can see for herself and Mary can use her help while she recuperates. I'd like having you around so we can talk about how to patch up our country."

"Telegraph after the baby's born and we'll take you up on your offer," he said.

"How about you and Sukie go with me when I return to New York tomorrow?" Mary had been after me to get her father to us out of what she feared would be anarchy in Virginia. I agreed. He was the only grandparent left to our children.

"I'd like to, but the trustees scheduled an important meeting next week. They want to ask General Lee to become our new president and want faculty endorsement."

"You can do no better than General Lee", I commented. "Not a man who fought with or against him doesn't respect him. You remember I met Lee before the war and came away impressed. A gentleman and very intelligent. Besides, if I remember correctly, he was once Superintendent at West Point." Absolutely the best man to lead George Washington College following the war. I much admired his conduct in arresting John Brown and as Jefferson Davis' military advisor and commander of the Army of Northern Virginia. President of a college would be a safe, comfortable position for him to retire, out of public eye.

"Faculty endorsement is foregone, but they want all the department heads there and that includes me."

"How about I take Sukie with me and you come along after the trustee meeting?" I knew she wanted to come and saw her behind the kitchen door eavesdropping on us.

"Mister Payne, you are persistent and persuasive. Sukie'd like it and so will Mary. I'll find a way to take care of myself before

I leave." Allen turned to the kitchen door and said, "All right, Sukie, I know you're listening. Come out and let Sam tell you about your trip north."

Sukie stepped out from the kitchen, shyly grinned, and said, "Mistuh William, you nose I do no sich thing. But, whas dis 'bout me gwin' Noath?"

Sukie was a second mother to Mary, particularly after her mother died while Mary was a young girl. She had a good heart and I liked her too. Hard not to like someone who has your good as her chief concern. I told her, "Your little girl has children of her own. We can use your help for a few weeks after the baby's born. It'll give you a chance to see the big city."

"I don' know, Mistuh Sam. I's heerd deys wicked folks in New Yahk."

"There are sinful people in Lexington, but fewer of them. You don't have to go outside our home if you don't want to."

Sukie protested, "I didn' say dat. I jist wants to be safe from de debil's ways."

"I'd worry about the devil if he ever crosses your path," said Professor Allen as he suppressed a grin.

Sukie, acting indignant, answered, "He knows bettah dan come neah me and mine."

"Start getting your stuff together. I'll buy tickets for us tomorrow and telegraph Mary. She'll be pleased to see you and the Professor when he can join us."

Sukie rode in the same passenger cars with me back to New York, something that would never have happened before or during the war.

Over the course of the war, my relation with Horace Greeley grew steadily. He recognized I had a knack for gaining the confidence of nearly all I interviewed. As a consequence, my stories had depth and human interest. Best of all, it sold newspapers, which endeared me to him.

Greeley and I each enjoyed one of his Cuban cigars from the humidor on his desk. "Sam, I'm considering an Independence Day special, a wrap up of the war and all that has gone on the past five years. You've been there from start to finish. No one covered the war more or better than you. I'm thinking you should write the lead story."

"Thank you, Sir. But, what should I say?"

"We always want them to feel good about themselves. After much sacrifice, we and, by extension they, won the war. Best not to mention the riots, Copperheads, and how we nearly lost the war from lack of public support. At the same time, there are lessons from the war, mostly from mistakes I want you to include. The readers should be educated as well as entertained."

Starting with John Brown and interviewing top Union generals, I had a different view of the war. Different from Greeley, different from our readers. I began thinking of what I would say in this article. "With Grant, Sherman, Thomas, Sheridan, and even Meade, we finished well. But I wouldn't give a plug nickel for the other generals we've had."

Greeley readily agreed. "Nor would I, but don't be harsh on them in your story. In the end, it was the soldiers, not the generals, who won the war even as poorly led as they often were."

I needed insight for the story and the most perceptive man I knew sat opposite me. "Moving on from the war, how do you see the future, Mister Greeley?"

Greeley paused, sat back and took several puffs from his cigar, a vain man always impressed when someone asked his opinion. It was apparently a question much on his mind, but also apparently he had not framed an answer until I asked. Greeley continued to think about the answer as he talked using his explanation to help further develop his thinking.

"We're coming out of turbulent times. The North's bled, the South devastated, but I see rapid and uneven expansion in the future. Half our country is not settled. It will be over the next twenty or thirty years. The patent office is flooded with applications. It means rapid population and economic growth. America will return to western expansion after interruption of the war and the issues that led to the war. I see great wealth accumulation starting with the railroads. At the same time, most Southerners and settlers in the West will live in poverty. I don't know how we'll manage the diversity of wealth, but somehow we will. We always have."

"My wife's a Virginian," I said. "Her family's house slave, Sukie, is family to Mary and her father, but, by law, she's now free. Sukie's visiting with us and helping while Mary recovers from Victoria's birth. She asked me last week what's to become of the Negroes. I didn't have a good answer. Do you?"

"The Emancipation Proclamation made them free, but that's something different than equal. The Negroes in the North have been free for years, but never equal. It will be worse for them in the South – a century to equality, maybe never."

Chapter 21: Return

Fort Delaware, Pennsylvania and Blaylock Farm,
Fauquier County, Virginia,
April, 1865
Jim Cobb

The spring climate changed from sunny and warm to overcast and gloomy. The interior of Fort Delaware remained the same – dirty, diseased, and depressing. Cholera struck in late March. Warden Schoepf opened the courtyard to sick prisoners where we could stretch out on blankets in open air. A boon until it rained, which was often. As the epidemic spread, Schoepf paid local doctors to supplement the prison staff in making cursory calls on the most ill. Some infected prisoners survived, others died.

Pete Morgan caught cholera early. His health, marginal since he came to Fort Delaware, declined steadily over the next ten days. I went to see him daily to help and keep his spirits up. Then I became sick and unable to help my friend as he lay dying.

Scipio helped with other sick prisoners but concentrated on Pete and me. Despite Scipio's best efforts, Pete wasted away. He lacked whatever will to live those of us that survived possessed. To this day, I do not know why. He had more to live for than most. The war ruined the livelihood of nearly every prisoner in Fort Delaware. But, if the Morgan Plantation could be salvaged, Pete would inherit it and live like a country squire even with sharecropper labor. We did it successfully on the Cobb Farm. If he lacked imagination or motivation, I could show him how.

Maybe the thought of a permanently crippled leg disheartened him.

Until the end, he remained the same old Pete when I talked with him. I worried he would die after I came down with cholera. Another of the mindless war tragedies except this one happened to my college roommate, a man I hoped would be a brother-in-law.

Day laborers dumped Pete's body in an open pit filled with other dead Confederates. Gravediggers poured lime on the bodies, covered the unmarked mass grave, and left quickly. When I first got to Fort Delaware, a minister came out and said a blessing for the dead. But, by now, dead Confederates did not even get a perfunctory prayer. Just plant them and get on to the next group. Typical Yankees. Heartless bastards. I doubted there was one soul for every ten of them.

I desperately wanted to stand at the dead line and watch Pete's burial so at least one person who knew and loved him would note his passing but I lacked the strength. Instead, I lay in bed feeling useless and disgusted with myself.

Scipio came to see me after the burial and, in frustration with my inability to do anything, I lashed out. "Scipio, I swear to God, I'll never forget or forgive what the damned Yankees did to Pete. Wouldn't provide decent care. The least they could have done was give him and the others a Christian burial."

Scipio rubbed my forehead gently with a cool, damp rag and talked reason. "I nose you feels bad, Mistuh Jim. But dem Yankees ain't all evil. Deys 'fraid de kolra gwin git dem too. God nose dat and fohgib 'em."

I feebly grasped his arm and said, "But for you and the grace of God, I'd be in the grave with Pete."

* * *

General Lee surrendered the Army of Northern Virginia on Wednesday, April 12, 1865. Warden Schoepf petitioned Washington to release the prisoners the same day. When Scipio heard the news, he ran to me and asked, "Now de wah's dun, whas to 'come of us, Mistuh Jim?"

"We've discussed your coming to the Cobb Farm with me. You understand you are a free man," I explained. "You're free to live anywhere you choose. But keep in mind the Negroes on the Cobb Farm were freed five years before the war and they all chose to stay."

Scipio nodded. "Yessuh, I wants to go wid you to Noath Ca'lina." He shuffled his feet, looked down and continued, "Mistuh Jim, you nose I'se got a wife."

This was apparently the reason for his question. Scipio wanted assurance he would get back to his wife and they had a future.

Scipio looked up and smiled for the first time since Pete died as I said, "We'll first go to the Morgan Plantation and add your wife to our traveling party. Besides, I promised you I'd see Missy before I return home. We'll leave when Mother sends the money."

Scipio found a cleaner blanket, replaced mine, and replied, "I nevah thanked you fo' standin' up fo' me when Mistuh Cawlton whupped me. I node den you'se good folks. Pearl and me work hard and do our best fo' you, Suh."

Not as restrained as Scipio, I put my hand on his shoulder, squeezed gently and, with tears in my eyes, replied, "You are a good man, Scipio. A very good man."

Scipio somehow hid Pete's personal effects – watch, ring, medals, wallet, photo of his parents and sisters, and cash – from the guards who took everything not stolen earlier by the soldiers.

He handed me one hundred dollars in Union currency which appeared he had kept in his shoe. The bills were worn, but spendable. I knew the Morgans did not have the cash to give Pete.

I learned what I expected when Scipio explained, "De Yankee Cun'l gib it to me."

I wrote a short letter to William Morgan which expressed my sorrow on Pete's death and that I would return with Scipio and Pete's belongings on my trip home. I added a note to Missy at the bottom of the letter.

I have amazed everyone including myself by surviving. God willing, if I recover, I will come by on the way home. I look forward to another of our long talks. Until then take care of yourself and save me a dance.

Jim

I wrote an abbreviated telegram asking for as much of the family's Union money as Mother could spare.

In a separate letter home, I told her I would ensure that Andy, if he were still alive, made it home and would bring Scipio and his wife. I added that I might bring some of the unattached officers and men from the regiment with me to work on the farm and in the mills.

I thought our farm would prosper after the war. We provided what people needed – processed and unprocessed food and lumber - and we needed good men.

I handed Scipio the note and letter and said, "Scipio, please take the letter to the mail post and send it. Take the telegram to the telegraph office and ask them to send it. The address is in the note. It'll probably cost us three or four dollars to bribe the telegrapher, but pay him whatever he demands. If it's more than that, tell the greedy bastard I'll make up the difference when Mother sends the money. But, of course, don't call him a greedy bastard."

Scipio laughed and said, "No, suh" as I continued, "Before you leave, ask the regimental officers to gather in my room. Tell them I want to talk with them before they leave for home. On your way back from the telegraph office, go by the soldiers' prison and ask for Sergeant Andy Blaylock. If you find him, tell him to see me as soon as he can." I gave Scipio four tasks which he cheerfully accepted and ran out the door of our division to the courtyard.

* * *

The regimental officers came by individually. I loved them all, even the ones I gave unfavorable performance reviews. I asked the early arrivals to wait until the others came so I could speak to them as a group. Seven came. Two died and another had already left. I asked them, "Do you have a home to return to and a way to make a living when you get there?"

I waited for their answers which were all affirmative. I told them, "I'm pleased. Put the war and, most particularly, Fort Delaware behind you as fast as you can. It's what I plan to do. I want to tell you as a group and individually how honored I am to have served with you. You are all good men. I wish you the best."

Captain Sommerville, one of my favorites, asked, "Major Cobb, what are your plans?"

"Most of you know we have a large farm in Catawba County, North Carolina with a grain and lumber mill. We're counting on selling food and lumber to the Yankee troops and maybe start exporting some of our long staple cotton north."

Sommerville commented, "That'd be a change. Taking money from Yankees" and the others politely chuckled.

"Yeah, I'm thinking we'll package and label flour and meal from the mill and sell it. Or, maybe, I can establish a construction business using lumber from the saw mill. Maybe both. I'll need good men and who better than you? If any of your plans fall through, write me."

Each of the regimental officers came to my cot, shook my hand, gave and received heartfelt farewells. After they left, I rested and fell asleep. When I awoke, to my great joy, Andy Blaylock stood over me.

He asked, "How you doin', Major?"

I reached up, grabbed his hand, and squeezed. "Now you're here, much better. Sit down and let's talk. We have a future to plan."

Andy looked around to see whether Scipio was near, sat down on an adjoining cot, and asked, "Jim, who's the darky you sent to get me? Surprised to find he's been livin' in the officer's prison."

I still had a hard time understanding how Scipio got here, let alone explain it to someone else, but did my best with Andy. "Scipio was a house slave for the Morgans. He served as Pete's servant during the war and took care of him all through Yankee hospital and prison. Until I saw what he did for us in prison, I did not fully realize that a black man, any man, could have a heart and soul as big as his. Can you imagine anyone staying here that didn't have to? Amazing."

"He said he'd go with you to your farm. That right?" Andy asked.

"Yes, and we have planning to do for all of us."

Andy leaned forward. "I've done some thinkin' myself. First thing we do is take you to my home. Whatever's still ailin' you, Ma and Doc Burrus'll fix it."

I smiled, thinking about all the good meals I ate at her table. "Yeah, if your mother's cooking can't cure me, there's no hope. But, I expect the roads'll be crowded with desperate Rebs and vengeful Yankees. We'll need good men with us in case we get into some scrapes on the way."

"Scipio said you had money coming from home. Is that right?" Like me, Andy obviously dreaded leaving prison empty handed like most had.

"Yeah. Hopefully enough to get us and whoever comes with us home." It had not arrived, but I was sure Mother would find a way to get the money to me.

Andy seemed reassured. "We've got a long journey ahead of us. My place, then the Morgan Plantation, and finally your home."

I pointed out, "You don't have to go with me all the way. I'll take your offer to recuperate at your farm, but you'll be needed for spring plowing and planting. I can get myself home from your place."

"No, Major." He shook his head. "Like it or not, I'm taking you all the way home. After that, I don't know what I'll do, but I've seen too much to spend the rest of my life on a farm."

I did not want to argue. "All right, Andy, I won't try to talk you out of it, but don't short the folks. The first year or two will be hard on them keeping the farm and getting it built up to where it was before the Yankees ruined your fields and stole all the animals and crops."

With his finger, Andy pointed to locations on an imaginary map. "We'll go to the farm. When you're ready to leave and we'll go by the Morgans, then on to your farm. None of our men I wouldn't trust on the trip back, but it makes sense to take ones we can drop off along the way.

"Have anyone in mind?" I asked.

"Yeah. The best Corporal I trained is Robert Savage. Hot headed and good with a pistol. He stays with a job 'til it's done. He's a Texan. Any direction we take from here points him home. We'll send him off with food, a horse, saddle, and a few dollars when we get to your place. Henry Shelton lives just up the road from me. He takes orders well. He'll be the first we drop off. I'm thinkin' we should include two of the newer men, Gilbert Kinney and Malcolm Reed. The best shots in the platoon and they live in Roanoke on the way to your place. Finally, I want to bring Sam Fort. If nothin' else, he'll entertain us with his stories. Sam's from Wilkesboro and another Corporal I trained. We'll drop him off last."

Andy paused for my reply. It seemed to me he gave our return considered thought and had a workable plan. "Not much I can add. I'm sure you thought of it too, but for all the good meals they'll eat, the men we bring can help with whatever plowing and planting needed on your farm."

"Yeah, the thought occurred."

"If you'll pardon me, I'm about to fade again. I'll send Scipio over when we hear about the money. But, come by and see me as often as you can."

* * *

Andy returned to the soldiers' prison and searched out the traveling party. He told me he thought it best to talk with them as a group and brought them to his nearly vacated division. He got to the point. "The Yankees promised a train south, but no mention of when. We must make our own way back and there's not a dime among us."

"Major Cobb's sick. He has a bit of money and telegraphed his mother for more. I'll take him home with me until he recovers and then on to his farm in North Carolina. I'm looking for volunteers. You're no longer in the army. It's your choice if you want to go with us. But, if you join, I want you to stay with us until Major Cobb is well and I drop you off to your home. We'll provide food, deliver each of you on the way, and outfit Corporal Savage for his return to Texas." He paused and watched for any sign of dissent.

Robert Savage spoke first. "Count me in. I've been up nights worryin'. Other than beggin' and stealin', I ain't come up with how I get home. Besides, I'd like to do somethin' for you and the Major."

Each man agreed to escort me home and sealed the agreement with a handshake. Andy told them, "Move whatever you have over to my division. There's plenty of room. Most of 'em left or will soon. We'll leave when the money comes."

*   *   *

Other than a mass exodus of prisoners eager to return home with or without provisions and transportation, little changed at Fort Delaware. I looked at the rickety bunk beds and lice ridden straw mattresses and wondered if hell could be much worse. The hateful guards did not diminish, just became more obnoxious with increased time and little else to do. In the reverie between sleep and consciousness, I imagined using Mother's money to buy a rifle and ammunition and shoot them. Then I worried the bastards would steal the money. I awoke and my thoughts turned to a more pleasant idea.

Maybe Sydney Ross needs a way home. He's a nice young man, but think how grateful his sister will be when I bring him home. I turned to Scipio and asked, "Please find Lieutenant Sydney Ross and bring him to me."

Scipio returned thirty minutes later. I guessed what happened before he reported, "Mistuh Jim, I'se sorry to tell you Mistuh Syd dun died from de kolra today." If I had tears left, I would have cried. One last tragedy in the long, brutal, and ultimately futile war now, by the mercy of God, over.

*   *   *

Before our departure, Andy came to see me and check on my recovery. I felt better and invited him to sit down on an empty bunk. "What was it like on the soldier's side?" I asked.

"You saw most of what we did. Putrid water, disgustin' food, bed bugs, and paltry blankets, but it wuz worse for the soldiers. We never had enough to eat. Thank God for the rats. We did."

"We left the worst food in the ceilin' to draw 'em. Every day, I shook the rafters so the rats fell down where the men caught 'em. One of our boys, a cook, figured out a way to boil 'em so we could peel off the hide, slice 'em into strips, and fry the strips. Fried rat meat don't taste that bad. Sometimes, cats followed the rats into the rafters, but, as hungry as I was, I had no stomach for it. I kept thinkin' about our family cat."

"How many of our men survived?" I asked.

"Ninety eight went in, eighty two will leave. They mostly died of sickness. We got little or nothin' to treat 'em. The sick pretty much lived or died on their own gumption. Three men tried to escape while we wuz outside workin' on one of the farms. The guards shot 'em before they could make it to the woods. Most of the boys envied the ones that died. From what I've seen here, the cholera was worse in the officer's prison. But, our guards wuz meaner, dumber, and lazier than yours."

I shook my head thinking it would take a lot of incompetence to come in under the guards I saw. Andy continued, "I know you fretted over the decision to surrender at Petersburg, but most of the men who'll leave here would've died there. As tough as prison wuz, you gave us a chance to survive."

"The decision was not difficult," I explained. "It's just that prison was worse than any of us imagined. Many times I thought we should've fought it out with the Yankees." The decision to surrender had always been heavy on my mind. The first and only time in my life I could be accused of cowardice. And then maybe what Andy said was true. Better to live through prison than die a hero?

*   *   *

Within one week of sending the telegram to Mother, I received a return telegram stating she could not send the money to me. Union banks would not accept drafts from Southern banks. She offered to send Hannibal with the money.

I sent Scipio back to the prison telegraph office and kept the message short as we were charged by letter count. "Do not send Hannibal. Home soon." I saw no possibility of a Negro man coming to Pennsylvania with Union money. I trusted Hannibal, but not completely. Regardless of his loyalty, too many brigands, Union and Confederate, would quickly relieve a freed Negro of whatever he carried and probably kill him in doing it.

We would have to get back to Virginia with what we had which was not much – hundred Union dollars Scipio gave me to support seven men and me sick and a burden to the others.

The journey home began when Andy walked in with five regimental soldiers. They looked like scarecrows. Long scraggly beards, unkempt hair, ripped, tattered, dirty uniforms and overwhelming body odor. But to me, they were dear and precious. I greeted them with tears in my eyes. "It's the first day of a new life for us. We'll make the most if it."

I told Andy we did not have the money I thought would come. He seemed unperturbed. "I don't give a damn. We'll make do with what you have. Let's get out of here."

* * *

Andy told us a colorful story of his first outside encounter. He asked one of the vegetable sellers at the prison, "Sir, if I pay a fair price, would you sell me your pushcart?" Andy pulled Union greenbacks out of his pocket so the vendor could see them.

The vendor shrugged and said, "I'd like to help you, but I don't know 'bout sellin' my rig."

Andy sensed an opening. "I'll pay you in cash. War's over. Fort Delaware's out of business housin' prisoners. Be a while 'fore you sell more vittles here."

He waited while the peddler made a show of rubbing his chin. Finally, the peddler said, "Twenty dollars."

Andy grinned, "How about ten dollars?" The peddler shook his head and turned to walk away.

Andy pleaded, "We don't have much. I can maybe squeeze

out another five dollars. We need to get home soon. Our officer's real sick. Work with me."

The peddler seemed sympathetic and relented. "All right. Fifteen dollars and that's final."

Andy put out his right hand to seal the agreement. "I need to get the cart over to the officers' prison. I can pay you there. Will you go with me?"

The peddler grumbled, "Damn, ain't it enough I'm givin' away my cart?" Andy looked sad as he had when we solicited contributions from the churches. The peddler gave in. "I'll go with you."

Andy, with help from Sam and Malcolm, placed me in the cart on blankets Robert and the other men gathered to make a pallet. Andy pushed the cart with me aboard out through the prison gate.

When we left, I thought of me riding a pushcart all the way to Andy's home and the men pushing. Not a comforting thought. I did not know how we would do it, but so many things had happened in the war that seemed impossible. I had to get somewhere to recuperate, somewhere away from Fort Delaware.

I asked Andy to find a store to buy clothes for us and food for the trip home. He stopped at two stores and found the prices high. He bought a few provisions and suggested we get started and buy more on the way home.

Outside Delaware City, Delaware,
Thursday, April 20, 1865
Jim Cobb

At nightfall, we stopped near a group of soldiers posted along the road to Baltimore. State militia who, by appearance of their shiny new uniforms, had not seen action during the war. By then, General Johnston had begun negotiation for surrender of the remainder of our eastern army in North Carolina or at least they thought he had. We noted they freely passed around whisky bottles to continue the victory celebration.

Andy leaned over and whispered to me, "Looks like the town drunk organized this militia and recruited his bar fly friends. These boys have a definite likin' for John Barleycorn. Might relieve 'em of supplies tonight."

We made camp near them.

Later that night, Andy, with Sam and Robert, found the militiamen passed out. Andy selected the youngest for a ride to Virginia. He pulled out a paper slip on which he had written, "I took the horses to get fed and watered" and placed the slip beside the militia Sergeant.

Using hand signals, Andy instructed Sam and Robert to take four horses, two saddles, two of the stockpiled rifles, rations, two half empty bottles of liquor, two boxes of ammunition, and the drunken Private to a wagon the militia squad brought with them. He hoped and expected the theft would not be discovered until well after the guardsmen sobered. Andy wanted the militia Sergeant to think the missing soldier took the wagon, horses, rifles, and supplies until later in the morning when he failed to return. Andy envisioned the Sergeant reporting he and the detachment got drunk, were robbed, and one of the Privates kidnapped and considered it unlikely. By the time the theft was reported, we should be well down the road to Virginia.

They returned and gently lifted me into the wagon beside the unconscious militiaman and loaded the pushcart on the wagon beside us. We set out well before sunrise.

* * *

I awoke mid morning. Andy was gone. Sam drove the wagon. I asked him, "Where's Sergeant Blaylock?"

"Took off at sun break with one of the Yankee horses and a

rifle. Said he had bizness back at Fort Delaware. He'll catch up with us 'fore we get to Baltimore."

The militiaman began to rouse. Sam stopped the wagon so the captive could relieve himself.

As he escorted the young militiaman, Robert told our guest, "We've killed many Yankees in service of the Confederacy and do not care, even a little, in shootin' one more. Keep your mouth shut, stay calm, and do as you're told. You'll be released in Virginia. We'll give you one of the horses and money for your return."

The captive looked at Robert with a mixed expression of fear and relief and answered, "Yes, sir. I'll stay quiet as a mouse."

After they disappeared into a thicket, we heard a long and surprisingly loud stream. Sam leaned over to me and commented, "From the sound of it, our Yankee must've taken in Lake Erie last night."

I expected them to return immediately. Instead, I heard a rifle shot. Robert came back alone. No one said anything, so I asked, "Where's the Yankee?"

Robert replied, "Tried to run away."

I thought about the inhumanity of it. We used him to steal what we needed from the militia squad and then lied to him and killed him. Probably Andy's order. Harsh, but I had to agree. We ran an unacceptable risk in taking a Yankee captive with us. I imagined we were back in the war when killing Yankees was acceptable for any reason.

Andy cautioned the men not to use our real names while around anyone we met on the road. Even sick and delirious, the assumed names amused me. "Precious", "Moonshine", "Peachy", "Blossom", and "Biscuit". Each fit the man. They addressed Andy as "Hizzoner."

We drove the wagon hard to get as far away as we could first night. Late evening, we crossed over the Susquehanna River at Perryville, Maryland, stopped for the night, and made camp on the other side near Havre de Grace. I had been in and out of delirium all day and welcomed opportunity for a good night sleep which did not come. I woke up periodically and had enough presence of mind and strength to pee off to the side so I did not foul the bedding.

About three in the morning, I awoke and saw Andy ride in. He carried a bundle. I called out, "Andy, let's talk."

He dismounted, unsaddled the horse that appeared lathered from a long hard ride, tied it to a rope where we had the other horses tethered, and walked over.

"What've you been up to?" I asked.

"Got some supplies for the ride home."

"Yeah. I see you have something in the bundle you're carrying."

Andy untied the bed sheet and brought out cooking utensils, men's clothes, soap, a razor, comb, and other household items.

I already knew, but asked, "Where'd you get this stuff?"

"The guards helped out." I could not tell if Andy was being facetious or coy.

"Andy, I'm weak and barely able to talk. Why don't you just tell me what you did and let's go to sleep."

He gave me a half-smile and said, "I waited outside the gate and followed two of 'em home. They had a little place down the road from the prison. Looked like they lived together and split costs. One of 'em came out to dump wash water. I clubbed him and then smashed his head with the rifle butt. I got back in the house without the other one knowin'. Found a knife in the kitchen and took my time in killin' him. I knew him. I think the other worked on the officer side. I took a bed sheet and gathered up all their stuff I thought we could use."

Andy reached in his pocket and pulled out a handful of coins. "Found these in a dresser drawer. The bastards took 'em from our boys when they came in."

I did not want to argue with Andy. He did what I wanted to

362

do – kill the guards. But he took too much risk and pleasure in doing it and I told him so.

With the same half-smile, Andy answered, "Never have a better chance to take out some of 'em. Besides, we'll need this stuff."

* * *

We passed through Baltimore easily but feared Washington as it would be filled with Yankee soldiers. However, Washington was the only way back to the Blaylock Farm without going far out of the way. Andy wanted to get me home quickly. We decided to risk it.

Coming through Maryland, we noted the residents seemed exceptionally tense and hostile to ex-Confederate soldiers including our group. Much of Maryland had leaned Confederate before the war, but no more. We learned, from a storekeeper, President Lincoln had been assassinated and Washington was rife with rumors and frenzied search for other conspirators.

Passengers in wagons and carriages and civilians and soldier on the street hurled insults at us. We came on a group of young officers idling near the newly restored White House. One of them stepped out to the street, shook a fist at us, and shouted, "Get outta here Reb scum."

Andy tipped his hat and called back, "As soon as we can, your honor." Under his breath, he muttered, "Home Guard. Clean uniforms. Parade ground soldiers. The mouthy little bastard never saw a day's fight." He kept his head down, a smile on his face, and the horses moving as fast as traffic would allow.

On the road out of Washington, a Union patrol stopped us. A curt, surly Union Sergeant looked over Andy's shoulder into the wagon and asked, "You Rebs in a hurry? Where're you goin'?" He pushed the blanket back and saw the pushcart. "What's this?"

He appeared to be waiting for Andy to make a wrong answer so he could arrest us.

Our situation was perilous. In the current hysteria bordering on anarchy, we would face a firing squad or hanging for stealing Union property. With well placed shots and quick action, the Union patrol could be wiped out and maybe we could get down the road and escape capture.

Then I saw a side of Andy I did not expect. We had killed Yankees during the war and our time with Mosby and two prison guards. All we shot, except the guards, were less obnoxious than this bunch. I was surprised, and later amused, when Andy became meek and serious as he explained to the Union Sergeant, "We wuz released from Fort Delaware Prison earlier this week and on our way home." Andy motioned toward me as I huddled in back with my wan face looking out from under a blanket and said, "That's my corporal and neighbor. He's got the pox. Want to get him home before he dies."

The Union Sergeant backed away and said, "Get on down the road, Reb, 'fore I change my mind."

Andy waved and replied, "Thank you, Sir" and flipped the reins to get the wagon moving. He did not look back, but I saw hate and fear in the eyes of the Union patrol as we passed.

Andy's diplomacy saved what could have been an ugly and dangerous confrontation. If I had been in command, we would have shot it out with the Yankee patrol and would not have come out as well.

* * *

We were not discovered. Possibly, the militiamen were too drunk and then embarrassed to admit what had happened until we were too far gone to effectively respond. It helped that the roads were swelled with returning Confederates and most were as bedraggled as our traveling party. We never knew for sure, but only that we left Fort Delaware with needed horses, rations, and rifles and were not stopped.

On the way, we found other Confederates in miserable condition, but did not stop to talk or render aid. In hindsight, I regret we did not help some of the more pitiable stragglers. I remember one in particular. He sat beside the road near dead with his hands stretched out begging for help. May have taken off on his own and wore out. Or part of a group who left him. We did not stop. I count him among the men we killed in the war.

Andy found a general store desperate for cash and bought new clothes, including shoes, for each of us. He purchased a hatchet and hunting knife to cut fire wood and kindling for the remainder of the journey. He then bought provisions.

At a nearby creek, each of the men shaved, took off his ragged uniform, bathed, changed into the new clothes, washed and then dried what was left of his tattered uniform. Henry Shelton served as barber and treated each to a haircut and shave. Sam cut Henry's beard and hair, not nearly as well as Henry did his and the others.

I watched in amazement at the transformation. Until applying soap and cold water, I did not realize the amount of dirt and filth that had accumulated on them. The skin on their faces and chins, like the skin on their arms and legs after scrubbing, was pink when the scraggly beards came off and the grime removed. But as much as the physical transformation, I saw a noticeable change in expression and demeanor. Each seemed like a new man baptized and reborn in the waters of a Virginia stream.

With the men washed and shaved, Scipio gently assisted me in a thorough scrubbing and shave with cold stream water. I did not mind. I relaxed as he scrubbed away the dirt and shaved my beard. It was the best I felt since leaving Fort Delaware. Following our creek side revival, we set off for the Blaylock Farm.

The war ended and I was surprised at how easily and quickly the men accepted it and went on with our lives. I knew the

Confederacy lost the war at Gettysburg and reconciled myself to that fact two years earlier. I suspected the Confederate soldiers who stayed also knew the war was lost but fought anyway. It cost the lives of many and disabled and disfigured others, like Abel Robertson earlier, for a lost cause. Only pride and determination kept the war going. I thought it noble but futile and tragic.

The world did not come to an end when the Confederacy lost. Life went on as individuals, like our traveling party, simply did the best we could with what we had. In thinking back on what I knew of history, it seemed much the same for all people at all recorded time. As it turned out, life was no different than it was during the war except the South was now defeated. The men had families, sweethearts, and fields that needed plowing and very little to work with. They did their duty to the best of their ability and had nothing more they could do as soldiers of a lost cause.

I nudged Gilbert Kinney, who stood near where I rested, and asked, "What're you thinking?"

Gilbert seemed startled by my question, that his regimental commander would ask what he thought, but recovered and gave a moving reply, "I had a long time to look back on my life while I was in prison and what I would do if I got out alive. Like all of us, I joined the army to whip the Yankees so they'd finally leave us alone. When I got into the fightin', it wuz worse than I imagined. We wuz grateful when you decided to surrender and get us out of the war. In prison, I kept thinkin' I'd tell the pastor, when I got home, I fear no evil. I went through hell and came back. I just feel lucky to be alive."

He stopped and apologized, "I gave you a long answer to a short question."

I squeezed Gilbert's arm and said, "I think you stated very well how we all feel."

* * *

During lucid moments, I pulled myself up on the wagon side-board and looked out on the countryside we passed. I saw many burned and destroyed farms along the way. When the party came upon a prosperous looking farm that appeared untouched, Andy called back, "We'll stop here for the night. There's a stream where we can get water. Gilbert, you and Malcolm take the rifles. Shoot some rabbits before dark."

Scipio told me, "Mistuh Jim, I sees a loose chicken or two on dat farm we past. Maybe sum eggs too. I sho wud like roast chicken 'n eggs in de mawnin'. Speck' de men wud too."

I started to caution Scipio, but said nothing. Instead I watched him fashion a sack out of a blanket and start toward the farmhouse.

Scipio did not return. To my dying day, I will regret not ordering him to stay with us.

* * *

The next day, in early dawn, we were startled by sudden arrival of a mounted, armed band. Robert and Andy reached for the rifles and were immediately confronted by intruders with drawn pistols. I saw them dimly outlined in the early morning glow that, in my delirious mind, set off their features in a confused, devilish swirl. It seemed Satan and his attendants rode in.

I sat up and noticed their leader drop his right shoulder over his horse's neck as he withdrew a rifle from his saddle holster. A heavyset man tending to corpulence, he had sandy hair and a flat red face on a large head sitting on a thick neck. I particularly noted his cold, dark eyes as he looked down on us.

He pointed his rifle at Andy and announced, "I have somethin' for you Reb scum" and yanked on a rope he pulled behind his horse. Scipio's mangled body appeared, neck broken, face and body badly scraped and bloody from being dragged from the farm to our camp.

The bastard did not waste words. "I'd gladly shoot all you trash 'cept it'd bring in the Sheriff." Instead, he ordered, "Take their vittles, rifles, horses, and wagon. But, throw out them filthy blankets." They looked at the pushcart, but, apparently, it was no use to them.

Andy shook a fist and shouted, "You can't just ride in here and take our stuff."

Satan turned back and glared. "Watch me. You should've thought 'bout that 'fore you sent your nigger out to steal my chickens. If I find you here when I come back, I'll teach you another lesson."

With that he and his party rode off as abruptly as they arrived.

Stunned and infuriated, Andy went to a tree near the creek bank, lifted a stone, and retrieved Pete's belongings and the little money left. He said, "Damn it to hell. Son of a bitch hangs Scipio, rides in, and takes all our stuff. He'll pay."

Robert asked, "What d'you want us do with the Major and Scipio?"

Andy looked around and answered, "Cut off branches and use the blankets to make a stretcher for Scipio or what's left of him. We'll carry Major Cobb in the pushcart. Get busy. You heard what the bastard said. He's coming back and bringin' his posse."

"Hope he does. I'll kill him," Robert muttered.

"With what?" asked Sam.

"This knife," Robert replied as he scraped the cutting edge on a rock to sharpen the blade.

They wrapped blankets over the stripped branches and lifted Scipio's mangled body on the stretcher. I got up on the pushcart. Two miles down the road, we saw a farmhouse devastated like most we had passed since entering Virginia. It appeared the family were just able to save their home after the Yankees torched it.

As we approached, the lady of the house came out on the porch. Andy told her, "We're on our way home from Union prison. Your neighbor caught our colored man, hanged him, and dragged his body back to our camp. He took our wagon, horses, rifles, and supplies."

She spat and said, "It wuz that Son-of-Lucifer, Luther Perkins." The mention of his name seemed to set her off, "He's at war with the Confederacy and us. The reason his farm's untouched is 'cause the snake's been kissin' up to the damn Yankees since they took over the county."

Andy continued, "Ma'am, we'd much appreciate your lettin' us stay in your barn 'til we can get another wagon and get back on the road home. The man in the pushcart is our regimental commander. He caught cholera in prison and is in and out of fever. As best we can tell, cholera comes from bad water. It's not contagious if you stay clean."

She asked, "What's your name, soldier?"

"I'm Andy Blaylock, Sergeant in the Light Division." And then Andy introduced me and each of the men by rank as if we were still in the army.

She seemed to know, without further explanation, we saw heavy fighting during the war and spent miserable months in a Yankee prison. And, as Andy expected, she was sympathetic.

He asked, "Ma'am, may I ask your name?"

"Miriam Anderson. My husband, John, is out in the fields. Those are our young'uns." As she pointed back to the house, we saw three little towheads, in the windows, looking at us.

"Take your officer to the barn, but keep him away from the children. I can't take no chances. If you like, bury your colored man over there in the slave cemetery. You can use the shovel in the barn to dig the grave. You mentioned buying a horse. Do you have money?"

"Yes Ma'am, we were able to hide it from Perkins."

"I'll ask John, but I think he'll loan you a horse to ride into town, about eight miles from here, where you can buy vittles. Sorry to say it, but you'll likely find a bargain. We're just about broke ourselves." Again, Miriam Anderson spat.

Andy asked, "Could we buy food from you?"

"No, we ain't got none to spare. I'll feed you tonight. Repay me tomorrow from what you bring from town."

"Missus Anderson, we might help one another. Henry Shelton there," Andy pointed to him, "lives down the road 'bout twenty miles. What if I pay you to rent one of your horses? I can send Henry home to fetch a wagon to take us to his home."

"Talk to John," she replied, but seemed receptive to the idea.

Andy thanked her, turned to the men and said, "Take Major Cobb to the barn and bed down. Malcolm, you and Henry take turns with the shovel and dig a deep grave for Scipio."

When they finished, Andy told the men to bring Scipio's body and me out for the burial. I remained awake as Andy spoke to me.

"We'll give Scipio a Christian burial. I know you want to be there and I asked the boys to bring you out so you can watch."

"Thank you, Andy. You know what he did for me in prison and what he's done for us since we left."

From a Bible Miriam Anderson loaned him, Andy read First Corinthians 13, a favored passage on selfless love which fit Scipio perfectly. I was moved, as were each of the men, as they saw Scipio in the Apostle Paul's divine words. Each said good things about their former traveling companion. They buried Scipio under a blanket without a coffin or marker.

As Gilbert and Malcolm shoveled dirt over his broken and bloody body, I folded my hands and softly spoke a prayer, "Lord, let us never forget your servant, Scipio Morgan, and the injustice done to him."

I passed back into delirium.

* * *

When I awoke, Andy sat next to me. "I want to talk to you about what we do from here," he said.

"I can never repay Scipio, but I'll do two things for him if I do nothing else in what's left of my life. First, Luther Perkins is a dead man walking. Second, Scipio's wife will never want for anything as long as I'm alive."

"That's what I want to discuss with you. I talked with John Anderson. He'll loan a rifle and shotgun and provide shells if we go after Perkins. What do you think? Do we take him now?"

I shook my head. "No. You'd have to go through the men he brought with him. Shotgun and rifle aren't enough. Besides, I reserve the privilege of killing the bastard. Now's not the time. I'll do it when I'm well."

"Damn it, Jim, he stole our wagon, horses, rifles, and supplies. We'll sneak up on the house and take 'em before they know we're there. If nothing else, we need our stuff to get home."

"Yeah, I know. He's no better than the prison guards. But, remember the Good Book, Ecclesiastes 3. There's a season for all things under the sun. We'll settle with Perkins in due time and the time's not now."

My decision did not please Andy, but he understood. I wanted Perkins for myself and better to let time pass before coming back and killing the pig. I would need time to catch him out alone. I needed to be well when I did it.

Andy went to the farmhouse to talk with the Andersons after the children were put to bed. He learned that Luther Perkins came from a family of Whigs who went back several generations. Perkins became a Republican, perhaps the only one in the county, after the party was formed, and was a loyal Unionist throughout the war. During the back and forth battles in Northern Virginia, he provided food, cattle, and horses to the Union Army and refused to sell anything for Confederate currency. He held his sons out of service and later paid for substitutes when the draft began.

Since the end of hostilities, Perkins contracted with the Union quartermaster to continue supplying food and horses. To expand his growing business, Perkins was ready and eager to buy any farm that fell behind on taxes. Perkins was known to be a mean spirited and rapacious man. The Andersons feared he would buy out most of the county farms, including theirs, in tax court. They were not surprised with what he had done to Scipio and our party.

* * *

In the morning, Andy ordered Henry Shelton to his home with instructions. "Get a wagon. Here's two dollars for a deposit. Come back for us." Henry took off on a trip he should make the same day at quick pace.

Miriam Anderson fed me a thin soup I was able to hold down. She also cleaned the dirty blankets and hung them out to dry. Andy borrowed a horse from John Anderson for a trip to the nearest town. We relearned the purchase power of Union money in the postwar South. In a transaction between a buyer with cash and a desperate seller, he returned with enough food to repay the Andersons and for the return home.

Without looking at a mirror, I knew my appearance was emaciated. When I entered prison, I weighed about one hundred sixty pounds and less than one hundred twenty pounds when released. Without food I could digest, I became thinner and weaker. Andy knew my life depended on getting me somewhere I could be fed.

Late afternoon, next day, Henry Shelton came back with a wagon. He spent the night with us for an early departure next morning. In the morning, Henry gave Andy directions to his home and left on one of our horses to help prepare for our visit.

Before leaving, I thanked the Andersons for their kindness and told them I looked forward to seeing them again when I felt better. If the Andersons suspected my intention in returning, they gave no outward indication.

I sat on clean blankets in the wagon. We left for the Blaylock Farm.

Chapter 22: Robbery

Northern Virginia,
April - June, 1865
Jim Cobb

As our wagon approached, I saw Henry waiting on the porch of his home that also served as a general store. He went inside, brought out his family, and came toward the wagon to greet us. I told Andy, "We should have given him some stripes or a medal to show off to his folks."

Andy slowed the horses and replied, "I don't remember him doin' much to distinguish himself."

"He did better than most," I commented. "He survived and kept all his limbs."

Like other young men in Virginia, Henry Shelton enlisted in the local militia to defend his family, friends and home state. The Sheltons owned a small general store which carried some of everything – food, clothing, farm supplies, firearms and ammunition. They did not own slaves and Henry did not know anyone who did. Issues of slavery, states' rights, and preservation of the Southern way of life meant nothing to him.

Andy and the men got down from the wagon and joined Henry and his family on the front porch. Missus Shelton's eyes brimmed with tears as she hugged each man. She looked to me in the wagon and said, "Welcome, Major. We're honored."

Turning to Henry, she said, "Go in the house. Get pillers for the rockin' chair. Make the Major comfortable. The neighbors'll want to pay their respects when they come by."

After Andy and Malcolm helped me to the chair, she turned to her son and his companions and said, "You boys look starved." She brought a loaf of bread and a cheese slab from the house. "Make do with this 'til I get some vittles fixed. Get started. You've got a lot of catchin' up to do." They needed no encouragement and finished the bread and cheese in less than two minutes.

She called the children and told them, "Run tell the neighbors to come meet Henry's officer and men he served with. And tell 'em they're hungry." News spread quickly. Neighbors dropped by with food to add to the meal.

Henry talked with each as they came by. He did not break down and cry although he came close on two occasions when he heard the names of close friends who died in the war.

When she finished preparations, Missus Shelton called the men in for their first home-cooked meal and the most food they had eaten since Gettysburg. While they feasted inside, she gave me a thin, clear soup. "Ain't much," she said. "But Sergeant Blaylock says it's 'bout all you can handle."

I thanked her and she added, "Henry's Pa and me're right thankful to you fer bringin' our boy home alive."

I smiled, accepted her thanks, and did not point out that it was the other way around. The Sheltons treated the traveling party like family and would have gladly kept us for as long we wanted to stay. Despite my lingering illness, I politely refused their offer. Almost as much as Andy, I was anxious to continue on to the Blaylock Farm and be with my second family.

Andy offered money for use of the wagon to his farm, but Henry's father refused. "Just send it back after you get there."

We shook hands with the Shelton family, had parting words, and took seats in the wagon. Henry came with us to drive the wagon back. I felt pride and satisfaction. The first man came home to a loving family. We would have liked to stay longer, but the Shelton home was first stop on a long journey that would reunite each with his home and family.

Blaylock Farm, Fauquier County, Virginia,
Thursday, April 27, 1865
Jim Cobb

As Andy drove the wagon, I saw growing anticipation in his face and extra giddy-up on the reins. I shared his excitement. As the wagon clattered down the dusty dirt road, I raised myself up on an elbow and commented, "We're getting close. Won't be long before we see the folks."

"Yeah. Many times I thought this day would never come."

Despite fever and inability to digest solid food, my thoughts turned to Mary Blaylock's cured ham, fried eggs, and buttermilk biscuits. Even with a queasy stomach, I felt better just thinking about eating in her kitchen again.

As we later learned, Andy's letter from Fort Delaware recently arrived. It was their first letter from Andy since he sent a note from Petersburg in September. They worried Andy had died, but never gave up hope. As Andy hugged his father and brother, Mary Blaylock stood back and sobbed in joy at the sight of her son and concern with his gaunt appearance. Wasting no time, she sent Andy into town with a grocery list. She now had her own army and knew what they liked to eat.

She looked at the scrawny spectacle of Henry Shelton and said, "We ain't sendin' you back on an empty belly." She took him and the other men into the house for "fixins" she pulled together until Andy got back. While the men ate inside, Mary Blaylock came out to the porch where we talked. She wanted to know how long I had been sick and how I felt since I came down with the fever. She listened, nodded, put her hand on my forehead, and said, "Doc Burrus and I'll fix you. We'll send you home to your ma lookin' like a man 'stead of a near dead scarecrow." I knew she would and wanted to cry, but didn't have it in me, maybe in the future when the war and Fort Delaware were distant memories.

Malcolm and Robert brought me back to the bedroom, took off my clothes, and placed me in bed. I smiled weakly. "Thanks. I'll take some sleep now."

Before I dropped off I heard Mary talking with the men. She said, "Whichever one of you is the best shot take the shotgun and shells from the tool bin. The rest of you go out to the field and stir up rabbits. Bring back as many as you can." She added, "You'll like what I do with 'em."

That night, as the men feasted on roast rabbit, mashed potatoes, carrots from the garden, and strawberry shortcake, Mary spoon fed chicken broth to me in the bedroom.

*   *   *

Over the next week, Mary built up the soup gradually as my health and weight improved. I used a bed pan until I had strength to get up and go to the outhouse. As she had with Andy earlier, Mary shaved me and kept my hair combed. Day by day, I felt better and the periods of delirium diminished. By the second week, I ate solid food.

Andy put the men to work in the fields completing spring planting. Taking advantage of the added manpower, Christopher and his father finished fence repairs Andy and I started before we returned to the army. Periodically, Andy returned to the house to pick up cool well water and sandwiches his mother prepared for the men as they worked.

Late morning, Andy asked, "Up for some fresh air?"

I felt better and went with him to saddle a horse for a short ride to the fields. On the way, we stopped by to visit with Andy's father and brother working on the front fence.

As they shared a drink of water, John Blaylock looked at Andy and said, "Son, it's sure good to have you home. The war took Matthew. Don't know what we'd do if we lost you. After we heard you wuz captured, we feared you might die in Yankee prison."

Misreading his father's intent, Andy answered, "You have three sons. Christopher's the one to take over the farm when the time comes."

John threw down his cup and said, "Hell, Andy, it ain't that. You'll never know what it's like to lose a son 'til one dies and pray God that day never comes." John heaved and began to sob with a flood of tears held back from Matthew's death at Fredericksburg.

Andy did not reply, but simply pulled his father to him and hugged.

* * *

I sent a letter to Mother to tell her I made it to the Blaylock Farm and would be home soon. I sent another letter to the Morgans to let them know we would come by with Pete's things within two weeks. I appreciated the frequent inquiries about my health, but understood the men used my recovery as a gauge for when they could return home. When I put in a full day's work on the farm, they started talking openly about leaving.

They ate in the barn at night and adopted Christopher as a mascot. He took his meals with them. I usually ate with Blaylocks in the house. As before, they treated me like family. This night, we got into a discussion of the farm's future.

John told Andy, "We likely wouldn't keep the farm if you hadn't come home when you did and brought help. The Yankees took all we had and will hit us with a big tax at year end. I don't know how we'll pay it 'ceptin from the crops you planted."

Andy quickly replied, "We can't lose the farm. It's been in our family for over a hundred years. Somehow we'll get money to you." He looked to me and said, "I know Jim will want to help."

I asked John Blaylock, "Any idea how much the Yankees will tax the farm?"

He did not answer my question, but visibly stiffened and said, "No Blaylock ever took charity. Never will. You and Andy keep what you have for a new start."

Andy argued, "It's ain't charity. Just helpin' you, Ma, and Christopher out of a hole the Yankees dug for us. Jim hasn't forgotten how we took in Abel and him after they wuz shot up. He wants to help." I quickly agreed with what Andy said.

"I appreciate what you boys want to do, but no" John declared. "From what you dun in the war, helpin' me and Mosby, and suffered in Yankee prison, you've earned a shot at good lives. You don't need to worry none 'bout us. We'll find a way to keep the farm." Then, with a twinkle in his eye, added, "I have something I'll discuss with you and the boys later. It might get you off to a good start."

* * *

After supper, as we sat around smoking and talking about moving on, John Blaylock pushed his chair back from the table and told Andy, "Bring the boys in for a talk." When Andy returned with them, we sat in the front room, some on the floor. John began a long, rambling account of the Mosby Rangers.

During the war, Andy and I decided the fewer people who knew of Andy's, and by extension, his family's involvement in the Mosby organization the better. When questioned, we said little about our service with Mosby. As a result, what we did as Mosby Rangers was the subject of ongoing speculation and exaggeration within the regiment and, most particularly, the men who accompanied us on the return home.

Andy and I looked at each other quizzically. I could about

read his mind. If his father wanted to talk freely about Mosby with the men, why not? The war was over. We all had general pardons including, presumably, Mosby. Besides whom could they tell? But what was the point of bringing it up now?

John Blaylock stretched out the story to his appreciative audience. Amused at first, I noted he skipped over the payroll robbery until the end when he looked to me and then Andy, smiled slyly, and casually mentioned the payroll wagon still ran on the same route. He added, "Only now there's more Yankee soldiers, payroll's bigger, and they run the payroll durin' the day."

Andy and I exchanged glances. I saw a smile form on his face and jerked my head toward the back door. Andy took the hint. We excused ourselves and went outside.

I grabbed Andy's arm and asked, "You thinking what I'm thinking?"

"Hell, I reckon! Our new life is goin' down the road in a Yankee payroll wagon."

I said, "I'm thinking aloud. Work with me. Bigger payroll by daylight. They'll have more escorts. We need help."

"Don't worry about the men," Andy said. "I'll vouch for each. Besides, they deserve a chance at a share of Yankee money. Pretty sure it's why Pa had me bring 'em in to hear his Mosby stories."

"I know. I'm thinking we need a diversion to pull off some of the escort and your father knows it too."

Andy scratched his head. "Maybe we can round up some neighbors."

"Do you think there are Rangers in the county who could help out?" I asked.

"I bet Dad knows."

"Bet you're right. But, if you recall, the payroll we took two years ago was mostly currency. I suspect it'll be the same for what they carry now. Currency has serial numbers and can be traced. Whatever else happens, we don't want any of this to lead back to us or your family."

Andy agreed. I continued thinking through a scheme as we talked. "We'll figure out some way to convert the currency where the Yankees won't find us and give the coins to the Rangers."

"Save the farm and start a poke for the future. I like it, but the first thing the men will want to know is shares. What d'ya think?"

I had not gotten that far yet and told Andy, "Off the top of my head, how about you and I split half; ten percent of our shares to your father, and the men divide the rest? You and I organize, plan, and lead the robbery."

"How about you and I split sixty percent and each of the boys takes an even ten percent?"

I grinned and said, "I like your numbers better. They probably can't figure twelve and a half percent. Let's go back in and put it to them. If anybody wants out, we won't think the less of him."

John Blaylock still entertained the men with Mosby stories as we walked back into the house. "We wuz sittin' right here when Mosby and his Lieutenant rode up. Dressed like he run off from a circus somewheres." The men laughed and he interrupted the story by asking Andy and me, "What's you two been talkin' about, as if I don't know? Want to share it with me and the boys?"

Andy laid out the plan as he and I discussed and ended in polling the men, "Are you in?" He looked around the room. All heads nodded.

Sam spoke up first, "Take money from Yankee soldiers and get in a last lick for the Confederacy, hell yes." He stopped and remembered Mary Blaylock stood nearby. "Oh, sorry Ma'am. Ma taught me better'n to cuss where womenfolk can hear."

Mary laughed and reassured him, "Don't worry. I won't tell your mother. Truth be told, I've heard worse and from your Sergeant."

John Blaylock clapped his hands, laughed along with his

wife, and said, "We'll hit the Yankees where it hurts. I've seen 'em get in line Saturday waitin' for their pay. Soon as they get it, they take off at a dead run to town. Can't wait to spend it on cheap whisky and women. They'll be madder'n wet hens when their pay don't show."

Malcolm Reed, who generally said little, grinned and commented, "Now, that'd be plumb awful won't it?"

None of the former soldiers thought of the risk in taking a Union payroll in daylight. They knew with any mistake a nasty gunfight would ensue. We could be outnumbered by as many as four to one. But it did not matter. In the war, they put their lives on the line daily and often in situations where they faced worse odds. The simple act of taking a Yankee payroll in a surprise encounter paled in comparison.

I cautioned the men, "Union marshals will be all over this. They'll work hard to find us. We'll be taking their payroll at the same place where we took it two years ago as Mister Blaylock told you. Andy and I rode with Mosby. John Blaylock served as head of Mosby's organization in Fauquier County. He, Andy, and I'll be suspects in the robbery. The money trail cannot lead here. I want each of you to swear absolute secrecy now and forever. And that includes your family, wives, kids, friends, pastors, everybody." I looked around the room and again each head nodded in agreement.

To make sure they did not forget, I asked Mary for the family Bible. I put it on the table. Each of the men, in turn, placed his left hand on the Bible, raised the right hand, and swore secrecy.

We discussed the robbery into the night. It could not be a simple replay of the earlier robbery. The Yankees lost a payroll and would be twice cautious now. In keeping with our experience as Mosby Rangers, Andy and I would check all details carefully before settling on a final plan.

Andy asked the key question, "Pa, are there Rangers left in

the county? We need them to draw off and occupy the escorts while we take the payroll."

Without ever telling us he did, I figured John Blaylock had pretty much thought of the same plan we came up with. "Yeah, there's a few still around. Good men. They know the county too."

"You recall the uniforms Jim and Abel wore when they came?" Andy asked. "Ma patched them up. We need those uniforms and four more when we take the payroll."

John asked, "What do you need the uniforms for?" Maybe he saw us risking a gunfight with the escort.

I explained, "When the Rangers pull off most of the escort, we'll only have a few minutes to take the payroll. The uniforms will fool the escort left with the wagon. We'll draw down on them, take their horses with us, and ride off before the others come back."

He nodded and said, "Turkey to a trotline the Rangers know where to find what you need. Morris Clymer was one of our lieutenants. He lives down the road. I think he can get uniforms, horses, saddles, and pistols and Rangers to pull off the Yankees."

"Like us, he and whoever he recruits must keep their mouths shut. Do you trust him?" I asked.

"Yep."

I never knew John Blaylock to be wrong about anything and trusted his judgment now.

Fauquier County Virginia,
May 24 – June 4, 1865
Jim Cobb

Andy and I positioned ourselves along the path of the payroll wagon being careful to stay concealed. As before, we stationed ourselves ten miles apart, timed the arrival of the wagon, and counted escorts. The payroll wagon stopped at the bend in the road where we took the payroll with Mosby. Fourteen of the twenty escorts scoured the woods looking for bandits. They returned fifteen minutes later and the payroll wagon proceeded to town and Yankee soldiers eager to spend their pay.

Incredibly, the Yankees weakened the escort and paused precisely where they needed the most protection. I told Andy and John, "It won't be the first time we took advantage of their stupidity. But, we must be convincing enough to deceive them into chasing the decoys and leave the payroll wagon."

When we reported what we found John Blaylock worried. He pinched his face and said, "You're shaving it close, Major."

I agreed, "Yes, Sir. No time to waste. We'll need the Rangers to tie up most of them in the woods."

"We found a side road 'bout two miles up where we can drop the wagon. After we open the strongbox and take out the money, we'll take off in different directions." Andy added to help ease his father's concern.

"Like you did when the Yankees nearly caught you at the Gillison Farm?" John asked.

"Yeah. They'll look for us mounted in Union uniforms. We'll bury the uniforms, hide the saddles and pistols, lose the horses, and walk back to the farm. All goes well and we'll be back here late afternoon and night."

Our plan required preparation which I explained to John Blaylock, "The men don't know the area. We'll take them out to dig a hole for the uniform and then to and from where we will stop the wagon. We don't want anyone lost after the robbery. We have a week to prepare."

Andy looked to his father. "Pa, pull out your map and help us pick good places to bury the uniforms."

As we looked over the county map, I pointed to a road leading west. "Andy, bury the currency here before you return. We'll pick it up on the way out."

Fauquier County, Virginia,
Friday, June 2, 1865

I felt exhilarated and excited. My cholera was gone, Mary's food tasted wonderful, and, best of all, I felt strong for the first time since before prison. I walked to the house from the barn where the men and I slept and saw Andy outside watering the horses for what would be a long, eventful day. I asked, "Andy, how're you feeling?"

He replied, "Pretty good."

"Are you nervous?" I asked.

"You know me. I always have an edge before a fight. But we scouted this one. Should go well. Will go well."

"There's a lot that can go wrong, but I like our chances. You've done an excellent job training the men and getting them ready."

Andy grinned. "Sort of like Mosby ain't it?"

"We must have learned something riding with the Gray Ghost." I asked, "Do you think we should wear disguises?"

Andy shook his head. "They'd get in the way. If it goes as planned we don't need them. If it doesn't, I'm not sure disguises will help. But, cover your scar. If they see nothin' else, the Yankees'll remember the gash on your head."

After breakfast, I went back to the barn, used pine tar and shoe polish to cover the scar. Before riding out with Andy and the men, I put on my uniform, the one Abel and I took from a Union sentry.

As we assembled to ride out, I cautioned the men again, "Don't shoot unless it's absolutely necessary. Gunfire'll bring back the other Yankees before we get away."

I glanced at Andy and the men. All were anxious, but no one appeared nervous. They joked and kidded one another about going out as Yankee cavalry. I noticed something not evident earlier. The uniforms did not fit well. They looked to be one or two sizes too large except for the Lieutenant uniform Robert wore, the one I took from the Union hospital. They were also dated; what the Yankees wore earlier in the war with more ornate stitching and smaller chevrons on the sleeves. I thought, What the hell? It can't be all perfect and ordered, "Let's ride."

* * *

From concealment, we saw the payroll wagon and escort pass slowly up the road. I waited five minutes and ordered the men to fall in behind moving at the same deliberate pace carefully staying behind the escorts. In another ten minutes, we heard small arms fire as the Rangers exposed themselves, fired high, and retreated into the woods. As expected, the Yankees took the bait and pursued the Rangers into the woods and out of view. Based on what we observed last week, I estimated they would pursue the diversion for ten to fifteen minutes before returning to protect the payroll wagon.

We drew our pistols and raced up the road as a patrol coming to assist. As the payroll wagon came into clear view, I noted that ten, not six as expected, of the escort remained. A young Lieutenant, who apparently commanded the detachment, briefly looked back at us. He and the escorts stared intently into the woods and only glanced back occasionally at us. We rode up on each side of the wagon and escorts with our pistols drawn.

As rehearsed, Robert Savage posed as our leader. He asked the escort Lieutenant, "What happened?"

While gazing into the woods, the Yankee officer replied, "We saw Rebs in the woods and are driving them out."

Savage replied, in his distinctive Texas twang, "You're wrong, Lieutenant, the Rebs have you surrounded."

As the Union Lieutenant turned around, he saw our pistols pointed at him and his men. One of the Union troopers turned to fire at Robert and caught Malcolm's pistol along his head. He dropped to the ground with an audible thud.

With the Yankees looking down at the fallen trooper, Savage said, "Lieutenant, best if you and your men do as you're told. Now, all of you dismount." He pointed his pistol at the Lieutenant's head and ordered us, "Disarm the Yankees."

I took the Lieutenant's pistol and held out my hand for the scabbard. His hand shook as he handed it to me. I spoke briefly to reassure him. "Relax, Lieutenant. War's over. We only want the payroll."

Each of us took pistols and horse reins from two of the escort. Andy tied his horse to the back of the wagon, jumped up in the seat, pushed out the driver, turned the wagon around, and started back up the road. It seemed to take a long time, but, by my watch, I counted less than two minutes.

Before he left, Robert looked down at the Union Lieutenant and told him, as rehearsed, "We have sharpshooters in the woods. They have you in their sights. They'll leave when we disappear down the road. Remain silent 'til we're gone. We'll not harm you or any of your command." With that, he tipped his hat and rode off to catch up with us.

As soon as Robert left, I heard the escort shout and holler. They apparently did not believe the sharpshooter story, but gagging and tying them would have taken too much time.

The top heavy payroll wagon could not be driven rapidly, but Andy had the horses running as fast as possible. A hay wagon came into view. Andy ran it off the road losing no time as we followed close behind. From the side of the road, the unlucky farmer cursed but did not get a good look at us.

The horses, and particularly the wagon, left a noticeable dust trail from the dry road. I changed plan and motioned Robert and the others to take the stolen horses further up the road leaving a dust trail beyond where Andy turned off.

Andy slowed down and carefully turned up the side road into

the woods. The slowdown diminished the dust trail as the wagon disappeared into the woods. I followed and noted the wagon tracks were indistinguishable from other recent traces on the road and side road. No sign of pursuers.

When the payroll wagon reached the planned stop, Andy halted, jumped off, and pulled down the payroll box. It felt heavy and that was good. It was sealed with a heavy lock and that was anticipated. I pulled out wire shears Andy used to cut off the lock. Inside we found thousands in Union bills, but the coin amount disappointed. Andy took no time to count. He hastily stuffed the coins and currency into a haversack, and threw it over his shoulder. We departed in different directions without wasting time in conversation.

As I rode away, I reviewed the robbery. Execution was nearly flawless. We did not expect the departing wagon to leave a dust trail and anticipated fewer escorts would stay when the Rangers created the diversion. But these were inconsequential to the final result. I glimpsed the payroll as Andy dumped it on the ground. Looked like a good haul in crisp, newly printed bills. The operation was a success. Mosby couldn't have done better.

Chapter 23: Vengeance

Blaylock Farm, Fauquier County,
Virginia, June 2 - 3, 1865

For Andy and me, the escape went exactly as planned. We buried our uniforms, hid our saddles and set the horses loose. We saw no Union soldiers until walking back to the Blaylock Farm. Vagrants, many ex-Confederates carrying haversacks, filled the roads in Northern Virginia. We did not stand out.

I felt better than I had at any time since Chancellorsville. We took the payroll and killed or seriously hurt no one. But, then, I began to worry.

I ordered the men to ride on past the payroll wagon. They would not be able to use the carefully rehearsed escape routes and did not know the area well. Some of them might become lost. Then I remembered Andy carefully trained them. In the end, as occurred often in the Mosby raids, last minute changes negated planning and required improvisation.

On the long walk back to the Blaylock Farm, I pulled out the pistol taken from the Yankee Lieutenant and examined it. I had not seen one like it before - a Remington New Model Army 44 caliber revolver, a finer weapon than the Colt revolvers Morris Clymer provided for the robbery. Nicely balanced, the pistol had a solid feel. I wanted to fire my new pistol while walking back, but thought better of it. I decided to buy cartridges when I returned and test it.

Andy carefully counted the bills at $24,176. The amount exceeded our highest expectation. Andy would have stopped and had a party of one except he had no time to waste and, instead, buried the lockbox. But he only counted $996 in coin which he rolled up in the haversack along with his pistol and walked home.

I arrived at the Blaylock Farm first, and then Andy, everyone except Sam Fort straggled in. We waited until after supper to worry, but he did not return. The others went to the barn to sleep while Andy, John Blaylock, and I stayed up discussing what to do about Sam.

"Damn, wish that boy'd show up. No telling what happened to him," John said.

"Pa, that's the point. We don't know. He'll never give us up, but, if the Yankees have him, we'll have to figure some way to spring him. We'll need to do it soon," Andy commented.

"Let's find out what happened first," I suggested. "Mister Blaylock can you give us a list of safe homes along Sam's escape route? Andy and I'll start in the morning and see if we can find someone who knows something."

"We don't know if he ever got back to where he was supposed to be," Andy pointed out.

"We've got to start somewhere and where he should have been is the place to begin."

"You boys had a long day," John said. "Get some sleep. We'll have a late breakfast."

I joined the men in the barn, but no one slept well.

In the morning, after breakfast, Andy and I went to the barn and saddled up for the ride along Sam's planned escape route. We had John Blaylock's list of names. As we prepared to leave, Andy looked up the road, saw a traveler walking toward the farm, and asked, "Is that who I think it is?"

Feeling immediate relief, I said, "Yeah, it looks like our tardy Corporal."

I dismounted and Andy took my horse to pick up Sam Fort and bring him the rest of the way to the farm.

Relieved to see him, Andy asked, "Where you been young man?"

Sam replied, "Sorry, Sarge. I got lost. But, here I am alive and well with the Yankees none the wiser."

"Before you get started telling me what happened, mount up and ride back with me. You can tell all of us when we get there."

As the men gathered around to greet Sam, I got him started by asking, "What happened?"

Andy grinned. "Careful, Major. We're about to be treated to one of Corporal Fort's tall tales."

I knew Sam welcomed the opportunity to tell us about his latest adventure and maybe enhance it a bit. He stood in the center and began his heroic story of resourcefulness and subterfuge. "After we split up, I couldn't find where we dug the hole for my uniform and then along came a better opportunity."

Gilbert Kinney, who stood behind Sam, said, "You couldn't find your fanny with both hands."

Sam grinned and spun around quickly to take a swing at Gilbert as he moved out of range. Sam turned back and continued the story, "As I wuz sayin' before bein' rudely interrupted, I saw a road gang – two niggers and a white boss. They wuz burnin' a big pile of brush. I used my Kentucky accent and asked, 'Seen any Rebs? We had a payroll robbery today and everybody's looking for 'em. There's a reward if you point 'em out.'

None of 'em answered. They didn't even look up. I hung around and then told 'em, 'I'm posted here. If'n you want to go home, I'll keep an eye on the fire and see it don't spread.' The boss thanked me and they lost no time takin' off."

Sam started to hit his stride when Robert Savage dryly commented, "Your Kentucky accent's awful. They probably run off to tell the Yankees and collect a reward."

Sam grinned. "Mine's better'n yours, Tex. Let me finish the story and then decide if'n it's true." Sam paused briefly and proceeded, "When the road gang wuz out of sight, I took off my

Yankee uniform and throwed it in the fire. I made sure it burnt real good 'til there wuz nothin' left but the buttons and buckles. I unsaddled the horse and set it goin' home. It wuz gettin' dark so I propped the saddle up under a tree and spent the night."

"Next mornin', I hid the saddle and pistols and started down the road toward where I thought the farm wuz. And, then, damned if I didn't see the same road gang comin' up the road. I walked by and said nothin'. They didn't remember me out of uniform and on foot. On down the road, I stopped a man and got directions to the Milby Crick Bridge I remembered bein' near here."

It was Malcolm's turn to tease Sam. "You wuz likely goin' the wrong way when you met the man on the road."

Sam joined the laughter at his expense, but acted offended and said, "You ignernt, ungrateful sons of bitches. You wouldn't know a good story if'n it wuz to come up and bite you on the butt. From now on, even if you wuz to beg and plead, I ain't tellin' you no more of my amazin' adventures."

Gilbert looked earnestly at Sam and asked, "Is that a promise?" and took off running with Sam in pursuit.

John Blaylock came out and told Andy, "When he's through chasin' Gilbert, bring Sam in for breakfast. Ma'll give him a double helpin'. I'll take the wagon and Christopher and pick up the saddles and pistols the boys left. When I get back, I'll take Sam out to find his. Keep out of sight of Yankee patrols."

He looked at me and said, "Bill Woodruff at the general store carries 44 shells. When you get back, there's a hollow near the crick bend 'bout three miles away. Christopher'll show you when he gets back. You can try out your new pistol, but don't draw attention to yourself or stay there too long."

* * *

When he returned with Sam, John Blaylock told us, "Got stopped by a Yankee patrol. They wuz suspicious of Sam. Hadn't seen him before. We hid the saddles and pistols under blankets."

"Glad it wuz Sam," Andy commented. "He can talk his way out of 'bout anything."

"No, I talked us out of this one, but don't want to do it again. Before the Union Sergeant said anything, I asked what I could do for him."

The Sergeant had seen me earlier. He said he wanted to know where he could find the Rebs who took his payroll.

I acted surprised. "Someone stole the payroll?"

"Don't act dumb, old man. You know everything in the county."

"Not everything," I told him. "Sorry, you missed your pay, but I can't help you with findin' the robbers. Think they wuz local boys?"

"The Union Sergeant looked at me mean like and said, 'You tell me. Found a buried uniform. Looks like they're back to civilian clothes'." He shifted his gaze to Sam and asked, "Who's this?"

I told him, "My apologies, Sergeant. This here's Judson Mills, my wife's cousin's son from North Carolina. He's back from the war helpin' out on the farm 'fore he goes home."

I didn't practice Sam, but he dun well anyway. He smiled at the Sergeant.

"What d'ya have under the blankets?" the Sergeant asked.

"A saddle", I replied. "Judson's going with me to ride a horse back from the Clymer place. We're on our way to pick it up."

"Didn't Clymer ride with Mosby?"

"Wouldn't know, Sergeant?" I replied.

They hesitated and then the Sergeant waved us on. "Hear anything about the payroll robbery, come by the Provost Office."

"Yes, sir, I'll do that."

* * *

We loaded the wagon with Clymer's saddles and pistols and piled hay on top. Robert put nine hundred and six dollars in Union coin in the haversack and buried it in the wagon bed. John Blaylock coached Robert on a concocted story of delivering hay to Morris Clymer who was known locally as a horse trader.

After returning, Robert told us of his encounter with Morris Clymer. We were not pleased.

When Robert handed him the coins, Clymer frowned and said, "Milburn Taylor got winged while we lured the Yankees for you. He only got away because we went back and pulled the Yankees off. Our man'll have to stay out of sight 'til his shoulder heals. Only five of the horses I loaned came back. Nine hundred Yankee dollars ain't enough for what we done."

Robert replied, "Sorry to hear about your man. You have the pistols, saddles, and most of the horses. I just gave you nine hundred and six dollars. Nine hundred and six dollars for two hours work by four men. We'll get extra money to the wounded man, but that's all the coin there wuz in the Yankee payroll. We'll get him more money when we convert the currency."

It started out cordially, but Robert knew that had changed. After an uncomfortable pause, he remembered what I told him earlier and said, "Be careful when you spend the money. Don't draw attention to yourself."

Clymer snarled, "I don't need no damned Texan tellin' me how to spend my money."

Robert looked at him sternly and said, "Don't be stupid. The Yankees'll be lookin'. Start spendin' big now and they'll be all over you. Wait, maybe two, three months when things calm down 'fore you bring out the big coins and then carefully."

Pleasantries and small talk were no longer an option. Robert excused himself and left for the Blaylock Farm. He worried about Morris Clymer on the ride back.

* * *

I went into town, avoided contact with Union soldiers, and purchased two boxes of 44 caliber cartridges. When I returned, I took one box, the revolver, and Christopher to the hollow John Blaylock suggested. Christopher served as lookout while I tested my new weapon. The pistol had strong recoil, but I learned to control it. By the time I got through the first box of shells, I hit everything within fifty feet I aimed at. It was indeed a fine, accurate weapon.

That night, I took the pistol to the barn to clean, oil, and pack in my knapsack. While I was occupied with the pistol, Andy walked over and asked, "Have time to talk?"

I put down the pistol and answered, "Sure, what's on your on your mind?"

Andy sat down on a hay bale facing me. He seemed worried which made me concerned. Andy said, "I've been talkin' with my folks. They'll have a hard time of it 'til I get some of the payroll money back to them and there's no telling when that'll be. The Yankees took our cattle, all but one pig, and most of the crops and vegetables. Hell, they would've taken the seed corn if Christopher hadn't hid it."

I wasn't sure what he wanted. I already knew the Blaylocks would have a hard time holding on to the farm. Not much we could do except get usable money quickly and get some back to the folks. Andy and I had discussed throwing in together after the war. Maybe it was time to formalize our relation.

I agreed, "There'll be no milk or meat if they don't have cattle and pigs to replace what the Yankees took. They'll need money to pay taxes and tide them over. As soon as we convert the payroll currency, we'll get money to the folks."

Andy looked relieved, but leaned forward like he had something more on his mind. So did I. I told him, "I don't know what the future holds for us, but I want you with me when we convert the payroll and, long term, I don't know anyone I'd rather have as a business partner. Is it something you'd consider?"

Andy got up, reached out to shake my hand, and said, "You have a partner. I told my folks I'll send back money as soon as it's safe. There's nothing in writing, but I'm turning over my share of the farm to Christopher."

He relaxed, sat back down on the hay, and said, "You had somethin' on your mind when I interrupted. Want to talk about it?"

"I'm going back to settle with Luther Perkins."

"I thought so. I heard the racket you made down by the crick today. Christopher tells me you're pretty good with your new pistol."

"Good enough to kill Perkins," I replied.

"We better get started to the Morgan Plantation first thing in the morning. The county's crawlin' with Yankee patrols looking for the payroll. I'm uneasy 'bout Clymer. You heard what Pa told us 'bout what happened with him and Sam. I wuz worried that the ruckus you made would draw Yankees."

"Yeah, I saw them too. I'm thinking I'll take off when we make camp the first night and then catch up with you on the road to Lexington after I finish with Perkins."

Andy replied, "Sounds good, but I'm goin' with you."

Not what I planned. I wanted Perkins for myself. "No you're not. I'll take him down and I'll be careful, but there's always possibility of being caught. I don't want you and the others involved. It's my look out. If anything happens to me, split my share of the payroll."

"You're not going alone. If nothing else, you need someone to cover your backside. We're partners and it starts now."

I knew I was beat. Andy would go with me whether I liked it or not and, without admitting it to Andy, I felt relieved.

I said, "All right, we'll talk with Corporal Savage. If we

don't come back, he and the men should go on to the Morgan Plantation, drop off Pete's stuff, and then divide the payroll. I don't want them to know why we're leaving."

Andy shook his head and replied, "They'll know."

"You're probably right, but I don't want them to know for sure."

We agreed on a travel plan - pick up the buried payroll, proceed about twenty miles toward the Morgan Plantation, and camp out.

* * *

With the Union coins Robert held back from the payment to Morris Clymer, Andy rode into town and bought provisions to take the traveling party through to the Cobb Farm in Piedmont North Carolina.

We shook hands with John and Christopher. When they reached her, Mary Blaylock gave each a hug, and kissed him on the cheek. She took on the role of all the mothers they were returning to see. We deeply appreciated her care and hospitality, the inspiration and support John Blaylock provided for the robbery, and Christopher's hero worship. In addition, thanks to Mary's fine meals and our work on the farm, we left in much better shape.

We stopped, dug up the payroll currency, and continued on toward Lexington. Andy and I rode the horses, one ahead of the wagon and one behind, to look for Union patrols and highwaymen. Savage drove the wagon we took from the Blaylock Farm, Sam sat beside him with Gilbert and Malcolm on the blankets in back. They rotated positions during the day.

We experienced no problems the first day. To others on the road, including Union patrols, our traveling party was simply what we appeared to be – former Confederate soldiers returning home. We carried little visible baggage and hid the lockbox and provisions under the blankets. They took no notice of us. Returning former Confederate soldiers filled the roads of Northern Virginia. We did not stand out.

In the morning of the second day, Andy pulled Robert Savage to the side for instruction, "Major Cobb and I will go back to the farm for some things we forgot when we left."

Savage looked at Andy incredulously. He was not convinced and Andy knew it. Andy continued, "Keep goin' to the Morgan Plantation. The Major and I'll catch up with you on the way. If we don't, split the payroll with the others as you drop them off. Go ahead and take the wagon on to Texas."

Corporal Savage remained unconvinced, but Andy left it at that, saddled up, and rode off with me.

After we were on the road a while, Andy came up beside me and said, "We got our lives before us and over twenty four thousand dollars in Yankee currency. What do you think we can do with it?"

"I don't know. Everything happened so fast. The only thing I know for sure is we must get it out of the country and find some way to convert it. When I was younger I made plans. Now, I'm day to day. Right now, I want Luther Perkins dead. There's plenty of time to figure out what we will do when we get home. There's always opportunity whenever something big happens like end of the war. We're young. We're smart. We'll figure out something and make ourselves rich doing it." I gave Andy a summary of my thoughts such as they were.

"I know. But, it's excitin'. I keep seein' myself as a grandfather tellin' the grandkids what Major Cobb and I did. We're makin' it up as we go along."

"It's us two, but, thanks to your father, it's us two and what's sixty percent of twenty four thousand? Over fourteen thousand dollars. A good leg up on the rest of lives."

Andy said, "Yeah, if we don't get caught. So far, so good. We need to keep it up. Nothin' foolish when we find Perkins."

I thought to remind Andy that it was I, not Andy, who called off rash action earlier, but let it pass. We would execute Perkins professionally, Mosby style. No one would prove the murder back to him or me.

On horseback, the trip to the Perkins' Farm went much faster. We decided to start with the Anderson family, good people who hated Perkins. We needed local information and had to trust someone. Andy agreed no chance the Andersons would turn on us and help the bastard Perkins. They wanted him dead.

Loudon County, Virginia,
June 5 - 8, 1865
Jim Cobb

We arrived near nightfall as John Anderson came in from field work. He shook our hands vigorously and welcomed us inside. Miriam watched it all from the kitchen window and I suspected she added food to the oven before we walked in. John Anderson opened a cabinet door, reached up to the top shelf, and pulled down a bottle of good whiskey. He took out four glasses and poured drinks for the guests, himself, and Miriam who sat down with us.

After a supper of cornbread, beans, and ham, the Andersons put the children to bed. I asked if Andy and I could speak confidentially with them. They cleared the kitchen table and brought in a kerosene lamp for light. We pulled up chairs and began talking. I told them, "I want to repay your kindness to the men and me" and placed ten dollars in Union coin on the table.

John Anderson protested, "Major, you don't have to do that. We're grateful for what you dun in protectin' us in the war." But he took the coins.

I pointed out, "From the looks of your half burned home

and barn, we didn't do that good a job." The Andersons laughed along with us.

Then I made another offer. "I'll pay another ten dollars. Please use it to buy a headstone for our colored man. He was dear to me. If you would, have it inscribed 'Scipio Morgan, 1843-1865, Friend, Companion and Beloved of God'" and wrote the words on a sheet of paper I handed to John Anderson. Then I got down to Perkins.

"From what we saw and you told us, Luther Perkins is a greedy, selfish pig. He turned his back on the community, ingratiated himself with the Yankees, and is trying to buy the neighbors' farms out from under them. We need to know everything you can tell us about him and most particularly where and when he is during the day."

The Andersons looked at each other, smiled, and told us everything they knew. We learned he had a sour-tempered wife and three sons aged sixteen to twenty-six; likely some of the men with him on the raid to our camp. Extremely tight with his money, Perkins did not trust banks or paper money. Some thought he held his wealth in coins in a safe in his house. But, most significantly, Perkins kept to a regular schedule. Each Wednesday morning, he rode into town, paid his bills with currency he received from the Union Quartermaster, took the remainder to the bank, and converted it to coins he brought home. The Andersons described Luther Perkins as a powerful, feared, and hated man. No one crossed him. He rode alone.

After the Andersons retired, Andy and I went to the bedroom they provided for us and discussed our options in killing Perkins.

Andy led off, "We can ambush him."

I shook my head. "No, it's flat here and the woods have been backed off the road. Difficult to hide or sneak up on him unawares. But, more than that, I want the bastard to die knowing who killed him and why."

"We can find a place to gun him down on the way back when he goes to town. That way we kill him and take whatever coins he's bringin' back from the bank. It'll make the Sheriff think Perkins wuz killed for the money."

I had not thought about profiting from Perkins' killing, but Andy had a good idea. "I need to be within fifty feet to hit him with the first shot." Neither of us thought that would be a problem.

* * *

Though careful not to mention killing Perkins, we swore the Anderson family to secrecy and included the Anderson children. It would serve no one's interest if the Sheriff discovered the Andersons talked with two outside gunmen. They agreed and swore the children to keep the secret. I figured one of them would talk, but, hopefully, long after we left.

At breakfast, Andy nudged me and pointed to the kitchen calendar. Someone had circled the following day, Wednesday, June 7.

We traveled the road from the Perkins farm to town and back. The road went up and down a small hill or, more precisely, a rise about four miles outside of Leesburg.

Andy stopped and said, "This is it. I'll climb a tree on the other side of the rise and signal when I see Perkins. You wait for him on this side, move out on my signal, and kill him."

We waited thirty minutes and no one passed nor did we see anyone on the road. I commented, "The road's lightly traveled. We're not running much risk of someone coming up on us when I kill Perkins if we catch him about this time tomorrow."

Andy agreed, "It's not a perfect plan, but we've worked with less."

We woke early on Wednesday morning. Miriam Anderson provided a generous breakfast of biscuits, eggs, and the little bacon she had left. We thanked her for the meal and told both Andersons we would not return and to forget our names. The Andersons smiled and wished us the very best of luck.

John and Miriam must have known we planned to kill Perkins and why. They did not come out and say it, but it was obvious from the questions we asked and in swearing them to secrecy. Years later, I learned The Andersons and their neighbors met earlier to consider ways to kill Perkins before he, with help of conniving fellow scalawags and carpetbaggers, stole their farms. The timely return of Jim Cobb and Andy Blaylock was, in effect, a blessing for them and other farmers in the county. Perkins had curried favor with the occupying army. Much better someone outside Loudon County did the killing.

Outside Leesburg, Virginia,
Wednesday, June 7, 1865
Jim Cobb

Mid-morning Wednesday, we spotted Perkins on the road. We fell in behind, keeping a proper distance so he would not see us. As the Andersons predicted, Perkins went to the livery stable, feed store, and dry goods store. When he headed for the bank, we went back up the road to the hill.

Andy tied his horse to a bush out of view from the road and climbed a tree on the town side to the fifth branch up. He polished his knife the night before in preparation. With brief trial and error, Andy found the right position and angle to wiggle the knife to catch the sun and signal me on the other side of the hill. We waited, but not long.

A horseman came into view and Andy signaled me to come out, but it was soon apparent the rider was not Perkins. Andy frantically waved me off. After some confusion, I figured it out and backed into the woods before the traveler saw me.

After another ten minutes, Andy spotted Perkins coming up the road at a brisk pace. He gave me the wigwag signal and I moved out to the road and started toward the crest of the hill. Perkins did not seem surprised when I suddenly appeared in front of him. I stopped and turned my horse to block the road.

Perkins called out, "Damn you. Get out of the way. Who the hell do you think you are?"

"I'm the Rebel scum you ran off at the creek last month."

Perkins sneered. "What do you want?"

I felt an odd mix of rage and satisfaction. I had killed other men, but did not hate them or enjoy it. This execution would be different. "I came to settle with you. I'll give you a minute to think back to the young Negro you hanged and dragged back to our camp. Ask forgiveness. God may forgive you. I won't."

"Took pleasure with his mammy did you?" Perkins smirked.

I waited. Perkins gave me an evil grin and fixed me with his black eyes, something I presumed he did to intimidate. Then he dropped his right shoulder. Perfect.

I fired a precise shot that caught Perkins squarely in the chest. As he staggered and fell to the ground, I signaled Andy who quickly climbed down and retrieved his horse.

I rode over to where Perkins laid groaning and twisting on the ground. His horse backed off. I watched him bleed and cough up blood. He would die slowly and miserably as his lungs filled with blood. My first thought was to let him die a slow and painful death. But then I thought the hateful bastard might live long enough to tell someone who shot him. I dismounted and held the reins to Perkins' and my horses, aimed my pistol, cocked the hammer, and fired a bullet into his head.

I steadied the horses, reached into the side pouches of Perkins' horse, and found two coin bags. I did not count the coins, but the bags felt heavy. Andy rode up and we lifted Perkins body over his horse, careful to limit stains from his blood. We led the horse into the nearby woods. When well out of sight from the road, Andy pushed Perkins' body off the horse.

"Good horse and saddle. Let's take it with us," Andy said.

I looked at the horse and replied, "The horse has blood stains. Might draw attention on the ride back."

Andy pointed toward the stream where we had earlier camped, "We'll wash off the blood in the crick."

We needed another horse. Perkins owed us far more than a horse. Wouldn't begin to make up for what he took from us.

I handed Andy one of the coin bags. He commented on the weight and said, "No telling how much Perkins has stored in his safe."

I straightened up in my saddle and looked at Andy as he continued, "With what he's already stashed, there's probably enough Yankee coin in his safe to buy out every farm in the county. And that's probably what his no good sons will do with it."

"And...?" was all I replied. I knew what Andy was getting at but wanted him to say it.

"And maybe we go to his farm and ..."

I cut him off, "No, we have what we came for and then some. We need to put miles between us and Luther Perkins and his hateful brood now."

I looked down at the corpulent, blood soaked corpse on the ground, spat and turned my horse back toward the road. Andy grabbed the captured horse's reins and followed.

Chapter 24: Courtship

Morgan Plantation, Brownsburg, Virginia,
June - July, 1865
Robert Savage

My only outside connection to the robbery was Morris Clymer. What if he talked? What if he told the Yankee Provost it wuz Paul Mason, me, Robert Savage, who asked him to set up a diversion for the payroll robbery. Clymer wuzn't pleased with his share. Maybe the Yankees found him and he traded what he knew of Paul Mason to curry favor with them. Major Cobb gave me Union coin to give him and told me to stress again that the Rangers should not bring attention to themselves by flashin' around their money.

When Texas joined the Confederacy, I left school and enlisted in the Texas Brigade as a seventeen year old Private. Until the Wilderness, I survived injury and sickness that took out most of the brigade until the "L" where I caught a bullet in the shoulder. After three weeks in the hospital, General Early cleared out the walkin' wounded and assigned me to the 78th North Carolina Regiment. I served in First Corps earlier and knew no one in the new regiment before coming over. Major Cobb wuz just another officer although I heard stories of him and Andy servin' with Mosby.

The others called me "Tex." I took pride in servin' as a Confederate soldier, but bein' a Texan wuz better. Andy Blaylock picked me for promotion and brought me into his platoon for trainin'. I didn't like him — too army, too sure of himself, too hard on the men. Over time, I came to take to the soldierin' and understood it wuz lack of it that held me back from makin' Sergeant earlier. But, our surrender ended my trainin' and shot at another stripe.

I rode up to Clymer's house, tied my horse to a hitch in front, and knocked on the door. Clymer ordered me to come in.

I never asked, but wuz sure by looks of the place, Clymer did not live with a woman. I pulled out fifty dollars in Union coin, handed it to him, and said, "I told the boys what happened to your man. Here's extra money to help 'til he heals.'"

Clymer snatched the money out of my hand without sayin' nothin' and counted it.

As Major Cobb ordered, I added, "I caution you again 'bout spendin' too much of this at one time or one place."

Clymer snarled, "This ain't enough" and staggered into me, drunk and angry.

I had enough of Morris Clymer and told him, "That's all there is 'til we convert the currency and that'll take time. If you give me the name of the wounded Ranger and where he lives, we'll get more money back to him, but I can't promise when that'll be."

Clymer put his face in front of mine. I smelled 'shine whisky on his breath. Never much cared for the son of a bitch even when we planned the raid. Kind of had a low life look 'bout him. I wondered from the git go how he ever got to be an officer. Figgered Mosby wuzn't that partiklar 'bout who he took in. Maybe Mosby jist needed Clymer to git him horses and made him a Lieutenant for that reason.

"We put our lives on the line for you and all we get is nine hunnerd in coin," Clymer screamed. "It ain't enough. The Yankee payroll box had a lot more and you know it."

He lurched forward. My neck stiffened. "We gave you all there wuz in coin and scraped up another fifty dollars on account of your man wuz wounded. I told you at the start the payroll would be mostly currency and you're not gettin' a dollar of that. We lived up to our end and thanked you for the diversion. It kept the Yankees off us. But, you can live a year for the few hours work you did for us. You have all the money you're goin' to get for now."

Clymer snarled, "You're a liar. I've a good mind to take it out of your sorry hide."

I wanted to club him on the head, but stayed calm, barely. I told the Ranger Lieutenant, "You can try. Right now'd be a good time" and dropped my hand toward the Colt pistol in my holster.

Clymer backed down, but kept gripin' we dun him wrong. I listened, wanted to smack him in the mouth, but waited for the name and address. Only fair he get more, but not from Clymer. Finally, he gave up, wrote out a name and address, and handed it to me. I left right away. If I ever see the bastard again, it'd be too soon.

I paid a quick visit to the Blaylock Farm and learned one of the ex-Rangers had gotten drunk and run his mouth.

John Blaylock said, "Tell Jim and Andy the Yankees know for sure it wuz Rangers who pulled off the robbery. I've been hauled in twice. They know I wuz in on it but can't prove nothin'."

I asked the question most on my mind, "Wuz it Morris Clymer who talked?"

"Could be. The Provost's investigators questioned everyone who rode for Mosby. They never told me what they know. But it appears, from their questions, they know the Rangers and outsiders took the payroll."

I told John Blaylock of my meeting with Morris Clymer and he said what I thought, "It's why he wuz angry when you brought him the money. Probably drunk talkin', but drunk talk is often truthful talk. He should've been pleased. I'm sorry now I recommended him. The best thing you can do is get as far away as you can as soon as you can."

I nodded. "Yes, Sir. But, that they're still callin' in you and others shows they don't know who did the robbery."

"Let's keep it that way," he said.

I handed fifty dollars in Union coin to Mister Blaylock. "Andy and Major Cobb asked me to bring this back to you and Missus Blaylock."

He took the coins, looked at them, and said, "I think I know where these came from. I think you do too."

"Yes, Sir. I jist wish they'd let me have a shot at the bastard," I said. That Andy and Major Cobb didn't include me in gunnin' down Perkins still peeved me.

"Jim and Andy care about you and the men," he said. "There's risk in takin' out a scalawag like Perkins. No tellin' who he knows in the Yankee Army. They'd rather deal with it themselves than expose any of you to more danger."

Mary Blaylock came out of the kitchen with ham sandwiches and boiled eggs wrapped in a napkin for me to take on the ride back. But, before she gave me the food, I got a hug and kiss.

On the ride back, I thought about what John Blaylock told me and thought it fittin' for a man who wuz like a father to us. I took extra care to avoid Union patrols on the ride back, duckin' out of sight when I saw a blue uniform.

*   *   *

When I returned, I found Major Cobb sick again. It took away the anger I had for bein' left behind when he and Andy took out Perkins. The Major slept in fits and starts. Andy fed him broth, but it wuzn't the same as what Mary Blaylock, Miriam Anderson, and Henry Shelton's mother had dun.

I handed Andy the note Morris Clymer wrote and gave him

a full report of my meetin' with Clymer and what his father told me.

Andy clapped me on the back and said, "Well dun, Corporal, but I suggest you work on your Kentucky accent and use it any time we're near strangers. The Yankees'll look for a Texan travelin' with a group that ain't Texans."

Next day, Andy sent me ahead to the Morgan Plantation to tell 'em we wuz comin' and Jim wuz sick. I took a fresh mount, the horse they brought back, and rode to the Morgan Plantation less than a day ahead.

I arrived in late afternoon. The fields wuz torn up, fences knocked down, gates off the hinges. Should've been some plowed fields and wuzn't. I guessed the niggers had run off.

I knocked gently on the door and then harder, but no one answered. I heard movement inside the house and hollered out, "Hello, I'm Corporal Robert Savage. I have a message for you from Major Jim Cobb." No answer.

I gently opened the door, and came in. Hat in hand, I stood inside the front door. An older woman, probably the mother, came at me lookin' mad. She pointed to the door and said, "Get out. We have nothin' to feed you."

I started to back out the front door when I heard a younger woman call out, "Did you say, Major Cobb?"

I stopped and answered, "I'm not here to beg food. I have a message from Major Cobb."

The younger woman came running to the front room. She said, "We're expectin' Major Cobb's visit. I'm Missy Morgan. I apologize for our appearance. You met my mother when you came in. Are you with his party?"

I felt stunned and awkward. Major Cobb had not told me how pretty she wuz. The prettiest woman I had seen since goin' off to war. I stammered, "Yes, Ma'am. I'm Corporal Robert Savage. I served in Major Cobb's regiment and wuz with him in prison at Fort Delaware. Sergeant Blaylock, me, and some of the boys from our regiment are takin' the Major home."

She extended her hand. Not knowin' what else to do, I shook it. "Thank you for coming. Is Jim all right?"

I told her honestly, "He's sick with the fever that took many of us in prison."

"How sick is he?" From the look in her face, I knew right then that she wuz more'n a friend to the Major and envied him.

"When I left this mornin', he had the fever, but we've seen him sicker. Sergeant Blaylock sent me ahead to tell you the Major'll be here tomorrow mornin'."

She looked relieved and said, "Thank you, Corporal Savage. Please eat supper with us and, if you would, join me in the kitchen. I'd like to talk with you more."

I remembered the mother just told me they had nothin' to feed me and made a point to reply, "Thank you, Ma'am" as I walked past the mother toward the kitchen, "it'd be my pleasure."

Missy sat me in a chair and gave me cookies and a glass of buttermilk. She smiled at me often and cheerfully talked as she and the nigger cook worked fixin' supper. I remembered army debriefings less thorough. She asked questions about the war, surrender of the regiment, prison, and our return. I answered each question as best I could.

She commented, "In his letter, Jim wrote that Scipio died. We loved him. His wife, Pearl, will be distressed when she learns how he died."

I wanted to tell her about the Major and Andy settlin' with Luther Perkins, but decided against it. That they killed the bastard would not bring Scipio back and the less who knew, in Virginia partiklarly, the better.

Supper with the Morgans wuz better'n I thought it would be. They asked me questions about Texas I answered and maybe helped a bit. I gladly accepted Captain Morgan's offer of a bedroom for the night. The last time I slept in a stuffed bed wuz home before I left for the war. One of the whores workin' in Fredericksburg had a stuffed bed, but I wuzn't in it long.

Morgan Plantation, Brownsburg, Virginia,
Saturday, July 1, 1865
Missy Morgan

Late morning next day, I stood with Corporal Savage and my parents and watched as a group of gaunt young men drove up to the front door. Two rode horses beside the wagon. I presumed the man driving the wagon was Andy Blaylock whom Jim discussed in his letters and Corporal Savage recently mentioned.

Jim wrote of the poor living conditions and disease, but I hoped and prayed he would be spared, especially after we received the tragic news of Peter's death. When I heard Corporal Savage's message and saw the party approaching, my hope of marrying Jim Cobb became real and my heart swelled. I prayed Oh God, please let things work out as they should by Your purpose and to Your glory. Let me be joined to Jim Cobb as his wife.

Mother, Father, and I came to the front porch with Corporal Savage as the dilapidated wagon pulled up and stopped. The driver jumped down to talk with us. "I'm Sergeant Andy Blaylock," he announced, "of Major Cobb's regiment. These are soldiers from my platoon who came with us from prison." He pointed to each as he introduced them. "This is Corporal Sam Fort, Private Gilbert Kinney, and Private Malcolm Reed. You met Corporal Savage earlier."

I noted each man politely removed his cap and nodded as Sergeant Blaylock introduced him. Their mothers taught them well.

"We're on our way to the Cobb Farm in North Carolina. At Major Cobb's request, we came by to deliver personal possessions of your son, Peter Morgan, Scipio held before he died. With your permission, Major Cobb will invite Scipio's widow to the Cobb Farm where she'll be cared for. As a favor, we ask if we can remain until Major Cobb is well enough to go home."

"Jim Cobb's like a son to us." Father said. "You're welcome to stay as long as you need, but our food stores are low."

"It's all right, Mister Morgan", Andy replied. "We saved some coins and brought food with us. We can replace whatever of your food we eat while we're with you."

I knew how little food was left before the fall harvest and, like Father, appreciated Sergeant Blaylock's offer.

As the men stood awkwardly, I walked to the wagon and looked down into the bed. I almost cried when I saw the handsome man I loved lying motionless on soiled blankets. Rheumy eyes, pale skin, two day beard, stringy hair. What happened to the gallant, handsome officer I last saw?

I turned to Sergeant Blaylock and said, "Please help me carry Major Cobb to the guest room."

Sergeant Blaylock and Private Reed gently lifted Jim from the wagon and followed me into the house and up the stairs. At my direction, they took off Jim's outer clothing and put him in bed. They left and I went downstairs, got a basin, sponge, and soap, and returned. Jim lay where they placed him. I began to worry he was sicker than I was told. I took pleasure in giving Jim a sponge bath. It relaxed him and he lost control of his bladder and bowels. I ran and got a bed pan before the linens became badly soiled. Sara came up and we changed the linens.

I fluffed pillows for his head and pulled a light cover up over him. I kissed Jim softly on the brow. He appeared lifeless except for soft breathing when I left to join the family and our guests downstairs.

* * *

Father told me, "I told Sergeant Blaylock to quarter in the barn."

I objected, "Father, we housed Yankee officers, but ask Confederate soldiers to sleep in the barn. Is that right?"

"It's what Sergeant Blaylock wanted," Father explained, "and, besides, I don't think your mother would be comfortable with them staying in the house." I knew then why Andy and Jim's men had been put off to the barn.

Mother said, "Dear, you know we're very fond of Jim. You tend to his care and we'll take care of the men he brought with him. We all want Jim cured of his disease before he goes home."

Father added, "Same disease that killed your brother." His comment reminded me that I might yet lose Jim.

Mother directed Sara to cook a simple supper for the family and "guests." Following Andy's suggestion, I prepared a thin broth to take up to Jim. He ate some of it before drifting back into delirium.

During supper Sergeant Blaylock made a welcome offer. "We thank you for housing us until Major Cobb's better," he said. "My apologies for mentioning it, Mister Morgan, but there's a lot of damage to your plantation. With your permission, while we're here, we'll make as many repairs as we can with what materials we find."

Father quickly accepted. "Sergeant Blaylock, thank you. I take it you have experience?"

"Yes, Sir. The Yankees tore up our farm and the men worked with me on repairs and spring plantin' 'fore we left to take Jim home."

"Sergeant, if you're agreeable, I'll assign some of the field hands to you. The plowin' and plantin' are finished. Mostly weedin' now and we can let that go for awhile."

"Yes, Sir. We'll get even more done if your field hands take orders from me. I'll work 'em separate from the men."

Mother took me aside and said, "Imagine our feeding these

scarecrows. They're nothing like those smart, young Yankee officers. But, the Sergeant says they'll make themselves useful while they're with us, get repairs started."

I did not reply. I could think of nothing to say of the sacrifice and basic decency of Jim's men, our men, Mother would understand and appreciate. I felt shamed.

That night, as they left to bed down in the barn, I took Sergeant Blaylock aside. I knew he was more than a former First Sergeant to Jim and sensed a common bond, our love and respect for Jim Cobb, maybe an ally. I hoped he could help.

I began, "Sergeant Blaylock, how sick is Jim?"

"Miss Morgan, if you would, call me Andy and, with your permission, I'll call you Missy."

I nodded and asked, "Can we make him well?"

"It looks worse than it is," Andy reassured me. "He nearly died of cholera fever at Fort Delaware."

Thinking of Peter, I dropped my gaze and lowered my head. My eyes moistened. I turned and dabbed them with a handkerchief. Andy politely paused before continuing.

"The fever came back after we thought he wuz well. My mother started him on a thin broth and gradually built it up until Jim ate regular food. He'll come back quick when we get him back to solid food."

I felt better and said, "Losing Peter was bad, very bad. I don't know what I'd do if I lost Jim."

Andy looked at me intently, as if examining, and said, "No finer officer or better friend in the army. We've thrown in together, partners in some venture, but I don't know what it'll be."

Andy's comment confirmed what I thought. This man is a boost or obstacle in my winning Jim. I did not know Andy Blaylock and considered carefully what to say next. I decided to go with my instincts. Let Andy come to me.

I asked, "Has there been any women in Jim's life since you've known him?"

Andy replied, "Between war and prison, we saw very few women. Jim and I talk a lot. There's no one who has his affections." Then he asked, "Are you romantically interested in Jim?"

It was a simple question, but his directness caught me by surprise. I simply reacted, "Yes." And then, "I want to marry him."

I saw a slight smile form as Andy said, "It seems you skipped a step. You'll need a marriage proposal somewhere along the line."

I laughed nervously and confessed, "I wish I knew how to make Jim love me as much as I love him" and waited anxiously for his reply.

"As you asked, I'll speak frankly. He needs a good woman in his life. We all do. But, Jim deserves someone special."

I thought, oh God, he doesn't think I'm good enough for his friend. Then I saw concern and kindness in Andy's face as if he regretted what he had just said and sought to reassure me, "I'm not sure he ever thought of you in a romantic way. But, if you'll pardon me for sayin' so, you're very pretty. You're straightforward and intelligent as Jim describes his mother and you probably know he adores her. Heck, he loves my mother too. But, like you, I'll stick my neck out. I think you'd be a good wife for my friend and partner. What can I do to help?"

I relaxed and inwardly rejoiced. I gambled and crossed the first hurdle. I gained an important ally, a man I knew would play a significant role in Jim's and, by the grace of God, my future life.

Andy was not like the men I knew. Coarser, more direct, less educated. But I saw strength, intelligence, and compassion which appealed to me. He seemed to have many of the same qualities I admired in Jim.

"You're a good man, Andy Blaylock, as I'd expect of Jim's partner. Just keep on being his friend and looking out for him."

* * *

Good to his promise, Andy organized the remaining field hands and the men he brought and began work on repairs starting with the most obvious. I noted he seemed self-assured, easily took charge, and enjoyed farm work and making himself useful. Good partner indeed. After customary soldiers' grumbling, the men settled into a routine that left them tired and hungry at day end. Sara and I made sure they were well fed. I noted the physical improvement of Andy and the men which I presumed began at the Blaylock Farm and shuddered thinking about where they started after leaving Fort Delaware.

I followed Andy's recommendation and fed Jim broth and then soup and then stew on successive days to test what he could keep down. And, as Andy predicted, Jim responded well to my care. We had what I thought was the start of a conversation when I bathed and shaved him on the third morning. But it was soon apparent his mind was clouded by the fever.

When I came into Jim's room on the fourth morning, I found him awake. He said, "We've got some catching up to do."

I sat down on the bed, curled my leg underneath me, and asked, "Where would you like to begin?"

"How's Sissy doing? Pete and Scipio told me she married a Yankee Colonel in February."

He can't still be in love with her I thought. Maybe it was just something to get started talking about the family and the plantation.

"I thought you knew. Yankee officers billeted here in January."

Jim nodded. "Pete and Scipio mentioned it."

"The Yankee Colonel fell in love with her and she married him. She's up North as we speak."

"The Yankee Colonel. What's his name?" Jim asked.

"Colonel Jonathan Hamilton Curtis. He's from a wealthy textile family in Lowell, Massachusetts."

"If your mother had anything to do with it, and I'm sure she did, Colonel Curtis is wealthy." Jim teased me and I knew he felt better.

"Shhh. You know Mother'd never do anything like that." We both laughed.

I genuinely liked Jonathan and wanted Jim to like him too. "Jonathan Curtis is a good man. You'd like him if you ever meet him. He reminded me of you when I got to know him."

"How so?"

"Don't get a big head, Major Cobb, but I thought he was intelligent, considerate, and a perfect gentlemen. He's even handsome."

Jim laughed and said, "Sounds like a great guy. Why didn't you pick off a rich Yankee while they were under roof?"

For the first time since I had known him, I blushed, more from anger than embarrassment. I thought that he had no idea I loved him.

I finally stammered, "You know me. The wallflower little sister." I saw what I hoped was a slight gleam in Jim's eye and regained my composure.

Jim told me what Scipio did for Pete and later for him and his death at the Perkins farm. I listened to his story and asked, "What happened to Luther Perkins?"

My question surprised Jim. He grinned and said, "Appears you did a pretty good debriefing of Corporal Savage or was it Andy?"

"Corporal Savage told me a scalawag farmer hanged Scipio and I remembered his name was Perkins. I wasn't prying. Just a few questions." I tried not to appear defensive, but noted, in passing, that Jim had deflected, not answered my question.

Jim said, "I want to make sure Scipio's widow has a good life. If your family and she agree, I'll bring her to the Cobb Farm to live and work."

"You may be getting more than you bargained for. Pearl's

pregnant. Apparently, when the Yankees let Scipio come back for Peter's things, she and Scipio got an early start on their family."

Jim shook his head and said, "Doesn't matter. We'll take care of Scipio's son or daughter" and I knew he meant it.

I always admired Jim's basic kindness and decency and now loved him for it. Our discussion was calm and rational with a little humor and good-natured banter thrown in, like nearly all our prior conversations, a conversation between two good friends who knew each other well. I had to change that and did not have much time to do it.

Inside, I felt giddy with mixed and conflicting emotions. I was responsible for Jim Cobb and wanted to mother him and bring him back to full health. But, now that he showed signs of restored vigor, I wanted to take off my clothes, jump in bed with him, and make love. I took pleasure in both thoughts. But, then Jim turned serious.

"Missy, there's something I regret having to tell you, but I must. You remember Ken Johnson?"

"Yes." I dreaded what he might say next.

"Ken died at Cold Harbor. I'm not sure but he may have been killed by gunfire from my regiment. We found a letter he wrote to his folks." Jim's eyes misted as he talked about our friend.

"I remember how nice Ken was to spend time with Pete's little sister while you courted Sissy. He never talked down to me, listened to all my stories, and talked with me about what he was doing. He was the first young man who treated me like a lady. He made me feel important and special. I was honored to accompany him to the parties and balls. Even gave me my first kiss. I'll always remember him fondly."

Jim struggled with his reply like a hurt little boy not the senior officer he had become. "It was the saddest day of the war for me. Sorry, take that back. The low point was lying sick while Pete died and I could not do anything, not even see he got a decent burial."

My eyes misted, too. I took Jim's hand and squeezed. Ken's death, Peter's death, our lives in the past two years, the horror of my rape, and fear of losing Jim gripped me. I lowered my head and began to sniffle.

I held Jim's hand tightly. He asked, "Want a hug?"

I leaned into Jim, put my arms around his neck, buried my face in his chest, and sobbed. Jim ran his hand through my hair and stroked my back. He whispered, "Missy, I'm so grateful to you. Often I wonder what's real. Holding you just now, I feel alive again. Whatever happened in the past, we will make it better."

I moved my hands to the back of his neck, closed my eyes, and pursed my lips for our first passionate kiss. I felt my body quiver even as memories of Peter and Ken flooded my brain.

* * *

Fifth day, mid-morning, my parent were outside, Sara and Pearl busy in the kitchen and downstairs rooms, while Andy supervised outside repairs. Sunlight streamed in and a soft breeze wafted through the house, gently swaying the drapes and curtains. Even our skittish cat seemed content to curl up in a corner of my room and purr gently.

I knew rest was the best cure for Jim and made sure he slept late into the morning. This morning I quietly came into the guest bedroom to check on him. As I leaned over to fluff the pillow and straighten the covers, my hair caressed his face and woke him from a light sleep. Jim opened his eyes and muttered, "I like your perfume." He reached up, pulled me toward him, and gave me a soft kiss on the lips.

I jumped in bed with him and pressed my body to his. Our lips parted, tongues touched as our bodies melded, his hardness pressed against my thigh. I felt his hand caress my breast. Except for a rustle from the hall that jerked us back to unwelcome reality, I have no doubt where the encounter would have ended.

Thoughts of the rape returned and I had mixed feelings of elation and terror.

I sprang up quickly, straightened my clothes, and avoided his eyes knowing that, if anyone walked in now, my rosy blush would give us away.

Jim lay back in bed seemingly stunned by his own impulsive reaction. I hoped he finally understood that he wanted – no - had to have a woman in his life - me. He always liked and respected me, but, until last night, never indicated he thought of me as more than a good friend and Pete's and Sissy's kid sister.

Jim looked up and shyly said, "I think I feel well enough to come down and eat with the family and the men tonight."

I replied, "We cleaned and folded your clothes," and motioned toward the dresser in the room, "but you might be more comfortable in some of Peter's clothes. I'll bring them in for you. But, either way, I can help you get dressed."

Jim seemed to consider the possibilities of my offer, but politely declined. I imagined he thought about who had washed him, shaved him, and changed his bed pan over the past four day and became embarrassed. I enjoyed his discomfort. He had started thinking of me as a woman.

* * *

At supper that night, we tried to avoid looking at each other but did anyway. After the table was cleared, Andy and the men lingered. Andy brought in Peter's personal effects which Jim presented to Mother.

Father asked Jim, "What was it like in prison?"

Jim stayed with as much of the positive as he could, but finally gave up and told the plain truth including Andy's account of life in the soldiers' prison. When he finished talking about their experiences in Fort Delaware, he thanked Mother for the nice things Scipio brought in and which Peter shared with Jim and the others.

Then Father asked Jim how his regiment had been captured. The men mostly forgot their manners and had their elbows on the table as he spoke. Jim presented the simple logic of his decision – fight and die or surrender and maybe survive prison.

Father listened to the story and replied, "You made the right decision". I felt reassured to have Father's confirmation. Jim had acted honorably, but, more important, he survived. Others would see it as Father did.

Mother asked about the scar in his scalp she had apparently not noticed on his earlier visit. Jim told me he did not like to talk about his war experiences, but it was too late to pull back. He told his story of being wounded at Sharpsburg and escape from the Union hospital and included that hospital security was much more severe by the time Peter was hospitalized. He told of his encounter with the looter and moved the story on to Abel Robertson, meeting the Blaylocks, Andy, the raids they made with Mosby, and return to Confederate lines.

He surprised me and, I think, himself by talking most of an hour and recounting activity of the Light Division and his service as chief of staff and regiment commander. When he finished, Father asked, "Are you aware General Hill and his aide were killed at Petersburg during the last week of the war?"

Jim had not heard and the news saddened him. He shook his head and replied, "Another of our great generals lost in the miserable war. His aide, Major Titus Palmer, was a good friend. I'll miss him and so many others."

Jim's account of his war experience had been analytical, dispassionate, like the staff officer he once was. But I knew he respected General Hill and, other than Andy, Titus Palmer was his best friend in the army. It wasn't the jolt of Pete's death or Dorsey Pender's or Ken's, but it hurt him.

Under the table, I reached out, took his hand, and held it. I understood the hurt he felt.

Jim stated, "The war was lost at Gettysburg." No one at the table seemed surprised or upset with this statement.

Father asked, "How?"

"General Lee picked a bad time to become stubborn. The Yankees held the high ground. General Longstreet pleaded with him to pull out, flank the Union Army, and move on toward Washington to take a more favorable defensive position. But, General Lee wouldn't hear of it. I agreed with General Longstreet then and now. I don't know if we could've ever won the war, but I'll always wonder what might've happened if we did what we should have at Gettysburg."

Father commented, "It's gratifying to me and Margaret to see the young cadet we knew come back a competent and highly placed officer. We're proud of you." I said nothing, but listened intently, held Jim's hand, and took everything in.

Over the years of his service, I had picked up bits and pieces of his career. Jim served as Chief of Staff to Generals Pender, Hill, and Mahone at nearly every major battle our army fought. I considered it a miracle he sat beside me. So many times he could have been killed in battle and or died at Fort Delaware, but came back to me. I believed stronger than ever we belonged together.

Noting Jim tire, Mother shooed everyone from the table and said, "Jim, you've been up too long. Don't overdo on your first day back with us. Go on up and get your sleep."

I saw Jim motion Andy to accompany him to the guest bedroom and discretely followed them up the stairs pretending to go to my room. Instead, I went to Sissy's bedroom which shared a wall with the guest room. As a girl, I learned I could hear everything said in the guest room if I pressed my ear to the wall. Sissy showed me how to do it.

When they sat down, Jim related what happened with me in the morning.

Andy said, "I wuz beginnin' to wonder if you'd ever wake up and discover she's sweet on you."

"What should I do?" Jim asked. I wanted to throttle him.

"What do you want to do?" Andy asked.

"I don't know. I'm scared. I've known Missy since she was a gawky thirteen year old girl. I can't count the number of conversations we had while I was a cadet. Outside of my mother, she's the most clear-headed, intelligent woman I know."

"Yeah, and she grew into quite a looker. Why're you scared?" Andy asked what I would have if I could.

"What do I do? Do I just ask her?"

I doubted Andy knew anymore about proposing than Jim did. But, at his point I felt giddy. Jim was talking to his best friend about marrying me.

"You do want to marry her?" Andy questioned.

"I think so, but do I just come right out and ask her to marry me? And if she says yes, what do I do?"

"She'll say yes."

"How do you know? I wasn't good enough to marry her sister. Her mother looks down on me."

Andy said, "Missus Morgan isn't too sure about any of us, but you see where I'm going with this. You outranked their son, saw more action, counseled with the generals, and brought back Pete's stuff. You're a noble man in their eyes and most particularly with their daughter."

"Maybe the younger daughter," Jim answered, "but they liked me fine even as Missy's sister broke off our engagement and told me I wasn't good enough for her."

"I don't know Sissy and don't know if I care to. She sounds too much like her mother for me, but I think you got the best part of the deal." I wanted to reach through the wall and hug Andy.

"Do I just ask her?"

Playing the older brother, Andy said, "I don't know much

about women either, all boys in my family too. But, I know this much. If they're interested in marriage, they'll let you know."

He did not know I listened to their conversation, but Andy told me what I needed to do.

Chapter 25: Marriage

Morgan Plantation, Brownsburg,
Virginia, July 1865
Missy Morgan

After rapping gently on the door, I heard Jim stir. Figuring he was awake, I asked, "Are you decent?"and heard him reply, "As decent as I'll ever be. I'm lying here on this nice, soft bed thinking pleasant thoughts."

"Do your pleasant thoughts include me?" I asked as I walked in.

Jim took my hand. "You don't know how good it feels to wake up well and see a pretty girl smiling at me."

"Do you say that to all the girls you meet?"

"Yes, all the girls at Fort Delaware, Peebles' Farm, Petersburg …" I interrupted him with a kiss on the forehead. He took my other hand and pulled me to him for a firm kiss on the lips.

"That was nice. Very nice." I reluctantly stepped back and continued to what I came to ask, "I have an invitation for you. Do you feel well enough to join me in a picnic?"

"Yes."

His reply was instant and eager. I begin to feel tingly as I laid out my plan and hoped he would be up to what I had in mind.

"I have a favorite spot where Sissy and I held our picnics. Peter ate most of the food. It's something we did to entertain ourselves as children, but I thought even a broken down old Major might enjoy it."

Jim laughed.

"What's funny about that?" I asked. I knew he wanted to tease me and went along with it.

"Nothing, absolutely nothing," he said to bait me.

"You don't get off that easy. Tell me why you think a picnic with the Morgan children is so funny."

Jim raised his hands in mock surrender. "All right. As you described it, I saw the two of you in pretty little pinafores feeding fancy finger sandwiches to Pete who gobbled them down without noticing or caring they were fancy. It struck me as funny."

I stifled a laugh. "It wasn't exactly like that, but close enough. Come down when you're dressed and we'll plan the picnic."

* * *

Jim came to the parlor. His appearance was still underweight and weak, but handsome to me. No longer a boyish cadet or even the young staff officer who came to visit before Gettysburg. He had the same pleasant smile, but now had lines on his face and sadness in his eyes. Jim told of his service in the army. He was a man, a strong man, a man I much needed in my life. He suggested, "How about we take a ride to build up an appetite. I haven't seen the place since we came."

I readily agreed. "What should I put in the picnic basket?"

"Anything but finger sandwiches," he replied and we both laughed.

"Seriously, what do you want to eat? I need to tell Sara what to prepare before we leave on the ride."

"Anything you put in the picnic basket, including dainty, little finger sandwiches, is fine with me."

I went back to the kitchen to talk with Sara and then changed into my riding dress. I came out in knee length boots, a riding skirt, blouse, jacket, and a jaunty riding hat with a bright feather and yellow ribbon that fell down my back. I picked this outfit to dazzle him and I succeeded.

Jim looked at me intently and began speaking words I had dreamed he would say to me someday. "You are absolutely stunning."

I caught my breath, but managed to reply, "Do you want anything to eat before we leave?"

"No, I'm saving my appetite for the wonderful picnic you and Sara are preparing." We laughed again. Everything that morning seemed amusing.

I went back to the kitchen to give Sara instruction for the picnic basket and told her I would return in two hours to pick it up. She smiled and gave me a big hug before we left, and then smiled broadly at Jim from the kitchen.

A pair of groomed, matching saddled chestnut mares waited for us in the stable. "What's this?" Jim asked.

"We can thank our friend, Andy. I mentioned taking you on a picnic and he bet me you'd want a ride first."

"You and Andy struck up a friendship?" Jim asked. I knew then Jim was not aware of the alliance I had formed with his best friend.

"Yes, as you well know, Andy Blaylock is a good man. I am pleased to count him as a friend." I smiled at Jim with all the innocence I could muster.

* * *

Three months earlier, Jim nearly shared an unmarked grave with Peter. Now his head was full of life and hopefully me. Nothing either of us could do to erase the ugly memories of war, but, miracle of miracles, praise God, we were finally together.

As we rode, Jim looked out over the broken fences and overgrown bridal path and commented, "Sad to see what's happened."

He remembered wooden fences with hinged gates enclosing each of the plantation's fields and pastures. Live oak trees provided shade along the paths in the summer and protection from the wind during winter. Flowerbeds and rose bushes surrounded the main house and rose vines hung along the fences and outbuildings. Several small bridges carried the riding path over a meandering stream. In the spring and early summer, our plantation was an artist's palette – green fields and pastures, darker green oak leaves, white, red, pink, and yellow roses along the fences and paths, and a gently flowing clear stream separating our Plantation from the Carlton's.

All of it was in disrepair – splintered fences, gates hanging by one hinge, flowerbeds trampled, bridge rails missing, unplowed and torn up fields, massive damage from recent conflict and neglect.

"You and I remember when it was beautiful," Jim commented.

"It will be again." I patted the neck of my horse, as she became restive when we slowed down and came together. "We appreciate what Andy and the men are doing to get the repair started, but we'll soon have ample funds to completely restore the plantation. Part of Colonel Curtis's charm was his promise to send money, after the war, for repairs. I suspect Sissy made it a condition in accepting his proposal."

I deliberately brought up Sissy to gauge his reaction. His response surprised and pleased me. "With carpetbaggers and scalawags stealing farms all over the South, Sissy did what she had to. I'm pleased for her, you, your parents, and even Colonel Curtis."

Earlier, I'm sure Jim would have been highly offended by the thought of Sissy selling herself to a Yankee officer. But, all of that had changed. The war was lost, the South destitute, and I hoped his affections were now firmly fixed on me. Memories of Sissy seemed to no longer pain him.

We came upon Andy and the men repairing a fence. Andy saw us, grinned, and barked out, "Detail, attench-hut!" They dropped what they were doing, stood at attention, and rendered salutes.

Jim played along, returned the salute, and called out, "At ease, men." In passing, we heard "take it easy Major", "are you sure you're comfortable?", "can I ride along with you?"

Out of their hearing, Jim said, "I've never seen them happier. They're thinking of home and sweethearts they left."

"No one more deserves a good life than you, Andy, and the men. I'm pleased for all of you," I said and meant it. Every Confederate veteran was a hero to me.

Jim took my hand. We rode silently, hand in hand, for several minutes. Finally, he said, "I still cannot believe it. The war is over and we are alive. Battle after battle I felt like a dead man and then Fort Delaware and hell...." his voice trailed off.

Jim dropped my hand and said, "I am being morbid. Let's ride back for the basket, go on to the picnic, and have fun."

We rode back to the house and came out with the basket and blankets to sit on. Jim demonstrated some of what he learned in the army in rolling up the blankets and tying them down behind the saddles. He helped me mount sidesaddle. He seemed to shiver as I lightly ran my hand up his back and then picked up the basket, mounted, and we rode off.

* * *

On arriving at the picnic site, I waited until Jim stood directly in front of me for dismount. I leaned forward and put my hands lightly on his shoulders. He gripped my waist firmly as I slowly descended while caressing his chest with my body. Jim put his arms around me, drew me close, and kissed me firmly on the lips. Our mouths parted and our tongues touched.

We separated slowly. Jim took down the blankets and spread

them out. I did not like the placement - still visible from the house and the men working in the field - and suggested we would be more comfortable on a grassy knoll near a clump of bushes out of sight from the main house. Jim picked up the blankets and put them where I directed.

I placed the basket on a blanket and sat down beside it. Jim sat down beside me. I opened the basket and took out plates and the food – fried chicken, potato salad, strawberries, and lemonade to drink – Jim's favorites.

Jim looked at the food and declared, "This is the best I've seen since I left home." He added, "Or at least since I left Mary Blaylock's kitchen".

We playfully fed each other and exchanged pleasant small talk, mostly discussed the good times we had during his many visits as a cadet. By degrees, the pleasant talk turned romantic. Lying side by side on the blanket while watching puffy summer clouds drift by, I rested my head on Jim's chest.

After a few minutes, his hand moved slowly up my waist and lightly caressed my breast. I hoped the time was right and whispered, "James Cobb, do you love me?"

Without hesitation, he responded, "Yes, with all my heart."

I tilted my head up slightly, looked at him intently, and said, "I think now would be a good time to show me how much you love me." I reached over and unbuttoned the top button of his shirt.

I thought about and planned this moment since the first kiss, particularly in the following mornings when it would have been easy to climb in bed with him. I drove out memories of the rape and thought instead, this is what it should be. Making love to a man who loves and respects me.

Jim unbuttoned my blouse, removed it, and then fumbled around to find where the riding skirt was fastened and finally gave up. I felt relieved he seemed amateurish. He did not find the skirt button. I found his belt buckle, loosed it, and began unbuttoning his pants. Suddenly, he jumped back and I watched as he hastily took off his boots, shed his pants, and returned.

He kissed my neck, moved on down to my breasts, raised my skirt, and pulled off my underpants. A bit hasty, I thought, but I was eager too. I spread my legs, felt his arms under my shoulders as he propped himself over me, and then felt the hardness that excited me in our first passionate kiss. It hurt, but nothing like the rape. The difference, a huge difference, was coupling with a man who loved me, not a pig seeking pleasure.

When our passions cooled somewhat, Jim kissed me and whispered, "I'm very sorry if I hurt you. I never want to hurt you. I don't know what came over me and apologize for my rough behavior."

I thought, he really has not been with a woman before, and felt even more special. To reassure him, I curled up in his arms, put a finger on his lips, and whispered, "Darling, do not apologize. You were wonderful and are wonderful".

He looked down on me in my glory and declared, "After this, we'll have to marry."

It was what I dreamed since learning he was still alive and yet the suddenness and casualness of the proposal startled me. He smiled and waited.

Jim said nothing for a moment and then asked, "Want to talk about it?"

I sat up and said, "I have something I must tell you and wish to God I did not."

"What is it?" I saw surprise and hurt in his eyes and regretted what I must tell him.

I wiped my damp cheeks with the back of my hand and started. "I love you with all my heart. I hope you know that."

Jim leaned forward, took my hands. "Yes, I know you do and I love you. But…"

I could not go into marriage with a lie. It would be the hardest thing I had ever done, but I had to tell him. Tears streaked my cheeks. "Tuesday, September 27, the same day you surrendered your regiment, Yankee bummers came to our home. Nobody around but Sissy, Pearl, Sara, and me. They demanded money and food. We gave them all we had and fed them. Then three of them took me to the bedroom and ..."

Jim squeezed my hands. "Don't go on. Scipio told me what happened."

I could scarcely believe what he said. He must think me a low woman. No turning back now. Looking up through my tears, I said, "I'm...I'm a soiled woman. You deserve better. I'm not worthy of you."

Having exposed my shame and fear that he would reject me when he knew bummers had raped me, I broke down and began sobbing. Jim put his arms around me and pulled me to him. My body shook and rhythmically pulsed against his. He found the pins I used to hold up my hair, removed them, let my hair fall down over my shoulders, and gently stroked my back. More than anything he could say, I felt loved and protected by the man I adored and began to recover my composure.

After a few minutes, I stopped crying and felt Jim's hand under my chin. He lifted my head, looked lovingly into my eyes, and said, "You did nothing wrong. In fact, you showed remarkable courage in a very ugly situation. You were a victim. I'm not ashamed of you. I'm proud of you. I know idle tongues will wag, but we'll leave Virginia soon and go where you'll be Missus James Cobb. No one will ever say anything bad about you, not in my presence. The best we can do is put the ugly incident behind us. Thinking on it distresses you and angers me and everyone who loves you."

"James Cobb, I've always loved you, but never more than now," I blurted out the first thought that came to mind and then added, "But, think about it. Do you really want to marry someone Yankee bummers treated worse than a whore?"

I saw the look of determination I had seen on his face before.

He said, "I love you. I want to marry you and take you home. It's as simple as that. Nothing else matters. Andy and the men delayed coming home so I could become well and court you before moving on. They'll be disappointed if you turn me down. What do you say?"

"I say, let's marry here and take us and your men home."

Jim smiled. "Perfect. But, I don't have a ring to give you."

"I don't care." I really didn't. "I'll enlist Mother and, believe me, we'll be married within two weeks rings and all."

"I believe you." He said and then Jim asked, "Think we ought to get back?"

"Not yet."

I put my arms around his neck and pressed my breasts into his bare chest. I kissed him firmly and slowly fell back to the blanket. I arched my back so I no longer sat on my dress as he removed it. I held up one leg and then the other as he removed my riding boots, items we had neglected in the earlier haste. We were both entirely naked as he entered me again. But, this time, less aggressively, slowly and rhythmically until the end. I enjoyed the love making even more than before. Afterward we lay quietly enjoying our closeness.

He kissed me and whispered, "When we go back, I'll ask your father for his approval. It's the right thing to do."

Just like him to worry about propriety. I ran my hand through his hair. "Go ahead, but I know he'll say yes. My parents love and respect you too."

We dressed and gathered up the basket, blankets, and food scraps and then repeated the earlier mounting routine. I thought we would never be more in love. One week ago, I wasn't even sure he loved me in the way I wanted to be loved.

* * *

Jim walked over to Father and said, "I apologize for being forward, but I seek your approval. I want to marry Missy and as soon as possible."

Father smiled broadly, looked over to me. "I presume you agree with Jim." He knew my answer, but I beamed and nodded. He extended his hand to Jim, and said, "Welcome to our family. Margaret and I always hoped you and Missy would marry. You've been part of our family since Peter first brought you to visit and now we'll make it official."

The fortunes of war changed everything. It should have been Jim and Sissy going into a marriage I know would have been miserable. Instead, I would marry Jim Cobb, but at a terrible price in terms of what our family, the plantation, and, most particularly, what Jim and I had each suffered.

Mother stood at a discreet distance, facing away. As Jim approached, she turned and opened her arms for a hug. I knew Jim was sincere in his affection for Mother, even knowing her faults. During one of our serious conversations, he told me he thought she was, at heart, a woman who wanted the best for her children and that made it easier to overlook her manipulation, pettiness, and pretense. And, best of all, he told me I was nothing like her.

* * *

Jim went back to his room for rest while I sat in the parlor and talked with Father. He said, "Next to you and Jim, I may be the happiest person in the house. But my happiness is tempered by the prospect of losing my little girl."

The past two hours had completely changed my life. No longer just my father's girl, I was Jim Cobb's lover and soon-to-be wife. I patted Father's arm. "Another time, I would marry a planter's son, have children, and carry on the tradition we hoped to establish. But thank God Jim Cobb's alive and will marry me. Before I leave, there's opportunity to help turn around our situation."

Father looked at me quizzically. "I think about your sister. We can only hold on to the plantation because she married Colonel Curtis. At the same time, her marrying a Yankee officer destroyed what little standing we had. We'll never be accepted. Maybe your children, not Sissy's, and not in our lifetime. With Peter dead and our daughters gone, I'm thinking the Morgan Plantation dies with your mother and me."

"Have you thought through what my marriage might do for our standing in the community?" I asked.

Father leaned back in his chair. "Even when you were a little girl, you talked with me like an adult. But, you have an idea I'm not followin'."

"Sissy did what she had to. Jim understands, but the neighbors will never forgive us. However, you now have the antidote. You heard what Jim told us. Invite the neighbors who would not attend Sissy's wedding. You and mother tell everyone you know about what he did in our army. We'll see how many decline to attend my wedding to Major James Cobb, A P Hill's Chief of Staff."

* * *

After supper, one by one, Andy and the men passed by, shook Jim's hand, and patted him on the back. By now, Jim must have realized everyone in the house knew he would marry me before he did.

Malcolm Reed stood last in line. When he got to Jim, he extended his rough, burly hand, and said, "Major, I'm pleased for you. Miss Morgan's real purty and a fine lady. She'll be a good wife for you. I wish both of you the best."

Jim had not talked privately with Malcolm since coming down sick on the ride to the Morgan Plantation. He put his hand on Malcolm's shoulder. "I wouldn't have this opportunity if you and the others had not taken care of me on the ride back from Fort Delaware. Missy and I much appreciate your kindness and devotion. Thank you and our best wishes go with you."

The others had moved on so Jim and Malcolm lingered to talk briefly. Jim asked, "Is there someone special waiting for you?"

Malcolm's broad face broke out in a grin as he answered, "Yes, Sir, there is. She sent me a letter in prison and it somehow got through. She said ifn the Yankees didn't kill me, she'd be waitin'."

"If you would, tell me about her."

I noted it took little encouragement for Malcolm to talk about 'his girl'. Apparently, she had been much on his mind since he left to join the army. "Major, she's a purty little thang. Too purty for a big, ugly man like me, but she loves me anyways. She's the parson's niece and wuz workin' to fix my bad speech and manners 'fore the war."

Jim smiled. "She will have the opportunity to continue when we get you home. I regret I've delayed your return."

"Don't give it a thought Major. We're pleased to hep' you."

* * *

After supper, we sat alone in the parlor holding hands. I moved closer to Jim and pointed out, "Darling, we need to discuss the wedding."

As he told me earlier, Jim understood women planned, organized, and ran weddings; men served best by just showing up and doing what they're told. Knowing it would happen anyway, he replied, "I'd be appreciative if you take the lead and let me follow."

I smiled and allowed that Mother and I had made a few notes.

In summary, we would have a Confederate military wedding;

Jim would be fitted in Peter's formal uniform altered to show Major's rank; a formal sergeant's uniform would be found or sewn for Andy whom we assumed would be Jim's best man; the wedding would be simple with only the best man and a maid of honor as attendants; male guests would be encouraged to wear their uniforms. Mother promised to make best effort to find suitable attire or repair the uniforms of Jim's men; and Reverend Cuthbert would be asked to forego the usual banns so we could marry Saturday of next week.

When I finished, Jim smiled and replied, "Fine." I knew he was not enthusiastic about being outfitted in formal uniform again and doubted Andy and the men would be either. He looked at me plaintively and asked, "Can't we just get it done and I take you home."

I did my best to reassure him the wedding would not be too agonizing. I was anxious to leave too, but not before helping my family regain community standing with my marriage to a true hero of the Southern Army.

Jim held out for wearing his uniform in the wedding. "This uniform's special," he explained, "Dolly Hill, the general's wife herself, altered one of the General's uniforms and gave it to me after I rejoined the Light Division."

I replied, "Yes, dear. But it's also tattered and beyond repair. We want you looking your best."

Jim argued for a while, but reluctantly agreed to wear Pete's altered uniform during the wedding service.

During the next week, Mother and I engaged in the myriad of details that even a simple wedding entails. Jim wrote a quick letter to his mother informing her that he would marry me and started working with Andy and the men on repairs. He seemed to enjoy the outside work and exhaustion at the end of the day. Careful not to repeat the earlier relapse, he paced himself and his strength and weight improved daily.

By the wedding day, I felt both anxious and exuberant. As

Jim's wife, I would have the life I always wanted and my own small army for an exciting journey to Jim's home in North Carolina. To enjoy the moment, I deliberately refrained from thinking about what I would do when I arrived as the second Missus Cobb.

St Mark's Episcopal Church, Brownsburg, Virginia,
Saturday, July 22, 1865
Missy Cobb

Neighbors, who did not approve of us, resented our housing Yankee officers during the war, and highly offended by Sissy marrying a Yankee officer, came to wish Jim and me well. Our neighbors, but I knew they came to honor Jim, not the Morgans. Nevertheless they came.

During the twenty-five years we spent in the Brownsburg community, the neighbors had slowly separated the identities of our family. Father and I gained stature following the nasty business with the bummers. They admired our courage and swift justice rendered. Most of them seemed willing to temporarily set aside Sissy's transgression and celebrate my marriage particularly after what they learned of the bridegroom. I don't think the women of our community would ever accept Mother, but I knew she would keep trying regardless.

We married at the church with the reception in our home. No serious blunders during the wedding although Jim nervously attempted to put the family wedding ring on my middle finger.

The guests numbered about eighty including Andy and the men. Andy charmed and mixed well with all the guests as did the men. We picked flowers, including roses from the garden, and placed them in vases throughout the house. We served a rum-based punch along with cake and finger sandwiches for refreshment. Mother moved easily among the guests while Father, who told everyone how pleased he was with his son-in-law, served as gracious host. The wedding accomplished all I had hoped, not restoration of our family reputation, but a step upward.

During the reception, Reverend Elias Cuthbert spoke with Jim, Andy, and the men at length about his son and one of Peter's childhood friends, Captain Randall Cuthbert, who served as a company commander with General Longstreet and the First Corps. He described battles where Randall fought as if he had been there himself. Jim and Andy looked around briefly to find Randall until I whispered, "He died at Chickamauga. Reverend Cuthbert never accepted it; more grief than he can handle."

The men and some of the guests wanted to stage a raucous late night chivaree, but Andy talked them out of it. As a confidant to both of us during our brief courtship, he took partial credit for our marriage and felt protective of us.

That night, in deference to the family, we slept in one of the upper bedrooms and reluctantly agreed to postpone the usual wedding night pleasures until the next night when we would be on the road to Newton. Jim pointed out the vigor of our lovemaking would be heard throughout the house. I reluctantly agreed.

As a wedding present, my parents gave us a sturdy carriage and a team of horses for the upcoming trip. The men filled the wagon with my clothing and accessories, but left enough room for the tents and provisions. I noticed they carefully placed Andy's lock box under the load, out of sight.

Chapter 26: Farewells

Brownsburg, Virginia to Newton, North Carolina,
July 1865
Jim Cobb

I survived the marriage ceremony. At least, Missy told me I did well. But, like grooms before and since, I walked around in a semi-stupor. The names and faces of most of the guests were lost to me. I swapped war stories and did not remember most of it later.

It wasn't that I objected to the fuss of a formal wedding. I had much going through my mind. In the past four months, I had left prison near dead, took Union payroll, settled with the evil bastard who hanged Scipio, and discovered, to my great joy, Missy was the woman I had always dreamed of marrying. In my letter to Mother, I wrote of our mental and spiritual compatibility and it was true. But, it was her exciting, young, eager body that stirred me.

The night before our departure, while Missy packed all the stuff she wanted to take with us, I went downstairs to visit with Andy and the boys in the barn. On the staircase, I overheard Missy's parents talking about us. I knew they had mixed feeling, particularly William Morgan. Pleased Missy married the man she had always loved and leaving behind the shame of her assault, sad with the thought of losing his favorite child.

Margaret fretted, "I do hope she'll be safe. She won't have a fit place to stay until they reach Jim's farm."

Captain Morgan reassured her, "She has her own army. She'll be all right and Pearl's with her." He paused and asked, "Why is it Missy set her cap for Jim Cobb? She seemed fixed on him even when Jim and Sissy were engaged."

"Who among all the young men do you think she thought most like her father?"

"Do you think so? I'd like to believe she sees some of me in Jim."

"It'll be just you and me. We've got a lot of work to do. Restore the place and get it running again."

"Have you thought about what Jim suggested?" She asked.

"He's right about one thing. We don't have many choices. I'll talk with Jacob about takin' over as overseer and bringin' back some of the other slaves. Jim said their farm was more profitable after the Cobbs freed their slaves."

"Jim's family freed their slaves before the war?" Margaret asked.

"That's what he told me. Said they set up the slaves as share-croppers, provided food and housin', and gave them half the crop profit."

"Half the profit?" she exclaimed, "I thought Sissy married the Abolitionist."

* * *

Andy nudged me and pointed toward Missy. She had Malcolm fetching wood for Gilbert to chop into logs and kindling for the fire. Robert and Sam set up the tents where Missy directed as Pearl started supper. He commented, "Makes you wonder what they did before they had a woman around to tell 'em what to do."

"Seems they took a shine to Missy," I noted.

Andy winked. "Notice how they jump to whatever Missy asks or what they think she wants."

"Yeah, they even fight over who gets to do it. If they behaved like that in the army, we wouldn't need Sergeants, just women, or maybe Sergeants in petticoats."

Andy overlooked my feeble attempt at humor. He said, "You did well, Partner. I think all of us love your wife."

I motioned Missy to join Andy and me. Would have been more gentlemanly if we walked over to her, but I much enjoyed the alluring side-to-side sway of her hips as she approached. I turned to Andy and said, "Tell Missy what you just told me."

Andy removed his hat, held it to his chest, bowed, and said, "Missus Cobb, on behalf of 4th Platoon, D Company, 78th North Carolina, we decided you are the prettiest, most gracious lady we know."

Missy extended her hand, which Andy kissed, and replied, "Why Sergeant Blaylock, how you do turn my head with your flattery."

After supper, around the fire, Sam entertained us with a fanciful story about a wayward parson who encountered a bear in the Carolina mountains. When he finished, Andy looked at Missy and me, winked, and nodded toward a tent that had been set apart for us. "I think you two have better things to do than listen to Sam's stories."

Missy blushed, but jumped up and grabbed my hand. We went to the tent where we had just enough room to remove our clothing. I finished first, laid down on the pallet, and waited for Missy. Knowing I watched closely, Missy slowly and seductively undressed. Before I could pull her down to the pallet, she pounced on me and we began a leisurely night of coupling. I appreciated Missy's self-control in keeping our passion quiet and the stamina I maintained after being sick and delirious less than one month earlier.

Roanoke, Virginia, Tuesday,
July 25, 1865
Jim Cobb

Our party arrived late afternoon and stopped at the General Store. The owner, Julius Peden, saw Gilbert and Malcolm and said, "Lord be praised. You boys're live and well. We thought you wuz dead. Stay here. We'll have a shindig." He ordered his son, "Get over to the Reed Farm right away. Tell 'em Malcolm's here and then get on over to Gilbert's folks."

Within two hours, it seemed all the families in the Roanoke Valley gathered at the general store. The celebration continued as neighbors and friends arrived. A Union patrol came out to investigate and backed off when satisfied the spontaneous gathering simply honored two of Roanoke's returning veterans.

With the others inside, Andy told Robert, "One of us needs to stay with the wagon. I'll take first watch."

As the guests became comfortable with Andy, Robert, Sam, and me, they described missing sons, husbands, brothers, nephews, and sweethearts. They brought out letters and, in some instances, an old daguerreotype, photograph, or tintype to show us. Behind each story was a tragedy of a young man who died of disease or wounds or in a Yankee prison or simply disappeared.

We looked at the images and listened to the stories. I did not recognize any of the young men, but, in a larger sense, knew all of them.

One father drew Andy aside and said, "Sergeant Blaylock, you served in the Light Division. My son wuz a Private in the Virginia Brigade. Joined up after Gettysburg. Billy Redman. Did you know him?"

Billy's mother came over as Andy shook his head, "Sorry, Sir. I don't."

"Didn't git no letters in the last month 'fore he wuz killt. What wuz it like?" he asked.

"Mister Redman, I don't have to tell you your son was a brave man. The Yankees had us outnumbered and out supplied. Some quit, some walked away, but not Billy. No big battles after The Crater, but we skirmished Yankees nearly every day. The Virginia brigade got chewed up in the fightin'. I suspect that's what happened to Billy, caught a Yankee bullet outside Petersburg."

Billy's mother commented, "He worked with a surveyor. Would've come back to it, if'n he hadn't got killt." She took out a handkerchief to wipe her eyes.

"Billy have brothers or sisters?" Andy asked.

"Yes, Sir. He wrote to his sisters and younger brother. He had a girl he wuz sweet on." Her voice tailed off as Andy put an arm around her and hugged.

Billy Redman was like the men in his platoon. Like Andy. He, too, lost a brother and understood their grief.

Missy saw a pretty young girl run up, put her arms around Malcolm, and give him a long and extended kiss. They talked briefly before Malcolm looked up and saw Missy watching. He brought 'his girl' to us.

I whispered to Missy, "Pretty sure that's the parson's niece, Charlene Bates, the girl Malcolm told me about."

Missy put her arm inside Malcolm's and said, "You did not do this girl justice. She's even lovelier than you described her." Malcolm blushed while Charlene beamed.

I noted his unease and solemnly said, "Malcolm, it's been a long journey, but you're finally home. The war's over and you're back with your family and friends. What're your plans?"

"Sir, I'll go back to work on the family farm for now. Gilbert and I talked about throwin' in together later and buy or start a bizness when we can lay some money aside, maybe somethin' in bankin'. Might be good to lend money 'stead of always havin' to borrow."

"Gilbert's a good man. He'll make a good partner for you." As intended, Charlene looked up at Malcolm admiringly, impressed her man talked freely and seriously with his regimental commander.

I had a long talk with Gilbert Kinney's father. He told me, "We're much obliged to you and Sergeant Blaylock for keepin' our boy alive and bringin' him back to us."

I told him, "It's almost the other way around. Andy, Gilbert, Malcolm, and the others kept me alive since we left Fort Delaware. Your son's a good man, a very good man. I'm obligated to him. You should be very proud of Gilbert. I am."

*　*　*

We spent the night at the Reed Farm and were treated to a farm breakfast in the morning - eggs, ham, and biscuits dripping in red-eye gravy. Malcolm said grace for the meal, plain-spoken and sincere thanks for the food and deliverance of all in the traveling party. Gilbert Kinney rode over to say goodbye to us before we left.

I drove the carriage and felt glum. Missy asked, "Anything troubling you?"

"Very little I miss from the war, but I will miss Malcolm and Gilbert."

"Good men. I'm fond of them too," she said. "They're alive and back with their families. You and Andy should be pleased."

"I am, but I don't think I'll ever be as close to anyone as I am to my regiment, particularly these men."

Missy snuggled over to me and asked, "How about your wife?"

"You're different and special. We'll discuss it more tonight."

"Yes, Major, I think that would be in order. But, I'll miss them too."

Four days later, we reached the Fort Farm five miles east of Wilkesboro, North Carolina. Sam's mother, Bessie, came out to greet us. After she smothered her son with kisses and passed him on to his three sisters, she welcomed each of the men in turn, but stopped to talk with Missy.

"From a neighbor's son, we learnt Sam's regiment wuz took at Petersburg, put in Yankee prison, and then we heard nuthin'. We worried about him fierce 'til a letter come from the Blaylock Farm. Sam's a good son, tells funny stories, but he ain't much for letter writin'. Someday you'll be a mother and know how I feel."

"I just met you and Mister Fort. But, I know you're good people. You raised a fine son, a good man, one of my favorites." Missy replied and made an instant friend.

Bessie Fort pointed to the kitchen and said, "Why don't you come join me and the girls so we can talk."

"Appears you'll need to fix a lot of food. Please let me help," Missy offered.

"Nah. It's our pleasure just to visit with the Major's wife."

They sat Missy in a chair and had a long conversation. She told them what had happened with their son and brother since the regiment was captured at Petersburg. They were particularly interested in the story of her courtship and marriage.

Missy laughed, "I don't know if I could've caught Jim without the help of Andy, Sam, and the others."

Bessie raised a spoon, shook it at her, and said, "Major's the lucky one."

Missy nodded modestly to accept the compliment.

She told me later about her discussion with the Fort women and commented, "If they only knew." I hugged her. The rape would never leave her. Nothing I could do except love and take care of her and hope the memory would eventually fade.

* * *

Sam's father had recently slaughtered a hog and taken it to the smokehouse for curing. He built a fire behind the house, split the prize hog, and roasted it over an open spit in the backyard. He basted the meat with vinegar and served it as the main course for the party that started in the late afternoon.

As I watched the celebration, Missy joined me and said, "Sort of reminds you of the Parable of the Prodigal Son doesn't it?"

"Yeah. They killed a fatted calf and invited the neighbors. But, this time there's no envious older brother."

"And Sam hasn't exactly squandered his inheritance in loose living since he left home," Missy added.

As the guests arrived, I learned one of the neighbors, Jeremiah Dunston, operated a local whisky distillery. He brought several jugs of his product and passed them around. He too was fond of Sam Fort. Dunston told me, "I'm gettin' on in years. Young Sam's the perfect man to take over my whisky bidness. It's a good moneymaker. Local folks really like my whisky."

I drank a sample when offered and regretted my haste. It literally burned all the way down. I gulped and thanked Dunston, but politely turned down offers for additional sampling of the local 'nectar.' I warned Missy. She brought the moonshine to her lips in a cup and surprised me in taking a gulp. Her face turned red, but she also complimented Dunston. Andy and Robert had the same reaction, but not Sam and the Wilkes County neighbors. Definitely a local whisky for local taste.

I became curious. Stills were not uncommon in Catawba County. I recalled sneaking off with Emmett Shuford to see his uncle's still before the uncle ran us off after lecturing us about prying. I saw crude field stills in the army that produced brews

ranging from bad to awful. I suspected Dunston had a more refined still and wanted to see it.

I asked if I could visit his distillery. Dunston and Sam quickly
agreed.

Missy pointed to a young lady standing by herself. She asked,
"Do you think she's interested in Sam?"

I shrugged and replied, "Don't know, but she seems to have
come by herself. No escort."

Missy nodded. "We don't know if she's interested in Sam or
him in her. But, just in case, somebody ought to go talk to her.
Couldn't hurt."

Although totally unnecessary I suggested to Missy, "Why
don't you find out?"

"I'll do that." Missy walked over to the young lady. "Hello,
I'm Missy Cobb, Major Cobb's wife. What's your name?"

"I'm Celia Ralston, Ma'am."

"Are you a friend of Sam's?" Missy asked.

"Yes Ma'am. Reckon I am. Knew Sam 'fore he went off to
war."

Missy asked the question that always got others talking, "Tell
me about yourself, Celia."

"I ain't much. My father's a greengrocer. I keep books for
him. My older brother joined up with the 49th North Carolina.
Got killt in Virginia. Just me, my little sister, and Pa. Ma died
with the pox."

"Celia, pardon my asking, but you came by yourself and have
not gone over to see Sam. We have great affection for Sam and
are moving on tomorrow. I'd like to think we are leaving him
with someone who loves him. Someone other than his family. I'll
be blunt. Do you have a romantic interest in Sam?"

Missy's question startled Celia who blushed, but confided,
"Yes, Ma'am. Reckon I do. But he's been all busy talkin' with the
neighbors, your husband, and the others you brung."

Missy thought Sam deserved a good wife, maybe a wife who

could dissuade him from becoming a moonshiner, someone like Celia. This girl was pretty, seemed modest, and maybe had a level head. She took Celia by the arm and walked her over to where Sam talked with Andy and me. Missy introduced Celia to us and discreetly pulled Andy and me away so Sam and Celia could talk alone.

* * *

In the morning, Sam took Andy and me to visit Jeremiah Dunston. Robert stayed behind with Missy and guarded the wagon and lockbox. The ride to Dunston's Farm took longer than anticipated. His farm was six miles west of Wilkesboro and hidden away in a thick scrub pine forest. Dunston dedicated his farm to raising corn, the primary ingredient for his whisky.

On the ride over, I learned Dunston's clientele included most of Wilkes County, the Sheriff, and County Judge. Sam told me state tax agents knew a great deal of illegal liquor was distilled and sold in Wilkes County, but found local citizens highly protective of Dunston and his moonshine. Dunston had a profitable, if illegal, business for many years, even during the war when sugar and yeast were scarce.

Dunston took us back to his still which he located in a small hollow, a half mile from the farm house near a stream. He had earlier pressed corn so he could demonstrate how he processed the 'squeezins'.

Like my father and grandfather, I enjoyed learning new things simply for the pleasure of knowing and reasoned that I never knew when something I learned earlier might benefit me. I asked numerous questions and that seemed to please Dunston and Sam.

Dunston described the processing stages. "Fixins ain't no secret. We all use corn meal, sugar, yeast, and spring water. But, how we do it is what makes it diffurnt."

He pointed to a stone furnace, "Heat up corn meal in water to make the mash. Throw in sugar and then the yeast to ferment it. That tube comin' out the top of the still catches the alcohol and takes it to the tub beside the still."

Andy pointed to another tube and Dunston told us, "That's the cap arm. Catches the shine and takes it over to the thump keg, that's what we call the tank. It's just a heated barrel. I use it to filter out the mash."

"Any reason you use copper tubing?" I asked.

"Yeah, it carries the heat and don't leech into the shine. Bends easy too." Dunston added, "I put more mash into the thump keg to give my shine an extra kick."

He pointed to a coil coming from the thump keg to another barrel. "That there's the worm that goes into the worm barrel. See the pipe from the crick? I run spring water into worm barrel to cool down the shine steam."

"Then I guess you take the shine out through the hose coming out the worm barrel," I commented.

Dunston nodded. "Course you know I can't tell no one my secret fixins."

Andy and I talked while Sam had a private discussion with Dunston. Andy asked, "You surprised Dunston doesn't age his stuff?"

I shook my head. "His shine would take the hide off a cat. About the strongest moonshine I ever swallowed. It's probably the kicker he puts into the thump keg."

On the ride back to the Fort Farm, Sam looked at me and asked, "Major Cobb, what do you think of me buyin' Dunston's bizness?"

I knew Sam wanted my approval, but, for his own good, answered bluntly, "You can do better. We don't know what your share of the payroll will bring, but I'm sure it'll buy something better than a still."

Sam noticeably sagged and did not bring up buying the still again.

On the way back, a highwayman came out of the woods. He pointed a pistol at us and demanded our money. Andy calmly explained, "What you're tryin' to do won't work. Each of us is armed. We're all veterans and accustomed to close fightin'. Any one of us will drop you if you fire your pistol. What you demand won't happen. Why don't you think about it more and leave?"

The young would-be highwayman nervously looked back and forth across the three of us, backed up slowly, and withdrew into the woods.

* * *

Our traveling party was now down to Missy, Andy, Robert, Pearl, and me. That night, Andy brought out a half-filled jug of Dunston's whisky. "Might as well finish it before we get to Newton."

I shook my head. "Pour it on the ground."

Missy intervened, "Be fair. Sam liked it. You might like it if you try some more."

I looked at her curiously, but Andy and Robert, even Pearl, seemed ready to finish Dunston's shine. Each took a cup and managed to swallow it. I mixed water into mine and it still burned all the way down. Astonishingly, Missy and the others drank theirs straight.

Not long after, I felt my head swim and noted the others seemed woozy. Missy and I made it back to our tent and learned an early lesson in our marriage – inebriation did not enhance love making.

It had been the most exciting time of my life. I dreamed of being Jim's wife since I first met him. There was something special about Jim that made an immediate and lasting impression on me. It was the simple, unexplained, and unreasoned belief I was fated to be his wife. And, now, I was.

The unfortunate younger sister, victim of Yankee bummers was now the wife of a highly respected Confederate officer, adored by Andy and the men of my husband's regiment and their families. To me, my rapid transformation was a dream realized. I was very happy and, at the same time, anxious nothing go wrong as we came nearer the Cobb Farm.

On our ride to Jim's home, I had my husband to myself all day before we expected to arrive. It was his turn to drive the carriage while Andy rode scout and Robert took the wagon. I knew my husband was a highly placed staff officer during most of the war and wondered what he thought of the great Confederate generals who were already legendary in the South.

I started at the top and asked, "Jim, all of us heard only good things about General Lee. I know you disagree with his decision to stand and fight at Gettysburg, but, now you're no longer in the army, what do you think of him?"

"General Lee was not only a great general, but a great man. All the army loved and respected him. But, I wish he had commanded the Union Army."

I shook my head in disbelief and asked, "What in the world do you mean?"

Jim explained, "President Lincoln offered General Lee command of the Union Army. He declined and resigned his commission to serve in the Virginia Army. He placed loyalty to his home state over loyalty to the Union. We all did. But, if General

Lee had accepted Lincoln's offer, the Union Army would've had the competent commander it needed and never had. Could have ended the war two, maybe three years sooner. Think of the lives and misery that would have been spared."

"Do you think Lee was our greatest general?" I asked.

"No, that would be Stonewall Jackson. We lost the war when we lost him. He was that good."

As cadets, I remembered Jim, Ken and Peter discussing Jackson and wondered, "You've told me many times what a dull professor he was at VMI and he was a religious fanatic, somewhat unbalanced."

Jim grinned. "The army was divided. Some thought he was half crazy. The rest of us knew he was full crazy. But, that was Jackson off the battlefield. He was far and away the best field commander in the war."

I asked, "What about Jubal Early? You served under him for a while."

"I liked him, but most of the senior officers did not. Didn't bother Early. He was always quick to hand out criticism, but couldn't take it. But, that was Jubal Early off the battlefield. He was an outstanding field general. General Lee is probably the only man who could command him. Lee gave him an army, general directions, few supplies, and set him loose, sort of like Mosby with an army. I was amazed with what he accomplished, particularly late in the war. I would've gladly served under him. He was an aggressive general up to the end."

I perked up when Jim mentioned Mosby and said, "Speaking of John Mosby, he was the most mysterious and romantic officer we had. Most of the women in the South were in love with Mosby. And you and Andy actually rode with him."

"I know you meant to say Mosby was the most attractive officer in the Confederate Army besides your husband."

I smiled and patted him on the arm, "Of course, dear."

"Thinking back over his service record, I'm not sure why

General Lee picked him to lead a makeshift army behind Yankee lines. Probably because General Stuart talked him into it and they couldn't spare any of the regular army. But, they could not have made a better choice. Mosby was the most intelligent leader I served under. He never talked with anyone, except maybe Andy's dad, about where he would strike next. All the Rangers were devoted to him. It turned out to be a short term hitch for Andy and me, but we learned a lot working with him."

Since he returned from the war, I realized I knew little about his home, his family, the North Carolina Piedmont, and, most particularly, his mother whom I would soon meet. During our long friendship, I had many conversations with Jim on a broad range of topics but, in hindsight, I learned little about his upbringing and his family. More than anything, I wanted to please my new mother-in-law whom I knew my husband revered and suspected he had good reasons. I had to learn everything I could before we got to the Cobb Farm.

The solution to my problem sat beside me. I snuggled up to Jim and began a long conversation starting with my prime concern and worked down from there.

Chapter 27: Home

Cobb Farm, Newton, North Carolina,
August, 1865
Jim Cobb

Since we came together after the war, Missy had been happy. But as we came closer to home, she grew more pensive. She had a right to her private thoughts, but I became concerned.

I asked, "What's troubling you?"

Missy shook her head and turned away. "Nothing. I'm all right."

Her lips trembled and I thought her eyes might be tearing. I reached over and gently turned her face back toward me. "You've been jumpy since we set out this morning. Tell me what you're thinking."

"It's your mother," she confessed.

"My mother? She loves you even before she meets you. You're family. You're her daughter now."

"What if she thinks I'm not good enough for you?" Missy asked.

Her concern was ill founded, but, regardless, it was the first time I had seen her anxious.

I said, "Quit worrying. We'll be there soon and you'll see for yourself" and failed to reassure her.

Missy looked at me with tears in her eyes which I felt unable to prevent and it broke my heart. She said, "I felt incredibly fortunate over the past month. I had dreamed of marrying you and almost convinced myself I would never see you again. Or, if I did, you would be changed from war and prison, not to mention how I had been changed, that we would be strangers. Instead, you came back the same man I had loved all these years. You suffered and witnessed horror and brutality, but somehow retained the kindness and decency that charmed me as a schoolgirl."

"The past month has been all I had hoped, but, unfortunately, dreams end and reality set in. You will bring me to your home where you and Andy will develop some sort of enterprises that will make us wealthy. In the meantime, I will bear children and be the second Missus Cobb in a home that has a very capable first Missus Cobb."

"I do not know much about your mother except she is beautiful, intelligent, and an excellent administrator. In all our many conversations, you did not talk much about your home and family which will soon be my home and family. You would not be the man you are without coming from a strong family. That your mother, deceased father, and brother are good people do not worry me. But where I will fit in bothers me considerably."

Missy had blindsided me. I had no idea she felt insecure in coming home with me. As I thought about it, I realized she had pretty much run the Morgan Plantation even with her mother and sister there. Her father depended on her and she had come through. She wanted a home she could manage. But I knew, even if she didn't, her fear and anxiety would disappear when she met Mother.

* * *

We rode in silence for the next few miles before Missy said, "Do you realize you've been picking up the pace? Robert was a half mile ahead and now we're about to overtake him."

"You're right. I can't wait to get home," I said, and thought back to Andy doing the same thing before we got to his home and how wound up Gilbert, Malcolm, and Sam were on the last day before we took them home.

As the main house came into view, I saw Mother waiting on the front porch and felt my heart beat faster.

Robert drove the wagon and came in first. One of our Negroes, a young man I did not remember, went out to meet him. "Suh, heah. Bring de wagon heah. We tend to it."

Andy came in next on horseback and then Missy, Pearl, and I in the carriage. Mother came out to the yard before the carriage stopped to greet us. Lovely as ever, but grayer and I noted lines on her face that were not there before. I knew the war had been hard on her too and my perils had likely added to her gray hair and lines.

She ran to me, gave me a hug, and whispered, "It's so very good to see you alive and well, son."

"So good to see you!" I exclaimed, and held her close. Four years earlier, I held her tight before going off on an adventure and now held her thankful I had survived that adventure. I became lost in nostalgia until I remembered Missy.

Letting her go, I said, "And may I introduce someone very special?"

Mother turned to Missy. "Welcome, Missy. James has told me so much about you I feel I already know you." She gave Missy a warm hug.

Missy smiled for the first time that day and replied, "Thank you, Missus Cobb. It is very nice to meet you."

Mother smiled and said, "Better not call me Missus Cobb. Folks might confuse us. How about I call you Missy and you call me Anne?"

Missy's face lit up as Mother excused herself and walked toward Andy who had dismounted. He took off his hat and made a bow. Mother laughed, "You must be Andy Blaylock and, Mister Blaylock, you need not be formal with me." Her comment had the intended effect. Andy had a grin on his face when he looked up. She then hugged him.

Robert Savage approached carrying a lockbox. She must have known from my letter that the other man was Robert Savage, but she asked, "What's your name, young man?"

Robert set the box down, removed his hat, and solemnly answered, "I'm Robert Savage, Ma'am."

"Where are you from, Robert?"

"Nacogdoches, Texas, Ma'am."

She smiled and said, "Could you say that again?"

Robert repeated himself. Mother extended her hand and said, "Welcome to the Cobb Farm, Robert Savage. It's been a long time since I talked with a Texan. I love your accent and I want you to talk with me even when you have nothing to say." Robert also grinned widely after Mother hugged him. Mother surprised Pearl and gave her a hug. Having greeted our party, she walked back to Missy and me.

With all of us in front of her, she said, "I want to thank all of you from the bottom of my heart. Without you, my son would not be alive and standing before me." She turned to Pearl and said, "I know your late husband kept James alive in prison. I'm very sorry for your loss and much appreciative of what he did for my James."

She motioned toward the front door and we followed her into the house where Hannah had a meal waiting. Pearl started toward the kitchen to eat, but Mother motioned for her stay and eat with the rest of us.

Afterward, I heard Andy tell Robert, "There's something different about this farm. Union cavalry passed through here in the spring. The farms we passed show it, but not the Cobb Farm. And it's not because of Union sympathies."

Robert commented, "The niggers work hard. Look at the crops. Other farms we've seen, the niggers ran off as soon as they could. Not here. 'Pears they like the Major and his mother."

Cobb Farm, Newton, North Carolina,
Thursday, August 3, 1865
Missy Cobb

As mothers-in-law are wont to do, Anne Cobb arranged confidential and separate talks with her son and his bride starting with the daughter-in-law. While the men worked with Oliver, she invited me to take a ride with her to Newton and Hickory. It pleased me. I quickly realized the real purpose of the ride was for Anne Cobb to show off her new daughter-in-law, me.

On the ride back from Hickory, she started a serious conversation, "Missy, James spared me the details of his service during the war and in prison. He did not want to worry his mother and I'm thankful for that. But I suspect he opened up to you. I would appreciate your telling me what you know without the sugar my son often sprinkles on facts he thinks will upset me."

I did not know Anne Cobb well, but I already understood she had none of the coquette slyness that many upper class Southern women pretended to. My mother-in-law was amazingly direct and frank. The war was over and the danger her son faced over. I thought it best to answer in kind.

I remembered clearly the account Jim gave at our dining table when he first came down to eat with my family and his men. I had picked up additional information from my talks with Andy, Robert, Sam, Gilbert, and Malcolm. I did as my mother-in-law requested and told the story to her, direct and without embellishment.

When I finished, she grimaced, shook her head slowly, and said, "Thank God. What he went through is worse than I imagined. I cry every time I think of the mothers and widows who lost their men or seen them come back crippled. James is alive, well, and in one piece. I am eternally grateful that you, Andy, Robert, Scipio, and the others kept him alive to return home.

It's a miracle. Missy, I'm so glad he found you. His life is now complete and I'm very happy for both of you."

I asked her, "How has he changed? How has war and prison changed him?"

"He was always a sweet obedient boy. He'll be a good husband to you and father to your children. That will never change. But, he's a man now. I see a hardness that wasn't there before. He's driven to prove himself. You'll see that too."

A feeling of immense relief poured over me. The mother-in-law I had feared loved me and respected me. I found no deception or pretense in her. As Jim had described her, Anne Cobb was intelligent and direct in her thinking, speech, and actions. At the same time, she had a good heart and a delightful sense of humor. I saw much of his mother's personality in Jim. Without giving it thought earlier, I found myself drawn to qualities in her that are mostly lacking in my mother.

I did not have to guess what Anne Cobb thought of me. She told me, "I'm delighted James married a woman with good values, intelligence, and common sense. You're pretty and will likely produce smart, handsome, and well-behaved grandchildren. My James did well, but I expected no less of him. Are you pregnant?" she asked.

I blushed at the bluntness of the question and replied, "No, not yet."

"You may want to hold off for a while, but not too long. I'm looking forward to grandchildren as I imagine your parents are." She left it at that, but I knew there was something else she had not told me.

Cobb Farm, Newton, North Carolina,
Thursday August 3, 1865
Jim Cobb

After supper, Mother said, "Son, join me in the parlor. There are things we need to discuss." I excused myself and followed her into the parlor.

Mother handed me the last letter she received from my brother Tom. He wrote from Southampton, England where he waited for assignment on another ship.

Tom wrote of his long cruise on the Confederate warship, the CSS Alabama. For nearly two years, the Alabama terrorized Union shipping in the Atlantic and Indian Oceans, even made an earlier raid into the Gulf of Mexico as far as the Texas coast. Tom served as Third Officer and was proud of what they had accomplished, but seemed content that his part in the war ended. He supervised sale of captured Union cargo, collected his share of the prize money, and deposited most of it into a Southampton bank. He picked up a first mate berth on a merchant ship out of England and wrote before departure. Tom expected a shipping boom after the war and looked for an opportunity to buy a cargo ship and start making his fortune.

I put down the letter. "Mother, sure good to hear from Tom and know he's alive and well. Appears he's got a good future waiting."

"It's your future we need to discuss. Do you remember Ruth McCray from church?"

Puzzled, I nodded. "Yes, she's Doctor McCray's daughter. She had a younger brother, Geoffrey, who was a year ahead of me in Sunday school."

"Ruth works as a clerk and stenographer in the Provost Marshal's Office in Hickory. In going through the incoming mail, she saw a general dispatch several weeks ago and the details caught her attention. The dispatch alerted all the Districts of a small group of former Confederate soldiers who stole a payroll in Northeastern Virginia. The thieves were thought to be from out of the area of the robbery and likely on the move with the stolen payroll."

I tried to keep a calm expression even though I knew where Mother was headed. "Really?" I asked, straining to conceal my nerves.

"The presumed leader is a Texan named Paul Mason. The dispatch included suspects and descriptions. One of the suspects is described as a former Confederate soldier from the Western Carolinas with a long scar on the left side of his head above the ear."

"Like mine?" I said, asking the obvious.

Mother ignored my feeble attempt to divert her and continued, "What caught Ruth's attention was the list of suspects, former Mosby Rangers. The names included John A Blaylock, Sergeant, CSA and James G Cobb, Captain, CSA."

My face turned pale as she concluded, "I've noted the lockbox the three of you continually watch. He was not named with the suspects in the dispatch, but is my Robert 'Paul Mason'?"

When we were growing up, Mother always knew when her sons fibbed or did not tell the whole truth, so I made no attempt to evade her question now.

"Mother, how in the world could you know that?" I asked.

"I was not sure you were involved until Missy told me you and Andy rode with Mosby while you recovered after Sharpsburg. But, never mind how I know. If your Mother can figure it out so can a Yankee officer or a scalawag looking to collect a reward. You, Andy, Robert, and my precious daughter-in-law are not safe here. It's only a matter of time until the Provost Marshal learns you're here and remembers the dispatch. As much as I want you to stay, operate the farm, and present me with grandchildren, you must leave as soon as possible."

I looked at her and knew she was as disappointed as I was. I also understood the wisdom and finality of what she said. I felt helpless. Where could we go?

Before we left for home, Andy and I discussed a plan with the men to convert the stolen payroll. We decided that, after a few days rest at the Cobb Farm, Robert would take provisions for the long ride back to Texas and money for expenses along the way. Andy and I would take a few months to compile a list of possible purchases in Cuba or South America to bring home for resale. We would make a tour, return with hopefully salable items, and then sell them discreetly until we recouped the purchase cost and maybe a profit. If we spread the stolen currency around, as we planned, the Yankees would have a hard time tracing it back to us. The proceeds of the sale would be disbursed periodically according to the agreed upon percentages. The key would be to move slowly and not draw attention.

If the dry goods purchase did not work, we could simply swap currencies. We would likely lose money in the exchange, but most of it would be redeemed in clean money. Under no circumstances would any of the stolen currency be spent in the United States.

We had a workable plan, but not under scrutiny of the local Provost Office. Certainly Andy and I would be questioned when the Provost recognized our names on the dispatch and I fit a description of one of the suspects very well. We would have difficulty explaining an inventory of Cuban dry goods. And possibly worse, Mother and Missy could be harassed and that was totally unacceptable. Everything we planned was now worthless and there was no back up plan.

"Mother, are you disappointed in me?"

She quickly replied, "The only crime in stealing Yankee payroll is getting caught. I know from what the dispatch did not say that no one was killed or seriously hurt. As best I can tell, you made a clean escape. But the Yankees want to get their money back and punish you to discourage anyone else from trying the same thing."

I shook my head in disappointment and asked, "May I bring Andy and Robert in?"

"Yes, they should know of the Provost's dispatch."

*   *   *

"Damn," Andy muttered under his breath. Robert pounded his fist into his palm and began to pace. To lighten our gloom, Mother suggested, "The first thing you should do is have Robert practice the accent he uses around strangers. It sounds awful."

We laughed nervously and then Mother made a recommendation she considered since learning of the dispatch.

"I have a brother, Gustav Gerlach. He ran off to New Orleans before I married and joined a volunteer group that fought with the Texans in their revolt from Mexico in 1836. He accepted a land grant from the Texas government and stayed on following the war.

Gus has a son about your age who's a disappointment to him. He has written several times and asked if you or Tom could come out and help him manage a large estate he built up in Southeast Texas."

As Mother talked about her younger brother, her eyes misted. I knew she had strong feelings for him, but I had only a vague knowledge of Uncle Gustav Gerlach.

Mother looked to Robert for confirmation as she said, "Texas is a lawless state. No assurance you won't find Federal marshals there, but I understand you can go there and reinvent yourself. In Texas, you'll find opportunity to convert the Yankee payroll without drawing attention. If that doesn't work, try Northern Mexico. The French are down there now trying to take over."

Robert said, "'Fore the war I helped round up cattle for a

drive to Missouri. We got a good spread between the price of cattle in Texas and Missouri."

Andy poked Robert in the side with his elbow and said, "And knowin' you Texans, the price spread grows with each tellin'."

Robert was not in a kidding mood. He defended his recommendation. "I'm sayin' we use the payroll currency to buy Mexican cattle, take 'em up to Missouri, and make a profit on the drive."

I began to relax as the certainty of our move to Texas settled in. "It's something we'll consider. Getting the currency converted would be good. Multiplying it is better." I saw possibility in Robert's suggestion.

After briefly discussing and dismissing other options, we decided to accompany Robert Savage to Texas. Mother turned to me and said, "I suggest you bring your wife into this discussion."

I started to protest and then thought better of it. There would be no hiding the robbery from Missy. She would have to know soon. I could not tell her of the sudden decision to move to Texas without an explanation.

I brought Missy into the parlor and declared, "We've decided to move on to Texas with Robert. I have an uncle who has a large estate near Beaumont where we can stay until we're settled."

I hoped I could smooth over the sudden change in plans. It did not work.

Missy came back with, "Why are we going to Texas right after we came here?"

I gave an abridged version of what had happened hoping it would satisfy her. She was surprised when she heard what I said, but knew she did not have the full story.

She said, "James Cobb, we've not been married long, but now is not the time for us to have secrets. I want a full explanation and I want it now." Not a fight, not even a tiff, but the first time Missy had been cross with me.

I took her hands in mine, looked her in the eye, and said, "You've seen Andy's lockbox." She nodded. "It's full of stolen Yankee currency".

"And when did this take place?" she asked.

"You know Andy and I rode with John Mosby during the war. Among other raids, we robbed a Union payroll near the Blaylock Farm. With help from Robert, Sam, Gilbert, and Malcolm, we robbed the same payroll wagon at the same place as the earlier robbery. The currency's numbered and traceable. We must get the money out of the country to convert it."

"What has this got to do with our leaving for Texas?"

"Mother found a dispatch to the local Provost office. It alerts the Provost of a group of former soldiers moving away from Northeast Virginia. The dispatch lists Andy and me as suspects and includes a pretty good description of me."

Missy said, "You mean I married a thief who's now on the run?"

"I'm afraid so."

Missy shook her head. "None of this surprises me. I have seen the attention you pay to Andy's lockbox and the peculiar way Robert talks when strangers are around," she said and added, "Well, James Cobb, I certainly did not marry you because I thought you were rich and now I learn we are, but I wish you had stolen money we could spend." Her comment relieved our tension and caused the others laugh.

Knowing Mother and I were in a serious meeting with Andy and Robert and Missus Cobb wanted us to move on to Texas, Oliver knocked respectfully on the closed door to the parlor and asked if he could join us. He started slowly, but eventually got to the suggestion he wanted to make. "Too early to tell what price the new cotton will fetch wid Yankee buyers, but it grows good heah. Same cotton'll do bettah in Texas."

"Think so?" Andy asked.

Oliver nodded. "Wahma daht. It'll grow early and fastah dan

heah." He paused and added, "Go down ta LaGrange, Gawjaw. We gits de seed deah."

I asked, "What do you think we'll pay for seed?"

Oliver answered, "You'll git deah 'foe ginnin'. Last year wuz trubbl fo' dem. I spect you'll git bettah price dan we paid. Best pay in Yankee coin."

Mother agreed, "LaGrange's on the way and you young people can use an advantage when you get to Texas. Maybe plow some acres on Gustav's estate and get in a crop for next year. Should have good prices then."

As the others talked, I whispered to Missy, "What do you think?"

"On the run from Yankee marshals. I should be afraid, but it's an adventure. I like adventure."

I kissed her on the forehead and whispered back, "Me, too."

That night, in bed, Missy told me she loved, admired, and respected her mother-in-law, but wanted her own home. The idea of setting up in Texas with me and two men she had grown to regard as brothers appealed to her.

* * *

In discussing Pearl with Missy, I asked, "Do you think she'll want to go with us or stay here?"

"Let's ask her, but I think she will prefer Texas."

"She can have a comfortable life here. It won't be comfortable crossing to Texas while she's expecting."

"Pearl tells me your Negroes are close knit. They haven't made her feel welcome. But, part of it is Pearl. She was raised to be a companion to Sissy and me. Even took lessons with us. She can read, write, play the piano, and speak some French thanks to a tutor Mother hired for us. She likes you, Andy, and Robert. I think she feels more comfortable with us."

Next morning we invited Pearl to talk with us in the parlor. I told her we would move on to Texas and told her, "Pearl, I want you and your child to have the best life possible. At this point, it's a choice between leaving with Missy, Andy, Robert, and me for Texas and staying here with Mother. I talked with her and she's more than pleased to have you live and work here. So, think about it and let us know what you want to do."

Pearl replied, "Mister Jim, I've already decided. I'll go with you, Missy, and Texas."

I found Mother for a private talk and said. "Lot of things happened on the trip home, but I have a few dollars left. We'll need more to get to Texas and pick up cottonseed on the way."

Mother nodded and said, "I thought of that. I was prepared to wire three hundred Union dollars to you at Fort Delaware. As you know, I could not get any Yankee banks to complete the transfer. I want you and Missy to take it and get a start in Texas."

I protested, "I suspect it's all you have left in Union money. You need it here. We will make do with what we have."

Mother looked at me sternly. "You'll do no such thing. You can't spend any of the Yankee currency until you get it changed. I don't want you showing up hat in hand at Gus' home."

I put my arms around her and hugged her tightly. "Thank you. Thanks for everything. The hardest part of going to Texas is leaving you."

Mother sniffled. "Don't worry about your mother. War's over. We got a bunch of Yankee soldiers stationed here. They've got to eat and they pay in Union money."

I said, "You know the neighbors will talk."

Mother replied, "And you know I quit caring what they thought years ago."

Later, Mother found Missy and gave her three hundred dollars in Union coin. "You'll need this to get started in Texas."

If the cash gift temporarily put the Cobb Farm in a bind, Mother seemed unconcerned. She would make it work.

* * *

Oliver invited Andy and me to inspect the East Field with him. He produced a crop of long staple cotton in the prior year and had a current crop growing. He wanted to tell us all he knew before we planted the long strand cotton in Texas.

Oliver answered our questions and told us other things about the long staple cotton we did not ask. When we finished with the visit, Andy asked Oliver, "Why is the Cobb Farm in such good condition? I passed other farms on the way down that wuz burned out by the Yankees. Did they somehow miss this farm?"

Oliver smiled and said, "No, Mistuh Andy, but the Cobb Fahm not jis 'nodah fahm."

Andy said, "I see that, but why is it different?"

Oliver looked to me and asked, "All right if I tell Mistuh Andy?" I nodded. It was a favorite story and Oliver welcomed the opportunity to tell Andy.

"My Ma and Pa wuz sold ta Elisha Cobb, Mistuh James' grandfather, in eighteen o three. I wuz bahn on the fahm in eighteen o eight, same yeah as John Cobb, Mistuh James' father. The Cobbs wuz good mastuhs and treated us good. All de slaves tawt dey wuz lucky. I grew up wid John Cobb and knew him. He tole no one but me, but Mistuh John did not hold dat one man own 'nodah. He lef fo' school. I didn see much of him 'til he come back six year latah.

"Mistuh Elisha supervise de fields hisself. But, aftah Mistuh John lef, Mistuh Elisha askt me to supervise. When he died, Missus Maud Cobb askt me to take over 'til Mistuh John come home and den he askt me to keep on. I've run dis fahm since den. Mistuh John loved de fahm, but never liked fahm wohk. One of de smartest tings he dun wuz marry Missus Anne. She took over purchasin', de books, and de mills. Left me free ta wohk de fields and we had dis fahm hummin' since."

Andy said, "We have a farm in Virginia. I'm impressed with what I see here. The field hands seem to do things without being told. Why?"

Oliver broke out in a grin and said, "Deyse free and free fo' nine years." Andy was not surprised. I told him earlier we did not favor slavery.

Oliver continued, "Missus Anne tole me she and Mistuh John knew slavery wud not hold. De neighbors say dey cud not get back de money to feed and house deah slaves."

"October 19th, eighteen fifty six, de Cobbs invited me into de parlor. Dey tole me dey wud free all slaves. I always hoped and prayed my chilun wud be free, but never thought I'd be free. Mistuh John say he wud take any of us to a free state if'n dey want to go. But tole us not to tell nobody 'bout our freedom."

"I talk wid de slaves. Mos' cried when I tole 'em. Every slave, no 'cepshun, askt ta stay and wohk de fahm. The Cobbs give us food, houses, and clothes and sum of de profit. We wuz free and had a stake in de fahm. Mistuh Andy, it wuz de bes feelin' evah. I love wohkin' as ovahseah, but nose I cud leave if'n I want."

"Missus Cobb made another offah we 'preciate. She'd school our chilun in de mahnin 'fo dey turn out for chores. I node de neighbors talk, but she dun it 'spite 'em. We cud not read, rite, do sums, but, aftah a few years, our chilun cud."

"It's much easier ta work hard and be 'sponsible when you'se part ownah. Since de Yankees won de wah, all de slaves free. But, de Cobb Farm wuz de only farm 'roun heah dat free de slaves 'fo de wah."

I stood in awe as Oliver spoke to Andy. The longest I ever heard him talk about anything.

Later, Andy asked me about the Cobb Farm slaves. I said, "It's the reason I went to VMI seeking a career in the army. I agreed with my parents' decision to free them, but it changed the farm forever. I thought in terms of a military career and then buying land out west and starting over as my great grandfather did when he came to the Piedmont."

Andy said, "Blaylocks never owned slaves, but I'm not surprised you freed yours. You never held with slavery. Your parents didn't either."

"It doesn't matter now. The Yankees freed all the slaves. Maybe the only good thing to come out of the war."

"Partner, think about it. We're goin' to Texas with a fortune. We paid a hell of a price to get to where we could take it, but we got it because of the war."

"We're not there yet," I reminded him.

Chapter 28: Flight

Newton, North Carolina to Meridian, Mississippi,
August, 1865
Jim Cobb

When I returned to the main house, I found a family friend, Doctor Edward McCray, in the parlor visiting with Mother and Missy. Dr McCray delivered me and taught Sunday School at the Presbyterian Church in Hickory. I remembered him as well-liked and respected in the community. His wife died in the smallpox epidemic of 1857 that took my father. Most recently, his daughter, Ruth, informed us of the Provost letter. A really good family friend.

I knew Ruth and Geoffrey from church and asked Doctor McCray about Geoffrey. He told me Geoffrey had been severely injured in the war and recuperated at home. Doctor McCray wryly commented, "It puts me on equal footing with most of our community. About everyone has someone killed or wounded in the war. Thank God it's finally over."

Mother did not comment, but looked at me fondly and I noticed she patted Doctor McCray's hand. He excused himself with "I've got to get back to an office full of patients. But, before I leave I'd like to invite you and your mother for supper tonight at my home in Hickory. I know Ruth and Geoffrey would like to see you and meet Missy before you leave."

Mother accepted on our behalf, "Thank you, Edward. Six o'clock?"

"Yes, that'll be fine," he said as he headed for the door. Mother followed him and gave him a kiss on the cheek before he climbed back in his carriage and left.

Missy quickly picked up on Mother's relation with Doctor McCray, but I had a blind spot. I could not envision my mother with another man.

Missy told me she questioned Mother about Doctor McCray. Mother told her, "As you saw, he's intelligent, handsome, and pleasant to be around. Edward and I discussed marriage. We admire and respect each other but it's not the passion you young people have. For now, we're comfortable with just being good friends and spending time together."

"I left it at that," Missy said, "but I think she and Edward McCray will eventually marry." She turned to me and asked, "Are you comfortable with your mother marrying?"

I responded, "She's just teasing you."

Missy smiled at my remark and left it at that.

* * *

We found Doctor McCray a gracious and entertaining host. Initially shy, Ruth McCray gradually warmed up to Missy and me. Geoffrey McCray asked me numerous questions about my service in the army. I suspected he may have been intimidated by stories of the Catawba Wildcats which I knew were overblown.

"I didn't see the fighting you and the other Catawba boys had in Virginia", he told me, "but we fought a few scrapes in Georgia and Tennessee."

"More than scrapes," I commented. "As bad as we were outnumbered, General Lee sent Longstreet and the First Corps to help our army in the West."

Geoffrey made a sour face which I did not think was triggered by mention of General Longstreet. Many of our veterans had difficulty talking about their service simply because no one, besides other veterans, could believe what they said. Mother told me Geoffrey had been tight-mouthed since he returned. I thought he might open up to me and said, "If you would, tell me about your service."

"I worked as a draftsman in Atlanta when the war began. Without telling Dad and Ruth, I went down to the recruiting office and enlisted. I was assigned to an infantry division, but skilled artillerymen were in short supply. I knew engineering. I guess they thought it close enough and transferred me to an artillery battery.

We moved over to Chickamauga Creek for a big battle with the Yankees. Had them outnumbered and eventually whipped them, but I don't know how."

"You served with Generals Lee, Longstreet, Jackson, Hill, Early, and the others. From all I've heard and read, they were brilliant, but you wouldn't believe the sorry generals we had."

"Braxton Bragg was a friend and favorite of Jefferson Davis and a terrible general. Before Chickamauga, all the generals who reported to him, including Longstreet, signed a letter asking President Davis to remove Bragg. But, Davis wouldn't do it, as stubborn and pig headed as Bragg. Two of a kind."

"We had a chance to destroy the Yankee army, but Bragg sent our army in piecemeal and frittered it away. When we finally had them on the run, he refused to order an all out pursuit. Instead we followed them back to Chattanooga. General Forrest was fit to be tied."

"How'd you get injured?" I asked.

"One afternoon outside Chattanooga, we had an artillery duel. We fired a round and moved before the Yankees fired back. But, on one round, we were slow in moving and the Yankees hit the cannon next to me. It went up in the air and came down on me and two other soldiers who were killed. The cannon crushed my chest, left arm, and left leg. Dad's amazed I survived and I am too."

"They got the cannon off us right away, put me on a stretcher, and took me to a hospital. Thank God I was unconscious the whole time. The orderlies at the hospital put my bones back together as best they could but it was not a good job. I don't know which was worse, the battlefield or the hospital. The surgeons later put me under, broke, and reset some of the bones. It's been a long and painful recovery."

I saw the pained look in Mother's face as she listened to Geoffrey's story and refrained from telling about my experience in a Union hospital. It would only make Geoffrey feel worse to learn that the Union orderlies had done good work in setting my leg.

We were thankful to Ruth for alerting Mother to the content of the Provost Office dispatch, but made no mention of it. I knew Ruth noticed the scar in my scalp, tied it to the dispatch she read and passed on to Mother, but she said nothing about it.

* * *

The next morning at breakfast, I told Missy, "Whenever you're ready, I'd like to take you to Hickory to meet some friends before we leave."

Missy looked to Mother and asked, "Will you be all right if we are gone for awhile?"

Mother replied, "You young people go along. I know the friends James is speaking of and they've asked about him."

When we arrived at the town square in Hickory, I stopped and hitched the horses in front of the Wilkins Dry Goods Store. I escorted Missy into the store and asked the clerk, "Would you tell Captain Wilkins and Lieutenant Calvert their Second Lieutenant has come for a visit?"

The clerk went back to the office area and, with no apparent lapsed time, Henry Wilkins and Granville Calvert came out to greet us. Wilkins had a crutch and moved in a herky-jerky fashion that did not seem to slow him.

I smiled and said, "It's very good to see both of you."

Granville Calvert slapped me on the back and asked, "Who's this beautiful lady you brought with you?"

"This is my wife, Missy Cobb," I said as I held Missy's hand. She curtsied politely with my introduction.

Calvert feigned disappointment. "Shoot, I was hopin' you brought her here to introduce to me." Missy laughed. I did not tell her it was his standard response to every girl he met.

To explain to Missy, Henry Wilkins said, "I wuz busted up pretty bad in the Peninsula Campaign. Doctor McCray didn't think I'd walk again, but I fooled him. I'm thankful to be alive, particularly as I remember all our boys who did not come back."

I asked, "How many did we lose?"

"We took sixty to Raleigh. Countin' the three of us, eighteen came home alive and eight, like me, are cripples." It put a momentary pall on the reunion as each of us thought back on the Catawba Wildcats and the battles where they fell.

To break the momentary gloom, Granville smiled and asked, "You remember the promise we made the last time we talked?"

"You bet I do. That's one reason I came by today."

"And what's the other?"

"To show off my pretty new wife, of course." I winked at Missy and turned to Henry Wilkins, "Please entertain Missy. Granville and I have some drinks and stories to swap. I'll be back for her shortly."

Wilkins grinned and said, "Don't be in a hurry, James. It's not often I'm called on to keep company with a beautiful young woman." Missy took Henry Wilkins' arm as they went over to chairs on the store floor where husbands waited for their wives to finish shopping.

Granville Calvert took me back to his office. When we were

seated, he opened a desk drawer, pulled out a whiskey bottle and two glasses, and poured each of us a shot.

I said, "Before I take a drink, I'd like to thank you for what you tried to do at Peebles Farm."

Calvert shook his head. "We did the best we could. Even if I lost every man in the regiment, I could not break through to relieve you."

"I know. I was pleased when you turned back. Our situation was hopeless. No point in losing more men to rescue us."

"I felt bad, real bad for you and your regiment." Granville was not often serious as he was now.

"Yankee prison was awful, worse than we thought. But, men walked out of prison who would've died at Peebles Farm if we kept fighting. Let's drink the first one for all the men who did not come back."

With that, Granville and I touched glasses and drained them in one swallow. This was a skill and pleasure I learned and refined in my afternoon and evening "teas" with Dorsey Pender whom I remembered every time I drank good whiskey.

Granville refilled the glasses and said, "We'll drink the next one to a better future." After the toasts, we sat and talked. At one point in our conversation, he said, "My best years are behind me. We'll do all right with the store, but it'll never be as good as it was before the war."

On the ride home, Missy commented, "I enjoyed meeting your friends. Mister Wilkins is delightful. A real gentleman. But, I came away a little sad."

"Why?" I asked.

"He talked like his life's about over."

"Same with Granville. Makes me grateful. I've got you, Andy, Robert, and a chest full of Yankee currency. Our best years are ahead of us."

* * *

I stayed busy since I came home. Time was short. We needed to leave for Texas before the local Provost learned of our presence. But, there was one other person I had to see before we left - Hannah, my second mother.

Since I left for the war, Hannah mostly stayed in her home. Mother did not need her to work as housekeeper and cook as she did when I was growing up. She came to the main house once a week for cleaning, but there was little to do. Mother lived by herself and, true to her German heritage, was meticulously neat. Hannah came when Mother needed help in entertaining as when we arrived. But, even then, Missy and Pearl took over much of the housework and meal preparation.

I excused myself and rode over to the home Hannah kept for her husband, Henry and Hannibal, who still lived with their parents, and her other children. Hannah seemed pleased to see me. She fixed spiced tea we drank while visiting.

For me, it was like spending time with a favorite aunt. Hannah told me Henry and Hannibal would be married soon to girls who had recently been freed, but both her sons wanted to stay with the farm. Oliver and Mother had agreed to build additional quarters so that each would have his own home. Hannah looked forward to grandchildren. She teased me, "When's you and Missy gwine make Miz Anne a granmah?"

I laughed. "We're working on it."

Hannah laughed with me. "I'se got faith in you, James. You picked a good one. She's a fine young lady."

I thanked Hannah and went on to discuss life on the Cobb Farm. It was apparent to me that Hannah, like Oliver and the other Negroes, identified with and took pride in the Farm. Not a new revelation, but reassuring. I was concerned that the war and mass freeing of slaves would affect loyalty of the Cobb Farm Negroes. It didn't.

* * *

We swapped the wagon for a larger wagon from the Cobb Farm and filled it with tents, provisions, Missy's clothing and accessories, and a "few pieces of furniture" Mother insisted we take. She and Missy agreed on two stuffed chairs, a dining table, cabinet, chest of drawers, bed frame with head board, and mattress. I had no idea how all that and Missy's stuff would fit on the wagon, but it did. We covered and tied down the load with large waxed blankets to protect the contents from weather.

Earlier, I hoped to return to the farm I loved and use it as a springboard for a future life in business. But it was not to be. Most hurtful, I wanted the opportunity to give back to Mother the care she had given me. I saw Hannah and Oliver separately, said goodbye. After a sad farewell, in which Mother and Missy could not hold back tears, we departed on the long journey to Texas.

I felt subdued and contemplative for the first day of the trip. Sensing the reason for my depression, Missy told me, "Your mother will have a good life even without her son and daughter-in-law to look after her."

I wanted to believe her, but was not convinced. "Mother put on a good show for us. She looked forward to our return as much as we did. Now she's alone."

"She is not alone. Your mother and Doctor McCray have become good friends, maybe more later."

Missy still believed they would marry. I shook my head and drove on.

* * *

Missy drove as we approached Atlanta. Having taken my turn on guard duty the night before, I slept in the back seat of the carriage. When the city came into view, she reached back and shook me, "Jim, look at this. The Yankees burned it down. But look at all the rebuilding. Atlanta's coming back."

In the midst of burned out old Atlanta, a new city grew from a core around the railway station. I took it in briefly and commented, "Should rename the city Phoenix, like the bird of Heliopolis in Greek mythology."

Inspired by the rebirth of South's commercial hub, I decided we would stay in a hastily erected hotel for two nights and a day and hold the wagon and carriage in livery. I told Missy, "Let's spend some of our money in Atlanta and stay an extra day. It's not much, but you never had a honeymoon. I promise when we're settled, I'll make it up to you."

"You mean just us for the night?" Missy teased.

"Two nights, Dear. We'll splurge a little."

"Oh my, what will we find to do?" Missy asked as she gave me a wicked grin. We became lost in ourselves and may have embarrassed Pearl.

* * *

First night, we got everyone situated. The clerk recommended a colored family on the outskirts who took in traveling Negroes. We placed Pearl with them. Andy and Robert brought the lock-box up to their room along with the other luggage.

Several restaurants sprang up near the restored hotel and beyond the hotel stores, some in tents, offered their wares.

I took Missy to a newly opened restaurant and paid extra for a flower bouquet brought to our table. I took her hand and said, "I hope you feel special, Missus Cobb. You are."

She leaned forward and whispered, "You'll find out how special tonight Mister Cobb."

We did not sleep much the first night.

Next morning, after breakfast, Missy said, "I'm writing home. Help me."

She wrote:

I am in a new Atlanta hotel. It is hard to believe how much construction is underway here. Amazing.

And why are we in Atlanta? I will explain. Jim has an uncle in Texas with a huge estate near Beaumont. He asked Jim to come out and help develop and manage his holdings. Jim, Andy, and I are going out to start a new life in Texas. Robert Savage, who you may remember is from Nacogdoches, Texas, is also with our party. Pearl, too, decided to move to Texas with us.

You'll be pleased to learn that each of the men in Jim's regiment – Malcolm, Gilbert, and Sam – returned home on the way to the Cobb Farm in Newton. They come from good families. Malcolm and, I think, Sam rejoined sweethearts. We believe they will have good lives after their years of service to the Confederacy.

Jim's mother, Anne Cobb, is a marvelous woman. You will like her when you meet her. The qualities we love about Jim are in her. The Cobb Farm is very well managed by Jim's mother and their Negro overseer, Oliver. The Negroes have worked as tenant farmers for the past ten years. It will work at the Morgan Plantation as well. I talked with Missus Cobb about Oliver spending time with Jacob if you think it would help. Maybe after the harvest. Jim says Oliver is also agreeable to a trip to Virginia.

We are excited about our new life in Texas. It is a vast new land ready for development. Jim told me about his great grandfather who came to North Carolina from England and built a large farm. He wants to do the same in Texas.

By the way, are we related to the Revolutionary General Daniel Morgan? If so, he is an ancestor we can be proud to claim.

Goodbye for now. I will send letters along the way to Texas and give you our permanent address when we get there. Please pass along our regards to Sissy and Jonathan when you write them.

I read the letter and told Missy, "You don't need my help. You covered the reason for our move to Texas well. But, if you would, help me write a letter to the marvelous Anne Cobb."

* * *

Andy indulged in a newly discovered interest. Growing up, he saw few "store bought" goods and had a country boy fascination with them. He went through the retail stores looking at items offered and their prices. Robert went along, but did not share Andy's interest. Andy asked, "What do you like to do?"

Robert answered, "I'll show you when I get home."

"What'll you show me?"

"I'm gonna court the Parson's daughter like how we whupped the Yankees at Chancellorsville."

Andy grinned. "How long you been gone?"

"Four years."

Andy shook his head, "Don't be surprised if one of the local boys snatched her up. All the pretty girls I knew were gone when I got back."

Andy wrote home regularly, but, because of the constant moving, could not receive letters until we settled. We later learned Federal investigators were closing in on Andy's father. The fact the payroll had been robbed by Mosby's Rangers at the same location two years earlier focused attention to the former Mosby network.

From informers, the Provost Marshals learned John Blaylock served as head of intelligence for Mosby in Fauquier County where the robbery occurred. They called him in repeatedly for questioning. He steadfastly denied any connection to the robbery.

With no hard evidence implicating John Blaylock, the investigators pieced together information from their informers that tied Andy, me, and other former Rangers to the earlier payroll robbery and possible participants in the recent robbery. Interviews with the Union payroll detachment yielded descriptions of the robbers. By perverse fortune, the Union Lieutenant we robbed was an actor before the war and went back to a career on the stage after the war. He accurately identified local accents of individuals who spoke during the robbery.

Provost Office investigators compiled a list of known members of the Mosby organization, including Andy and me, and descriptions of the robbers. The list circulated in a dispatch to Provost offices throughout the South – the dispatch Ruth McCray saw in the Hickory Office.

* * *

Continuing the practice established on our ride down, we took turns guarding the camp at night. Missy made the sensible suggestion that the man who stayed up the night before ride with her and Pearl in the carriage. She and Pearl would do most of the driving and he could catch up on his sleep in the back seat as we traveled. The second man drove the wagon and the third man rode one of the horses in front of the party to look for possible trouble ahead.

With Andy in the carriage backseat after a night of sentry duty, he asked Missy, "Where's a fella to find girl like you when I get to Texas?"

She smiled, "Handsome buck like you'll have no trouble attracting women. But, you'll have a big advantage. Me."

"You'll check out whatever women I bring around?" Andy asked.

"And Robert, too," she promised.

"What if they don't pass muster?"

"You'll hear about it."

"I'd take it as a favor if you would. I joined the army when I was still a kid. No sisters. Other than Mother and a few girlfriends, I don't know much about women."

Missy nodded in agreement. "You and Jim are two peas in a pod. He doesn't know much either, but he's learning."

LaGrange, Georgia, Tuesday,
August 8, 1865
Jim Cobb

Andy rode ahead, asked for directions to the cottonseed broker, Aaron Chiles, and led the party to his office. Robert stayed with the women and the wagon while Andy and I went inside to talk with Chiles. We explained we were headed to Southeast Texas and wanted to buy seed for one thousand acres of long staple cotton.

Chiles told us, "During the war, I sold seed to growers in East Texas. They got around the blockade by shipping out of Matamoros, Mexico. They did well with the seed. I think you will too." Chiles spoke without emotion and seemed sad.

I told him, "For the past two years, my mother bought seed from you. You may remember her - Anne Cobb in Newton, North Carolina."

Chiles' face brightened briefly as he responded, "She and the Texans were the only ones who paid in Union coin. I gave her a better price than the others." Chiles then asked, "Where'd you boys serve?" He seemed to know, without asking, we were veterans.

Andy replied, "Army of Northern Virginia, Light Division, Third Corps. Did you have anyone in the war?"

"Two sons and three nephews, two in the Army of Tennessee and three in the Army of Northern Virginia. Only one came home, my brother's son." Chiles' last statement explained his glum demeanor. Not unfriendly, but depressed and preoccupied as a man who had lost two sons and two nephews.

I wrote down Aaron Chiles' address and told him, "If the

crop works out, we'll buy more seed next year." I paid Chiles in Union coin. He took us to a storage building in back and weighed out the seed we purchased. He said, "Watch me. I want you to know you're not being shorted."

Near Opelika, Alabama
Thursday, August 10, 1865
Jim Cobb

Two days out from LaGrange, we camped for the night in Alabama just over the Georgia border. Robert stood watch. He kept the fire going and the coffee hot through the night, filling his cup often.

Damp fog chilled the mid-summer night air blocking the quarter moon which made it difficult to see beyond the glow of the campfire. Robert disliked guard duty, especially on dark nights. He felt uneasy when he could not see well. His imagination played tricks, causing him to see and hear things that weren't there.

Robert huddled under a blanket and kept his rifle and pistol close. To stay awake and pass the time, he thought back to a favored memory – Catherine Hendricks, the parson's daughter. Andy's comment troubled him. He wondered who's sparkin' her now? Robert finished his coffee and got up to take another turn around the camp.

As he approached the trees where the horses were tied, he heard a sound – like someone or something stepped on a dry twig. Or was it? He stopped and looked in the direction of the sound. Nothing. Turning back to the campfire, he thought probably just my mind playin' tricks again.

Then he caught a glimpse of something moving. The horses snorted and stamped. He made out a dim figure creeping toward the horses. Robert looked further into the darkness for others and saw nothing. He put his finger on the rifle trigger. Any sudden movement or just looking at him and the intruder was a dead man. He saw him clearly – a young man creeping up on the horses. Robert moved fast. As the intruder looked up, Robert saw he carried a pistol and acted quickly. He swung his rifle and hit the young man in the gut. The intruder fell back and moaned.

Robert looked for others but did not see them. He knelt by the young man and rolled him on his back for a good look. Sixteen, maybe eighteen. The intruder opened his eyes and Robert asked, "Where're the others?"

The boy licked his lips but said nothing.

"Anybody with you?" Robert repeated.

The boy shook his head.

Robert slapped him across the face, cocked his pistol and put it beside the intruder's head, "Don't lie to me boy. How many and where are they?"

The intruder whispered, "Three." He closed his eyes.

Andy and I ran up, pistols drawn. Looking at the young man, Andy asked Robert, "You okay?"

We looked around and saw nothing. I asked, "Any more with him?"

"He said three before he passed out," Robert answered.

"Watch him. Andy and I will circle around the camp".

We found nothing, but heard horses moving up the road back toward LaGrange. Pearl and Missy found a rope Robert used to tie up the young man. It was near daybreak and, rather than going back to sleep, Pearl and Missy started breakfast.

We dragged the boy away from the campfire where we could watch him but he could not hear what we said. I looked at the boy with disgust. Buck toothed kid with dirty brown hair and the start of a stringy beard. He wore britches a size too short with patches across the knees and butt. Most came together during the war to help one another. Some, like this boy and his no good kin, stole from others. Worse than the Yankee bummers who plagued us. At least the Yankee scum weren't ours.

"Got ourselves a problem," I said.

"Why don't we cut his throat and hide the body back in the woods?" Robert asked.

"No, somebody'll find him. Might remember us passing through and tie it to us." Andy commented.

"But, if we turn him loose, he'll run his mouth 'bout what he saw," Robert replied.

"What did he see?" I asked. "Three men with a woman and a darky woman headed west. Must be hundreds like us came through here. We don't want to alert anyone about the lockbox, but he didn't see that and won't. Let's turn him loose with a lecture, no horse. It'll take him awhile to get home. We'll be long gone by the time he talks to anyone." Robert looked for agreement.

Then I asked Robert, "How about you talk with him before we send him on his way?"

"My pleasure, Major."

We circled around the campfire and brought the captive into the circle. Pearl gave him a plate of food. Even with his hands tied, the boy ate like it was his last meal.

When we finished, packed, and ready to leave, Robert pulled the young man to his feet and cut the rope that tied his legs and wrists. He looked at him and asked, "What's your name?"

He shuffled his feet but did not look up. "Kendrick Prior."

"Kendrick Prior, I could've killed you. I wuz a soldier in the late war and killed more men than I can count. Think about that. Men you rob cud be like me. Next time you cud be dead. If your sorry family's makin' a livin' stealin' from others who have no more than you, it's time you strike out on your own. Go where nobody knows you or your worthless kin. Make a new life for yourself."

Robert paused until the young man looked up and added, "If

I find you stealin' again, I'll drop you. Don't take what I say as a threat; it's a promise."

The young man hung his head and did not look up again. He sullenly walked away as we left for the next town - Opelika, Alabama.

Robert rode in the carriage with Missy and Pearl, but did not immediately go to sleep. He said, "I wonder about the young man. Maybe he'll turn out good. More likely, he'll keep on until he does jail time or worse."

"You did all you could for him," Pearl said. 'What happens to him from here own is not your look out."

After a few miles, Robert stretched out on the back seat and slept.

Alabama and Mississippi,
August 11-25, 1865
Jim Cobb

We continued to see the grim side of Southern life – rural poverty – in the farms and communities we passed. Many plantations and farms lay idle and in disrepair. We saw listless towns with little apparent commerce going on and numerous Union patrols, but they too seemed bored and indifferent.

While we stopped for lunch, a group of former slaves passed by, looked at us hungrily, and camped beyond us. Barefoot, with threadbare clothes, they appeared starved. I walked over to their camp, introduced myself and Pearl, and said, "We have food. We can give you some of it."

One of the former slaves, the apparent leader, removed his hat, stepped forward, and said, "Thank you, Suh. We'se pow'ful hungry. Anyting you gib iz 'preciated."

I turned to Pearl and instructed her to "Give them all we

can spare. We'll pick up more supplies in the next town." Pearl motioned for two of the women to follow her to the wagon.

I asked the Negro man, "Where're you from?"

He mentioned a plantation near a community in Southern Alabama unfamiliar to me.

"Where're you headed?" I asked.

"We's heerd dere's wohk in de Noath and askin' as we go."

"You couldn't stay on the plantation and work?"

The Negro shook his head and said, "No, Suh. De mastuh he died in de wah and de Yankees came. Dey sed deys got no wohk foh us, but go Noath and we get fohty acres and a mule?"

"Have you found any Yankees with forty acres and a mule to give you?" I asked.

The Negro shook his head. "No, Suh."

Pearl returned with the women, carrying foodstuff for the party. I reached into my pocket, took out a five dollar coin, and handed it to the Negro who slowly lifted his hand to accept the coin. I said, "Good luck to you. I wish you the best."

He gripped my hand gently and replied, "God bless you Suh. You'll be 'membered in heb'n. Jesus sed dat 'even as ye dun it to de least of dese, ye dun it to me'" and released my hand.

I thought This man knows the Bible, probably their spiritual leader, might have been praying for relief when we came up.

I was struck by what the Negro minister said and regretted I could not do more for them. I came away from Fort Delaware with renewed conviction God had spared my life. Too many times I could have died and didn't. The only explanation was God had work for me to do. But I knew most of my attention, since prison, had gone to gaining wealth, exacting vengeance, and lust for my young wife's body. I knew I must reorder my priorities and appreciated the chance encounter as a reminder. Maybe God sent the Negro minister to me rather than the other way around.

* * *

We passed several communities with vigilance committees. The vigilantes included former soldiers who rode out during the night, under white sheets, to frighten and intimidate the recently freed and enfranchised Negroes and, in some instances, exact vengeance from scalawags and carpetbaggers.

In a community near the Mississippi border, I rode scout and came upon an angry mob that literally rode a man out of town. The "guest of honor" had been stripped naked and covered with tar and feather before he was mounted on a stout pole for a quick exit. About a half-mile out of town, the men carrying the pole tired and unceremoniously dumped him beside the road and started walking back.

I dismounted and talked with them while I walked my horse toward town. Their guest of honor slinked into weeds beside the road hoping, I guess, someone would come along to help him.

I asked one of them, "What did he do?"

"Scouted for the Yankees and had the gall to buy a neighbor's farm for back taxes."

"Where's the Sheriff?" I asked.

"I am the Sheriff" he answered.

* * *

In our time alone at night, Missy asked an occasional question or made comment about Mother to draw out my feelings. She picked the right moment to say, "Your mother seems so comfortable with Doctor McCray."

I replied, "We've known him a long time. Been our family doctor for as long as I can remember. Church elder. Good man. Sure, we're all comfortable with him."

Missy asked, "Do you think he might be more than a friend to her?"

I reacted sharply. "No. She's my mother, my father's wife. She's no one's sweetheart, if that's what you mean."

Missy waited briefly and then gently pointed out, "She's also an attractive, intelligent, and accomplished woman. I think Doctor McCray is interested in her and she in him. Think about it. Your mother's a loving woman. She needs to be needed and is there anyone more worthy of her attention than Geoffrey McCray? He needs a purpose for his life and, maybe, when he gets better, he could work the mills. Your mother and Doctor McCray may marry."

"Did she tell you that?" I asked.

"No, but don't be surprised if it happens and it would be wonderful for both of them."

I did not respond, but Missy put the seed in my head and nourished it with her endorsement. Same thing worked well with me before we married.

*   *   *

In the dark of early morning, I awoke and became aware I sat straight up on the stuffed blanket Missy and I used for a mattress. Outside our tent, Andy, Robert, and Pearl surrounded us and looked concerned and uncertain. Missy huddled in a corner of the tent.

I had no idea what had happened, but felt cold sweat on my forehead and the soaked sheet on which I had been sleeping. I turned to Missy for an explanation and could see she was shaken.

Missy spoke hesitantly and softly and said, "Darling, you had a nightmare."

I knew there was more to it and asked, "Why are you frightened and why's everyone looking into our tent?"

Missy started to explain and then broke down and sobbed. I took her in my arms to calm and comfort her.

Andy said, "I heard screamin' and shoutin' comin' from your tent. Mostly stuff I didn't understand, but, I heard you call out 'fall back', 'look out' and other words I could make out. I thought someone might be attackin' you and came pistol cocked. I saw Missy in the corner shakin' while you sat wide-eyed in the middle of the tent with your arms thrashin' around. Robert and Pearl came runnin' at the same time."

I had no recollection of anything that happened after I went to sleep, but did not doubt Andy told me exactly what he saw. I turned to Missy and said, "Missy, Honey, I'm so sorry. The last thing in the world I want is to frighten you. I have no idea what I dreamed, but it had nothing to do with you or our life together." I reached out and pulled her to me as I spoke. Missy, still shaking, put her head on my chest and sobbed gently. Andy, Robert, and Pearl excused themselves and went back to their tents. We lay down again, but neither of us slept.

Chapter 29: El Dorado

Laurel, Mississippi to Orange, Texas,
August 26 – September 7, 1865
Jim Cobb

Near Laurel, Mississippi, Andy rode scout and came upon a badly beaten young man lying unconscious beside the road and stopped to help. The victim wore a Confederate shirt and jacket with Corporal chevrons. He was badly bruised and dehydrated, but had no broken bones.

The remainder of the party caught up and took pity on the unfortunate traveler. We cleared a place in the wagon, put down blankets and pillows for the young man, and assigned Pearl to attend him.

That evening, he awoke and told a story of being set upon by robbers who took his money and horse and left him for dead. He thanked us for giving him aid and comfort. "I'm Victor Tenant and on my way home to Columbia when robbers attacked me."

I asked, "Where'd you serve?"

"I wuz detached from the army after the fight at Franklin. I joined a group of soldiers like me. We worked behind Yankee lines until the war ended. I wuz walkin' home when I found a stray horse the day before they robbed me."

His story seemed to check out. He gave us details of the Army of Tennessee that only a veteran would know. His shoes were worn down as if by someone who had walked over two hundred miles. We offered to drop him off at his destination,

Columbia, Mississippi, as the party would pass through there in three days. Over the next two days, he recovered with regular food, water, and rest and was a perfect guest in helping out wherever he could.

I thought of the unfortunate Confederate soldier we left in Virginia when Missy pulled me to one side for a private talk. "Have you noticed how Victor's eyes constantly shift even when he sits doing nothing?"

"Guess he's nervous. Been through a lot before we found him. I had not noticed his shifty eyes, but I've seen soldiers do strange things. It might just be some sort of battle weariness."

Missy said, "Pearl has something she wants to tell you" and motioned to Pearl to join us.

Reluctant to say anything, Pearl, with Missy's urging, finally told me, "Mister Jim, there's something wrong with that man" as she nodded toward Victor Tenant who talked with Robert.

Noting her unease, I said, "Don't be afraid. Tell us what you're thinking. You need not give me facts just tell me what's on your mind."

"I think he's a thief. He says thieves attacked him, but I think he ran with thieves when he fell out with them."

Missy joined in, "I can't put my finger on it, but I agree with Pearl. Victor's not telling us the full truth."

I looked at Pearl and asked, "Have you seen him do anything suspicious?"

"In the wagon, he's always looking at your things, particularly the lockbox. When we're alone, just him and me, he isn't polite and respectful like you and Mister Andy and Mister Robert or the way he is when you're around. He questions me often about what's in the lockbox."

I said, "Thank you, Pearl. Say nothing of this to Andy and Robert. I'll speak with them later."

Pearl left, I turned to Missy, and asked, "What do you think we should do?"

"Keep a close eye on Victor. I don't trust him."

Missy's and Pearl's suspicions were sufficient "evidence", particularly when Pearl mentioned the lockbox. We had worked too long and too hard for the stolen currency to risk any possibility of loss. Could leave him without explanation, but who would he talk to and what would he say? Could put a bullet through his head, but we had no evidence to convict him of being anything other than shifty-eyed and maybe two faced. I decided to keep a close eye on Victor and drop him off in Columbia as promised.

I spoke separately with Andy and Robert out of Tenant's hearing before resuming the journey. I started with Andy.

After I told him of Missy's and Pearl's suspicions, Andy took some time before replying, "Missy's right. His eyes shift a lot. I don't doubt what Pearl told you either. Tomorrow's my day to ride scout. What if I circle back into Columbia after we drop him off and see what I can find out?"

I replied, "I was thinking the same thing. If you learn anything, catch up with us as soon as you can."

Robert was more direct. "I don't trust the little shit either. Why don't we just shoot him and be done with it?"

I reprimanded Robert, "We don't know enough to kill him. I don't know if Tenant has anything in mind or not. But, we can't go around killing everyone that looks at us crosswise."

Robert mounted his horse, looked down at me, and said, "If you change your mind, say the word, and I'll take care of it". Robert rode out as scout.

Columbia, Mississippi,
Friday, August 18, 1865
Jim Cobb

Next day, mid-morning, we dropped off Victor Tenant at the town square. He thanked each member of the party before departing.

As we left town, Missy and I saw a Union Provost Office and felt uneasy. In late afternoon, Andy caught up with us.

Robert and I turned the carriage and wagon off the road and gathered to hear his report. Andy told us, "It's worse than we suspected. When I went back into town, I saw the little shit, sorry Missy, coming out of the Provost Office. He didn't see me. He went to a livery stable, rented a horse and saddle, and headed north. He saw me and turned to run. I caught him about five miles out of town, shot him in the leg, and pulled him off his horse. I finally got the truth."

"Pearl was right. He rode with an outlaw gang. His name's not Victor Tenant. Victor Tenant is one of the victims of the gang he rode with in Southern Mississippi. When they found him stealin' from them, they beat him and left him for dead. I came on him the next morning. His name's Thad Riley and a deserter. They didn't operate behind Union lines, but spent their time robbin' and lootin' in Mississippi and Alabama. He and his gang were nothin' but thieves and cutthroats, bummers."

I noted Missy cringed when Andy said "bummers" and asked, "Did you find out what he told the Provost?"

"He denied everything. I rolled my pistol handle over his leg where it was broke. The second time, he told me what he did at the Provost Office."

"He saw how we watched the lockbox, how little Pearl would tell him about what's in it, and how we avoided Union patrols. He figured the Provost might have an interest in us and lucked out. The Provost remembered the same dispatch Jim's mother told us about and thought we might be the travelin' party in the dispatch particularly when he told them you had a long head scar. The Provost gave Riley fifty dollars to take four of his marshals out to arrest us. Riley told the Provost he would get a horse from the livery stable and come right back to lead them to us. He rented a horse, saddled up, and took off."

Robert said, "They know we're headed west from Columbia.

Lucky we ain't seen a Yankee patrol. Must be lookin' for him, maybe us. We have to throw 'em off."

"I've been thinkin' about it" Andy replied. "For now, we should stay in the woods. They'll look for us farther down the road. The lockbox must be hidden. We need to buy lumber and nails and build a little nest under the wagon bottom. They'll look for a front rider, a carriage, and a wagon as Riley described us. We need to split up and travel separately. We can come together at night to camp, but we need to maintain more distance between the wagon and carriage."

Missy spoke up, "I have a better idea. Pearl and I can sew pockets inside my petticoat. I know there's a lot of currency, but I have a lot of petticoat. No Yankee will dare search a Southern lady's underclothing and a Southern lady is expected to wear her petticoat when she travels. And, I'm a Southern lady."

Andy grinned and said, "I like that. What do you think, Jim?"

I shook my head. "Mother always said no good deed goes unpunished. She must have had Thad Riley in mind. We've had no problem with Union Marshals until now, but I think our luck just changed. They know we passed through Columbia and are in the area. The Provost must've thought Riley identified the party with the stolen payroll."

"I agree with you and Missy. But, we need to take it a step further. We've been angling for Orange, Texas in a west, southwest direction. We should drop south about one hundred miles from here and then go due west. It'll put us on a different route than what Riley gave the Provost."

Robert said, "Yeah, we'll be in Louisiana swamps."

"Better Louisiana swamps than Yankee patrols" Andy pointed out as the good Mosby Ranger he once was.

"Did you kill him?" Robert asked.

"I was tempted, but no. If the Yankees found his body, they'd know we got to him first and maybe alerted us. As it is, Riley's hidin' from the Yankees. But, if I ever see him again, he's a dead man."

I liked Andy's thinking. It was the smart thing to do. Andy added, "One other thing. We need to keep Jim and the wagon separate. It won't take much for the Yankees to tie Jim, description of a suspect with a head scar, and the lockbox together."

I said, "The currency will be in Missy's petticoat. They won't find it."

"The Yankees may figure we hid the money somewhere else and start lookin', who knows, maybe even Missy's petticoat" Andy replied. "We need to keep you away from the lockbox during the day. It means you can't drive the wagon for the rest of the trip. It'll slow us down and because I took pity on a piece of trash along the road."

I said, "Don't be hard on yourself. We all would've done the same. It's what we're taught in church – take pity on the less fortunate. This one turned out to be a snake, but we must maintain our values."

We drove the carriage and wagon out of sight and made camp for the remainder of the next two days. Missy and Pearl stitched pockets inside Missy's petticoat and stuffed the pockets with stolen currency. Andy and I laid out a new route to Texas and filled the lockbox with papers and other valuables. We considered dumping it, but that would raise suspicion as most travelers carried their valuables under lock.

* * *

We left at daybreak, traveled twenty miles west, and found the road south to Hammond, Louisiana. Two days later we headed due west toward Baton Rouge and maintained a one hour interval between the carriage and wagon. For the remainder of our journey, Yankee patrols stopped and searched all carriages and wagons on the road.

We practiced our stories each night. Outside Hammond, a Union patrol ordered Robert to pull off the road for an inspection. As he talked with them, Missy and I rode by in the carriage, showed curiosity, but no recognition. I drove on until we turned a bend and got out to watch from behind a clump of bushes. After a few minutes, Andy joined us.

Robert stood before a Union Sergeant who demanded to know, "What you got in the wagon, Reb?"

Robert pointed to the furniture pieces and said, "Takin' furniture to my grandfolks in Vermilionville." The Union Sergeant circled around the wagon, lifted the cover, pointed to the tents, bedrolls, and pots, "What's this?"

"Stuff we used in the war. I'm takin' it home to my folks in Texas."

"We'll take a look in the lock box you're carryin'."

"Yes, Sir. Here's the key."

A Corporal grabbed the key from Robert's hand, opened the lockbox and spilled the papers on the ground. Documents, jewelry, and such.

"Anyone travelin' with you?"

Robert shook his head and anticipated the next question.

"How is it you're goin' west with all this?"

"Left Fort Delaware after the war. Stayed with an uncle in North Carolina 'til he lost his farm in tax court. He asked me to drop off the furniture to the grandfolks."

"How about the tents and the other stuff?"

"Found 'em along the way. Some of your boy's must've dumped 'em." Best lie is closest to the truth – Fort Delaware, Cobb Farm furniture, and Union tents Rangers captured during the war.

*   *   *

After daily stops and questioning, we became a bit jaded. Andy and Missy rode in the carriage. I had lookout and Robert the wagon for the day. Missy spotted a Union patrol up the road, turned to Andy, and said, "Let's have some fun with this one."

By the time the Yankee patrol ordered them over for an inspection, Missy and Andy were deep in a marital argument making it up as they went along.

"I never told your mother that," she screamed at Andy as the Sergeant rode up. Andy looked up searching for relief.

"Where you headed?"

"Baton Rouge," Andy answered.

"What's your purpose in goin' to Baton Rouge?"

"To see my folks," Andy answered.

"Not if you don't tell them the truth about what I said," Missy interjected.

"What you said. What did you say? I forgot," Andy replied.

"You don't remember anything. If you love me, you'll tell your mother the truth. You don't care. Whatever's easy. And don't think I forgot what you promised before I married you."

Andy looked at Missy exasperated and blankly said, "What promise?"

They bickered and ignored the Union Sergeant until he finally waved them on.

Out of sight, Andy pulled the carriage over. They both erupted into laughter.

Andy asked, "Ever consider a career in the theater?"

"How about you? You have the henpecked husband perfected. Fooled the Yankees, didn't we?"

Andy nodded. Fortunately, he had remembered to put on my wedding ring that morning.

Baton Rouge, Louisiana
Wednesday, August 30, 1865
Jim Cobb

We came into a culture and people we had only read about. The farms grew rice and sugar cane. The rural folk spoke a French dialect and ate rice, beans, okra, shrimp, crawfish, and pork seasoned with peppers and other spices - a strange and fascinating land of moss laden oak trees.

Near Baton Rouge, we found a ferry owned and operated by Pierre Landry, a boisterous, colorful Cajun. While crossing the big river, he asked, "Hey, you Confedrett?"

Robert nodded and said, "Light Division, Army of Northern Virginia."

Landry asked, "Any yuh officuh?"

Robert pointed to me, "Major Cobb was our regimental commander and aide to General A P Hill."

I smiled and tipped my hat. Landry broke out in a wide grin. "Ma boy, he wuz aide ta Genral Mouton. Yuh heard uh dat Genral Mouton?"

I nodded and said, "Yes."

Landry seemed delighted. I had heard mention of a Confederate General Alfred Mouton who led an army active in Louisiana and Texas during the war.

As we crossed the river, Landry proceeded to tell us, at length, about his son and the much revered and celebrated Cajun General Mouton. Landry seemed sympathetic to Confederate soldiers returning home particularly after he learned Andy was a top sergeant like his nephew. He refused to take the customary fee for bringing us across.

Landry directed us to a nearby camp to spend the night. The local residents had planned an outdoor shrimp boil near the camp and he invited us to attend.

The spicy boiled shrimp, actually mostly crawfish, with corn and rice tasted delicious. We drank a local brew that was not bad. After taking a drink, Andy commented, "Seems like they started with rice instead of barley in makin' their beer."

A small band with fiddle, squeeze-box, and te fere kept the night lively with 'conky-conk' music we came to enjoy. The Cajuns put down wooden planks for a floor. Missy danced with each of the men in an attempt to copy the two-step she saw the locals dance.

She told me, "Not a Lexington cotillion, but a lot more fun."

In talking with Landry, I learned the shrimp peel was one of a series of parties the locals organized to welcome their men back from the war. Landry introduced his guests to other Cajuns and exaggerated our story some to make it more colorful although it was hard to tell. He mostly spoke in the Cajun dialect.

Many of the celebrants came over to talk and swap war stories, but it was difficult. The Cajuns picked up some English during the war but it was mostly not understandable. Missy and Pearl learned French from a tutor William Morgan hired for his children when they were young, but they forgot much of what they learned and the Cajun dialect was decidedly different from formal French. With hand motions, facial expressions, gestures, and some French we carried out a semblance of conversation. Pierre Landry, who was mostly conversant in English, helped out.

One of the Cajuns came over with a jug he passed among the guests. Knowing it was impolite to refuse a drink, each of us, in turn, wiped off the spout with his sleeve and took a swig that was as powerful as Jeremiah Dunston's moonshine we sampled in Wilkesboro. But this brew had a distinct cherry taste. From the Cajuns, we learned the drink was, as we suspected, distilled from fermented cherries.

I left money for the band, but none of the organizers of the party would accept reimbursement for the food and beer.

I thought Missy looked particularly fetching in the simple skirt and blouse she wore for the party. I mentioned it to her and found her aroused in our tent that night leading to one of our more memorable nights of raw, naked sex.

* * *

Two days after leaving Baton Rouge, Missy felt ill in the morning with an upset stomach that made preparation of the morning meal difficult. The smell of bacon frying and coffee, which she normally enjoyed, nearly caused her to vomit. Pearl took over breakfast. By mid morning, Missy felt better. When Pearl suggested she might be pregnant, Missy had already guessed. She waited another day to be sure and then told me I would be a father.

I offered to discontinue love making until the baby was born, but Missy assured me, "I'll be fine until about two months before delivery."

I felt relieved. The closeness, affection, and thrill of our lovemaking had become an important part of my life.

Turned out Missy knew more about childbirth than I thought. On plantations, the owner's wife typically took part in birth of slave children, particularly the house staff. Not Margaret Morgan and not Sissy Morgan, but Missy attended births often and learned.

A wagon axle broke near Vermilionville and required us to rent another wagon, unload the broken down wagon, and drag the wagon to a blacksmith for repair. It took three days to complete the repair that would have been done in Virginia or North Carolina in a day and, even at that, the wagon was iffy all the way to Texas. It had been a long, hard journey from Newton to Vermilionville of over one month and, by now, we felt it.

We used the delay to sample local food and walk around as we had in Atlanta. I insisted Missy and Pearl see a local doctor although both assured me they felt fine and I was wasting money. Pearl's pregnancy was seven months along and she noticeably showed. The doctor confirmed both were fit and, barring sickness or injury, should have fine, healthy babies.

* * *

On leaving Vermilionville, Andy rode lookout, Robert took the wagon while Missy, Pearl, and I rode in the carriage. We followed the routine we established after our escape outside Columbia, Mississippi. Andy left at daybreak, Robert waited thirty minutes and departed, and we left thirty minutes behind Robert.

About ten miles out of town, we came across a Union patrol. They had stopped Robert and seemed to be questioning him. The Union Sergeant saw us and rode over. He asked, "You James Cobb?"

My blood froze and I thought fast. Robert did not tell him. They somehow figured out we are the party they tried to arrest in Columbia.

I recovered and asked, "Is there a problem, Sergeant?"

As two others in the patrol came over, he replied, "There is if we find the stolen payroll on you. Your man, Paul Mason, there played dumb. We searched the wagon. It's not there. You must have it. We find the payroll and we have it and two of the ones that took it."

He gave us a chilling smile and ordered, "Step down Captain Cobb."

I complied. Nothing else I could do.

The Sergeant dismounted and searched my coat and pants pockets. "I didn't expect you'd carry any of it on you." He took the pistol I carried under my coat.

"Where's Blaylock?" he asked.

"Who?"

"You know. Your Sergeant. The one that's been riding with you."

I told him, "I haven't seen him in a while." It was literally true.

He looked to the carriage. "That your sweetheart?"

"No just a woman and her servant we met in Vermilionville. We offered her a ride to Beaumont."

He chuckled. "Sure you did, but the doctor says she's your pregnant wife."

That's it, I thought. We were spotted in town. Someone contacted the Provost Office and they pulled up a report on us.

He seemed to admire Missy's beauty, I'll give him that. He said, "We'll have to search her and the nigger."

I protested, "Sir, in the South, men do not search women."

"We'll go easy on her." He winked while he leered at Missy. "Tell her to step down so we don't have to pull her out of the carriage."

I motioned Missy to join me. "Yankees have no respect for women. Best do as he orders."

Missy came to me. I put my arm around her indicating they would have to go through me to search her.

The Sergeant told Missy, "That petticoat of yours seems to be hanging heavy. You can take it off behind the wagon and hand it over or we'll have to search you while you're wearing it."

It's over I thought. I turned to speak with Missy and saw deliverance in the distance. The Lord looked after us. Andy rode toward us at a slow pace, as a traveler going to Vermilionville.

I leaned down and whispered in Missy's ear. "Andy's coming. Take Pearl behind the carriage and stall."

Missy nodded, motioned Pearl to join her, and went behind the carriage.

I then did the act of my life – the indignant husband. I stormed and ranted while Andy came closer. When he came within pistol range, I threw a punch at the Sergeant.

The two Privates were immediately on me. I used all my strength and broke lose and went after the Sergeant who joined in subduing me.

I heard a pistol shot. They looked up and relaxed their hold. I yanked the Sergeant's pistol from his holster and shot him in the forehead.

In quick order, I backed off and shot each of the two Privates, didn't kill them but took them out. I looked over where Andy had dropped a trooper and winged another. The sixth trooper raced back up the road until Robert shot him in the back with a rifle he carried in the wagon. I wasn't sure Robert got him until we saw him sway and then fall off his horse.

I called Andy and Robert over for a quick conference. Andy spoke first, "We've got to kill 'em all."

I did not want to do it. These were innocent men simply doing their duty at the wrong place and time. But, I knew Andy was right. We had to dispose of witnesses. I nodded.

Robert said, "We got to move quick 'fore someone else comes along."

"Yeah. Cut the throat of anyone still alive. Load them on the wagon. We'll use the shovel and bury them."

"How 'bout the horses?" Robert asked.

I hadn't thought that far. I shrugged. "Maybe keep one or two and trade the rest the first chance we get."

I went back to the carriage where I found Missy and Pearl huddled together shivering.

Missy looked up and asked, "Was that like one of your gun-fights in the war?"

I nodded and said, "Yes and I don't want you to watch what comes next."

Missy surprised me when she said, "We can't let any of them live and testify against us. Pearl and I can help bind them up so there won't be so much blood spilt." She looked at Pearl and asked, "Will you help me?"

Missy and Pearl ripped blankets into strips and used the strips to stanch the troopers' wounds including four with cut throats. They bled profusely. We loaded the bodies on the wagon which Robert drove to a rice field with soft dirt. Andy and I took turns with the shovel and quickly dug a wide, shallow grave. Missy and Pearl cleaned the wagon while Robert gathered the Union horses. He unsaddled each horse and tied them to the back of the wagon and added our two spare horses to the back of the carriage.

God protected us. We saw no one in the two hours it took to dispatch and bury the Union patrol. But, undoubtedly, others would come out looking for them when they did not report back. We were about ninety miles from Texas. We had to move quickly and look for a place to get rid of the horses.

Sabine River,
Thursday, September 7, 1865

The ferryman had a small farm which he worked until someone came along for transit across the river. We stopped at the farmhouse where his wife came out. I could barely understand her. We motioned to the river and conveyed that we needed to get across.

She sent the older of what appeared to be five children to the field to get her husband. He rode back on a mule with the ten year old boy running beside him.

I told Missy, "Occupy the wife while Andy and I talk with the ferryman."

He gave his name as Luis Hebert. We used false names. We were in grave danger every minute until we left Louisiana and passed to another army district. I asked Hebert, "You serve in the war?"

"Yes, Suh. I wuz Corpr'l in de 20th Louisiana. Yankees damn near kill me at Pittsburg Landing. Marry dis widah woman after de wah and scratch out a libin' on dis fahm. You want ferry to Texas?"

"As soon as you can."

He looked at us warily and asked, "You runnin' from de law?"

I asked him, "Do Union marshals come around asking questions?"

"Dey do, but I doan tell 'em nuttin' or I make up lies." Before we could question him, he lifted his trouser legs to show scars on his lower legs and repeated, "Dey damn near kill me. Lotsa folks runnin' from de law come heah to get to Texas."

I took a chance. We had little option. I said, "Mister Hebert, we have six Union horses. They are yours if you take us across the river and forget you ever saw us."

Hebert did not seem concerned. Instead he replied, "Yankees find me wid stole horses, take 'em away, I got nuttin."

I reached in my pocket, took out a ten dollar coin, and said, "You have the horses and ten dollars and you say nothing. Right?"

Hebert nodded and replied, "I take yo' money. I got five chilrun to feed but I doan say nuttin' to dem Yankees."

"If the Yankees ask you about the horses, tell 'em you bought 'em at an auction. Keep one to replace the mule you ride and sell off the rest as quick as you can to buyers far away."

Hebert's face lit up. We just handed him a windfall. "Git loaded. I take ya across."

We crossed the Sabine River near where it enters the Gulf of Mexico.

* * *

When we arrived on the Texas side, Hebert asked, "Where ya goin'?"

I didn't answer. He already knew too much about us. But,

Hebert persisted. "Mite's well let me tell ya. Nex un you talk wid mite parley wid de Yankees."

He had a point. I said, "We're headed to the Gerlach Estate near Lumberton. Ever hear of it?"

He told us Gus Gerlach was a local legend. According to Hebert, Gus was one of the few veterans of the Texas Army left and had a big spread. He not only gave us directions to Lumberton but also to the Gerlach Estate.

It was the first time I heard anyone, other than Mother, speak of Uncle Gus. I was pleased to hear he was a respected land-owner.

On parting, Hebert asked, "Yuh gon start new in El Dorado?"

I had not heard the term before, but saw Robert nod. I asked, "What is El Dorado?"

Hebert looked at me blankly and said, "You start over dere." He paused and then added, "Leave de trubbl at duh rivah. Texas is uh big lann. Take a new name if yuh want. Texas is duh El Dorado."

We rode on, happy to finally be in Texas. Out of hearing distance, Andy asked, "What's to stop him from takin' money from the Yankees and tell them we went to the Gerlach Estate?"

I answered, "Nothing. But, there's something about these Cajuns. I think they value honor over money. Just in case, we'll keep the currency in Missy's petticoat."

Andy agreed.

Missy asked, "Robert, you seemed to know what the ferry-man meant by 'El Dorado'. What is it?"

Robert explained, "It's a story I heard in school and else-wheres. A Spaniard, Coronado, looked for a city of gold called El Dorado on the High Plains. For me, it's the search to reach your highest dream."

"Did Coronado find the gold?" Missy asked.

"Not that I recollect," Robert replied. "I think it's just the idea of going after what you want."

We decided to make camp early, leave in the morning, and arrive sometime around mid-afternoon. I knew little of Uncle Gus outside of what Mother told me, the letters from him she saved, and the recent comments of the ferryman. I knew even less about Aunt Pansy and Cousin Rene. Missy knew less than me about any of them and was apprehensive. But, in the back of our minds, we had the thought the Cajun ferryman planted. Maybe Texas would be our El Dorado.

Footnotes

In my story, I recalled or found information that help explain what I wrote, but, as my friend, Sam Truscott, and my wife suggest, interrupt flow of the story. I have collected my notes of added information in this section.

General

My stories include Confederate names for battles in which we fought. The Yankees won and the history books call these battles by Union names familiar to readers. These include

Confederate	**Union**
Manassas	Bull Run
Seven Pines	Fair Oaks
Sharpsburg	Antietam
Pittsburg Landing	Shiloh

My story so I used the names I know.

Chapter 5: War

At the beginning of the war, Confederates named their Eastern Army "Army of the Potomac". We used that name until General Lee took command of our army and renamed it, more accurately, as the Army of Northern Virginia, a name I used throughout. The Union named their Eastern army "Army of the Potomac" which I used throughout for the Union Army we opposed.

Chapter 7: 1862

I took classes at VMI taught by Thomas J Jackson. Later, I served with and occasionally under him in the Army of Northern Virginia. I have always thought Jackson our best field commander and that his untimely death was a major reason we lost the war. I have learned, over time, that Stonewall Jackson was not only the best general in our war, but one of the great all-time generals.

His Shenandoah Valley campaign is taught at West Point and other military institutions worldwide as a case study in how to effectively use an interior position to defeat a superior enemy force. A large measure of his brilliance was due to serving under General Lee, but time and again I saw him outwit and outfight larger Union forces thrown against us.

Chapter 10: Mosby

John Blaylock's concerns were well founded. As the war progressed, partisan raids on Union supply trains, intercept and disruption of communications, and depot raids in occupied areas escalated. In return, Union retaliation became increasingly harsh. The Union Army torched homes and farms simply because they were near where a raid occurred.

Later, in the war, to set an example for Mosby, Union General George Custer captured and hanged six Rangers. Mosby retaliated by selecting seven captured Union soldiers and hanged them. He pinned a letter on one of the unfortunate captives stating 1) he regretted the hangings, and 2) there would be no more executions of captured Union soldiers provided there were no more hangings of his Rangers. Executions stopped thereafter.

Chapter 11: Chancellorsville

The term "Hooker's Girls" that described "Fighting Joe" Hooker's camp followers was simplified to "hooker", one of many synonyms for prostitute. The term did not begin with Hooker's debauched camp, but his notoriety amplified its use. A well known prostitution area in Washington was appropriately named "Hooker Town" to "honor" Fighting Joe Hooker.

A P Hill played a pivotal, if underappreciated, role in the Army of Northern Virginia. It came out in the dying words of his commanders, Generals Jackson and Lee. I included Jackson's comments in delirium in the chapter.

I learned that General Lee, when he died ten years after Jackson, in his final delirium, said "Tell Hill he must come up" and then, finally, "Strike the tent."

Chapter 13: Gettysburg

Unlike the Union Army, Confederates funneled replacements into veteran units. The older and seasoned soldiers had a calming and steadying effect on the new recruits. Soldiers are very much inclined to react like other nearby soldiers. In most battles, the veteran Confederate soldiers stood and fought as did the replacements who followed their example.

By contrast, until late in the war, the Union Army raised new companies and sent them into battle intact. Too often, one inexperienced and frightened soldier broke and ran and then another until the new company dissolved. It happened much less often in the Confederate Army because of how new soldiers were dispatched to battle.

Chapter 14: Cold Harbor

In reading journals of men who fought at Cold Harbor, a prophetic quote from one of General Meade's staff officers caught my eye. About a month before the battle, he wrote "It is a rule that, when the Rebels halt, the first day gives them a good rifle-pit; the second, a regular infantry parapet with artillery in position; and the third a parapet with abbatis in front and entrenched batteries behind."

A Confederate artillery officer called the trenches on the morning of June 2 "mere little ditches that a calf might run over." By nightfall, however, the defenses changed dramatically. All day Lee, his engineers, and his subordinate commanders supervised construction of the trench line and the placement of the supporting artillery. Their work was masterful. The trench line zigzagged, not only to provide traverses, but also interlocking fields of fire.

In other words, no matter which point Union forces assaulted, they would find themselves trapped in crossfire. They also contented themselves with not just one but, "two and in places three, following the uneven terrain, snaking in and out of gullies and clumps of woods. They placed their cannon not just behind their main line but also in works projecting forward, sighted to fire across the front of attacking forces."

Attacking infantry would not only meet rifle crossfire, but artillery as well. Basically, by dawn on Friday, June 3, most of the Confederates would be more thoroughly dug in and ready than on any morning since the spring campaign began. More than anything else, we won the battle at Cold Harbor with the spade. That and the extra thirty-six hours Meade provided in shifting Hancock's Corps across the Union line.

Chapter 23: Vengeance

For decades after, the murder of Luther Perkins remained an unsolved homicide and robbery in Loudon County. Alarmed when he did not return, Perkins' family searched for him. The sons found his blood-stained body in the woods. No attempt had been made to conceal the body and the coins Perkins picked up at the bank were missing.

In their report to the Sheriff, the sons mentioned running off a group of Confederate stragglers in the prior month. They provided details of hanging a Negro after catching him in the henhouse and then taking the wagon, horses, rifles, and supplies of the stragglers as compensation for the attempted theft.

The Sheriff wrote it into his report, but many former Confederate soldiers passed through the county after the war. The Sheriff could not and did not want to trace all of them as suspects and had no solid evidence any of them killed Perkins. Perkins family offered a reward for information, but no one came forward. The Sheriff made a half-hearted investigation and then gave up on the case. Like many others in the county, he detested Luther Perkins.

Years later, one of the Anderson grandchildren told the "family secret" to a newspaper reporter. As it turned out, the newspaper account was fairly accurate and included the names of Jim Cobb and Andy Blaylock. By the time the article was published, in May, 1915, local officials refused to prosecute the case. The reporter even included the fact that Luther Perkins was roundly hated in the community as a Union sympathizer and scalawag. Perkins' descendants living in the county wrote angry denials to the editor published in subsequent newspaper issues.

Chapter 29: El Dorado

I inherited and expanded a large estate located north of Beaumont, Texas. The Gerlach Estate is near the present community of Lumberton which did not exist until years after my uncle, Gus Gerlach, created the estate. But, as an aid in telling my story, I used Lumberton as the location for the Gerlach Estate throughout.

Introduction to Memoirs of a Texan: Redemption

Memoirs of a Texan is a three part saga based on the life of Jim Cobb. We hope readers of the first book will want to continue reading the story of Jim & Missy Cobb, Andy Blaylock, Robert Savage, Jonathan Curtis, and other characters introduced in the second and third books in the series. The second book, subtitled Redemption, starts with the following excerpt from the first chapter.

Chapter 1: Uncle Gus

Gerlach Estate, Lumberton, Texas
September 8 - 15, 1865,

After reaching Texas, we settled in early for a long night sleep. The next day would be the first of the grand adventure we envisioned.

Before setting out in the morning, we scrubbed up and put on their best clothes. But early September in Southeast Texas meant hot and humid. We had been on the long journey for over one month before finally arriving at the Gerlach Estate. Despite best efforts at "sprucing up", we appeared haggard and tired which matched how we felt.

Missy asked, "What do they look like?"

I replied, "Don't know. I've never seen a photograph, daguerreotype, or any impression of Uncle Gus. I suspect he'll look something like my mother, Aunt Melissa, Uncle Ernst, and Grandfather Gerlach."

"Tall, German, strong jaw, blond hair, blue eyes?"

"Something like that. He's a Gerlach."

"Why did he leave Salem?" Missy asked.

"Not sure. Mother never talked about it. Something he did, but I don't think it was serious."

"Serious enough that he left." Missy stopped momentarily on Gus and asked, "What of his wife and son?"

"I know he has them, but no more than what Mother told us. He has a good wife and apparently a worthless son."

"I hope we do not look too poorly."

I replied, "I hope they take us in."

*   *   *

Pansy and Gus came out of the main house with their son, Rene, who had a mix of their features – light brown hair, thin mustache, slender and oddly delicate hands and wrists, tall, like his father, and the beginning of a paunch. Rene had a noticeable limp and perpetual scowl on his face. He stood in contrast with Aunt Pansy, a short, dark haired, handsome woman with pretty brown eyes and winsome smile. At fifty two years old, she had maintained her looks.

Without realizing we could hear him or caring that Rene did, Gus told Pansy, "That's our salvation ridin' in."

Pansy looked at him, "What?"

"You saw what Anne wrote in her letters" Gus said, "Chief of Staff to General Hill. Commanded a regiment. My nephew's a leader. Anne raised him to manage their farm in Newton. She says Sergeant Blaylock is a good overseer. They can get our place turned around."

"Gus, they may have no interest in building our estate."

Gus was not deterred. As I learned, he suffered many prior failures. He replied, "This is it. When the hounds chase a rabbit, there has to be hole when he jumps."

Pansy gave up and waited for us to stop and dismount. Rene stood and sulked at her side.

As it was a meeting of total strangers with the single bond of kinship between Gus and me to link us, I took the lead in getting everyone in our party introduced - first Missy then Andy and Robert. When I got to Pearl, I said, "This is Pearl Morgan. She is part of our family."

Uncle Gus gushed, "You're a fine lookin' man, James Cobb, handsome enough to be my nephew." He looked approvingly at Missy and said, "You sure married a pretty one." Addressing Andy and Robert, "I'm glad you brought strong men with you. There's more work here than we'll ever get done." Gus acknowledged Pearl by nodding in her direction.

Gus had the handsome features of his Gerlach kin, but, at the same time, he seemed bloated with a ruddy face and red nose, like someone who drank too much. I saw many like him in the army.

In an effort to make pleasant small talk, Robert approached Rene and asked if he had served in the war. He pointed out, "I grew up in Nacogdoches. You may have served with someone I know."

Rene replied without bothering to look at Robert, "Yeah, me and a bunch of starvin' bastards fought the Yankees at Vicksburg while you soaked up the glory back east."

Robert looked at Rene dumfounded. I heard him mutter, as he walked away, "Gettysburg, The Wilderness, Petersburg, glorious?"

Later, Andy asked Rene how the crops were doing. Rene, in Missy's and his mother's hearing, replied sharply, "Not worth a shit, but now you're here, you can show us how we've fucked everything up."

Andy tensed and started toward Rene as if to deck him. Missy slipped between them and whispered to Andy, "No. Don't do it."

Andy stopped, but, still angry, said loud enough for the rest of us to hear, "He can't talk that way in front of his mother and you."

Missy took Andy's arm firmly, leaned closer, and whispered, "Not now. Not the first day we meet him."

Andy stood down, but gave Rene a hard stare which he ignored.

Uncle Gus looked embarrassed and quickly said, "You young folks need a place to stay. I've got a tenant house down the road. The worthless overseer lived there 'til he took off. Not much, but you're welcome to it."

Humble as it may be, we welcomed the privacy of the overseer's house. It also got us away from Rene. Trouble from the start. I doubted it would get better after we knew him better.

Missy answered, "Thank you, Uncle Gus. We're appreciative."

Gus offered, "I'll take you now if you like."

Pansy finally spoke, "Gus, we prepared a meal for our guests. Take them to the tenant house afterwards."

Pansy led us back to the main house and a tasty meal we all appreciated after weeks of campfire cooking.

* * *

I rode beside Uncle Gus to the tenant house and talked with him on the way. Andy, Missy, and Pearl followed in the carriage. Robert drove the wagon. Gus reassured me, "I'm real pleased you came." He waved his arm in a wide arc and continued, "I put together a large estate. But, it's been hard to scratch out a livin'. The land's rich, but I'm not much of a farmer nor were any of the overseers I hired. The last one spent his time drinkin' and chasin' whores. He wasn't much good at that either. I mean the whore part.

After she married, your mother told me your family, the

Cobbs, have a large farm in Newton. I wanted to visit but never seem to find the time. She likely told you I've been after her for years to send you or your brother to help make somethin' of this place. It could be really good if it's run right." I listened to what my uncle said, but did not react.

Gus finally asked, "What do you think, James?"

Instead of answering directly, I replied, "I'd like a tour of the estate when you have time and I want to bring Andy and Robert with me."

Gus said, "Get settled in and we'll do it tomorrow, first thing after you, Missy, Andy, and Robert have breakfast with us in the morning."

"Please include Pearl. She's dear to us" I said.

Gus nodded, "She'll have to eat separate."

I nodded back, "All right."

* * *

We found the tenant house small and a mess. The former oc-cupant took off, without notice, two months earlier in search of better paying work and, no doubt, better access to women.

Without apology or even noticing its poor appearance, Gus opened the door and invited us to go in. After saying a few words to Missy, he got on his horse and rode back to the main house from what had become our new home.

It was obvious the prior tenant had paid little attention to housekeeping. Missy and Pearl changed clothes and got busy with brooms, mops, and washcloths borrowed from Pansy who suggested they take them. Robert, Andy, and I went back to the bedroom, changed, and came out to help Missy and Pearl. She worked us hard and, after a few hours of combined effort, we had the house clean from top to bottom. Our anticipated "rest" turned into heavy work which, mercifully, ended.

The front door of the small house led to an open room

adjoining a small kitchen with a back door off the kitchen and two small bedrooms to the side. The overseer left rudimentary furniture including a large dining table and chairs and beds, chairs, and dressers for the bedrooms. The house had a water well in front and a small outhouse in the back. Missy added the furniture from the Cobb Farm and made the small home livable.

After supper, following the hard day cleaning and moving furniture, we gathered outside on the front stoop and rested. We finally reached the end of a long, tiring journey and felt comfort that comes from completion of a major, necessary task.

I looked at Andy and asked, "How long's it been, Partner."

Andy counted on his fingers, "We took the payroll on June 4th, you and Missy married on July 2nd, left Newton on July 18th, and arrived here September 8th. Would've got here three days sooner if the wagon hadn't broke down in Vermilionville." He thought a minute and added, "Yep, it's been a long journey."

I put my arm around Missy. She put her head on my shoulder and said, "I know this house's not much, but your uncle has a lot of land. May be even more than the Cobb Farm."

I nodded, "I think he does."

As we looked to the setting sun, a flock of pure white herons flew by and settled in a nearby field. Pearl asked, "What kind of birds are those? They're so pretty and graceful." We admired the elegant birds for several minutes before the flock moved on to another field.

Robert said, "Don't know, Pearl. Lived in Texas all my life 'cept when I wuz off fightin' Yankees. Never seen anything like 'em in Nacogdoches. Must be birds that live on the Coast."

For the interim, Andy and Robert slept in the hayloft of an adjoining barn and ate meals with Missy, Pearl, and me. Pearl slept in the second bedroom. No complaints from Andy and Robert. It was much like what they had done at the Morgan Plantation and much better than when they ate and spent nights along the road.

Printed in the United States
219338BV00001B/3/P